PRAISE FOR

"Nelle's comedic talent shines in *Baby D[addy]*...
caught fire from the steamy chemistry be[tween]...

I adore everything about Nelle Lamour's romances! *Baby Daddy* is no different."
—*Whitney G., New York Times Bestselling Author*

"Funny, sexy perfection. Equal parts Emma Chase and Christina Lauren."
—*Adriane Leigh, USA Today Bestselling Author*

"I couldn't put it down. Drake Hanson is the perfect cocktail of sexy alpha meets sarcastic wit. I loved his transformation most of all. Five Fabulous Stars for *Baby Daddy!*"
—*Raine Miller, New York Times Bestselling Author*

"Another brilliantly written story by Nelle L'Amour. You will fall in love with Drake, Dee, and Tyson. *Baby Daddy* is a page-turner. I would give this book 10-stars if I could!"
—*Bookaholic*

"Laugh! Cry! Swoon! Nelle will make you go through all the emotions as she tells a story you'll soon not forget."
—*As You Like It Reviews*

"Sexy and fun! Nelle writes male POV like nobody's business!"
—*The Book Bellas*

"Unputdownable. It's got everything in it to make it a great read—mystery, humor, and most important, sizzling hot chemistry."
—*Love Between the Sheets Book Blog*

"5-Sexy Shmexy Stars. Nelle L'Amour keeps the perfect balance of sexual innuendos, hot, hot sex and laugh out loud moments."
—*A4Alphas B4Books Blog*

"A great blend of suspense, action, humor, and sexy times that kept me glued from the beginning to the end."
—*April's Blog of Awesomeness*

"Hot and steamy. On the wall, on the floor, everywhere steam!"
—*Three Chicks and Their Books*

"Awesome book! Oh, how I loved these characters. I loved the flow of the story, the storyline itself, and every steamy, swoony moment, but precious Tyson stole the book for me.
—*Reviewers for Authors*

"Nelle is up there with the best, such as Sylvia Day and E.L. James."
—*Goodreads Reviewer*

BOOKS BY NELLE L'AMOUR

Unforgettable
Unforgettable Book 1
Unforgettable Book 2
Unforgettable Book 3

Alpha Billionaire Duet
TRAINWRECK 1
TRAINWRECK 2

An OTT Insta-love Standalone
The Big O

THAT MAN Series
THAT MAN 1
THAT MAN 2
THAT MAN 3
THAT MAN 4
THAT MAN 5

Gloria
Gloria's Secret
Gloria's Revenge
Gloria's Forever

An Erotic Love Story
Undying Love

Seduced by the Park Avenue Billionaire
Strangers on a Train
Derailed
Final Destination

Writing as E.L. Sarnoff
DEWITCHED: The Untold Story of the Evil Queen
UNHITCHED: The Untold Story of the Evil Queen 2

Boxed Sets
THAT MAN TRILOGY
THAT MAN: THE WEDDING STORY
Unforgettable: The Complete Series
Gloria's Secret: The Trilogy
Seduced by the Park Avenue Billionaire

Baby Daddy

Baby Daddy

New York Times Bestselling Author
NELLE L'AMOUR

Copyright © 2017 by Nelle L'Amour
Print Edition
All rights reserved
First Edition: May 2017

This is a work of fiction. Names, characters, places, and incidents are either the product of the author's imagination or used fictitiously. Any resemblance to events, locales, business establishments, or actual persons—living or dead—is purely coincidental.

No part of this book may be reproduced, uploaded to the Internet, or copied without permission from the author. The author respectfully asks that you please support artistic expression and help promote anti-piracy efforts by purchasing a copy of this ebook at the authorized online outlets.

Nelle L'Amour thanks you for your understanding and support. To join my mailing list for new releases, please sign up here: http://eepurl.com/N3AXb

NICHOLS CANYON PRESS
Los Angeles, CA USA

Baby Daddy

Cover by Arijana Karcic, Cover It! Designs
Proofreading by Mary Jo Toth and Gloria Herrera
Formatting by BB eBooks

In memory of my beautiful baby girl, Luna.
I will always love you.

*Destiny is not a matter of chance;
it is a matter of choice.*

—Zoltar

ABOUT

A new standalone romantic comedy told in dual POV from the *New York Times* bestselling author of *THAT MAN* and *Unforgettable!*

I have three cardinal rules:
1. Never mix business with pleasure.
2. Never let a woman spend the night.
3. Never date a woman with kids.

Kids freak me out. God only knows how many this baby daddy has. Man, what was I thinking when I was in college? Me, Drake Hanson. God's gift to women. Aka Donor 5262. It was a piece of cake and two hundred dollars a deposit (in sperm bank speak) came in handy. Wank, bank, and go. I just didn't think about the consequences. One day, some kid is going to call me Daddy and I'm going to get hit up with child support. Big time.

Now, my father is pressuring me to settle down because the investor who's looking to acquire his animation company doesn't want a player running a family-oriented business. Just in time, she came along. The temp. Dee Walker. The minute the hot as sin brunette with her killer curves and those chocolate brown eyes stepped foot in my office and saved me from an ugly disaster with her magic hands, I wanted her to be mine. Except she's totally off limits. And there's someone else she loves with all her heart and soul that I can't replace.

Can my temp become my forever before my past catches up with me? I'm willing to break *all* the rules.

Baby Daddy

PROLOGUE
Drake

Ten Years Earlier

"Hi, handsome."

"Hi, gorgeous," I replied with a wink. Constance, the buxom blond receptionist, was far from gorgeous, but I sure knew how to charm her. Minoring in What a Woman Wants had its benefits. A big smile lit up her face.

"Sheila will take you back to Room 2."

"Nah, it's okay. I know the routine." Sheila was her recently divorced co-worker with the spray tan and fake boobs. I knew she had a thing for me. Except I didn't have a thing for her and fooling around with the staff was definitely a no-no.

Swinging open the heavy door that led to my destination, I walked down a short corridor, past several administration offices, marveling at how many times I'd walked this path before. I did some mental calculations—I'd frequented this place three times a week regularly for the past four years. So, that was over five hundred times. By now, I could walk to infamous Room 2 with my eyes closed.

Room 2 was at the very end of the hallway, and when I got there, I cranked open another door. I took in my surroundings. Not a thing had changed from the last time I'd been here two days ago. In fact, nothing had changed since the first time I'd set foot in this room.

It was small and sterile, a lot like a doctor's examining room. Except instead of an exam table, there was a TV, a DVD player, a rack of familiar magazines, and a chair covered with a disposable towel and holding a jar labeled with my name. Forcing myself to not overthink the fact that hundreds of dudes had gotten off in this room, I bypassed the porn (at this point, I'd seen the DVDs a hundred times and leafed through every *Hustler*), grabbed the specimen jar, and sat down in my wanking throne, ready to get to work.

Setting the jar between my legs, I zipped down my fly and freed my dick. I cast my eyes downward and stared at it. It might be eight inches of limpness now, but in a few strokes, it was going to be ten inches of rock-hard, pulsating magnificence. A smile warmed my lips and pride soared in my heart as I curled my fingers around my already swelling length and aimed it at the jar. I should mention some dudes wore goggles they provided just in case they missed, but me, the hockey player, never missed a goal.

Call me God's gift to mankind. Not only was I going to give some childless couple a family, but I was also going to make the world a more beautiful place with my premium genes. These couples deserved the best. They were dropping upwards of $40,000 per child, so it sure as hell well be the Rolls Royce of babies. Not a freak. And man, the lucky kid who got my package.

It's good thing I didn't have a steady girlfriend. The only downside of this job was that I couldn't have sex for forty-eight hours prior to reporting for active duty. So, I could only hook up a few nights a week. But don't feel sorry for me. The amount of action I got totally compensated for my days off.

Staring down at my long, thick shaft, my mind wandered. Who should I think about during today's session?

Jasmine? Amber? Carrie?...yeah, she was good. I loved the way she went down on me the other night with that big mouth of hers, taking me to the hilt. Imagining her soft pillowy lips clamped around my rigid length, I began to slide my hand up and down, picking up speed until I was pumping fast and furiously. My eyes squeezed shut, I felt my cock swelling in my palm, the blood rushing to it. In five, four, three, two, one, I had a blast off as I fantasized coming in Carrie's warm mouth, my load coating her throat. I peeled my eyes open and watched as my jizz dripped down the interior of the jar. Grinning, I screwed on the lid and put it on the shelf where I always did. Baby gravy.

My fly still down, I headed over to the sink area where I washed up.

Wank, bank, and go. Tonight, I was going out on the town and was going to fuck my brains out. A couple of hundred dollars would come in handy at the high-end club I was planning to go to and plunk down some big bucks.

I tucked my spent dick back in my jeans and zipped up my fly. Seriously, jerking off for money was the best damn job in the world.

But when I graduated this year, my father had other plans for me in the kids' biz.

CHAPTER 1
Drake

It was the most dreaded day of the year.
Not Black Friday.
Not Valentine's Day.
Not Tax Day.
It was fucking Bring Your Kids to Work Day. The third Wednesday in May. God, I hated this day. It wasn't even nine o'clock and dozens of kids were flocking the halls of Hanson Entertainment, the animation company founded by my father.

My legendary old man, Orson Hanson, loved this day. Kids were after all what made him a multi-millionaire ten times over. *Danger Rangers,* the series he created when I was eight, was an overnight sensation. The theme song, "Go, Go, Danger Rangers," became a national anthem among children and stores couldn't keep the toys in stock. Now in its second decade, the show was still going strong on Peanuts, the children's television network owned and operated by Conquest Broadcasting. Over the years, our slate of animated series had expanded and included many other hit series. Approaching the ripe old age of sixty-five, my father was looking to retire . . . sell the business and achieve what he'd always wanted—to become a billionaire and be ranked among the world's moguls on the Forbes Top 40 list. No matter who he sold the company to, he wanted me to continue to run it.

The kids' business—not the cartoon kind—had netted me a small fortune too. My old man sent me to UCLA, but he insisted I get a job while I was taking classes. To see what it was like. To build a work ethic and values. And to keep me out of trouble. Dad knew I was a party animal, a lazy son of a bitch, who'd rather screw around than study and who had trouble keeping his pants on. Well, I found the perfect job: Wanking off.

The minute I saw the ad for "Sperm Donors Wanted" on a bulletin board at the campus coffee shop, I knew I was a shoe in. I went online and filled out the form. I was perfect breeding material. Six feet two inches tall (no shorties or fatsoes wanted), dark, thick hair (no gingers allowed because no one wanted a carrot top), baby blue eyes, and straight as an arrow (sleeping with guys eliminated you immediately). I was healthy and came from a family where almost everyone lived to be a hundred. Plus, I had an amazing skill set—I was athletic, could sing like a rock star, and had a 150 IQ. Okay, I goofed off and my C grades reflected that (I lied and said I had a 5.0 GPA), but the potential was there. Plus, I was hung like a horse. I had no STDs and my specimen past the test with flying colors—getting a higher score than I'd ever gotten on any academic test. My sperm count was worthy of the *Guinness Book of Records*, their morphology museum-worthy, and the real clincher was my little testicular tadpoles were Olympians that could swim like Michael Phelps.

The sperm bank was conveniently located in Westwood Village, a few blocks away from the UCLA campus. It was the perfect "job." I only had to go in two to three times a week, whenever I chose, and it took ten minutes or less to complete the task. An easy peasy fifteen hundred dollars a month. Not bad for a few hours work. Some called it a sperm bank; but I called it the wank bank. Wank, bank, and go!

"Be a hero!" proclaimed the home page of the website. "Give a childless family their dream." Looking back, what the hell was I thinking? My nightmares had started a few years ago right after my best bud, Brock, dragged me to see the Vince Vaughn movie, *Delivery Man.* Vince played a hapless dude, who, like me, had given batches of his seed to a sperm bank while he was in college. Fast forward several years, the sperm bank was being sued for a shit load of money by the women he impregnated, demanding to know his identity. Had I known what the movie was about, I would have never gone to see it.

Given how many batches of Donor 5262 (as I was officially known) sperm I deposited (in sperm-bank speak) and had frozen, half the kid population in LA might be some form of mini-me. Okay, I'm exaggerating a little, but still there were likely hundreds, if not thousands. And right here, right now in our studios, a few might be roaming around. Though I didn't do open donation where the parent and donor mutually agree to let the kid contact and meet you at the age of eighteen, I still constantly felt the inevitable would happen. One day, I would run into a clone of myself and my life would change forever.

After taking a sip of my coffee and a bite of a glazed donut that I'd purchased at a nearby Donut King on the way into the office, I booted up my computer. The day, filled with one parent-child activity after another, was going to be a total time suck. I had a lot of shit on my plate, including readying a pitch to Conquest Broadcasting, so the last thing I needed was a presentation to all the little brats about the cartoons we produced. Last year was a fucking disaster . . . one of the kids started throwing his chicken nuggets at me and before long the entire screening room had erupted into a nasty food fight. This year could easily be a repeat. Even worse.

Studying my calendar and looking less and less forward to the day ahead, I looked up when I heard an unexpected voice.

"Mister, can you tell me where the bathroom is?"

My eyes landed on a chubby little boy, wearing shorts and an Astro Camp sweatshirt. Probably eight or nine, he was a freckled carrot top and wore large horn-rimmed glasses that covered most of his pudgy face. His eyes beneath the thick lenses looked glazed.

"It's down the hall on the right," I replied as I sized him up. Nah. For sure this little nerd wasn't one of mine. From my research on genetics, one could only be a redhead if both parents had the genes in their ancestry. Not one ginger existed on either my mother's or father's side of the family.

"Could you please show me?" His voice grew smaller. More watery.

"Fine." I mentally rolled my eyes. I had better things to do. Reluctantly, I stood up from my desk and strolled over to the youngster who didn't budge. As I neared him, he paled and clutched his stomach.

"What's the matter?"

The boy's mouth opened wide as if to say something, but instead a loud *BLEGH!* dislodged from his throat.

The sound shot through my ears as a spray of hot molten lava with chunky bits splattered across my T-Shirt.

Jesus!

BLEGH! Another round of projectile vomiting, this time hitting me below the belt. All over my crotch.

Christ!

The kid began to cry. I'm talking big fat ugly tears that rolled down his face from under his glasses. "I want my mommy."

Shit! With his freckled face now the shade of puke

green, he looked like he might barf again. Parents shouldn't be allowed to bring their kids to work. When I became President of this company, this day was going to be eliminated once and for all. Covered in vomit, I inhaled deeply and regretted doing so as the odiferous smell drifted up my nose. I began to feel nauseated myself. Crap. What was I going to do? A new voice distracted me. It was soft and raspy, innocent and sexy at the same time.

"Hi, I'm Deandra. But you can call me Dee."

My gaze shifted to the doorway of my office. At the threshold, stood a shapely brunette wearing a gray fitted skirt, sensible black pumps, and a cropped red sweater over an ivory blouse. Her lustrous chestnut hair was swept up in a ponytail, showcasing her flawless complexion, doe-like brown eyes, full upturned lips, and cute as a button nose.

"Are you his mother?" I yelled out above the wails of the child. *Get him out of here.*

"Oh, dear!" exclaimed the attractive, twenty-something woman, taking notice of the disastrous situation.

The kid's sobs grew louder and he cried out again for his mommy. Obviously and unfortunately, this woman bore no relationship to him.

"Who are you?" I asked as she hurried toward us.

Keeping my eyes on her curvy body, I watched as she took the hysterical kid into her arms. "You poor baby."

You poor baby? Hello! What about me? I was the one who'd taken a barf bath.

Stroking the boy's copper curls, she made eye contact with me. "I'm your new assistant. The temp."

Her words sunk in. I'd totally forgotten that my regular, soon-to-retire assistant, Mona, had taken her overdue vacation time to visit her daughter, who'd given birth two weeks early. She would be away for at least three weeks, and always efficient, no matter what the circumstances, she'd managed to arrange for someone to fill in for her until she returned.

I met my new assistant's chocolate orbs. "Okay, then start by getting this kid the hell out of my office and find me something I can use to clean myself up." I was unable to look down at the damage and the stench was really getting to me.

"Sure," she replied with a small dimpled smile. Even in my distressed state, I had to admit this girl was cute. One hot little number. My eyes stayed on her as she escorted the kid, whose crying had subsided, out of my office, one arm wrapped around him in a motherly way. My gaze traveled down her taut body, spending way too much time on her spectacular heart-shaped ass and shapely calves.

I stayed in one spot awaiting her return, decorated with revolting chunky bits. Growing more and more nauseated and disgusted, I grew impatient. Where the fuck did she go? Five long, wretched minutes later, she reappeared, holding a thick stack of paper towels and a glass of sudsy water.

"I found his mother," she beamed as she approached me. "Everything's good. She's taking him home."

"Good," I mumbled, watching her soak a wad of the paper towels with the soapy liquid. "What are you doing?"

"Stand still. I'm going to try to clean up this mess."

"Hurry! I've got a presentation in an hour."

I stood as still as I could as she began to vigorously wipe the chunky bits off my T-shirt. Bit my bit, they disappeared, but the horrific smell lingered. "Work on my jeans now."

The disgusting red chunky bits (what the fuck did that kid eat for breakfast? Dog food?) were clustered around my fly with a few scattered down the legs of my jeans. After tossing the wet towels she used for my T-shirt onto the floor, she moistened another bunch and began to scrub my crotch with small, vigorous strokes.

"Jesus," I moaned.

Still working, she gazed up at me. "Am I hurting you?"

My muscles clenched as I felt my cock swelling beneath the denim. Holy shit. She was giving me a fucking hard-on.

"Rub harder," I gritted through my teeth.

At my command, her strokes grew faster and more forceful. I hissed. Christ. Didn't she know what she was doing to me?

"Don't stop," I breathed out, feeling the makings of a volcanic eruption between my thighs. I was so close to coming . . . about to cream my pants and scream out in relief. And then on her next stroke, I did, cursing under my breath, just as she stopped her ministrations.

"I'm sorry. This isn't working," she said, frustration in her voice. Oh, it worked just fine. If she knew I'd just had a full-on orgasm, she didn't show it. In fact, she probably thought I was yelling at her.

She examined her handiwork, no pun intended. "I've gotten most of the puke off, but I can't get rid of the smell."

I looked down at myself. Nope. This wasn't good. My *Danger Rangers* T-shirt was soaked and stained, and it looked like I'd taken a leak in my pants. And she was right. The horrible odor was palpable.

I dug my hand into a pocket and retrieved my cardholder, pulling out my Visa. Still feeling a hot, tingly sensation between my legs, I handed it to her.

"Listen, I need you to run to the Galleria and pick up a new pair of jeans and a T-Shirt. There's a Bloomingdale's there . . . they should have what I need."

"What size are you?" Her eyes roamed down my body, staying a little too long where they shouldn't have.

For a minute, my mind jumped to my cock. *Big, very big!* I bit down on my tongue and answered, "I wear a Size Large T-shirt and a 32 in jeans." And silently I added,

"While you're there, pick up some Calvin Klein briefs. The ones with extra support."

Without wasting a second, she flew out of my office.

CHAPTER 2
Dee

Less than five minutes on the job, I was out the door, shopping for my new boss. All I knew from Human Resources was that his name was Drake Hanson and he was the Head of Development for Hanson Entertainment. It didn't take a genius to figure out he was connected to someone who owned this animation company. And therefore some kind of big shot. After filling out the necessary paperwork, I was immediately escorted to his office.

Well, I certainly didn't expect my day to start off as it did, I thought to myself as I drove back to the office in what I was learning was typical LA traffic. Coming from a small town outside of Fresno, I still hadn't gotten used to the hustle bustle and it totally freaked me out. LA drivers were ruthless and I was surprised I hadn't already gotten into an accident.

My new boss wasn't going to be happy when I got back. New to LA, I didn't even know what or where the Galleria was. Googling my cell phone, I learned it was a mall in Glendale near Hanson Entertainment and then used my GPS app to find the fastest route via the Ventura Freeway. I got there in ten minutes . . . except the exit was closed off, and when I got off on the next one, I totally got lost and somehow ended up in Pasadena.

As I crawled along the freeway in my beat-up Ford pickup truck, my new boss occupied my mind. I could tell he was bossy and somewhat of a jerk. And the man seemed to hate kids, which was pretty ironic since he made kids' cartoons. I was familiar with most of them.

But one thing for sure, he was gorgeous. Sinfully gorgeous. My sister had told me that hot guys were a dime a dozen in LA, and yes, I'd seen a lot of cuties, but none compared with this man. His eyes were the bluest blue and could hold you prisoner while his body was pure manly perfection. He was the perfect height—probably just over six feet—with broad shoulders that gave way to chiseled biceps and ripples in just the right places that showed he must work out. And then there was that incredible thick length between his long, athletic legs. Holy shit! My breath hitched in my throat as I relived it growing hard beneath my palm as I tried to wipe his crotch clean. I could actually feel it pulsating against my hand and I swear he got off on me. How was I going to work for this sex god? Okay, it was just a temporary job for a few weeks until his regular assistant returned. But still.

Suddenly, a car on the right pulled in front of me. I slammed down on the brakes and cursed. A new reality set in: why was I worrying? I was probably going to get fired for taking so long or I was going to die in a car accident. Catching my breath and returning my full attention to the road, I prayed the latter wouldn't happen. I had something far more important than myself to live for.

CHAPTER 3
Drake

Where the hell was she? Dee . . . I think that's what her name was. I was lousy at remembering names. Always in one ear and out the other. It could have something to do with my selective hearing.

The Galleria was only a short ten minutes away, but she'd been gone for almost an hour. A disturbing thought knocked at the door to my brain. Maybe she wasn't *c*oming back. I mean, I'm sure I didn't make a very favorable impression on her. In fact, I probably scared the shit out of her. The minute she stepped foot in my office, I yelled at her and demanded she clean that crap off me from that damn kid.

Okay, that was bad enough—I don't know how she was able to tolerate the smell or even look at the gross vomit—but that was nothing compared to the fact that I practically came in her hand. And I was still feeling the aftermath of the orgasm shooting through my balls.

Seriously, how goddamn embarrassing! I can't believe she didn't react. There's no way she didn't feel my cock expand then grow as hard as a rock and feel my spasms as I blew my load. Seated behind my desk, now bare-chested and minus my jeans, I stared down at my package. Impulsively, I put my hand on it. The fabric of my briefs was still damp from my release and my cock was still enlarged and warm. The image of that girl with her dimpled smile flashed into my head and a surge of desire spilled through my blood.

Okay, this girl wasn't exactly my type. She was dark-haired and curvy when I preferred tall, willowy blondes, but there was something so fresh and sexy about her. It was like Rebecca of Sunnybrook farm had grown up and was milking the hell out of me. The bottom line, she turned me on like a light bulb. The temperature in the room had risen at least ten degrees. Maybe more.

Now acutely aware of the air conditioning blowing on me, I returned my attention to my computer screen. My door was locked shut because I sure didn't want another brat disturbing me and I sure as hell didn't want anyone from the company to see me almost butt naked. I glanced at the time. It was almost ten o'clock . . . the Bring Your Kids to Work Day breakfast was about to end and I was expected to give a thirty-minute presentation about our company—an overview—to the kids in our state-of-the-art screening room. Following the presentation, the kids would break into groups and visit various employees and departments, including our character designers, computer animators, editors, and our in-house recording studio.

My father hated tardiness. Moreover, Gunther Saxton, the German media mogul who was looking to buy our company, would be there observing me . . . to see if I was CEO material. Shit. What was I going to do? My eyes darted to the far right corner where I'd tossed my stinky, vomit-ridden T-shirt and jeans. There was no way I was putting them back on. And there was no way I was leaving my office. Damn that girl. I couldn't even call her to find out what was going on since I didn't have her cell phone number. I could only surmise she'd quit on me, giving new meaning to the word "temporary." Raking my fingers through my hair, I blew out a loud frustrated breath. This day was going from bad to worse.

A sudden loud knock at the door sounded in my ears. "Who's there?" I shouted out. I just hoped it wasn't my father. I didn't want him—or anyone for that matter—to see me like this.

"It's me, Dee. I've got your things," came a familiar voice from the other side.

Phew! Finally, she was back. Without saying a word, I leapt up from my chair and sprinted over to the door. Before I could get to it, the door swung open and a loud gasp filled the air.

CHAPTER 4

Dee

"Oh. My. God." After saying the last word, my mouth stayed wide open in the shape of an "O." A big "O." I couldn't get my legs to move or my eyes to blink. I just stood at the doorway, paralyzed, the large Bloomingdale's shopping bag dangling from my hand while he barked at me.

"Jesus. Just don't stand there. Hurry in and close the door."

Holy moly! Standing before me was my new boss. The sex god, wearing nothing, but his boxer briefs. And there was nothing that stood between me and his Calvins. I could feel his heat as my eyes drank in his exquisitely sculpted body. He was spectacular with his clothes on, but even more breathtaking without them. Six-feet plus of pure manly perfection. Broad, sculpted shoulders . . . chiseled pecs . . . the six-pack of a male model . . . and powerful, muscular arms and legs dusted with a fine layer of dark hair. Oh, and that perfect pelvic V that drew my eyes to a bulge in his briefs that was far bigger than the one I imagined. Only one word came to mind—humongous. My eyes stayed glued on it. I was in state of shock. I should have waited for him to open the door. Maybe he was putting on some sort of cover-up. But stupid me used the office key Human Resources had given me and barged in. What was I thinking?

"Hurry," he repeated, his voice urgent. Not giving me time to respond, he grabbed me by my elbow and yanked me into his office, slamming the door behind us.

Ruthlessly, he tore the shopping bag out of my hand. "Perfect," he muttered, reaching inside for the T-shirt and jeans.

"They only had ripped jeans in your size. True Religion. I hope you don't mind."

Holding them up, he quirked a smile. God, it was dazzling, with two heart-shaped dimples that kissed his lush lips. My eyes stayed on him as he hastily stepped into the faded denim pants and pulled them up over his long legs before focusing on his groin as he zipped up his fly over his extraordinary endowment. My nerve endings buzzed with the whoosh of the zipper and I could feel my heart galloping. The sexy jeans fit him perfectly, hanging low on his hips, just below that those pelvic V lines and that happy trail grazing his lower abdomen. Wordlessly, I watched as he pulled the V-neck T-Shirt over his head and tucked it into his jeans, his mouthwatering biceps flexing as he did. God, he looked gorgeous. Swoon-worthy, may I say as my legs turned to Jell-O.

"Good job," he said as he pivoted to retrieve his shoes—a pair of red Nikes nearby on the floor. I felt myself flush with pride—and arousal—as I admired his delicious ass. Well, at least I wasn't on his shit list. Or about to get fired.

"What took you so long?" he snapped as he bent down to slip on the shoes.

A lump formed in my throat as dread rolled through my stomach. Maybe I jumped to a conclusion too fast.

"Well?" He looked up at me as he fiddled with the laces. "My presentation is in five minutes."

"Um, uh, I got lost." I refrained from telling him that I

also made a stop at the lingerie department to pick up a new pair of panties to replace my soaked ones.

"Seriously? Everyone knows where the Galleria is."

My mouth twitched while words stayed trapped in my throat.

"Dammit," he shouted.

I held my breath and prepared for the worse. I was getting the ax.

"Get your ass . . .

Out of here . . . GULP!

"Over here and help me take out these damn knots."

Phew! I breathed out a sigh of relief and hurried over to him. Squatting down, I joined him, so close that our knees touched and his warm breath skimmed my cheeks. He yanked at a pair of the shoelaces and I could hear him curse again under his breath.

"Stop it," I reprimanded. "You're making it worse."

"Oh, so now you're an expert on knots?" His voice dripped with sarcasm.

"Yes, I am. Now please let go."

Reluctantly, he removed his hands, setting them on his thighs, while I went to work. The honest-to-god truth, I was an expert when it came to knots. I'd undone countless ones, from the simplest to the toughest that often took hours. And I was great with gnarly hair knots and tangled necklace chains as well. It was all part of my other job requirements.

Fortunately, Drake's knots weren't too bad. I felt his eyes on my hands as I maneuvered the balled-up laces, loosening and untangling them. It took patience and a fair amount of strategy. In no time, both knots were undone.

"Wow, you're really good," remarked Drake with a smile.

I returned the smile, though mine was fraught with smugness. "Let me tie your shoes for you the proper way so the laces won't get undone or knotted up again."

"You'd make a really good mother." Drake laughed.

His laugh was naturally sexy. Deep and sexy. Hot tingles danced down my spine as I finished tying both shoes.

Drake stood up, lifting me up with him. His hands curled around my upper arms while we stood face to face. His eyes burnt into mine.

"Thanks. I've got to run. You're welcome to come to the presentation."

"It's okay. I want to get acclimated."

"You sure?"

"Positive."

"Okay. I'll be back in a half-hour. And we'll talk about your job requirements."

"Oh, there's more to it than cleaning up vomit, shopping, and tying your shoes?"

"You're funny." And with that, he dashed out of his office.

CHAPTER 5
Drake

I survived Bring Your Kids to Work Day and my father told me Gunther Saxton was impressed by my presentation to the kiddies. Fortunately, there was no repeat of last year's food fight, and the kids were so well behaved you would have thought we got them from Central Casting. We were one step closer to making the deal happen.

The rest of the day went by without a hitch. With pitch season around the corner and the pending acquisition of my father's company by Saxton Enterprises, I spent most of my time out of my office... meeting with in-house character designers, storyboard artists, story editors, and animators as well as with ZAP!, the cutting-edge ad agency that was putting together a sizzle reel to show to network development execs. One thing worried me: while we had a full development slate, none of the shows we had in development felt like the next big hit. Both my father and Gunther were counting on me to find that needle in the haystack.

My temp, Dee, was doing a great job holding down the fort while I was in meetings. In fact, she was perfect, attending to my every need and whim, from keeping me on schedule to running to Starbucks to get me a much-needed Vanilla Ice Blended and warm chocolate chip cookie in the middle of the day. I, on the other hand, wasn't doing such a great job suppressing my feelings about her. While her behavior toward me was very professional and not the least bit flirtatious, something about her fucking turned me on. My dick was twitchy, especially when I caught sight of her taking off her sweater and unbuttoning the top buttons of her blouse, which exposed just the tiniest bit of her lace bra and made me fantasize about what lay beneath. From the way they pressed against the silky fabric of her blouse, I could tell her tits were full and firm with nipples that I imagined were succulent and rosy.

I hadn't been this turned on in ages. Maybe it had to do with my recent self-imposed period of celibacy, but I'd seriously never had so many fantasies about a woman. Most chicks were just one-night hook-ups that fit into the find, feel, fuck, and forget category. But Dee, ever since that barfing incident, had lingered in my head. I fantasized about her kneeling at my feet and giving me head, fucking her on the floor and over my desk, then banging her against a wall. She didn't wear any kind of wedding band, so I assumed she was single. I refrained from asking her because I didn't want to know she was off limits and have to say *adiós* to my fantasies. Plain and simple: I didn't bang married ladies; that's where I drew the line. Maybe I was a little bit of a manwhore (okay, understatement) and marriage-phobic, but I at least respected the institution. Enduring their share of ups and downs, including one horrific tragedy, my parents had stayed together for almost forty years and were still madly in love. Not a small feat by Hollywood standards. The number of celebrity divorces in this town had made my best bud Brock Andrews a millionaire. And somewhat of a celebrity in his own right.

Before I knew it, it was six o'clock. While I usually didn't leave the office until seven and sometimes later, tonight I was meeting Brock at the LA Kings Valley Ice

Center for our bi-monthly hockey game. I grabbed my laptop bag and headed out of my office. To my surprise, my new temp was still at her desk. Her eyes glued to her computer screen, she glanced up at me. She looked a little tired.

"Hey, you don't have to stay late."

She quirked a sweet little smile. "It's okay. I was just studying the "To Do" list your regular assistant was kind enough to send. I'll make sure I have your schedule for the rest of the week printed out and on your desk before you get in tomorrow."

"Thanks. See you in the morning."

"Night," she replied, her eyes already back on the screen.

I lingered, tempted to ask if she wanted to come watch me play hockey.

"Hey, do you have plans for tonight?"

"Yes, I'm going out later."

I hardly knew this girl, yet I felt a little dejected and rejected. I shouldn't have been surprised by her response. Cute, single chicks like her didn't stay home at night. If she didn't have a boyfriend, I bet she had a hot date every night.

I inhaled a breath while she ignored me, then bid her good night one more time and split.

Friends since kindergarten, Brock and I had both been playing hockey for as long as we could remember and now belonged to an amateur team known as the Mighty Dicks. The name of the team suited us well; combined, we were a bunch of spoiled rich pricks, who were determined to win and had enough testosterone among us to melt the ice. Suited up in my padded uniform and a protective helmet, it felt good to be on the ice. After a stressful day, it was my way of chilling and using my big stick to score goals. It was also my way of releasing my pent up sexual energy. And I had a lot of it. Not so much because I hadn't used my God-given big stick for over a month, but because ever since my sexy temp stepped into my office, I had the burning urge to bury it in her pussy and score a goal of another kind. My hormones were raging.

Tonight, we were playing the best team in our league. Our fiercest competition—the Manchots, which was French for penguins. The Canadian ex-pats, who composed this team, thought they were hot shots and born with pucks between their legs. So far this season, they were undefeated. Fuck them, I thought as the game went into sudden death overtime. My heart was racing, my focus on the puck. The puck flew across the ice to the other team, but one of our defensemen blocked it, hitting it straight to Brock, my fellow forward. Through our helmets, we made eye contact, and in a split second, the puck was mine. It was a long shot, but I had to take it. Without wasting a second, I whacked the puck with my stick and watched as it swept across the ice straight past the Manchots' stunned goaltender into the net. The score: 2-1. Victory was ours! Cheers and man hugs all around.

Brock high fived me. "C'mon, man, let's go out and celebrate." *And get laid.* "I'll buy."

I thought about his offer. It had been a while since I'd been out on the town. Gunther Saxton, whose holdings included amusement parks, electronic games, and pre-school brands, had made it crystal clear to my father that if I was going to take over and run his animation company I needed to change my image. "Form equals meaning," he'd stressed repeatedly. "I can't have someone like your son running an animation company who's out screwing every starlet and supermodel in LA. A family brand needs a family man.

Someone who is settled down with a wife and kids."

Every time he mentioned the wife and kids part I inwardly cringed. Settling down was the last thing on my mind. I was just not the marrying type, let alone the family man. And, of course, the mention of kids always reminded me of all the kids that might be mine as the result of being a sperm donor. I hated to think about the consequences if that secret ever got out. Whoof.

My past aside, the deal was majorly important to my father so I agreed to low key it for a while . . . stay away from the Hollywood scene and stay out of the tabloids. At first, it sucked balls, but I'd actually gotten used to it, and to my astonishment, I found myself not missing the meaningless hook-ups night after night or the superficial nightlife. Though this was the longest dry spell I'd endured in my adult life, I felt rested and productive. A sabbatical. Yet, despite my commitment to living a temporary celibate life until the deal was done, my buddy Brock managed to sweet talk me into going to a new Hollywood hot spot to celebrate our victory.

"Man, I think I've gotten too old for this shit," I grumbled, taking in the five-people deep bar.

"Bro, you've got to get back in the game. Your dick can only last so long without being laid. It can even fall off."

Mentally, I rolled my eyes. In his office, Brock thought with his brain; he was one of the sharpest, shrewdest attorneys in LA, specializing in high profile, sticky divorce cases and family law. But once outside his glass-and-steel tower, Brock thought with his dick. He didn't just check out attractive women. He checked out *women.* Fat ones, skinny ones, tall ones, and short ones. Women of all color though the equal opportunity player had a predilection for leggy blondes whereas I was an ass-man. He approached the opposite sex no differently than one of his high-profile cases—no risk, no gain. Score a win. His eyes roaming, he was already on the prowl. Brock the Rock had earned his name.

"Maybe you'll meet Miss Right here tonight," he chuckled, giving me a man pat on my back. "And make your old man happy."

"Yeah, right," I retorted, the sarcasm dripping. All skin, sex, and heat, this was no place to meet your future wife. Nor was I looking for one.

"Check out that babe at eleven o'clock," he said, pointing in her direction. "She's hot as shit."

My eyes followed his and landed on a tall, lithe blonde in tight-ass jeans standing at the bar. Yup. He was right. A margarita in her hand, she was definitely off the charts hot. The face and body of a goddess with radiant waist-length hair, mile-long legs, and spectacular tits that spilled out of her low-cut halter-top. But what really grabbed my attention were her defined, full lips. As she made eye contact with us, she took a long sip of her drink and then licked them. I felt my cock stir.

"Fuck," muttered Brock under his breath. "I saw her first. She's mine."

In addition to speaking three languages fluently, Brock was an expert on the body language of women. He could read exactly what they wanted and how they wanted it. Then say what they wanted to hear. He was ready to conquer. And score. Flashing a seductive smile, the blonde turned around so her back was to us.

"Check out that piece of ass," crooned Brock. "C'mon. Remember, I make the first moves."

A short minute later, we were at the bar. Luck had it that there was an empty seat next to Ms. Blond and Gorgeous.

"Hey, beautiful. Anyone sitting here?" Brock asked, pulling out the barstool while I stood next to him. I was already feeling like his sidekick.

She turned to face us. Up close, she was even more striking. Her skin porcelain, her eyes sapphire, and her luscious lips lightly glossed. They reminded me a lot of my new assistant's, especially the way the corners turned up like a Cupid's bow. They were lips made for cock sucking. She smiled seductively again.

"It's reserved for my sister. She went to the ladies' room. You can have it until she gets back."

"Great," said my companion, scooting onto the stool while I leaned against the bar.

"Watcha drinking, angel?" Brock asked, already on the make.

"A pink margarita." She took another sip.

Another almost empty margarita glass was on the bar counter where Brock was sitting. Probably the sister's. A little bit of salt still coated the rim.

The blonde finished her drink, but before she could set the glass down, Brock took it from her.

"Can I buy you another?"

Oh, man, he was slick.

"Sure."

"You know what, I'm going to order a pitcher." Brock turned to me. "Is that okay by you, bro?"

"Go for it." I really wanted a gin and tonic, but I wasn't about to fuck things up.

While Brock got the attention of a bartender, the blond babe smiled at me and then returned her attention to Brock after he placed the order.

"Why don't you introduce me to your friend, stranger?"

"Sorry. This is my buddy, Drake, and my name's Brock.

"Hi," she said breathily, sizing both of us up. That's what chicks did. Mentally, they were calculating how much money we made and how big our dicks were. The more the better. I guess we passed the test because she didn't brush us off. At least, not yet.

"I'm Lulu. So, what do you guys do?"

Yup. She was going for the jugular. Not wasting a second to see if we were worth her time. Or should I say, net-worthy. Brock responded.

"I'm a lawyer. And Drake's in the entertainment business."

Her eyes stayed fixed on Brock. "Cool. What kind of law do you practice?"

"Family law. Did you read about the woman who sued her sperm donor and won child support?"

My muscles clenched. Brock's cockiness was bad enough, but every time he brought up this case (he had no clue about my little extra-curricular college activity), I saw my life savings pouring out of my bank account like water. Given all the women I'd likely impregnated, I could be cleaned out for life. And I'm sure my old man would cut off my inheritance. Maybe even boot me out of the company.

Her eyes lit up. "Yeah, that was all over the news. You represented her?"

"Yeah, that was me." Brock flashed a big shit-eating grin. He could be such a pompous asshole. But I guess it took one to know one.

Lulu raked her manicured fingers through her mane. "Wow! You're like famous."

Rich and famous. Still smiling smugly, he did his Mr. Humble Pie bit. He really had his act down to an art.

"Yeah, kind of," he replied, eyeing her cleavage. Subconsciously, she adjusted one of her spaghetti straps. When it slipped down her shoulder again, Brock nimbly slid it back up.

"Thanks," she breathed out, batting her eyes at him. Oh yeah, she was on fire, and I was positive that whatever little lace panties she had on were melting. Things were looking good for Brock. The bartender returned with the pitcher of margaritas along with two salt-laced glasses, one for Brock and the other for me. As Brock filled Lulu's glass and then his, the chair to his right became vacant and I took it, taking my glass with me.

"So, Lulu, tell me a little bit about yourself," Brock lilted, setting the pitcher down in front of me. While most men wanted to talk about themselves, Brock was smart enough to know that women loved it when men took an interest in what they did. His favorite pick-up line was coming.

"Are you a supermodel or something?"

Flushing, Lulu giggled. "Hardly. I'm a Zumba instructor."

"Well, you sure have a great body."

That you can't wait to fuck.

"I bet you have a lot of great moves."

I could feel the heat rising between them. Sparks were flying.

She guzzled her margarita before saying, "Yes, you could say that."

"I have a few too."

That was for sure. His gaze traveled down her taut body. He was mentally undressing her. Eye fucking her. I just knew what was going on in his head. This beautiful babe butt naked, bent over with her sweet ass in the air. And him behind her, banging her hard. His own kind of Zumba. Or was that my fantasy? A familiar voice cut my ruminations short.

"Excuse me. You're sitting in my chair."

Holy shit! Could it be? I wondered as Brock stood up and I froze.

"Sorry," my buddy apologized, spinning around.

Lulu jumped in. "This is my sister . . . "

I heard her name on her lips before she said it.

"Deandra. But I call her Dee-Dee."

"Nice to meet you. I'm Brock and this is my friend, Drake."

"Drake?" Her voice cracked with a mixture of shock and disbelief.

My heart raced as I cringed. My head bowed down. But beneath the bar, my cock bounced up.

Hesitantly, I looked up and faced her. She looked as sexy as sin, dressed in tight jeans that showed off her curves and a sheer short-sleeve blouse that fell off her shoulders. Her thick, wavy hair was loose and grazed her shoulders like a whimsical cape. The silence between us vibrated as loudly as the dance music that was blasting.

"Come on, beautiful, let's dance," said Brock, taking Lulu by the hand.

With a saucy smile, Lulu told her sister she could have her seat.

Hopping onto the stool, Dee immediately grabbed the margarita pitcher and filled her glass to the brim. I would have done it for her, but she didn't give me a chance. I watched as she drained it, and as she took giant gulps, I contemplated what to say.

"What are you doing here?" I asked.

After another gulp, she set her glass down. "The same thing you are."

Looking for a hook-up? I refilled her glass and then poured myself an equal helping of the margarita. We were going to need it.

"And what would that be?" I asked after taking a chug of the intoxicatingly sweet, icy drink.

"You know, chilling. Checking out the scene."

The scene was a blur to me. The only person I was interested in checking out was the intriguing, sexy woman sitting beside me. Wanting so badly to touch her, I fumbled for conversation.

"Um, how did you like your first day on the job?"

"Great. I totally enjoyed it."

To say I totally enjoyed it, too, was the understatement of the century. At the memory of her making me come in my pants, my cock tensed. I squirmed in my chair, seeking relief.

"How 'bout another round?" I asked, noticing that her glass was verging on empty.

"Um, uh, sure," she replied, lifting her glass to those kissable lips once it was refilled. Sipping the drink, she swiveled her neck and took in the crowd of dancers on the floor.

"Looks like your friend is really into my sister."

Looking over my shoulder, I followed her gaze and found Brock and Lulu dancing up a storm. Brock was grinding her, and with her arms swinging high in the air, she was gyrating her hips to meet his every move. Brock loved to dance, and in no time, his hands were cupping her fine ass, pulling her closer until he was practically dry humping her. Let me tell you, Brock's cock was dancing *up* a storm too. And Dee's sister was enjoying every fucking minute.

"Do you come here often?" I asked.

"Hardly. This is a first. My sister insisted on taking me here to celebrate my first day at work in LA. I'm really kind of a homebody. What about you?"

"I get out and about."

"I saw a lot of pictures of you online with supermodel types."

I cocked a brow, unsure if the sudden pitchiness of her voice was to counter the loud, thudding music or the result of being buzzed. Or a combination of both.

"Oh, so that's how you spent your time while I was in meetings all day?"

My eyes stayed on her as she took another long sip of the frosty pink drink and then licked her sensuous lips.

"I just wanted to have a better idea of who I was working for." She unexpectedly hiccupped, and something about the little hitch in her breath was so damn adorable, my cock twitched. She excused herself before babbling on.

"Who's that redhead I saw in a lot of the photos?"

My breath caught. Krizia. Crazy, desperate Krizia. She'd been after me for years. "My parents' personal publicist. It's nothing."

"Well, it looks like she's really into you."

"She's a camera hog. She enjoys having her photo taken by the paparazzi."

"Oh, so she's like arm candy." Studying my face, she knit her brows. "You're not gay, are you?"

I practically laughed out the next sip of my drink, but swallowed just in time. "No, I'm not gay. What made you say that?"

Before she could answer, a familiar voice drifted into my ear. Brock. I spun around. A sheen of sweat coated his face, and an arm was wrapped around Dee's sister. Getting laid was inevitable.

"Yo, Drakester, get your ass on the dance floor."

"Yeah," echoed Lulu. "You should ask my sister to dance. She's an amazing dancer."

I turned to face my companion. Even in the dim light, I could see her cheeks flushing. She nervously bit down on her lip.

"Don't believe her. I can't dance."

When I turned to face my best bud again, he and Lulu were already locked in a heated kiss, her arms flung around his neck and his looped around her lower back—crawling to her ass. I hated being a voyeur. Impulsively, I grabbed Dee's hand and coaxed her off the barstool.

"I don't believe *you*. Let's dance."

"No, please," she protested.

"C'mon. Boss's orders."

Grabbing her margarita glass with her free hand and downing what remained, she set it back down on the counter and hesitantly let me lead the way. She was buzzed; I was buzzed. The thudding music quickened my gait and anticipation zipped through my veins. Weaving in and out of the crowd, I squeezed Dee's hand, not wanting to lose her.

As we stepped onto the dance floor, the music suddenly changed. Ed Sheeran's "Thinking Out Loud" was playing. The lyrics made me even more aware of Dee's soft warm hand in mine and think again of what that talented hand had done to me earlier in the day. It was time for a slow dance. Maybe it was all part of a plan.

CHAPTER 6

Dee

Lulu was telling the truth. I was a very good dancer, but in the arms of my sinfully sexy boss, I felt like was stepping all over myself. Maybe because I was so buzzed. And so turned on.

My hands rested on his broad shoulders while his arms draped around my back, holding me firmly and swaying me side to side as Ed Sheeran played on the sound system. With my five-foot-four body stuffed into my spikey heels, I was almost eye-level with him and close enough to feel his warm breath heat my cheeks. I soaked in his gorgeous face. His scorching blue eyes, manly straight nose, luscious mouth, and strong jaw that was laced with an oh so sexy fine layer of stubble. Call me drunk, but I was at a loss for words and knew that anything that came out of my mouth would be slurred or sound all wrong. I was hoping there would be no need for conversation. Wishful thinking.

"Your sister was right. You *are* a good dancer," he began with a sexy smile.

Heating, I managed a small thanks. I refrained from telling him that I was just following his lead. He was a great dancer himself. Smooth, fluid, and definitely in control.

"You okay?" asked Drake, gripping me tighter and drawing me closer to him. So close my breasts grazed his steely chest, my fingers longing to run over every ripple of his defined abs. My nipples hardened and a spray of tingles showered me from head to toe. I stared into his blue orbs.

"Are you sure you're not gay?" Why did I keep asking this question? Was I too blitzed to make intelligent conversation? Or was I simply looking for a reason to not be physically attracted to him?

He rolled his eyes at me and then a wicked smirk lifted his edible lips. "Geez. Do I have to prove it to you?"

On my next heartbeat, his lips came crashing down on mine in a fierce kiss ripped right out of a movie. In seconds, our tongues were dancing and my fingers were fisting his hair, pulling his face toward me and deepening the kiss . . . a kiss like none other.

God. It had been so long. He tasted warm and delicious, a mixture of sweet and salty from the margaritas. A bolt of electricity shot through me, igniting every cell in my body, causing an explosion of fireworks behind my eyelids. As he drew me tighter against him, his hardness pressed against my stomach, and I could feel the heat of it right through his jeans. My fingers clung to the roots of his silky hair, fearing that if I let go I would move my hand between his legs and do a crotch grab, that's if I didn't faint first. Or yank down his fly.

Finally, as the song ended, he withdrew his mouth from mine. The intoxicating taste of him lingered on my tongue.

"Are you satisfied?" he asked softly, his hooded eyes locking with mine.

I wanted his lips back on mine in the worst way. As if I was thinking out loud, his lips touched down again and this time my moans filled his mouth as I reclaimed it with equal hunger and need.

Another barrage of sparks bombarded me as I felt myself orbiting into the stratosphere. My head was spinning. Everything was spinning. Yup, I was leaving the planet.

CHAPTER 7

Drake

"If you're happy and you know it, clap your hands." *Clap Clap.*

I had practically carried my adorable temp off the dance floor and now she was seated at the bar next to her sister, singing at the top of her lungs. Brock and I flanked them, stomping our feet on the next verse. More and more off key, she sung on.

"If you're happy and you know it, shout 'Hooray!'"

"Hooray!" shouted Brock and Lulu along with Dee. Drinking another round of margaritas, they definitely looked happy. With his free hand, Brock was touching Lulu in all the right places and Lulu was loving it.

I pretended to be into the drunken fun the three of them were having, but I was more sober and pensive than I made out to be. I'd learned a lot about Dee on the dance floor. Not only was she a great dancer like her sister said, she was also a great kisser. And I learned something about myself: I liked holding her in my arms and kissing her. Who was I kidding? I more than liked it. She felt and tasted delicious. In retrospect, maybe I shouldn't have kissed her, but I couldn't resist.

"Whoo hoo!" shouted Dee, several decibels louder and brandishing her arms.

"Is she always like this?" I asked Lulu.

Lulu burst into laughter. "Never. She rarely drinks. I think she's sloshed."

That was for sure. Still singing at the top of her lungs, Dee reached for the margarita pitcher, but I stopped her midway.

"Boo!" she pouted, ruffling my hair. "Why'd you do that?"

"Because you've had enough."

"Please, pretty please. With a cherry on top?"

"I think she needs to go home." But I was speaking to deaf ears. Dee's sister was back to making out with Brock. I wasn't sure how my temp had gotten here. But if she had driven, there was no way I was going to let her drive home in her inebriated state. And if she'd come with Lulu, there was no way I was going to ask her to take her home and ruin my best bud's good chance of getting laid. And the third alternative—putting her in a cab or Uber worried me as she wasn't coherent and could end up in some gang-ridden neighborhood. So it was up to me.

Waiting outside the club for the valet to bring around my car, I clutched Dee by the waist in an effort to keep her standing. Shit faced, she'd grown even loopier, becoming very talkative and bold. She was vomiting words and that's all I hoped would spill out of her mouth. The thought of her puking inside my brand-new Maserati Gran Turismo scared the shit out of me.

"How are you feeling?" I asked, hoping my car would get here soon.

"Do you have a twin?"

Balls. She was seeing double.

"He's as hot as you are. Is his cock—*hiccup*—as big as yours?"

I couldn't help but laugh. "Shhh! Don't tell him I told you, but mine is bigger."

She glanced down at my crotch, her eyes sizing me up before darting to the "other" me. And then another hiccup. "I don't believe you. I want you to prove it." A hand flew to my fly, and as she groped my dick, my breath hitched with anticipation. Was she going to give me a hand job right here on the curb? As she began to fiddle with the tab of the zipper, the valet whipped around with my shiny black convertible. The top was down. My cock was up.

"C'mon," I urged, ushering her into the car. "It's time to take you home."

"But I want to see your cock first. Please. Pretty please?"

"Later," I replied as I buckled her in. Handing the valet a generous tip, I rounded the car and hopped into the driver's seat. With a screech, I peeled off the curb.

Shortly into the ride, I managed to secure Dee's address; her case of the hiccups didn't make it easy. Fortunately, she didn't live far away and given that there was little traffic, I could be there in about fifteen minutes. She was still talkative and tipsy. And totally adorable. She started singing again at the top of her lungs, totally off key and hiccupping non-stop.

"If you're horny and you know it, unzip your fly . . . if you're horny and you know it and you really want to show it . . ."

The hiccups kept coming. I wish she could get her mind off my cock. Though, to be honest, the thought of her lush mouth sucking it was making me hard again. My manhood throbbed.

By the time I reached Dee's residence, she was totally conked out. I was relieved because it meant my car had been spared a barf wash. After parking it, I dipped my hand into her purse and retrieved her key chain. One of the many keys must be for her house.

Dee lived in a funky Los Angeles neighborhood known as Silver Lake. It was home to lots of artsy types and aspiring actors. Her house, a small quaint Spanish cottage that was probably built in the twenties, sat almost at the end of a long winding hillside road. The house next door, which seemed vacant, was for sale, and on the other side was a deserted lot. There were bars on the windows, reminding me that this wasn't the greatest neighborhood for a single girl to live in. Or even a guy. Break-ins and car thefts were frequent. I put up my top and made a mental note to lock my Maserati.

After scooting out of it, I scooped my temp into my arms and had no choice but to throw her over my shoulder so I could unlock her front door. My other hand gripped her right below her perfect ass. I felt like *Captain Caveman*, one of the first animated series my father had created.

At the front door, I lucked out with the first key I tried. It opened easily with two turns and I carted Dee inside. Flipping on the lights, I soaked in my surroundings. I'd stepped right into her living room—typical of these vintage Spanish-style houses. My eyes darted from corner to corner. Her living room was smaller than the grand entrance of my parents' house, and it was filled with boxes suggesting she'd either just moved in or was about to move out. The sparse furnishings were definitely flea market finds, my attention drawn to the whimsical paintings on the walls of big-eyed children. Knowing a little about art from my mother the collector, I decided whoever painted them was very talented.

A hoarse mumble cut into my thoughts.

"Need to call Tyson."

Tyson? Who was that? Her boyfriend?

"Need to say goodnight."

"Who's Tyson?" I dared to ask.

"The love of my life." The words came out in slurred one-syllables. My chest constricted. There was someone in her life. Boner downer. Glumly, I headed over to the couch and set her down.

Without warning, she grew agitated and began to cry. Desperate words spilled out of her quivering lips. "Need to call my baby . . . Say I love you from here to the moon . . . Give each other a big kiss."

Ms. Happy and You Know It was a whimpering mess. I wasn't too happy either. Red-hot jealousy shot through my veins and I wasn't even the jealous type. I'd been played. Yet, despite my rising rage, her sobs were gutting me.

"C'mon. You need to go to sleep."

On my next breath, I set her down on the couch and she curled into a fetal position. Her sobs continued to fill the room. "I miss my baby."

There was no point in moving her to her bedroom, and I didn't especially want to see the bed where she and this Tyson guy fucked. Searching the living room, I spotted an afghan on a rocking chair and retrieved it. Gently, I folded it over her heaving body as her sobs subsided. In no time, she was out like a light. A much as I wanted to kiss her goodnight, it was my cue to leave.

CHAPTER 8

Dee

A loud pounding sounded at the front door. It was nothing compared to the pounding in my head. Slowly, I peeled my eyes open, one at a time. It was as if they were super-glued shut.

The pounding at the door persisted. And then the doorbell rang again and again. The banging and chiming were making my headache feel worse, if worse was possible.

Slowly, I sat up and took in my surroundings. I was home, but I had no recollection of how I got here. The blinding sunlight that was filtering through the window was my only clue that it was early morning. I rubbed my throbbing temples and, after swallowing, discovered how parched my throat was. In a word, I felt like shit.

"Dee-Dee, open up," shouted a familiar voice. "I can't find my key." It was my sister, Lulu.

Draping the afghan over my shoulders, I made it to my feet and staggered to the front door. At the sight of my sister still dressed in a halter-top and skin-tight jeans with her mane of hair in just fucked mode, the fog that clouded my mind began to lift. Panic set in.

"Brock was amazing!" she spewed as she made her way into the house we shared. "We fucked all night long. You wouldn't believe all the insane positions. And you should see his apartment. It's a penthouse on the Wilshire Corridor. I think he's loaded in more ways than one." Tossing her bag on the couch, she asked, "Did you get laid?"

Her question made my blood run cold. Oh God! Did I? I didn't know. My mouth couldn't form words.

"Brock's friend Drake was really into you. That kiss must have made the *Guinness Book of Records*. The longest kiss ever!"

"We kissed?" My voice quivered.

"Twice," replied my sister with a big grin.

Oh, Geez! How many margaritas had I drunk? What else had I done?

"How did I get home?"

"Drake gave you a ride in his car. You were pretty snockered." She sauntered in the direction of the kitchen. "I'm going to make a pot of coffee, okay?"

"Yeah, that would be great," I mumbled as I futilely searched my fuzzy mind for any clue of what had happened after Drake drove me home. Though I was still fully clothed, that didn't prove anything. A shudder rippled through me as Lulu returned with two mugs of much needed coffee.

"So, did you get laid?" my persistent sister asked again, handing me one of the steaming mugs.

The tantalizing aroma of the strong brew awakened my senses and just one caffeinated sip erased the stale taste in my mouth. It did not, however, restore my memory of last night.

"I don't know," I murmured as she plopped down on the couch where I'd slept. *And fucked Drake?*

Lulu rolled her eyes. "Well, I sure hope you did. He's hot as shit. Are you going to see him again?"

Fortifying myself with a deep breath, I just blurted it out. "Lulu, he's my new boss."

About to take a sip of her coffee, Lulu froze. "Whoa!"

"Yeah . . . whoa. How am I going to face him?"

Pensively, Lulu sipped her coffee and then looked up at me. "You're just going to be yourself. Trust me, he really liked you. And if he did screw you, he's going to like you more."

I processed her words. So much of me wanted to crawl into bed and stay under the covers for the rest of my life. But I couldn't afford to lose my job. I needed the money and temporary jobs were hard to come by.

"What time is it?" I asked with resignation.

My eyes stayed on her as she pulled her cell phone out from her jeans pocket.

"It's five after nine."

"Oh shit! I'm late for work. And I need a ride." Wait! Maybe I should just call in sick. The thought of having to face my gorgeous boss after all that might have transpired last night sent a shiver down my spine. Dread filled every crevice of my body.

"Did you tell him about Tyson?" asked my sister as I trudged to the bathroom to shower.

Tyson . . . my true love. At her words, a heart-wrenching thought stabbed me. I hadn't called last night to say I love you. And now it was too late.

As late as I was, I stopped at the coffee station before I headed to my desk. My mind was in a frenzy. What was I going to say to him? *Thank you for kissing me, and by the way, did you fuck me?* How was I going to look him in the face, oh that sinfully beautiful face, without imagining his lips on my mine as his tongue swept through my mouth and sent me orbiting? Anxiously, I slogged down the hall to my desk, pondering answers to these questions and more. The coffee wasn't giving me any clarity.

His office door was closed when I got there. As I sat down at my desk and booted up my computer, I remembered he had a meeting this morning with some animation director. Maybe it would last all day.

I hadn't even taken off my sunglasses when I heard his door click open. I felt my shoulders stiffen and my stomach tighten.

"Well, good-morning." His voice was business-like.

"I thought you had a meeting out of the office," I spluttered, not looking away from my computer screen.

"It got canceled." From the corner of my eye, I watched as he rounded my desk. He was now facing me, seductively posing, with his strong, muscular arms folded across his broad chest. He was wearing his basic sexy uniform—a yummy T-shirt, low slung jeans, and Nikes. An unnerving smirk curved his lips. "How are you feeling?"

"I'm fine." *I'm dying here.* I chewed on my lip. "About last night, I'm sorry—"

He cut me off. "There's nothing to be sorry about. We've all gotten a little plastered."

"N-no, really I'm sorry if I did anything out of line. I'd totally understand if you want to fire me."

To my surprise, he laughed. "Trust me, you didn't do anything too drastic. You're actually quite a funny drunk and I have no intention of firing you."

"Really?" I squeaked, still not knowing how far I'd gone with him.

"Really," he smiled back and then winked. "I hope I convinced you that I'm not gay."

What was he implying? I let him fuck me? Before I could get my mouth to move, my cell phone rang. "Excuse me. I hope you don't mind, but I need to take this." The phone kept ringing.

"Go ahead . . . by the way, nice shades."

Fumbling, I reached into my purse and found my phone. Upon seeing the caller ID, my heartbeat quickened as I put the phone to my ear. As I listened to the voice on the other end, my thudding heart leapt into my throat and every muscle in my body clenched.

"Oh my God! I'll get there as soon as I can." Every nerve in my body was crackling with fear and I felt tears welling up in my eyes. I met my boss's concerned gaze as a few escaped.

"What's the matter?"

"Oh my God. It's Tyson!"

His brows furrowed. "Your boyfriend?"

"No, my daughter. She's in the emergency room!"

A look of shock washed over Drake's face. His brows shot up. "What happened?"

"She was stung by a bee during recess and had a seizure."

"Jesus."

"I-I've got to get to the hospital. I need to call for an Uber."

"Don't bother. C'mon, I'll take you."

CHAPTER 9

Drake

I mentally hit my reset button. So, my new temp had a kid. A little girl named Tyson who was in kindergarten. I sure wasn't prepared for the K-bomb. Or the explosion of questions that accompanied it. Was Dee married? Divorced? Separated? As much as I yearned to know, this wasn't the time to probe. This was an emergency.

For the second time in less than twenty-four hours, my assistant was sitting next to me in my car. Taking the I-5, my Maserati wove through the five-lane freeway en route to Children's Hospital where her daughter had been taken. I kept my eyes glued to the road but occasionally shot a look her way. The wild tipsy look from last night was gone, replaced by a somberness that bordered on fear. After thanking me for the ride, a tense silence prevailed over the whoosh of the wind and traffic. Speeding down Los Feliz Boulevard where I exited, I glanced into the rearview mirror.

"Shit!"

"What's the matter?"

"There's a cop behind me. He wants me to pull over."

"Oh my God! NO!"

There was no way I could pull over on the busy thoroughfare so I activated my right turn signal to let the cop know I was turning onto the next residential street. He got the message and followed me.

Pulling up behind me, the cop got out of his car and approached me. "Sir, do you know you were going way over the speed limit?"

Before I could get out a word, Dee broke down in tears. "Oh, Officer, we're so sorry. My daughter was rushed to Children's Hospital, unconscious from a bee sting."

A look of compassion washed over the officer's ruddy face. "Ma'am, I totally understand. That happened to one of my kids from a peanut allergy. C'mon, just follow me and I'll get you there in no time."

With tears still dripping down her face, Dee clasped both hands to her heart. "Oh, thank you, Officer." And I thanked him too.

Thanks to Officer O'Riley, we got to the hospital in five quick minutes. I clutched Dee's icy hand as we raced to the information center. I didn't think about it much; it just felt right. And she didn't resist. Breathlessly, I introduced myself, and in no time, thanks to my VIP status, we were in the critical care unit where Dee's daughter, Tyson, had been transported. A silver-haired nurse named Mary immediately met us.

"My daughter . . . can I see her? Is she all right?" Dee blurted out in a panic.

"She went into anaphylactic shock."

"Anaphylactic shock?"

"A rare, life-threatening allergic reaction to a bee sting," I offered solemnly, flashing back to my own childhood experience with a bee sting. While I didn't quite go into shock, I broke out in hives, my tongue swelled, and I couldn't breathe. Bees still freaked me out.

"Exactly," replied Nurse Mary.

Dee's eyes widened. "I had no idea she was allergic to bees. She's never been stung before."

"According to her teacher, she initially broke out in hives, but when her face began to swell and she complained she couldn't breathe, she immediately called 9-1-1. The paramedics got there just as she lost consciousness and injected her with adrenaline to counter the severe reaction."

"Oh my God! Is she still unconscious?"

"She returned to consciousness, but she's sound asleep now." The nurse smiled. "She's a very lucky little girl. Everything seems stable."

Dee let out a loud sigh of relief. The hold on my hand loosened, but she still clung to it like a lifeline. "Can I see her?"

"Of course, follow me."

"I'll wait here," I murmured.

"No, please come with me. I'd love for you to meet her."

"No, really, I'd rather not. I'm not good with kids. And maybe I'll scare her."

Dee relaxed for the first time and let out a small laugh. "Trust me, nothing scares her. Well, except maybe bees do now."

I don't know what made me do it, but I stayed with Dee and followed Nurse Mary down the hall to Tyson's room. I kept my eyes straight ahead of me, not wanting to glimpse the critically sick kids in this ward. My philanthropic mother, God bless her, did a lot to cheer these children up, from putting on magic shows to sponsoring therapy dogs who put big smiles on their faces.

Tyson's room was at the very end of the long corridor. I felt bad there were so many sick children in this world. I didn't know how parents coped with that awful fate. A normal kid was a big enough responsibility. But a sick one?

A disquieting thought hit me. I hoped that none of the women I'd impregnated had to go through that. Yet another good reason not to have kids.

As we stepped into Tyson's small sterile room, Dee let out a gasp and ran to her side. The little girl was sound asleep, but hooked up to IVs and had a breathing tube in her nose.

"Oh my God. What are all these machines and tubes?" Dee asked as she caressed the child's angelic face.

"They're just intravenous fluids to regulate her heartbeat and circulatory system. The breathing tube is just an extra precautionary measure."

"My poor baby."

"Don't worry, Mrs. McDermott—"

Dee stopped her short. "I go by my maiden name, Walker. So does my daughter."

Unfazed, Nurse Mary continued. "Most likely by this evening, all the tubes will be removed. We'd like to keep her here overnight for observation."

"Of course," Dee said softly, still caressing her little one.

"I'll be back shortly to check on her," said Nurse Mary as she headed to the door and then disappeared.

My eyes stayed on Dee and her daughter. Despite my macho façade, the scene tugged at my heartstrings. There was something about her maternal love for this child that toyed with my emotions and made my bones weaken. I found myself inching closer to the two of them until I was standing beside Dee.

"She's beautiful, isn't she, my little mighty girl?" Dee whispered, never taking her eyes off her daughter.

"Yeah," I swallowed. Up close, the child was indeed a little beauty with ivory skin, an upturned button nose, and two long, thick dark pigtails. And despite the breathing tube, her full ruby-red lips curled into a little smile. The rise and fall of her chest and her soft breathing mesmerized me.

"How old is she?" I asked, keeping my voice down. "Five?"

"She'll be six at the end of the week. This Sunday."

"Well, you definitely have a reason to celebrate."

"That's for sure." Dee's voice grew watery and before long she was sniffling again.

"What's the matter? She's going to be okay."

Dee brushed away her tears with a hand. On the nightstand, I eyed a box of Kleenex and handed her one.

"Thanks," she choked out after blowing her nose. "I'm just overwhelmed. If something ever happened to her, I don't know what I'd do. She's everything to me. My universe. If she died, I would die too."

Her words left me speechless. What was I going to say? I understand. No, self-centered single forever me didn't really understand this intense level of love and loss even though my parents had many years ago experienced an unexpected life or death tragedy that tested their mettle. And their love for one another.

"I should get back to the office," I said, floundering for words.

"Do you mind if I stay here until she wakes up?"

"Take the day off."

"Are you sure?"

"Positive. I don't have a lot going on. I'll be fine."

I wasn't prepared for Dee's reaction. She turned around and flung her arms around me, giving me a big hug.

"Drake, I don't know how to thank you."

Oh, I could think of a couple ways as I felt the beginnings of an erection beneath my jeans. She felt delicious, so soft, and feminine, and her vulnerability made her even more appealing. I'd never been so attracted to a woman. Not even to stunning supermodel-like Krizia. There was just something about her.

CHAPTER 10

Dee

Only a few hours ago, I was hung-over. A total trainwreck. This life-and-death encounter had sobered me up fast. In fact, I felt horribly guilty about getting plastered last night. I could have done something really dumb that endangered my life. As I watched Ty stir, I vowed never to lose my precious baby. And to never again do anything that could take me away from her. I didn't want to be my mother, the drunkard who passed out nightly and abandoned us for days at a time during her binges. Even worse was the possibility that she'd end up with her father. I trembled at the thought.

The face of another man broke into my dark thoughts. Drake. My gorgeous new boss. Though I still wasn't sure if he'd taken advantage of me, he'd been there for me last night and he'd been there for me today. Somehow his presence helped me weather this nerve-wracking storm. He comforted me, made me feel safe. And he'd put up with both my drunken stupor and my deep-rooted fears. Even my tears. When I hugged him, I felt myself melt into him and didn't want to let him go.

While watching over Tyson, I called my sister to let her know what had happened. She was greatly relieved to hear that her treasured niece was going to be okay. Between

Zumba classes, she was going to run to the house and grab a few of Ty's favorite things as well as her PJs. I told her to also pack a small bag for me with a few necessities because there was no way I was going to leave my baby alone in the hospital. Not even for a night. Lulu promised she would be here later in the afternoon.

Soon after I hung up with Lulu, a hospital attendant stopped by carrying a huge basket with a large "Get Well" balloon attached to it. Inside, were adorable hand-drawn cards from Tyson's kindergarten classmates. Each one put a big smile on my face, and I knew she would love them. I made a call to her teacher to thank her and update her on Ty's condition. While I spoke with her, a warm feeling saturated me. I felt blessed I would be teaching art at this school in the fall and be among these lovely children and teachers. Mrs. Dunne was thrilled to hear that Tyson would likely be back in school sometime tomorrow. The hospital was sending us home with a couple of adrenaline-filled Epipens, one for me and one for her teacher, that could be used to inject her should she get stung by a bee again and have another severe reaction.

As I was reading through the cards, a familiar little raspy voice sounded in my ears.

"Mommy! I'm thirsty!"

Joy filled every molecule of my being. My little girl was awake. Leaping to my feet, I placed the basket of cards on the chair. Fighting back happy tears, I ran over to her and smothered her with kisses.

"Oh, cupcake, I'm so happy you're okay." I reached for the sippy cup on the nightstand and held it to her lips. "Drink slowly, my baby girl." Sitting up, she guzzled the water.

"How do you feel, my love?" I asked as she took her last sip.

"Much better, Mommy." She took a deep breath and

exhaled loudly. "I can breathe perfectly fine. What are all these weird machines and what's this yucky thingy up my nose?"

"They're just some machines to help your heart beat better and make it easier for you to breathe. They're going to come out soon."

My feisty little girl screwed up her face. "No, now! I want to go back to school."

My gaze turned to the basket of cards. I stood up and fetched it. I set the basket on the bed.

"Look at what all your friends made."

"Cool!" She began leafing through the colorful cards and then started laughing. "Look! Chandra drew a picture of us."

"Let me see." Chandra was her best friend, whose house she had slept over. It was a stick figure drawing of two little girls holding hands, one with short curly hair, the other with long braids.

"It looks just like you! Oh and by the way, your teacher, Mrs. Dunne, sends you a big hug."

"She told me that the bee that stung me is going to die. Is he going to go to heaven, Mommy?" Her eyes grew wide with worry.

My sweet little girl loved all creatures, great and small. She was perpetually rescuing ladybugs and stray animals, and loved to leave food for birds and squirrels. I told her the bee probably wasn't going to die, but if he did he was going to go to honeycomb heaven to be with all his brothers and sisters.

The afternoon whizzed by. Nurse after nurse stopped by to meet my sweet, precocious daughter, who by now could recite the bee-sting story in full drama queen mode. With the television tuned to the Peanuts channel, we both had lunch, which was surprisingly good for hospital food, and devoured the extra Jell-Os with whip cream. Lulu stopped by with all the things I requested and brought along a cute stuffed teddy bear to add to Tyson's collection; she loved it and named him Honeybear. My sister stayed for about an hour. Just after her departure, Tyson's doctor stopped by to remove all her tubes, including the breathing aid in her nose. He put cartoon character Band-Aids on her arms where the IVs had been. Hanson Entertainment's *Danger Rangers*, one of Tyson's favorite shows. My mind drifted to Drake for a minute and a hot tingle shot through me.

"You know, I'm working for the man whose company makes *Danger Rangers*."

"That's so cool, Mommy. Do you think I could meet them?"

"I think I can arrange that, Mighty Girl."

My heart skipped a beat as ticklish shivers skittered down my spine. Drake!

"Yay!" shouted Tyson.

I shifted my body so that I was facing Drake at the doorway. His sparkling blue eyes, which were close in color to Tyson's, met mine and a dazzling smile lit up his swoon-worthy face. My heart thudded, and butterflies fluttered in my stomach.

"Um, uh, honey, this is Drake Hanson. The man I told you I work for."

"Hi," said Drake with a wave of his hand.

"Hi, Mr. *Handsome!*"

I flushed. Oh, God was he!

"I've brought along a few things I thought you might like."

Drake stepped into the room and my eyes popped as a hospital attendant wheeled in a dolly piled high with toys, all inspired by Hanson cartoons.

"Wowee!" exclaimed my overjoyed little girl.

"Drake, you shouldn't have."

I was totally, utterly blown away by my boss's kindness. For a guy who wasn't crazy about kids, he sure had a weird way of showing it.

"Drake, seriously, I don't know how to thank you." For the second time today, I found myself uttering these words.

A devilish grin crossed Drake's face. "I do. Have dinner with me."

"B-but, I'm staying overnight at the hospital. I can't leave Tyson."

Drake flicked the tip of my nose, a small gesture that set every cell on fire. "You won't have to. We're not going anywhere."

CHAPTER 11
Drake

It wasn't hard convincing Dee to have dinner with me in the hospital cafeteria after Tyson fell asleep. She was starving and now that Tyson was well on her way to recovery, she felt comfortable taking a short break. As we stood in line waiting for our cheeseburgers and fries, I wondered if I should consider this our first date since I did in theory ask her out. Nah. It was just dinner. And I didn't date.

The cafeteria wasn't crowded so we found a table for two easily. Dee set down her tray, which also included a small Coke like mine, and I helped her into her chair. I took a seat facing her. We simultaneously bit into our burgers. I was starving too.

"Wow, this is so good," she exclaimed.

I swallowed my man-size bite. "Yeah. My mother's a stickler about good food."

She looked at me quizzically. "Your mother is a chef here?"

I almost choked from laughter on my next bite. My mother in an apron behind a stove? I. Don't. Think. So. We'd had professional chefs cook for us for as long as I could remember. We even had a sushi chef that worked for us on weekends or whenever my father entertained Japanese guests at our house. After taking a swig of my Coke, I responded, laughter still in my voice.

"Hardly. She's on the Board of this hospital and is very vociferous. My father made a huge donation to build the Trauma Center that bears our family name so they bow down to her."

Her face lit up with a mixture of awe and surprise. I don't think she knew how rich our family really was thanks to the phenomenal success of *Danger Rangers*. A shrewd businessman and investor, my father liked to joke he made as much money in his sleep as he did awake.

Dee played with her straw, swirling it around in the soda cup. "Are you involved with the hospital too?"

"No, not really. Except on Christmas when my father dresses up as Santa and makes me be his elf."

A winsome smile blossomed on her face. "You're a little big to be an elf."

My cock flexed. "I'd say I'm way big."

She blushed and immediately took another big bite of her burger. God, she was cute even with the ketchup left behind on her lips.

"You've got ketchup on your mouth."

"I do?"

She flushed another shade of red.

"Lean forward."

She did as I asked and with an outstretched hand, I wiped the ketchup off her sensuous mouth with my index finger, sweeping it across her soft, Cupid-bowed lips, longer than I had to, remembering how good they felt against mine. I'd never kissed a girl so hard, so relentlessly. Did she remember? I sucked the ketchup off my finger as her eyes stayed on me. The flavor of her cherry lip-gloss mixed with the condiment and was delicious enough to bottle.

"Thanks," she murmured.

"You've got great lips. They're just like your daughters."

"Thanks," she said again softly, almost embarrassed. "That's one of the few good features she got from me."

"Oh, the rest come from her father?" I suddenly realized I was entering unchartered, potentially dangerous territory. Her face darkened.

"I suppose."

"Does he know what happened?"

Dee's jaw tightened and she fiddled again with her straw. "My husband is in prison. He doesn't know anything about our lives."

My brows shot up. Boy, I sure wasn't ready for that one. I was strapped for words. "I'm sorry," I mumbled, not knowing what else to say.

Dee took a sip of her soda. "Don't be. He's a piece of shit and deserves to be behind bars."

"What did he do?" I ventured.

Dee narrowed her eyes and took in a deep breath. "He assaulted me when he found out I was pregnant. Social services made me press charges." She paused for another breath. "I had to be hospitalized. I almost lost Tyson."

"Jesus. Does Tyson know this?"

"Tyson doesn't even know she has a father. I told her he died in a car accident just before she was born. I didn't want her to know what kind of man he is. For all intents and purposes, he *is* dead to me."

Rage filled her every word. I wasn't sure if I should pursue the subject, but I persevered. "For how long will he be serving time?"

"Ten years. Maybe less if he gets paroled, but I doubt the badass will."

I reflected on the fact that she hadn't once referred to him as her ex. A question burned on my tongue. "Are you divorced?"

"We're separated," she answered bluntly.

"Have you thought about divorcing him?"

"Plenty. But the asshole won't grant me one."

"Why?"

"I think he just wants to make my life difficult and punish me for getting him sentenced. Revenge."

"Isn't there a law that would allow you to?"

"Wishful thinking. A felony used to be grounds for divorce in California, but it no longer is. He's got a very shrewd lawyer named Luis Ramirez and is contesting my plea for irreconcilable differences. I can't afford to keep paying an attorney to fight him."

"That sucks."

"Tell me."

"Is it unlawful for you to see other guys?"

"The court said I can, but truthfully, I haven't wanted to. I've needed to be protective of Tyson. I just don't need another bastard to fuck up our lives. Or hurt us."

I processed her words. Dee came with a lot of baggage. Ugly baggage. Plus, I was her boss. Temporarily, but still. A warning sign should have flashed in my mind, but it didn't. Instead, that kiss, that incredible kiss from last night, was all I could think about. I was intrigued and attracted to her though most guys would be running the other way. I wanted to spend more time with her . . . get to know her better and her cute kid too.

Relationships weren't part of my DNA. And getting involved with someone who worked for me, let alone was still married and had a kid, were hard limits for me. I finished my cheeseburger, unsure of what I was starting.

CHAPTER 12
Dee

Things returned to normal the next morning. Tyson was released from the hospital and was eager to go back to school and tell everyone about her hospital adventure. Since I was carless—my pickup truck was still probably at that damn club and might even be towed—I asked Lulu to swing by the hospital. To my surprise, she was driving my truck, which was fortunate because her Mini was way too small to accommodate all of Drake's stuff. My sweet little girl planned to share the toys with her classmates and even left some behind for the children at the hospital.

"Thanks for picking up the truck," I told my sister as I buckled Tyson into her car seat.

"Don't thank me," she replied, already in the front passenger seat.

"What do you mean?"

"Drake arranged to have it brought to the house."

"Drake, the man you work for, Mommy, who gave me all these toys?" interjected my daughter.

"Yes, cupcake."

"He's the *bestest* man ever!"

My precious little girl was right. Drake was too good to be true. And as I got into the car, it frightened me as much as it excited me.

Drake was out of the office all day. His schedule included several meetings as well as auditions for a new animated series he was developing. I held things down in the office, answering emails, setting up pitches, and doing some filing. In between tasks, my mind drifted to him. It was impossible not to think about him.

I felt beholden to him for getting me through the Tyson crisis. In the course of twenty-four hours, he'd gone from being a jerk to being my hero. Though I still wasn't sure if he screwed me and I wasn't going to ask, his recent actions spoke louder than words. I tried hard to keep myself busy because every time I thought about him, my heart pitter-pattered and a cluster of tingles danced between my legs. He was gorgeous, funny, and successful. I'd never met a man like him nor had I ever been so attracted to anyone. But I didn't have to do a lot of soul searching to know I didn't stand a chance with him. I wasn't his type and what hot, rich single guy would want a woman with a kid, who came with baggage that could sink the Titanic *and* was still married, to a felon no less. Fucking Kyle. I tried to bury him in the back of my mind, wishing I could bury him six feet under.

Facing my glum reality, I heard my cell phone buzz mid afternoon. A text. It was either Lulu because she was the only person in my life who texted me or my wireless carrier telling me I had a payment past due. I reached into my purse for my phone and my heart skipped a beat as I eyeballed the message. It was from Drake! How did he get my cell phone number? Had my sister given it to him? Or maybe he'd gotten it from Human Resources? With an unsteady hand, I read it.

Drake: I'm bored. This audition is dragging on. The

actors can't get their lines right.

Me: I'm sorry. Didn't they practice?
Drake: Nah. Voice actors can be lazy.
Me: It must be fun. Have you ever tried?
Drake: Once. I played a leprechaun prince and had to contort my voice.
Me: What did you have to say?
Drake: I've screwed everyone in this kingdom, but I only have eyes for you, my frog princess.

I almost dropped my phone as I laughed out loud. I could also feel my cheeks heating and wet heat pooling between my legs.

Me: LOL! You didn't really say that.
Drake: I did. Boy Scout Honor.
Me: LOL! You were never a Boy Scout.
Drake: That's true. I was a Girl Scout.

I laughed out loud again. My boss was witty. It was time to show him again that I could be witty too. I could have made some transgender comment, but I went in a different direction.

Me: And what kind of girls did you scout for?
Drake: Cute brunettes with perky boobs and big fat ponytails.

A heat wave flashed through me and the flutters between my legs intensified. Holy shit! He was describing me! He texted again before I could respond.

Drake: What are you doing tonight? Big plans?

I hesitated to reply. Ty had convinced me to let her sleep over her friend Chandra's house again, and with all she'd been through and her birthday around the corner, I couldn't say no. I texted Drake back. With the truth. *Pity party for one*.

Me: Nada.
Drake: :-)

My blood bubbled. The cocky bastard was happy I was alone on a Friday night? Was there a flip off emoji I could send him? Before I could find one and lose my job, he sent me another text.

Drake: I'm coming over. I want you to listen to the auditions with me and help me cast the voices. I can't think straight.

Neither could I. My boss had a dizzying affect on me.

Drake: And you'll be paid overtime.

The extra money, despite how much I needed it, had nothing to do with my sudden temperature spike or giddiness. It was a work date, I told myself. Just a work date.

∽

I got home a little after six. Lulu must be teaching an evening Zumba class as her car wasn't parked in the driveway. I could never keep track of her frenetic schedule especially since it seemed to change weekly. In addition to her group classes at gyms all over the city, she was building a strong client base as a personal Zumba instructor.

Tossing my purse on the couch, I made a beeline for the kitchen, hoping to find a bottle of wine in the fridge. I was both excited and anxious about Drake coming over and hoped a glass of Two Buck Chuck would relax me. *It's business, just business* I told myself, my nerves buzzing.

I stepped into the kitchen and froze. All the air left my lungs.

"What the hell are you doing here?" My voice was filled with shock and rage and I could feel fear pouring into my veins.

A beer bottle in his hand, he turned around and glared at me with his steel blue eyes. A wicked smirk crossed his lips. "Nice to see you too, darlin'. You're lookin' good."

I met his predatory gaze. Kyle! He hadn't changed much . . . still tall and sinewy, but his face was now lined and bearded, his russet hair longer and in some kind of man bun. Jetting from his befitting wifebeater, the sleeves of tattoos that had once so turned me on repulsed me.

He took a long chug of the beer and strutted my way. I was too afraid to move as he swaggered up to me. I could feel the heat of his breath on my cheek and smell the stench of the alcohol. He was for sure drunk. Drunk as usual.

Still holding the bottle, he leaned into me and, with his other hand, yanked hard at my ponytail, pulling my head back. "You let your hair grow. It looks good."

My breath hitched. "I-I thought you were still in prison."

He laughed. "Nope. Been there. Done that. Got out for good behavior. Just call me Mr. Goody Two Shoes." He laughed again.

"How did you find me?"

He snickered. "Piece of cake. I have friends everywhere."

"How did you get in here?"

He snorted. "Looks like someone left the backdoor open."

Dammit. Lulu sometimes did that when she took the garbage out. "Why are you here?"

"I want you back."

My blood turned to Freon as my heart raced in my chest.

"Kyle, it's over. I want you to leave."

His long, pointed tongue slithered across his upper lip. "I'm not going anywhere, babe, until I get a taste of you."

I jerked my head away as his slobbering lips smacked down on mine. He nudged me to open my mouth for his tongue, but I kept my lips clamped. He slid the hand holding the beer between my legs, and began jabbing me with the bottle. Forcefully, harder and harder. He was hurting me.

Moans and groans clogged my throat. And then I did it—I slapped him across his face. So hard the whack stung my hand. He pulled away.

"Why the fuck did you do that, bitch?" He rubbed the rosy handprint I'd left on his right cheek.

"Get the hell out of here."

He snarled. "I'm not going anywhere until I get a piece of your ass and see my kid."

My already rapid heartbeat quickened. I could feel my pulse in my throat. Fear surged in my blood vessels as I tried to think rationally. With his violent streak and drunken state, there was no telling how far he'd go.

"Tyson isn't here. Now, leave!"

"Bullshit. Let me see her or I'm going to give it to you."

"Kyle, if you don't leave, I'm going to call the police."

I impulsively turned on my heel, but as I took a step, he grabbed me, knocking me to the kitchen floor, flat on my back.

"Oh no you're not," he growled, pouncing upon me and holding me down with the weight of his body and the force of his hands. I writhed and wailed. "Let go of me!"

"Shut up, cunt!" he yelled with a sharp whack across my face that made me wince with pain. Tears stung my eyes as he squeezed me prisoner with his legs.

"Please don't hurt me," I begged, the tears now falling. I was trapped by him and helpless. Screaming for help at the top of my lungs wouldn't help as no one lived on either side of our house and rarely did anyone walk by it.

Setting his beer bottle on the floor after another guzzle, he popped the button of his jeans and zipped down his fly. Thank God, he wasn't commando. He rubbed his cock vigorously and I watched it swell beneath the fabric of his black boxer briefs. He breathed heavily against me.

"Remember good ol' Joe Cocker?"

I never wanted to hear that name again. His pet name for his dick. I bit down on my trembling lip.

His mouth twisted into another diabolical smirk. "Well, if you don't, let me refresh your memory."

I shuddered as my breath caught.

"Open your legs for me, sweetheart, or I'll open them for you."

"No, please!" I sobbed out, my entire body shaking. I could already feel the pain of his penetration even before he entered me. How could I have ever fallen in love with this man? This monster.

"Are you wet for me?"

I couldn't get words past my constricted throat. My lips quivered as sobs wracked my body.

"Answer me, bitch!" Without warning, his hand crashed across my face again, this time even harder, leaving a burning sensation in its wake. I cried out in pain. And then my eyes grew wide.

"Get the fuck off her." Two large hands pulled Kyle off me by the edge of his wifebeater. Drake! My knight in shining armor. He shoved Kyle forcefully against the kitchen counter, one hand gripping his neck, the other his shoulder.

"Who the fuck are you?" Kyle choked out, turning red with rage as I scrambled to my feet.

"Your worst nightmare."

"Drake, watch out!"

It was too late for a warning. In one swift move, Kyle grabbed an empty beer bottle off the counter and smashed it over Drake's head. The glass bottle broke in half. I watched in horror as Drake, dazed, recoiled, stumbling on his feet and holding a hand to his head. Blood trickling down his face, he cursed under his breath and groaned.

Stepping backward, I ended up plastered against a wall as Kyle pulled up his worn jeans and took angry giant steps toward me. He pressed his hard, wiry body against me and poked his index finger into my throat, holding it there like a gun. A terrifying thought assaulted me. What if he actually had a gun? Terror filled every cell of my body.

"So, is that your motherfucking boyfriend?" he growled in my face.

"I'm more than her boyfriend," came Drake's enraged voice, "you fucking cocksucker."

Before I could blink, Drake lunged toward Kyle, hurling him off me once more.

"You're going to pay!" Spinning Kyle around, Drake punched him in the face with ear-splitting force and then gave a hard kick to his balls. Cursing, Kyle clutched his crotch.

"And here's another one for good measure, fuckface." With his powerful knee, Drake jabbed Kyle in the balls again. Groaning loudly, Kyle bent over in pain and then staggered out the backdoor. Rather than going after him, Drake took me into his strong arms.

"Are you okay?" he asked, tenderly brushing a strand of hair out of my eye.

Still shaking, I nodded and held him in my gaze. Kyle had cracked open Drake's head and blood was pouring down his face from the sizeable gash above his eyebrow.

"You're hurt."

"I'll live. Who was that motherfucker?"

I heaved a deep breath. "My husband."

CHAPTER 13
Drake

Dee forced me to sit down at the kitchen table while she went to get first aid supplies. My head was fucking killing me and the washcloth full of ice she made me hold to the gash wasn't helping much. That motherfucker! I should have gone after him. Given him what he deserved. But I wanted to stay with Dee.

Dee returned in no time with a small plastic tray holding a box of Band-Aids, a bottle of peroxide, a clump of cotton balls, and a jar of Advil.

"How are you doing?" she asked as she approached me.

"I'm okay."

"Let me see." Gently, she lowered my hand and examined the damage. "Shit. You're going to have a big bump, but the cut doesn't seem too bad. I don't think you'll need stitches."

Stitches? Fuck no. I had them once under my chin when I fell off a jungle gym at the age of seven and then again at seventeen after being hit in the shin by a hockey stick when I was in college.

"Stay still," she said, setting the first aid supplies on the table.

I watched as she opened the peroxide and soaked a couple of cotton balls with the antiseptic solution.

"Shit! That hurts!" I yelped as she dabbed one of them on my wound.

She smiled and continued to dab away. I squirmed in my seat.

"You're worse than a six-year-old."

The fact was all men were big babies. We could take a knife to our heart, but when it came to the little things like a small cut it was like we'd been to war. And don't get me started on guys getting sick. Did you ever hear of a guy with a cold? No, it was always the flu and we were always sick as a dog.

Dee stepped back and examined my face. Her eyes narrowed. "Good. The bleeding is stopping. But you need to keep this cut covered so it won't get infected."

I kept my eyes on her as she opened the box of Band-Aids.

"Are you fucking kidding me? You're going to make me wear a *Danger Rangers* Band-Aid? Those are for six-year-olds."

"That's right. They're Tyson's favorite. And right now, I'd say you're acting like a two-year-old."

I started to roll my eyes at her, but it hurt too much. Instead, I grimaced as she affixed the bandage. Okay, confession. I was enjoying every minute of her attention. I loved the way she was so maternal. So different from all the women who were after me, especially Krizia, who didn't have a maternal bone in her body.

My temp stepped back to examine her handiwork and flashed a proud smile. "All done. You'll be as good as new in a couple days."

My eyes stayed on her as she traipsed to the kitchen sink. Her heart-shaped ass was fucking gorgeous and her gait had a sexy little bounce. Opening a cabinet, she removed a glass and filled it with water. She returned and handed it to me.

"Take some Advil. It'll help with the pain."

Wordlessly, I unscrewed the ibuprofen jar and then downed a couple of the tablets.

Setting down the glass of water on the table, I gazed up at her. "Didn't you forget something?"

Puzzled, she stared at me.

"You know, you need to kiss the boo-boo."

"Oh, right."

As she bent down to kiss me, I impulsively drew her into my arms until she was straddled on my lap. I began to kiss her slender neck, trailing soft kisses from under her chin to her ears, then along the nape. Delicious, sexy little sounds, which were totally turning me on, filled the back of her throat.

"You do a lot of things well," I whispered between kisses, my dick hardening.

"Like what?" she breathed out, arching her back.

"You're great at undoing knots . . . "

"Yeah . . . "

"And you're a terrific dancer . . . "

"What else?" she asked, her voice low and seductive.

"You administer first aid like a pro . . . "

"And . . . "

"You're one hell of a kisser . . . "

Without giving her time to respond, my lips latched onto hers, the kiss hungry and fierce. Her hands moved to my hair as I parted her lips and thrust my tongue into her warm mouth, tangling it with hers. A symphony of moans and groans accompanied the wild clashing of our warm wet vessels.

Without warning, she pulled away. No smile lifted her glistening lips. Instead, a look of regret and confusion washed over her face.

I tipped up her chin with my thumb. "What's the matter?"

"Everything. I wish you didn't have to meet Kyle that way. And we shouldn't be doing this. I'm your assistant."

I kept my thumb pressed to her soft skin and looked straight at her. "Hey, it wasn't your fault he was here and quite frankly, I'm glad I showed up when I did. Lucky thing you didn't lock your door, which in the future you better do." I moved my thumb to her lips, those magical lips, and swept it across the sensuous curves.

She held back a smile. "We should call it a night."

"There's no way I'm leaving because that motherfucker might come back."

"Please, Drake. You don't need all this drama."

"I'm part of the drama now," I countered. "And besides, this is supposed to be a date. I mean a work date."

I quickly corrected myself. "Let me take you out for dinner and then we'll come back here and listen to the auditions."

Folding her arms across her lovely breasts, she pressed her lips thin, contemplating my words. "Okay. Here's the deal. One . . . this is definitely not a date."

"Call it what you want."

"Two . . . forget that I ever kissed you."

I had to bite down on my tongue to stifle my laughter. Was she kidding? I could still taste her on my lips. It almost hurt to say the next words: "Sure. No problem."

"And three . . . we'll stay in and I'll cook."

Victory. My eyes blazed into hers. "Oh, is that another one of your amazing talents?"

She stood up and grinned. "You'll soon find out."

Deal.

CHAPTER 14

Dee

It took me no time to whip up spaghetti and meatballs along with a hearty salad. Rather than eating at the kitchen table, I set up dinner on the coffee table in the living room and managed to find a few votive candles for atmosphere along with a bottle of wine to accompany the meal. Soft jazz, thanks to handy Drake, drifted in the air. The candles, wine, and music should have had a calming effect on me, but I was all aflutter.

I'd be lying if I said he didn't affect me. And it wasn't just physical. He was funny and caring. And I felt beholden to him for saving me from Kyle. It had been years since I'd spent quality time with a man—let alone, one I was insanely attracted to. He looked even more crazy gorgeous in the candlelit room even with the silly Band-Aid above his eyebrow. I was going to have to control myself. Act professional for the rest of the evening. Keep the conversation casual. And pretend that I didn't want those luscious lips all over me.

Sitting on the floor cattycorner to me, Drake inhaled the heaping plate of spaghetti. "Mmm. This smells awesome."

"Thanks. It's Tyson's favorite."

"Where is your daughter?"

"She's at a sleepover. She'll be back in the morning."

"Man, it's a lucky thing she wasn't home."

"Tell me." The thought of her witnessing my encounter with Kyle sent an icy chill down my spine.

"Is she all recovered from the bee sting?" inquired Drake, stopping me from going down an even darker path.

"Yes, totally. Thanks for asking. She was the star of her class. Everyone wanted to know what it was like to be in an ambulance and in the hospital." I poured us each a glass of wine. "And of course, sharing all those toys you got her with her classmates didn't hurt."

"She's a really great kid."

"Yes, she's special. I feel very blessed. Thanks."

He smiled at me and lifted his wine glass. "Bon appétit."

"Bon appétit," I repeated, clinking my glass against his. We each took a sip, and after we set the glasses down, I piled some salad into our bowls. Mental note: Do not drink on an empty stomach. I sure didn't want a repeat of the other night.

Drake immediately dug into the spaghetti and meatballs, twirling a bountiful amount of the long pasta strands around the tines of his fork. My eyes stayed riveted on his bronzed, beautiful biceps, which flexed as he put the forkful to his mouth and sucked in the sauce-covered bundle. Then, silently he went for a meatball.

"Shit!" he blurted out as the meatball disappeared.

My heartbeat sped up with worry. "What's the matter?"

"This is fucking amazing!"

I inwardly sighed with relief as I helped myself to a forkful of salad.

"Where did you learn to cook like this? From your mother?"

"Hardly. My mother was a drunk. She was either screwing someone or passed out so she never made us dinner. I had to take care of my little sister Lulu so I taught myself how to cook by watching the Food Network."

If privileged Drake was shocked by this revelation, he didn't show it. After digging into the salad, he asked, "Where did you grow up?"

"Outside Fresno... in a trailer park." There was no point in hiding the truth. "This kids in school called me trailer trash."

"I'm sorry," Drake said, compassion in his voice. "Some kids can be so mean."

While I took another long sip of the wine to stay loosened up, he twirled some more spaghetti around his fork. "What did your father do?"

I swallowed hard. "I don't know. He abandoned us when Lulu and I were both very young. I have no recollection of him. And have no idea if he's dead or alive."

"How long did you live there?"

"Too long."

"With your sister?"

I shook my head. "No, she was the rebellious one. She hated our life and ran away to LA when she was sixteen. She begged me to join her, but I couldn't leave my mother alone. She was dying of cirrhosis." I paused. "Then I got married."

His face darkening, Drake poked at the other meatball with the tip of his fork. "To Kyle?"

"Yes." I swallowed his name as the memory of our encounter tonight flashed into my mind. I took another big gulp of the wine to banish it.

"How did the two of you meet?" He took a sip of wine, waiting for me to answer.

"In high school. He had a band. I was one of his groupies and then he asked me to do backup for him."

"Singing?"

"No, backup dancing. And then one night after a performance, we both got loaded and... I became his girl." Yeah, I lost my virginity, but the thirty-seconds he was inside me were hardly memorable. He came prematurely.

Drake cut the memory short. "Were you in love with him?"

"I don't know. I think it was more of an infatuation. He was sexy and dangerous."

"Oh, so you like your men dangerous?" A bit of sarcasm laced his voice.

"If you mean with guns and knives, the answer is no. And if you mean men who physically abuse women, the answer is no again."

"So, why did you marry him?"

I was young. Only eighteen. It was a way out of my rut. We both had dreams—him to score a record deal and hit it big, and I wanted to be an artist. But he also had a problem. He wasn't patient. And the more his dream eluded him, the more he turned to drugs and booze. I thought if I gave him a child, he would have something to live for; he'd turn his life around and we'd have a future together. He was all I had. I didn't want to lose him." I paused and my voice grew rueful. "But it didn't work out."

Drake's eyes held mine. Compassion was written all over his face. "You've had a rough life, Dee."

"I guess, but I'm turning it around. Soon after Tyson was born, my mother died. I sold her trailer and moved further south to get away from Kyle who was incarcerated. People in small towns talk and can be cruel, and I didn't want Tyson growing up with the stigma of having a father in prison. I put myself through college to get a teaching degree. On the side, I made a small living, giving art lessons to kids. I finally scraped up enough money to move to LA to be with my sister and to give Tyson a better life. One with love, culture, and opportunities. Los Angeles . . . the City of Angels, right?"

"Yeah, right." His eyes circled the living room, stopping

on the boxes that were scattered on the floor.

"Did you just move here?"

"A couple of months ago. This is my sister's place. She had a spare bedroom because her roommate got a job in Chicago, and because the girl's new employer covered the rest of her lease, Ty and I got to live here rent-free. But at the end of the month, we're all moving out because this house is being demolished to make way for a condo complex. Hence, the boxes. We've begun to pack."

"I hope you're looking for a more secure place."

"Yes. I've been looking at some apartment buildings close to Ty's school that have an intercom system."

"That's good." He flashed that dazzling smile that again made my heart dance.

Avoiding eye contact, I glanced down at his plate; to my delight, it was scraped clean. "Enough about me. Would you like dessert?"

"Depends. Is it as delicious as you are?"

The temperature in the room suddenly went up ten degrees. I felt myself flush at his sexual innuendo. Words once again were caught in my throat. I laughed nervously.

The temperature kept rising. I gulped down what remained of my wine and stood up after collecting the spaghetti and salad plates. "I'll be right back."

A cocky grin played on his lips. "Surprise me."

CHAPTER 15

Drake

My eyes stayed on her as she returned to the kitchen. She was trying to play it cool, but she was on fire. I just knew it from the way she played with her food and kept drinking her wine. And from those little blushes. After our conversation, I found myself even more wildly attracted to her.

I liked the fact that she wasn't stuck up or money-hungry.

I liked the fact that she was both honest and humble.

I liked the fact that she was a fighter and a survivor.

I liked the fact that she was funny and caring. Her laugh was adorable like the rest of her. And she made me laugh too.

Yup, I liked a lot of things about my temp, even the fact that she could cook like *America's Top Chef*, but I *loved* the fact that she totally turned me on. I craved more of her like a little kid craved more candy. She was irresistibly delicious. And not good for me. The warning sign was there in bright neon—Steer Clear!—but I found myself not heeding it. Why was it men wanted more of what they couldn't have? Fuck. She wasn't even available. My chest clenched as I fought the urge to follow her into the kitchen and bend her over the counter.

"You're going to love this." Dee's bright voice cut my mental ramblings short. My eyes instantly darted in her direction. She was heading my way with two sundae glasses piled high with whip cream. Long spoons stood up from the glasses.

"Shit. Is that what I think it is?" My mouth was watering as she set one of the fluted glasses in front of me. She sat down again in her spot and placed the other glass on her placemat.

"Uh-huh, it's a hot fudge sundae. Tyson loves them."

I immediately dug in and put a heaping teaspoon of the creamy vanilla ice cream, warm rich fudge, and fluffy whipped cream into my mouth. I moaned as I swallowed. "Jesus, Dee, this is crazy good! I haven't had one since I was a kid."

"Your mother made them for you?"

"Hell no. My nanny Blanca did. She made them just the way you do. I fucking loved them." I ingested another big spoonful. "You're going to kill me."

She laughed. The cutest, sexiest laugh. "Don't die on me. I've had enough drama for one night."

I laughed too. That was a fact.

Dee dug into her sundae. My gaze stayed fixed on her as she put an equally heaping teaspoon to her mouth. A sexy little "mmm" spilled out as she savored the delectable desert. It was so refreshing to be with a real woman who had a healthy appetite and didn't pick at lettuce leaves or call a blueberry dessert. A little bit of the whip cream stayed behind on her kissable lips. My cock flexed as she licked it off with her tongue. She had no clue how fucking sexy she was and that's what made her sexier. My deviant mind wandered to all the places I could lick whip cream off from her. Her pussy was one of them. My cock twitched at the delicious thought.

"Do you want my cherry?" she asked, giving me a jolt. What kind of loaded question was that? Oh God, Lord of the Boners, I wanted to eat her pussy, oh pretty please with a cherry on top.

"You don't want it?" I managed, almost choking on my words.

"Uh-uh. I don't like them. I just put it on to make the sundae look pretty. Tyson loves them. She once ate a whole jar of them."

"A girl after my own heart. I did that once, too, when I was her age."

"So, you want it?" she asked again, already dangling the bright red candied fruit in front of me by its stem.

What a fucking tease! With a boner raging under my jeans, I snagged it out of her fingers with my mouth and sucked it, squeezing out the juice. I had the burning desire to kiss her, to share the sweetness, and to taste hers. It took all I had not to pull her into my arms and devour her. I wasn't getting kudos from any little voice in my head or from my throbbing cock. I went back to the sundae and consumed it until there wasn't a drop to be had.

"Should we listen to the auditions now?" Her voice was hesitant.

"It can wait till Monday." The truth is I didn't even bring them along.

She shifted uncomfortably. "Well then, I guess it's time to call it a night."

A short stretch of silence followed until I broke it. "Dee, I don't think you should stay here alone tonight. It's too risky. The asshole may come back."

She weighed my words. "What are you trying to say? That I should check into some hotel?"

Or come home with me. The thought of her all naked in my bed sent my cock into a tailspin. Before I could respond, she continued.

"I don't think so. I need to be here for Tyson when she comes home in the morning."

"Then let me stay here."

"You can't. One bedroom belongs to my sister who will likely be home later; the other is mine. Tyson shares it with me."

"I'll sleep on the couch. C'mon, think about it. I won't come near you." I paused for a beat. "Unless you beg."

She flushed and then flung one word at me: "Fine."

In no time, I was stretched out on the couch, my eyes closed with dirty dreams ahead.

CHAPTER 16

Drake

"How's my new patient doing?" she asks, her voice cheery.

Nurse Dee. I sit up and soak her in. Fuck. She looks so unbelievably sexy in that little white nurse's uniform that stops mid thigh just above her fishnet stockings and that cute cap with the Red Cross that holds back her lustrous hair. My cock aches at the sight of her.

"My head is still killing me," I lie. Well kind of. It's the head of my cock that's throbbing, not the one above my shoulders.

"Poor baby," she pouts with those luscious glossed lips. "It's time for your cherry medicine."

"Will it make me feel all better?"

"All better," she purrs as she gets on the bed and straddles me, her knees bent up. My eyes get a glimpse of what's between her legs. Holy shit. She's not wearing panties. My temperature shoots up.

I watch as she reaches into a pocket and pulls out a ripe cherry. Her tongue runs sensuously around it, moistening and warming it. Then, she puts the shimmering fruit between her legs and rubs it on her pussy.

"Drake, you look feverish," she says with concern, palming my forehead with her free hand. "Oh my God, you *are* hot!"

She's not kidding. I'm on fire. Burning up with desire. My temperature soars as she hikes the skirt of her uniform above her hips and spreads her legs further, fully exposing her glistening pink pussy.

"Be a good boy, Drake, and take your medicine."

On my next heated breath, I go down on her, burying my face in her sweet, cherrylicious pussy. My tongue sweeps across her slick folds, then flicks and licks her pretty little clit. Her moans fill my ears. They grow louder, more savage, and I love that she can't manage words. I work my tongue more vigorously, arousing her further, her ass lifting, her hips bucking with madness as I suck her off. Her fingers clench my hair as she rides my face to ecstasy.

"Oh, Drake," she cries out, finally finding her voice, "You're an exceptional patient. I'm going to come."

Yeah, baby, if you're happy and you know it, come for me. On my mouth. On my chin. On my nose. Shower me with your pleasure. With a shout of my name so loud it could wake the dead, she explodes all over my face. Her whole body shakes with endless spasms. As she rides her orgasm out, I lift her up by her ass and reposition her so that she's sitting on my enormous cock. I rub the crown along her wet, swollen, pulsing clit, stimulating myself as I stimulate her.

"Oh, Drake. You still feel so hot. I think you need another dose of medicine."

I do. My aching cock hungers for her. I want her so bad. Soaked with her wetness, it's so ready for action. I'm ready to plant my seed inside her, give her another orgasm she'll never forget. One I'll never forget either.

"Cure me of my need, baby. Take all of me. Ride me hard."

Her breathing labored, she circles her fingers around my thick length as I help her guide it deep inside her. Her warm pussy walls expand to accommodate my size and I thrust into her with a grunt, hitting her soft womb. She groans. God, she feels so fucking good. So hot! So wet! So tight! Gripping her hips, I begin to pump into her. Harder. Faster. It feels so fucking amazing. Did anyone ever say that a good fuck is the best medicine? Well if they didn't, I'm saying it now. My balls tighten, my cock readies for the inevitable . . .

And then . . .

⁓

"I'm home," a little voice in my head cried out.

But it wasn't mine. Snapping my eyes open, I abruptly awoke from my dream as the double click of a door unlocking sounded in my ears. Confused, I bolted to a sitting position, my eyes shifting to the door as I remembered where I was and what had transpired last night. Shit. Was that motherfucker Kyle back? Jumping off the couch, dressed only in my boxer briefs, I eyed the empty wine bottle Dee and I had shared and grabbed it. My heart thudding, I strode to the door and yanked it open, ready to strike. I froze and my eyes grew wide. A smile as bright as sunshine greeted me.

"Hi, Drake! Did you do a sleepover with my mommy?"

Tyson! Dee's little girl. And next to her was an attractive African-American woman in her thirties whose suspicious eyes gave me the once over before bugging out.

"Oh, Lordy!" The woman fanned herself as I lowered my arm holding the bottle. "And you are . . . "

"Mommy's new friend," chirped Tyson before I could get a word out.

"Hi," I said with a sheepish smile that I could only hope masked my embarrassment.

"You are one fine man."

Mortification raced through me as Tyson thanked the woman for letting her have a sleepover with her daughter.

The woman, still flustered, said goodbye to Tyson and hurried to her car. As she drove off, Tyson's sparkling blue eyes met mine and she began to giggle.

"Did you get an owie?" she asked, her gaze glued to my face.

Nervously, I rubbed the Band-Aid above my eyebrow. There was still a bump and it still hurt. "Yeah, I bumped my head," I said, thankful I could come up with a fast answer.

"That must have hurt." Her eyes traveled down my bare torso. "Wow! You have really big muscles!"

"Yeah. I work out."

"Is that a big muscle between your legs?"

I glanced down. Christ. She was referring to my boner. My morning wood. And thanks to my wet dream, Little Miss Blow It All had rudely interrupted, it was bigger than usual. A ten-inch block of concrete that was ready to burst through the seams.

"Yeah, it's a really big muscle," I sputtered, mortification racing through me.

"Cool beans. Can I feel it?"

"Um, uh, not today. I worked out too hard. It hurts." I wasn't lying. My raging hard-on was killing me. Crying out for relief.

"Maybe my mommy can make it feel better."

Oh, could she! At least in my dream. Before I could say another word, a voice sounded from behind me.

"Tyson, honey!" It was Dee. Naughty Nurse Dee. The little girl went flying to her mother. Spinning around, I watched as Dee lifted her into her arms and gave her a big hug.

"Did you have fun at Chandra's house?"

"SO much fun!" She reached into her backpack. "Look

what Chandra's daddy gave me."

She held up a four-inch-long white squiggly character sporting a Mohawk and sunglasses. Holy shit!

"What's that?" asked a perplexed Dee.

"Mommy, it's a sperm magnet!"

Dee and I gulped in unison. My mouth went dry. *Sperm.* I had an aversion to that word. A big one.

"Chandra's daddy is a *gynosaurus*. He helps mommies make babies. He got *Spermy* at a *furility confwence.* Can we put him on the fridge?"

"Um, of course," stuttered Dee.

"Yay! Did you have fun with Drake?"

Dee's eyes met mine and a slow, diffident smile curled on her luscious lips. "Yes, baby girl. We had a very fun . . . playdate."

"Did you feel Drake's big muscle between his legs?"

Dee's eyes fell to my crotch and I thought they might pop out of their sockets. Jesus. I should have covered up my boner with the blanket . . . a pillow . . . even my hands. Whatever. I quickly chimed in, sparing her from having to say a thing.

"Um, uh, I think I better be leaving."

Tyson frowned. "Don't you wanna come ice skating with us, Drake? My mommy promised to take me today. It's my first time."

Dee's expression turned equally glum. "Ty-baby, I'm afraid we can't go today. Aunt Lulu just texted me—she's busy and can't make it. I don't know how to skate so it won't be any fun, and I don't want you alone on the ice."

Tears welled in Tyson's eyes, and in no time, they began to trickle down her cheeks. Her rosebud lips pouted. "But, Mommy, you promised!"

Dee affectionately ruffled her hand through Tyson's loose hair, which fell almost to her waist. "Sweetie, we'll do it some time . . ."

Call me a sucker, but the little girl's tears were gutting me. I cut Dee off.

" . . . later this morning. I'm a great skater and I know just the place to go."

While Dee looked at me with a puzzled expression, Tyson ran up to me and gave me a big hug. The frown on her face gave way to a huge smile. "YAY!! I can't wait!!! I'm super duper excited!"

And so was I.

CHAPTER 17

Dee

The three of us were in Drake's gazillion dollar convertible, me in the front sitting next to him and Tyson in the back strapped into her car seat. The top was down and the radio was tuned to some Top 40 countdown station. Tyson had never been in a convertible before and was loving every minute as if it were an amusement park ride. Looking over my shoulder, happiness shot through me as I caught sight of her big smile and her braids whipping in the wind. Oh, my beautiful little girl.

It had been a busy morning. Right after I made a pancake breakfast for everyone (after I recovered from Drake's enormous erection), Drake took us to Big Five, a sporting goods store, to buy Ty and me ice skates; his, I learned, were already in the trunk of his car—hockey ready. "Why can't we just rent them at the rink?" I'd asked him. "And how much do I owe you?" I didn't feel comfortable accepting gifts from him. I was still taken aback from the boatload of toys he'd given Ty while she was in the hospital.

"First of all," he said, handing the cashier his credit card, "the ice skating rink we're going to doesn't have rentals. And secondly, I'll come up with a way in which you can pay me back." He shot me a wicked grin that sent a fiery arrow to my core.

For the rest of the ride, my eyes skipped back and forth between the glorious sight of Drake's profile and the spectacular canyon we were driving up. Wearing sexy Ray-Bans, Drake managed the sharp curves with precision as if he'd navigated them a thousand times before. Stately mansions with preened gardens dotted either side of the winding road. It was hard for me to imagine a skating rink in the middle of this magnificent neighborhood.

Midway up the canyon, we turned onto a tree-lined street. The ginormous houses that came into view made the ones along the canyon look like cottages. I'd never seen anything like them. They were practically fairy-tale castles. For sure, we had entered the land of the rich and famous. This must be some very elite skating rink. A cloud of intimidation swept over me.

"Are we there yet?" demanded Tyson from the back seat.

"Almost." Drake smiled. "It's right behind the big gate on the left."

"Where are we?" I asked, following his gaze.

"Beverly Hills. More precisely, Beverly Park."

Wow! This is where movie stars lived. I was totally awestruck as he stopped at the guardhouse outside the ornate gate. With a smile and no questions, the guard opened the massive iron structure and let Drake in. The sprawling houses sitting on acres of land made my eyes grow wide and took my breath away.

"Wow, Mommy!" squealed my little girl. "Look at all these pretty hotels."

Drake chuckled. "That's my parents' house on the right."

Holy cow! It was the biggest house I'd ever seen. Two massive stories of gray stone with turrets that made it look like a French castle sitting on acres of grass so green I thought for a minute that I was Dorothy in the Emerald City. Nope, we weren't in Kansas anymore. My mouth was agape as we pulled into the circular drive that could easily hold two dozen more cars.

"Are we stopping here for a reason?" I asked as Drake put the car in park.

"Yup. This is where we're going skating."

Five short minutes later, Drake was escorting us through his parents' vast backyard. It was more like a golf course with grassy hills and vales, and as we walked toward our destination with our skates tied together and slung over our shoulders, I even saw two men playing golf in the distance. Drake told me it was his father and Saul Bernstein, who headed up Conquest Broadcasting, the parent company of the kids' channel, Peanuts. It was their weekly Saturday game. Along the way, we passed a grotto-like swimming pool with a waterfall and pool house, a tennis court, and exquisite patches of flowers and shrubs, although oddly not a tree in sight. Drake told me this is where he'd grown up. It was nothing like the trailer park I'd grown up in and a deep feeling of inferiority gnawed at my stomach. Tyson, on the other hand, who was skipping ahead of us, was acting as if she'd just been sucked into the pages of an enchanted fairy tale. Like she was born to live here.

Shortly, we reached a palatial glass pavilion. As Drake led us inside, a chill in the air descended upon me while classical music filled my ears. The skating rink. In the center, a lone figure was doing some kind of intricate spin. She was tall and slim, with long toned legs that looked even longer in her ice skates and short sparkly skating outfit. Her almost white platinum hair was held back in a bun that hit the nape of her swan-like neck. She was in a word, elegant. A sight to behold.

"Who's that?" I whispered to Drake.

"My mother."

His mother? She looked no older than forty.

"She works out here daily. She used to be a champion ice skater and toured with the Ice Capades. My father built this rink just after I was born for her thirtieth birthday."

"Mommy, she's such a good skater!" piped Tyson while I mentally calculated her age to be about sixty. "I want to skate like that."

My eyes stayed riveted on Drake's stunning mother as the music concluded and she finished her routine with a graceful leap. Spotting us, she skated our way, her speed astonishing and her form magnificent.

"Drake, darling! How good to see you! What a wonderful surprise!" She leaned over the railing to give Drake a kiss on each cheek. I could see the resemblance between them—the deep-set eyes, chiseled bone structure, and flawless skin.

She zeroed in on the gash above his eyebrow that was now uncovered despite my insistence to keep the Band-Aid on. "What in heavens happened to your face? Please don't tell me it's another hockey mishap."

"No, Mom. It's just um, uh, a shaving nick."

While I shuddered at the thought of what really happened, she twisted her lips with disapproval. "Well, darling, don't pick at it or it'll leave a scar."

Her focus then switched to Tyson and me. "And who might your friends be?"

"Mom, this is my temp, Dee, and her daughter, Tyson."

I held out my hand and she shook it firmly with her slender one. "So lovely to meet you, my dear."

Before I could say a word, my daughter blurted out, "You are SO pretty!"

I felt myself blushing, but Drake's mother was totally flattered. "What a delightful child!"

"Thank you, Mrs. Hanson."

She smiled warmly. "Please call me Alexis."

She kept her eyes on Tyson, studying her. A wistful smile formed on her face before she looked up and focused on Drake.

"She reminds me of your sister."

Drake had a sister?

Drake cleared his throat, clearly uncomfortable at the mention of his sibling. "Yeah, a little bit. The same blue eyes."

Drake had blue eyes too, similar in color to Kyle's, but Tyson's had a rim of gold around the pupils that was rare.

My eyes darted between Drake and Tyson as his mother stepped off the ice. In her ice skates, she towered over me.

"So what brings you here, darling?" she asked, directing her question at Drake. "Don't tell me you stopped by just to see your dear old mother."

I liked her. She was warm and funny. Much more personable than the society doyenne Drake made her out to be.

"Drake's gonna teach us how to ice skate," beamed Tyson before either of us could respond.

"Wonderful! He's an excellent skater though I still think he should have chosen figure skating over ice hockey. Such a vulgar sport."

Drake scrunched up his face. God, he was cute! "Mom, let's not go there again. Real men don't figure skate."

"Whatever, darling!" she breathed out as she sat down on a bleacher, unlaced her skates, and then tugged them off. Reaching for a close-by hand towel, she cleaned off the blades and covered them with protective rubber guards. After slipping the skates into a large monogrammed bag that seemed custom made for them, she stepped into her shoes. A pair of metallic gold ballet flats. She stood up.

"My love, have fun! If you have time, do stop by to have lunch or say goodbye. I'll be working on the seating arrangement for the gala we're hosting for Gunther. I can't believe it's only a week away. I hope you've put it in your calendar."

Drake rolled his eyes. "Yes, Mom, I have."

"Too-de-loo" She blew her son a kiss, and clutching her skate bag, she waltzed off.

"Okay, who's ready to go ice skating?" Drake asked.

"ME!" shouted out my little eager beaver, jumping up and down.

"I think I'm going to sit this out for a while." I'd never skated before, and though I could dance, I was never as coordinated or as athletic as my sister. Or my daughter for that matter. The thought of falling on my ass and making a fool of myself was enough for me to pass.

"C'mon, Mommy, it'll be fun!"

"Maybe later."

Drake shot me a cocky look. "Have it your way. There's a hot chocolate machine on the other side near the restroom." And then he swept Tyson into his arms. "C'mon, Mighty Girl, let's get your skates on." He shot me another cocky look. "And we're going to get your mommy into skates, too, just in case she changes her mind."

I gave him the evil eye. No way.

Way. Fifteen minutes later, we were all laced up in our skates thanks to Drake's help. The skates felt weird on my feet and I had trouble balancing on them. I wobbled like a toddler taking her first steps. Tyson, on the other hand, was prancing around in them on the rubber matting as if she was born wearing them.

Drake took her hand and led her onto the ice. My heart leapt to my throat as she lost her balance on the slippery surface. Thank goodness, Drake reacted in time to break the fall and keep her on her feet. My little girl was gleefully laughing while I was seriously freaking.

"Drake, be careful with her. Don't let go of her. And don't go too fast."

Drake smirked at me dismissively. "Stop worrying. By the time I'm done with her, she'll be ready for the Olympics."

Pompous jerk. I let it go as they, hand in hand, began to slowly circle the rink. In no time, my anxiety dissipated, giving way to pure joy.

Still clutching Drake's hand, my baby took what looked like baby steps around the circumference of the rink. She looked so tiny next to his broad six-foot-two frame. The pleasure I got from seeing the mixture of excitement, happiness, and accomplishment on her face couldn't be measured. I could tell that Drake was enjoying every minute instructing her. They looked so cute together, my big built boss and my fragile little baby, both wearing jeans, wooly sweaters, and knit beanies. Standing at the edge of the rink, I pulled out my cell phone and began taking photos and videos.

As they progressed, Ty's steps grew more confident and fluid, and her speed picked up a bit.

"Hi, Mommy!" she hollered, waving her free hand, as she and Drake passed by me. "Look at me skate!"

"You're doing such a great job, baby girl!" I shouted back with a big smile.

"What about me, Mommy?" mock-shouted Drake.

"Not nearly as well as Tyson."

He stuck his tongue out at me like a pouty three-year-old. I found it incredibly sexy, and the memory of it gliding in my mouth last night sent a heat wave through me despite the chill in the air. Head to toe tingles zapped me as I imagined what that deft tongue was capable of. A shiver of lust skittered down my spine.

Halfway through their next spin around the rink, Drake

let go of Tyson's hand. To my great surprise and delight, she was able to manage all by herself. Thank goodness, Drake stayed close to her in case she took a spill. But she didn't. I watched as Drake led her over to the side of the rink. While she stood against the railing, he gave her a lesson in stroking. Holding up my phone, I shot a video while he made Tyson imitate his smooth moves. With her little arms outstretched, she pushed off from the wall and, to my amazement, skated to him. My heart melted when he took her into his arms and lifted her high in the air to celebrate her small victory. My little skater, full of laughter, was a natural and her instant connection to Drake undeniable. A pang of guilt knifed through me. She'd been deprived of a father. A daddy to love and who could love her back. Maybe having only me wasn't enough.

With Tyson skating on her own close to the railing and Drake by her side, the twosome skated over to me.

"Mommy, skating is SO much fun! You should try it!"

"She's right," Drake chimed in.

"I'm afraid I'll fall."

"But, Mommy, you have a big butt so it won't hurt."

Mortification raced through me. I felt myself turning as red as a beet. Kids say the darndest things, right? Wrong! My sassy almost six-year-old had no filter.

Drake broke out into hysterical laughter.

I clenched my fists. I wanted to punch him. "It's not funny."

"Dee, you have a great butt. Now, get your ass on the ice."

"C'mon, Mommy," Ty pleaded. "Please, pretty please with a cherry on top."

Drake's laughter let up. "Mighty, why don't you take a spin around the rink? You're ready to skate all by yourself. Stay close to the railing and hold on to it if you have to."

"Yay!" On my next breath, she took off. My breath caught in my throat, but she seemed to be managing just fine.

Drake stayed behind. All that separated us was the waist-high railing. He leaned into me. His sparkling blue eyes flickered with a mixture of determination and mischief while his warm breath heated my cheeks. His hands tugged playfully at the ends of my wool plaid scarf.

"Aren't you going to skate with Tyson?"

He glanced in her direction. She was already halfway around the rink. "She's doing just fine by herself. She's a total natural. She reminds me of myself at that age. I took, like her, to the ice like a penguin."

"But what if she falls?"

He shrugged. "She'll get up." He tugged again at my scarf. "C'mon, Dee, get your big beautiful butt on the ice."

"No way."

"That does it."

My eyes stayed on him as he skated with amazing grace and speed to the entrance of the rink, stormed off the ice, and marched my way. In a single swoop, he hauled me over his shoulders.

"What the hell are you doing, Drake?"

"Getting you on the ice," he responded, marching back to the entrance, one hand gripping me right below my ass.

"Put me down!" I began to kick my feet in protest.

"Behave! And stop kicking. Skate blades are sharp and can be very dangerous. I don't want you to cut off my dick. I'd like to keep it intact. And the same with my balls."

Rage filled every bone in my body. The asshole! He'd made me his captive like some kind of caveman. "Stop," I shrieked at the top of my lungs as he marched us back on the ice and then raced around the rink at breakneck speed. We quickly caught up with Tyson.

"Hi, Mommy!" she yelled out as we flew by. I could hear her giggling as the whooshing sound of Drake's skates sung in my ears.

Speeding around the ice, draped over Drake's shoulder, I was getting dizzy. My arms hung loose like a ragdoll's within groping distance of his perfect buns of steel. Blood rushed to my head. I'd had enough.

"Put me down!" I breathed out.

"Are you ready to stop acting like a brat?"

"I am not a brat!"

Without warning, he swatted my ass with his free hand. The slap stung straight through my thick leggings, but the incendiary sting strangely turned me on. A barrage of tingles blazed through me, clustering between my inner thighs.

"Put me down," I yelled again.

He didn't say a thing. Coming to a braking halt that left a skid mark on the ice, he set me on my feet. Standing behind me, he kept his hands anchored on my waist to keep me balanced. I stood as frozen as the ice, hoping he'd never let me go. Partly because I was nervous as shit. And mostly because it felt so good to have his hands touching me. The sparks coursing through my body were definitely not going to help with skating.

"Okay, I'm going to teach you how to skate. Trust me, you're going to be the next Dorothy Hamill."

I couldn't help a nervous laugh. "I. Don't. Think. So."

He laughed his sexy laugh. "Think again."

"Seriously, Drake, I don't think I can do this."

"Come on. If your five-year-old daughter can, so can you."

My eyes darted to Tyson, who was circling around the rink. Her strokes were a little awkward, but she was definitely skating. And doing it well.

"Tyson is fearless," I countered.

"What are you afraid of?" he breathed into my ear. The warmth of his breath sent a chill down my spine.

"Of falling." *Of falling for you.*

"You won't. I've got you. Now push off with one foot and then the other."

Trembling, I did what he asked. My legs wobbled, but I moved three feet forward. A small victory on the slippery ice.

"Nice. Now do it again. But this time push from your hips, not your knees."

"Okay," I stammered. I did as he asked and noticed how much steadier and more powerful my strokes were. Still holding me firmly, he asked me to repeat the movements and I did so several more times. I'd probably skated a total of twenty feet.

"You're doing great!" He let go of me with one hand.

Gah! Don't let go of me.

And then he tugged at my ponytail before repositioning himself so that we were side by side. He laced his fingers with mine. My heart pounding, I squeezed his hand.

"What are you doing?" I asked, my voice as contorted as my face.

"What does it look like? I'm holding your hand. We're going to skate around the rink."

"No, I'm not ready for this!" I protested. "I want to get off the ice."

"Fine. You can get off by yourself. I'm going for a spin. See ya."

To my utter horror, he let go of my hand and skirted off—skating backward, no less, the damn showoff, facing me with a Cheshire grin plastered on his face.

"Please, Drake," I begged.

My begging only made his grin grow bigger. "Please what?"

"Please don't leave me." I'm not sure if he heard me because my voice was so shaky and small.

His grin morphed into a wicked smile, and in a few frantic heartbeats, he was again by my side. His fingers entwined with mine once more. How warm his hand felt next to my cold and clammy one. He gave my hand a little squeeze.

"I'm never going to leave you, D-baby."

My heart jumped. He called me baby. He probably called every girl that, but the way he said it so tenderly made me think I was the first. Following his lead, I began to skate with more confidence. Loving every minute of our togetherness.

For about the next five or so minutes, we circled the rink, Drake holding my hand, me improving with each stroke. Once or twice I turned to look at him, and somehow at those moments, his gaze met mine. No words were spoken. Just silent smiles.

Midway around the rink, *my* baby called out to me. "Look, Mommy no hands!"

Half elated, half fearful, I craned my head in her direction, losing focus on my strokes. Suddenly, one of my blades caught with Drake's and my heart lurched in my chest at that horrible sensation that I—we?—were taking a tumble. "Shit," I heard Drake mumble as the inevitable happened. On my next rapid heartbeat, I was flat on my back on the ice and he was splayed on top of me. We were a breath apart, his heart beating against mine. The warmth of his body caging mine was a sharp contrast to the cold ice beneath me.

"Are you okay?" he asked, the heat of his breath warming my cheeks.

"Yeah. You?"

"Totally."

I gazed at his face. His lips were parted, his eyes smoldering. The heat of his body was melting the ice beneath me. Melting the distance that separated us.

The weight of Drake's body kept me from moving. "Can you help me up?"

"Not yet. I like being on top of you."

I like you on top too. "It can't be that hard—"

"Yeah, it *is* that hard. Very hard." He rocked his hips against me.

Gah! *It* was hard. Very, *very* hard.

His eyes blazing into mine, he traced my lips with his fingertip and then leaned in closer until I could practically taste his minty breath. I could feel my heart pounding, hear my breathing grow labored. My lips parted, partly because I needed to get oxygen into my lungs and partly because I wanted him to devour them. I wanted him to kiss me so badly I could scream. As his lips were about to touchdown, a little voice caused us both to jolt. Tyson.

Giggling, she skated up to us. "You guys look so funny!"

Yes, we were a tangled pile of arms and legs. But it was more than just the physical. Our emotions were all tangled up too.

"I'm hungry," said my little girl.

Drake's eyes burned into mine. "Me too."

"Me three." I'd never hungered for a man as much as I did for my new boss, Drake Hanson.

I should have felt relieved that Tyson didn't catch us kissing, but instead I felt bereft.

CHAPTER 18
Drake

Leaving our skates behind in the trunk of my car, which was still parked outside my parents' mansion, we headed inside to say goodbye to my mother.

The interior of our house was even more majestic than the exterior. Comprising over twenty thousand square feet, there were over thirty rooms, including a home gym and a special Japanese dining room where guests dined seated on pillows around a table built into the floor. My father, who regularly entertained Japanese businessmen, got the idea for the dining room from his golf buddy, Conquest Broadcasting head, Saul Bernstein, who had a similar one in his neighboring house. Keep in mind that being a neighbor in this über-exclusive gated community meant living a mile away.

My focus stayed on Dee as she stepped into the grand entryway, which was larger than her entire cottage. Clearly, she'd never been in a house of this magnitude. The expression on her face was a mixture of awe and intimidation. Her eyes widened, taking in the fine antiques and artwork, French rugs and furnishings, and towering vases filled with exotic fresh flowers.

"Mommy, this is just like Cinderella's palace," exclaimed little Tyson, who was as happy as a clam and didn't share her mother's inner reservations. "Look at this really pretty egg," she chirped, picking up the jeweled, pink enameled one that stood on a gilded stand on the entryway console.

"That's a Fabergé egg dating from the nineteenth century. It belonged to the Czar. My father won it at an auction and gave it to my mother for her fortieth birthday. He paid a record twelve million dollars for it."

Terror washed over Dee's face. Call me a bastard, but I found it amusing.

"Ty, put that down immediately, and don't touch anything else." She snatched it out of her daughter's hand without giving her a chance and nervously set it back on the stand.

I couldn't help but laugh. "Seriously, Dee, don't worry so much. Everything in this house is replaceable. My mother doesn't fret over her possessions no matter how grand or rare they may be. I was brought up with the philosophy not to love things that can't love you back."

"I was brought up with nothing." The somberness of her words struck a chord, and I suddenly realized that I took my privileged upbringing for granted. I couldn't fathom what it was like to grow up poor and unloved in a trailer park.

As we continued through the house, Dee began to relax a little even when Tyson insisted on trying out every overstuffed Louis the Whoey chair, pretending she was a princess. Her eyes wandered across the paintings lining the walls.

"Your parents collect paintings?" my new assistant asked, staring at an original Picasso.

"Yes, for years. They're one of the foremost collectors of twentieth century art in the world."

"What about that painting over there?" she asked, pointing to a life-size portrait of an elegant little girl with blond braids and golden halos circling her big blue eyes, much like

Tyson's.

My sister. "That's by the late painter who went by the name PAZ. Payton Anthony Zander, the father of my buddy Jaime, who does some of our promotional trailers."

Moving closer, she studied the canvas. "It's really well done. I love his technique. The little girl reminds me of—"

"My mommy is a painter," interjected Tyson brightly, sparing me from having to reveal the story behind the painting.

Dee's cheeks flushed pink and my mind flashed back to the whimsical portraits scattered on the walls of her living room. I had meant to ask her about them.

"The paintings in your house . . . you did them?"

"Yes." Her voice was small but laced with pride.

"My mommy wanted to be an artist when she was growing up."

"Tyson, please—"

Before she could reprimand her precocious kid, I cut her off. "You're very talented, Dee. Have you ever thought about exhibiting?"

She let out a little laugh. "Hardly. I can barely afford to frame them."

"You should let my friend Jaime take a look at your paintings. In addition to his ad agency, he owns an art gallery in West Hollywood."

Moving away from the painting, she digested my words. "Maybe after I get settled in my job at Tyson's school in the fall."

"My mommy's going to be an art teacher there," chimed in Tyson.

My chest tightened. I was reminded that Dee was just a temporary fixture in my life. The temp. As soon as my regular assistant Mona returned, she'd likely be out of my life. And so would sweet, rosy-cheeked Mighty Girl. But maybe introducing her to Jaime would be a way to extend our relationship. My mood lightened.

We made our way to the dining room. My mother, now clad in a stylish velour jogging outfit, was seated at our massive dining room table, mapping out the seating arrangement for the Gunther Saxton gala. It was as if she was putting together the pieces of a giant jigsaw puzzle. She had a system in place, but neither my father nor I knew how she did it. Nor did we want to.

Upon hearing us enter, she stopped what she was doing and gazed up at us. A smile graced her porcelain-skinned face. She'd stayed out of the sun for years to avoid wrinkles and now her self-discipline had paid off. While all her friends were constantly getting Botox injections and subjecting themselves to myriad youth-inducing procedures, my mother had never undergone either the knife or a needle and looked stunning.

"Why, hello, children," she began, her voice breathy and regal. "How was skating?"

"It was SO much fun!" exclaimed Tyson, holding Dee's hand. "Drake says I'm a natural girl, but I don't know what that means."

Dee shot her a stern look. "You mean 'a natural' which means things came easy to you. You shouldn't be boasting."

Tyson gave her a puzzled look. "What's boasting?"

"Showing off."

I quickly came to the little girl's defense. "Mom, she's not showing off. Tyson did amazing. By the time we were done, she could skate around the entire rink by herself and do a bunny hop."

I watched proudly as the twinkly-eyed child demonstrated the rudimentary jump. My mother's face lit up. It was no secret she had always wanted another child—a little girl—but that never happened after the tragedy.

"Darling, you're a child after my own heart. I began skating at your age, and my son took to the ice almost as soon as he could walk."

I felt myself reddening. But that was a fact. Before I could say a word, Tyson tugged at Dee's sweater.

"Mommy, I want a pretty skating costume like Drake's mommy's."

"They're very expensive." I detected a bit of frustration in Dee's voice. It must be hard to not be able to give your kid whatever he or she wanted. But then I remembered that despite their extreme wealth, my parents made me work for what I wanted. And save up. Even in college. I so fucking wanted that Mustang convertible, but it took being a sperm donor to finally get one. My parents had no clue how I'd earned the money. I told them I worked in the campus bookstore (fat chance!) and they believed me. My wanking-off-for-dollars days filled my head and distracted me. So, when I heard a familiar breathy voice call out my name, I was startled.

My heart jumped, hurtling me back to the moment. Standing at the entrance to the dining room was Krizia Vanderberg, the stunning daughter of my father's financial advisor, Karl. Once an aspiring actress, she now had her own public relations firm and counted us among her clients. We'd grown up together, and both sets of parents thought we were a match made in heaven. They were wrong. I had no interest in Krizia and never had. She was pushy, abrasive, and manipulative, qualities that served her well in her new career. And qualities that turned me off along with her relentlessness to get me into bed and put a ring on her finger. A wild party girl, she stalked me at events and once went as far as throwing a glass of champagne in my face when I refused to take a photo with her. And then there was the time she tried to unzip my fly and grab my cock. The list went on and got worse. With her acute mood swings, sometimes I wondered if she was manic-depressive or high on something. My father had recently been urging me to get to know her better—start up a relationship—especially since Gunther Saxton was looking for me to settle down. While my father thought highly of Krizia as a professional, he had no clue about her stalking tendencies or erratic behavior in her personal life. I held back on sharing this info with him because of his long-time relationship with her father. Moreover, she'd been instrumental in bringing Gunther and my father together. Gunther, it turned out, was also her client. So, I found myself walking on eggshells, risking setting Krizia off and upsetting the all-important Saxton Enterprises takeover.

I met her feline green eyes. I hadn't seen her in a while. She'd been away on a business trip in South America for several weeks. Holding a mimosa in one hand, she looked as beautiful as ever. Tall, slender, and bronzed. Fresh and rested. Her mane of flaming red hair cascaded over her shoulders in soft, lustrous waves, and her tight designer jeans and halter-top showcased her supermodel figure. Given how beautiful she was, neither my mother nor father could understand why I wasn't attracted to her. She was, according to them, perfect marriage material.

"Why aren't you saying hello, Drake darling?" she pouted, snubbing Dee and her little girl.

"Krizia, what are you doing here?" My tone was as cold as ice.

"Why just helping your mother with the seating arrangement for the upcoming gala. It's mega important that Gunther sits next to the right people."

My mother smiled. "It's such a Godsend to have her here. She's been so helpful."

"Thank you, Alexis. The party is going to be divine."

"Krizia literally just got back from Brazil," my mother informed me, "where she had a lot of work."

Shooting me a seductive smile, Krizia sauntered into the room. On closer inspection, it was obvious what kind of "work." Plastic surgery. Her tits looked noticeably bigger as did her lips, and that little bump on her otherwise perfect nose was gone. Her eyes shifted to Dee and Tyson, giving them the once over.

"Drake, why don't you introduce me to your friends?" Her voice was coated with disdain.

"I recognize you from the photos I saw of you with Drake online," Dee said before I could make the introductions.

A predatory smile snaked across Krizia's plump lips. "And you are . . ."

"Dee. Drake's temp."

Krizia's arched brows shot up. "Really?"

"Mona's daughter gave birth early. She's taking a few weeks off to be with her new grandson," I explained, trying my best to get through this uncomfortable encounter.

"Whatever," sniffed Krizia dismissively. Egocentric Krizia had little interest in the affairs of other people, and she detested children. Sitting down at the table next to my mother, her venomous gaze fixed on Tyson. "And who is this little imp?"

I cringed. Fucking Krizia. I wanted to stuff one of my mother's paper seating arrangements down her throat.

Tyson looked up at her mother, her eyes full of innocence. "Mommy, what's an imp?"

Dee protectively wrapped her arm around her daughter and then narrowed her eyes at Krizia. Poison darts were going back and forth between them and I was in the crossfire. There was nothing I could do except get the hell out of here as fast as I could.

Before Dee could respond to Tyson, I bit out, "Mom, we need to go. I promised I'd take Dee and her daughter to The Beverly Hills Hotel coffee shop for lunch."

"But darling, I've had Blanca prepare a lovely salad with fresh Alaskan king crab. Your favorite. Why don't all of you stay and join us?"

"Yes, why don't you . . . Drake?" echoed Krizia, taking a slow sip of her mimosa.

Dee answered for me. "I'm sorry, Mrs. Hanson. Tyson is highly allergic to crabs and so am I."

Krizia fired Dee a scathing look. My chest constricted. And I was allergic to bitches.

CHAPTER 19

Dee

We ended up spending the rest of Saturday with Drake. After lunch at the famed Beverly Hills Hotel coffee shop, where Drake and his father regularly lunched when he was a boy, he wanted to show us some sights. With his convertible top down, we drove through Beverly Hills, where he pointed out movie star mansions before heading into Hollywood to Grauman's Theater where we all went crazy comparing our handprints and footprints to every major movie star who'd ever laid their hands or feet into the cement. I had promised Tyson a movie and we ended up at The Grove, a fairytale-like outdoor mall with a tram, where they were playing a thirty-five-year anniversary edition of *ET*. My first time seeing it, I loved it as much as she did.

"*Drake no go home!*" begged my little one in her best ET voice over dinner at the adjacent Farmer's Market. "Can he sleep over again?"

"I'm afraid not tonight."

Tyson folded her arms across her chest and gave me her pouty look. "Not fair. Tomorrow's my birthday!"

Before I could utter another word, Drake jumped in. "What are you doing for your birthday?"

Tyson's face lit up with excitement. "Mommy's taking me to the Santa Monica Pier. Do you want to come with us,

Drake? It's gonna be so much fun!"

"Tyson!" I reprimanded, but what did it matter?

I knew in my heart that I had won half the battle and lost the other. I couldn't say no to my daughter. Especially in light of her birthday. Drake was coming with us tomorrow. I'd be lying, however, if I didn't admit that I wished I'd let him stay over. The threat of Kyle returning loomed. The house was secure. I had to wear my big girl panties. Truthfully, I was more afraid Drake wouldn't let me keep them on.

The rest of the night, thank goodness, transpired without any drama. Maybe Kyle was more afraid of Drake than I was of him. Drake did after all kick his ass and, with his size and strength, could do it again. I reminded myself that under his skin, Kyle was a coward. He'd given into failure rather than challenge it and succeed.

Drake picked us up in his convertible mid Sunday morning. Warm and sunny, the weather couldn't have been more perfect for a day at The Pier. Or another exhilarating ride in Drake's convertible. Drake once had the radio turned to some countdown station, and in the back seat, Ty was belting out the songs at the top of her lungs. I turned to look at her and my heart melted. She was now six. It was her "big girl" birthday. Time flew by so quickly, and part of me wished I could slow it down. No matter how big she got, she would always be my little girl.

"Ty has a great voice," Drake remarked, cutting into my bittersweet thoughts.

"I know," I said proudly, shouting above the blasting music and blaring wind. We were cruising down the 10 Freeway, which took us directly to The Pier.

Drake cast a glance at me. "I heard you sing the other night at that club."

I cringed. Gah! I must have been so drunk. "I'm sorry you had to endure that. My voice is so bad it could scare off aliens."

He laughed. "Oh, then Ty got her talent from her father?"

His unexpected reference to Kyle sent a shiver down my spine. "M-maybe . . . "

My companion instantly realized his faux pas. Kyle was dead to me. Dead to Tyson. "I'm sorry." His voice was low and remorseful.

"It's okay." Recovering, I asked him if he sang.

"Yeah. I have a pretty good voice if I must say so myself."

"You're so full of yourself. Prove it."

He smiled smugly. God, he was gorgeous in his Ray-Bans, T-shirt, and ripped jeans. His hair rippled in the wind, making it more sexily tousled than ever. I had the burning urge to run my fingers through it, but refrained. The next song came on—an Ed Sheeran one. A memory unexpectedly resurfaced. We'd danced to it at that club. I loved that song and I loved the way Ed sang it. Drake joined in.

Oh God. He did have an incredible voice. Soft with just the right amount of rasp. Pitch perfect, he harmonized with Ed. He was melting me. And then on the line about people falling in love in the most mysterious way, he took my left hand, entwining his long fingers with mine. A delicious flurry of tingles spun around in my body. I glanced at him, and his eyes met mine for a brief moment. He flashed a saucy smile as he continued to sing.

"Oh baby, take me into your loving arms," I sang the lyrics silently in my head as he faced the road again and finished the song, harmonizing perfectly with my favorite recording artist.

"Wow, Drake! You sing great!" exclaimed Ty before I could say a thing.

"You do," I agreed, my shaky voice a cross between awestruck and love-struck. Why was he kicking up an emotional dust storm inside me? I had never felt this way about a man. Not even with Kyle. What I had with Kyle was wild infatuation. Idol worship. The need to escape. What I felt with Drake was different. It felt real. Honest. Down-to-earth. I liked him. I actually more than liked him. He was giving me a slow burn that could turn into a wildfire if I didn't keep a lid on it.

The traffic was light and we got to The Pier in less than an hour. At the sight of the ocean and the rides, Ty squealed with excitement.

"Mommy, I want to do the roller coaster first! Please? Pretty please!"

The five-car roller coaster was whipping around a ginormous bright yellow track. People were screaming. I'd never ridden a roller coaster or a Ferris wheel. My drunkard mother never took us to amusement parks. Never. And now maybe I was too old for one. Ty, however, had been counting down the days to go to The Pier, and I hoped she was tall enough for the roller coaster. I'd read online you had to measure at least forty-two inches and Ty was borderline that.

"C'mon guys. This is going to be fun!" Drake hopped out of the car, unbuckled Ty's car seat, and then lifted her out of it.

"Drake, can you give me a piggyback ride?"

A smile that could light up the sky beamed on his face. "Sure, birthday girl."

I watched as he effortlessly slid Ty over his shoulders. "Drake, be careful with her."

He rolled his eyes at me. "Seriously, Dee?"

"Oh, Mommy, you're such a worrywart," Ty said with a laugh as Drake rounded the car to open my door.

"I could have done that," I said, unbuckling myself.

"Well you didn't, and I was brought up to be a gentleman."

A gentleman. A gentle man. I'd never had neither in my turbulent life.

"Thanks," I said softly.

That dazzling smile again flashed on his face, sending my emotions on a roller coaster ride of their own.

Traversing both the wide sandy beach and the white-crested waves of the Pacific Ocean, the iconic Santa Monica Pier, which opened in 1909, stretched almost a half-mile long. It was packed with people of all ages and races, families, friends, and lovers, gleefully united by their quest to have a day of fun. Despite my protest, Drake purchased a "family package" that included all-day wristbands for all the rides. I would be lying if I didn't say that's what it felt like—that we were a family, a family of three who'd been together forever. I was amazed by how comfortable Ty was with Drake and vice versa. They took to each other like bread and butter. At the sight of this sinfully sexy man with my pride and joy on his back, my heart swelled with an emotion I couldn't put into words. There was something about this spectacular man with my precious daughter that made everything inside me flutter. Wanting to remember them together, I took some photos with my phone while we waited in line for the roller coaster.

"Give me your phone and stand next to us," said Drake, Ty still riding on his back. "I'm gonna take some selfies."

Before I could blink, the phone was in Drake's hand and I was beside him.

"Smile . . . say cheese . . . make a face," he commanded,

snapping one photo after another as Ty and I obliged. "Now stick out your tongues."

Laughing, I turned to face Drake and did as he asked. To my surprise, his tongue met mine and flicked it. The warm, ticklish touch of it sent a bevy of butterflies to my core, and in my head, I begged for more . . . his lips on mine, his hands all over me. My eyelids lowered as his tongue continued to play with mine. I didn't know how long we'd been doing this when Ty's voice broke into my trance, snapping my eyes open. I immediately pulled away from Drake, who wore a wry smile. He licked his upper lip I bet just to incense me. Yes, I was on fire.

"Mommy! Drake! It's almost our turn!"

Gah! It was. Now at the front of the line, we would definitely get on the next car. My heartbeat sped up. My muscles clenched. I was freaking. I didn't want to do this ride. Having endured the long wait, how could I gracefully back out? I gazed up, taking in the speed of the cars whipping around the tracks and all the screaming people, and I knew this wasn't for me. I was a coward. The story of my life. Afraid to be daring. Afraid to make changes. My move to LA had been the bravest thing I'd ever done. Well, after conceiving Ty.

The bright yellow coaster came to a slow, chugging stop in front of us. And then came the big moment. Not mine. Drake set Tyson down on her feet so she could be measured by a mega-sized ruler. My heart hammered in my chest with anticipation. Please let her pass the height test! She wanted so badly to do this ride. She'd talked about it forever, even before we moved to LA. She just had to measure forty-two inches. In the car, Drake had told her to stand up tall, hold in her stomach, and puff out her chest. He'd even given her a few Kleenex to stuff in her Sketchers to make her a little taller. He was such a fucking scam artist, but so damn good. Holding my breath, I watched as my little one got measured. Following Drake's advice, she stood tall and as still as a statue against the mega-ruler, worry etched on her face. *"Taller, taller. Stand up taller. Lift up your shoulders. Tilt up your chin. Pray to the amusement park gods,"* I said silently, seeing she narrowly skimmed the required height. It could go either way. I was already feeling my daughter's disappointment if she didn't qualify. I think I felt it more than her. That's what mothers did.

"Let's move it." The attendant's gruff voice broke into my thoughts. It took a couple of long moments for his words to sink in. Yes! She'd passed. We were good to go!

"Yay!" shouted Tyson, jumping up and down as the attendant swung open the entrance gate and passengers clamored off the roller coaster, most bearing big grins and many saying they wanted to do it again. Really? Were they kidding?

And then there were a few who looked ghoulish green. Like they were going to barf or pass out. My stomach twisted with fear. That was going to be me! I'd never survive this hellish ride.

"Front car," said the attendant, ushering us onto the ride.

My heart pounding, it was now or never. I made a quick decision. *Never.*

"Cupcake, I'm going to wait for you here. I don't want to do the ride. And besides only two of us can sit together. You can go on with Drake."

A disheartened frown tugged at my Ty's sweet lips. It gutted me. That it was her birthday made it even more unbearable. She hugged me, her slender arms wrapping around my legs.

"No, Mommy. Please. I want you to come."

Drake chimed in. "I want you to *come* too."

Why did I read more into his words than I should?

"Please, Mommy. I'll sit in the front row and you can sit behind me with Drake."

In a few heartbeats, all three of us were in the car, Tyson sitting in front of me next to a jubilant silver-haired grandma and Drake sitting next to me, the safety bars lowered.

"Cupcake, are you okay," I asked Tyson, tapping her back and feeling terribly guilty that I wasn't sitting next to her.

She looked over her shoulder. "Yes, Mommy. I can't wait! It's gonna be so much fun."

The grandma, who turned out to be Drake's parents' neighbor, gave me an aside. *"Bubala*, trust me. It's as fun as *shtupping*. No need to *vorry shmorry*."

Her enviable fearlessness, like Ty's, did nothing to soothe me. "Drake, I'm scared!"

Laughing, he squeezed my hand. "Seriously, there's nothing to be afraid of. Driving in a car is way more dangerous. And the ride will be over before you know it."

My stomach tightened. I didn't believe a word he said. I wanted it to be over . . . now! Before it even started.

"Here we go!" shouted Drake, a fiendish smile on his face as the car chugged into motion.

Oh shit!

"YAY!" squealed Ty.

Oh, dear Lord! We hadn't even gone twenty feet or picked up speed, and I was already freaking out. In no time, we were making our climb up the first steep incline. *Chug. Chug. Chug. Chug.* Though the ascent was slow, every muscle in my body tensed. Butterflies swarmed my stomach.

"Dee, you're going to love it!" shouted Drake when we were almost at the apex.

"No, I'm not!" I gripped the safety bar so tightly my fists hurt.

The car paused at the very top. I looked down. Oh, God! The drop was formidable. My heart thudded so loudly I could hear it in my ears. Drake's voice broke into my fear.

"Dee, look at me."

Hesitantly, I did as he asked and on my next rapid heartbeat, my head was cradled in his hands. As I stared at him breathlessly, his lips slammed into mine.

Don't ask me what happened next. The car hurled down the slope at some ungodly speed as Drake gave me a kiss that sent my heart racing. My eyes squeezed shut, every organ in my body free-falling. I didn't know what was sending my heartbeat into a frenzy and turning my stomach upside down more—this extreme thrill ride or this extreme kiss that was consuming my breath and every cell in my body. Ty's joyous screams roared in my ears. My mouth smothered by Drake's, I screamed along silently.

I lost all track of time, and when Drake pulled away, we were now whipping around sharp curves. Before I could catch my breath, I was screaming at the top of my lungs.

"That's it, Dee, scream all you want. I love hearing you scream. In fact, scream as loud as you can."

My stomach lurched forward and my neck hyperextended. I felt like I was getting a severe case of whiplash.

"I'm going to fall off," I cried out as the coaster made another hairpin turn. Drake laughed at me. "You won't. I've got you." He wrapped his sculpted arm around me, drawing me closer to him.

Hold me tight! Don't let me go! You feel so good!

Though I felt safer with him holding me, I continued to scream my guts out, and as we whooshed around the serpentine track, the frantic sounds came out in loud pants.

"Look at the great view," Drake yelled out.

My eyes glimpsed the Pacific Ocean far below us for a brief second, and it made me even dizzier. In front of me, Ty was screaming at the top of her lungs, her arms raised high. Just like her octogenarian companion.

"Oh my God, Drake!" I blurted in a panic, the air rushing in my face. "She's going to fall off!"

Drake laughed. Insensitive man! He let go of me and mimicked Ty's actions.

"Look, Mom, no hands!" he yelled out with mockery, lifting his arms into the air.

Oh God! Please hold me!

As if he heard my desperate plea, he lowered his arms, this time removing one of my hands from the safety bar and placing it on his lap.

A rock-hard bulge met my palm. Holy cow! He had a hard-on. A full-on erection!

"I hope you're enjoying this ride as much as I am," he yelled out as the car swerved around yet another sharp curve.

To my relief, he wrapped his arm back around me. I couldn't stop screaming.

"Don't worry, Dee. It's almost over." He laughed as we mounted one more slope and then plunged toward the finish line.

Grinding to a halt, the ride finally ended. I knew it only lasted a few minutes, but it felt like an eternity. Drake helped me off. I was still shaken, my legs wobbly. Drake steadied me as I caught my breath. Though the ride was over, a roller coaster of emotions kept whipping through my system. That kiss! His erection! All the highs and lows!

"Mommy, that was SO much fun." Tyson's voice brought me back to reality. "Can we do it again? Please? Pretty please?"

I hedged and I hawed. Drake's voice broke into my trepidation.

"Don't worry, Dee. I'll hold you again."

Worry shmorry. I instantly said yes.

CHAPTER 20
Drake

I was having the best time of my life. Seriously. At least, in a very long time. Okay . . . maybe ever.

I hadn't been to the Santa Monica Pier in years. The last time I went was when I graduated high school. A bunch of kids in my class, including Brock, had gone there to celebrate. After college, I avoided it like the plague, worried that the kid-infested stomping ground would be filled with my offspring. Mini-me's, one of whom would recognize that I was his or her real father. But somehow, today I managed to put that ridiculous fear to the back of my mind.

My temporary assistant, Dee, was fucking adorable. I loved the way she screamed on the roller coaster—or should I say the boner coaster. She totally turned me on. My heart rate's reaction from the thrill ride combined with my physical attraction to this girl had increased my blood pressure and led to an erection of mega-proportions. It got worse. The whole time I was wondering—was this the way she screamed when she came? I was dying to find out. All throughout the Ferris wheel ride, which we did next, I kept fantasizing about her sitting on my lap and riding me. I was positive she knew I had a hard-on because I'd put her hand to my length on the roller coaster and her eyes never strayed from my face on the wheel. As the wheel spun around, wicked thoughts of coming with her were spinning in my head.

We went on several more rides, including the bumper cars and the old-fashioned carousel. After the rides, we grabbed some corn dogs and then played carnival games as well as arcade games. Dee found her calling with Skee-Ball, landing the almost impossible 100-point hole three times in a row, hence winning lots of prize tickets. I, in turn, managed to win one of those rigged carnival games when the ring I tossed slipped over one of the dozens of lined-up soda bottles. To the attendant's chagrin, I won Tyson a ginormous plush frog that was bigger than she was. Overjoyed, she named him Froggie and carried him proudly across The Pier, everyone we passed in total awe. The cutie-pie was having the time of her life. All day long, she laughed and wore a big smile. Knowing I gave her that smile made my heart swell with pride. I wanted to give her so much. And I felt the same way about her mother. I had a growing attachment to both of them that I was unable to fight. Each minute I spent with them, the more I liked them. Or should I say more than liked them? Was I was falling in love with a girl that was all wrong for me, at least on paper, and wasn't even available?

There was only one way to find out. One last amusement park attraction to visit. Zoltar. Fingers crossed that the mechanical fortune teller I fondly remembered from my youth was still here. Sure enough, he was. After all these years, he hadn't changed a bit. Still sitting before his crystal ball and sporting that jet-black mustache and goatee as well as his bejeweled turban and vest. The only thing different was he now commanded a dollar for your fortune instead of a coin.

"This machine is bogus," Dee protested. "We should go now. It's getting late."

Ty came to my rescue. "No, Mommy! I want to hear my

fortune. I bet I'm gonna get a really good one because it's my birthday."

"I agree." I shot Dee an already triumphant grin.

"Fine."

"Dee, you go first." I handed her a buck and watched as she inserted it into the bill slot.

His voice deep, Zoltar began to speak. "Destiny is not a matter of chance; it is a matter of choice."

"Cool beans!" shouted Ty. "He can talk!"

Dee rolled her eyes. A few moments later her fortune spewed out of the machine.

"What does it say, Mommy?" asked Tyson as Dee read the card.

"It says: You will fall in love with a tall, dark, handsome stranger." She rolled her eyes again. "That is *so* typical. I bet everyone gets that or something like: Life will bring you many riches." She turned to Tyson. "Cupcake, you do it."

After I gave her a dollar bill, the eager little girl repeated her mother's actions. She handed Dee the fortune. "What does mine say, Mommy?"

Dee smiled smugly. "Ha! It says: Life will bring you many riches and surprises."

"That's a good one, right?"

"It's a great fortune," I replied before Dee could respond.

"Yay!"

Dee turned to me. "Okay, Mister. Your turn." Her skeptical gaze stayed on me as I inserted a dollar and retrieved my fortune. Reading it, my eyes grew wide and my heart skipped a beat.

"Tell us, Drake. What does it say?" begged Tyson.

I caught my breath. "It says: You will meet a beautiful woman who will change your life forever."

Dee muttered a small, shocked "oh."

Our eyes met and I wondered if the ageless fortune teller in the glass case was always 100% right.

CHAPTER 21

Dee

We indulged in sugary sweet rainbow snow cones just before leaving The Pier at four o'clock. We'd been there for over five hours, and to be honest, I was a little weary. Ty, on the other hand, was still going strong and probably could have lasted until the amusement park closed at midnight.

On the drive home, we encountered light freeway traffic and got to my part of town in no time. Despite her energy, Ty fell asleep in the backseat, snuggled against the humongous frog Drake had won. I glanced back at her several times. My sweetie-pie looked so content. So peaceful. Drake had given her the best time of her life.

"Did you have fun?" he asked me as we turned off onto my exit.

"Yes. I had a blast. So did Ty. Thank you."

"No. Thank you. I had a great time too."

Memories of the day replayed in my head. From all the gnarly rides to all the fun games. I thought about our laughter. Our connection. His erection. Our smiles. How he held me tightly while I was screaming my head off on the roller coaster and spun me around after my first Skee-Ball game. Then, I thought about Zoltar, the fortune teller. My fortune was in my purse. Usually, I threw those ridiculous things out, but something made me want to hold on to it along with Ty's. When I got home, I was going to stick them on the refrigerator door with Ty's timely sperm magnet. Zoltar had turned a disbeliever into a believer—at least a wannabe.

Once off the freeway, the Sunday night traffic built up as we headed east on Sunset Boulevard. I was still getting used to it. Twenty minutes later, Drake parked his car in front of my house and Ty woke up.

"We're home already, Mommy?" she asked, rubbing her eyes, her voice a little groggy.

"Yes, cupcake. We're home."

"Is Drake coming to the rest of my birthday party?"

Lifting his brows, Drake shot me a surprised look. I gulped down a ball of guilt.

Before I could say a word, he invited himself.

"Mighty Girl, I'd love to. I even have presents for you."

He did?

"YAY!" screamed my daughter.

And silently, I screamed yay too. And so did my ovaries.

CHAPTER 22
Drake

A half hour later, we were sitting around the coffee table in the living room of Dee's modest cottage, devouring an extra-large pepperoni pizza. Her sister was there and, to my great surprise, so was Brock. Ty had also invited her best friend from school, Chandra.

Ty and Chandra retreated to the bedroom to play together while Dee and her sister retreated to the kitchen to get the cake ready. I caught some "guy time" with Brock, who I hadn't seen or spoken to for a few days. We were both drinking beers.

"How's it going?" I asked my best bud, whose arms had been all over Dee's sister from the moment they'd arrived.

"Fucking unbelievable." He polished off the last slice of pizza with a big bite. "Lulu's as hot as they come. Man, she's got the moves, and you wouldn't believe her stamina. Every time I've been her, she's given me a full-body workout."

I listened as he went into more detail, wondering if Dee possessed the same talents. The one thing I knew about her after our day at The Pier was that she was a screamer. Brock continued. You'd think he'd never been laid.

"The girl's insatiable. Last night, she came four times. And that was just in the first hour."

"Wow," I sputtered, not knowing what else to say.

"What's going on with you and Dee?" he asked, sparing me from the details. "She seems like she's really into you."

"It's complicated." I took a swig of my beer. "Hey, would you have any time for me to come by your office this week?"

Brock the Rock quirked a brow. "You have some legal shit going on?"

It became apparent to me that Lulu hadn't shared her sister's situation with my best bud.

"Not really. More like some questions," I replied, my voice unsteady. "I don't want to get into it right now."

"Sure, come by. Just call Stella. I'm sure she'll jump at the opportunity to squeeze you in."

Stella was his longtime super efficient sixty-something secretary, who had long harbored a crush on me. The double entendre of his words wasn't lost on me. Despite my rising libido, which had nothing to do with Stella, I laughed and told him I would set up an appointment.

Before I could say more, a pair of loud, off-key voices singing "Happy Birthday" captured my attention. Turning my head in their direction, my gaze fixed on Dee and Lulu heading our way, big smiles scrawled across their faces. Walking carefully with her sister by her side, Dee was holding a large plate with a lit-up birthday cake.

"Yay!" yelled a joyous Ty, who came running into the living room with her friend Chandra. While Brock and I joined in, harmonizing with the last notes of the traditional song, Ty reached the coffee table as Dee set the cake down.

"Make a wish, cupcake, and then blow out the candles," Dee said, wrapping her arms around her sweet daughter. I secretly longed to do the same . . . in fact, to wrap my arms around both of them.

My eyes stayed on the little girl as she thought for a

moment and then extinguished all six candles and the one for good luck on a single breath. While I wondered what she'd wished for, we all applauded and cheered.

"Mommy, can I open my presents now?" she asked as Dee removed the candles.

"Sure," replied Dee, reaching for a knife.

As Dee sliced the ice cream cake, Ty ran to the corner of the room where the presents were stacked and began to open them one by one.

First . . . an iPad from Lulu and Brock. Jeez. They were already buying things together.

"Oh my goodness," exclaimed Dee as she served the first slice of cake to ecstatic Ty. "Lou, you shouldn't have."

"Every six-year-old needs an iPad," replied her sister as Dee cut another slice, and Ty hurriedly tore open her next present after thanking her aunt and Brock, each with a big hug.

"That one's from me," said Dee, done with serving us each a slice of the cake. I dug in as I kept my eyes on Tyson.

"Yay! An Easy Bake Oven! Just what I wanted!"

A big smile beamed on Dee's face as her elated little girl gave her a big hug.

"Can we bake something later?"

"Maybe tomorrow. Open your other presents."

The next present was from her friend Chandra. A Furby doll, something I had growing up. There were two remaining presents—both from me, well sort of. Ty went for the bigger of the identically wrapped boxes.

"Is this from you, Drake?" she asked.

"No. Open the card first."

Dee lifted a surprised eyebrow as Tyson did as I asked. "Ooh, it's so cute," she cooed as she handed Dee the card, which featured a little bunny wearing ice skates.

Dee read the card and smiled. "It's from Drake's mother."

Upon unwrapping the box and removing the layers of tissue paper (my mother was a meticulous wrapper), Ty's face lit up like a Christmas tree and she let out a loud squeal. Then, she turned to me.

"Wow! A skating costume just like your mommy's!"

"How thoughtful of your mother," commented Dee before I could say a word.

Ty held up the sparkly purple costume against her body. "Oh, Mommy! Can I put it on?"

This time I got a word in. "Go for it. I'll take a picture and send it to my mother. I'm sure she'll love to see you in it. Oh, and by the way, the costume comes with a year of skating lessons."

Another "wow." Without wasting a second, Ty skipped off, clutching the costume. In a few minutes, she was back wearing both the costume, which fitted her perfectly, and the ice skates I'd bought her.

"Look, Mommy!" she exclaimed, twirling on the toe picks and swirling the skirt.

With my iPhone, I snapped a photo and then emailed it to my mother.

A few moments later, I got a reply.

So darling! xo

I replied with a happy face emoticon. My big-hearted mother had developed a fondness for Ty from the moment she'd met her. I'm sure the connection to my sister had something to do with it. Regardless, it was her idea to bestow the skating outfit when I told her about Ty's sixth birthday, a birthday my mother never got to celebrate with her little girl. When I suggested the ice skating lessons, my mother readily agreed to them. Little did she know that it was a ploy on my part to keep Dee and Ty in my life, long after Dee stopped being my temp.

There was one present left. Mine. As Ty reached for it, my pulse quickened. After my mother's perfect present, I wondered if she would like it. My eyes stayed on her as she peeled off the wrapping paper and took my gift out of the box. The puzzled look on her face made me uneasy.

"What is this, Drake?" she asked, examining the piece of red fabric.

"It's my magic cape. My father gave it to me when I turned six."

"That's so cool! Does it have magic powers?"

I smiled, feeling more relaxed. "In fact, it does. When you put it on, it protects you against evil and you can be anything you want." I watched as she unfolded the crimson triangle and flung it over her skating costume. Dee helped her fasten it and then gasped as Ty leaped into the air.

"Oh, my goodness! Tyson, you're going to hurt yourself!"

"No, I'm not, Mommy," retorted Ty, after another leap. "I'm Mighty Girl!"

Dee shot me a frightened look as I chuckled out loud. "Yes, you are!"

Ty leaped all over the living room, and when things calmed down, we all devoured the delicious cake. Shortly afterward, Chandra's parents came by to pick her up. Ty begged for her to sleepover, but unfortunately her classmate had her yearly checkup scheduled in the morning before she went to school. While Brock wanted to take Lulu to a movie, Lulu insisted on staying to help Dee clean up. Dee told her there was no need to since there was little to do. There were hugs all around, and as Brock ushered Lulu out the front door, he looked over his shoulder and fired me a conspiratorial wink. My face scrunched into a what-the-fuck expression as he formed a circle with his left forefinger and thumb and then repeatedly plunged his right-hand forefinger in and out of it.

"What's Brock doing?" asked Ty innocently.

"Jesus!" exclaimed a mortified Dee.

"Um, uh, it's just his special way of saying goodbye to everyone," I quickly said, covering up for him. *Fucking smartass! His way of telling me to get some pussy.*

The door closed behind him, and it was just Dee, Ty, and me.

Dee gathered up the paper plates and plastic utensils while Ty continued to prance around the living room in her skating costume, skates, and magic cape.

"Cupcake, I want you to get ready for bed."

"Aww, Mommy! Can't I stay up late? It's my birthday?"

I silently laughed, remembering how I used to try to bribe my parents to stay up late.

"It *is* late," Dee responded, her voice authoritative. "And tomorrow's a school day."

"Pooey," sulked Ty. "Can Drake put me to bed after I get into my jammies?"

Dee stopped to think while I grew a little anxious. Shit. I'd never put a kid to bed before.

"Please? Pretty please?" Ty begged, adding to my apprehension.

To my dismay, Dee caved in. "Fine. But only if you get into your pajamas right this very minute. And don't forget to brush your teeth."

"YAY!" Ty shouted before scurrying off in her skates. Five minutes later, she reappeared dressed in *Danger Ranger*s PJs and still wearing my cape. An ear-to-ear grin spread across her face. I had to admit she was so damn cute.

"I'm ready, Drake," she said brightly.

"Um . . . okay," I hedged and hawed as she skipped back to the bedroom.

"Don't let her trick you into reading more than one

book," Dee called out as I followed her daughter.

I looked over my shoulder and our eyes met. I shot her a nervous smile and assured her I wouldn't.

Ty's bedroom, which she shared with Dee, was the size of my walk-in closet. While Ty hopped into her bed, I eyed Dee's identical neatly made-up twin bed. I'd had plenty of experience with them in college. They were good for a quick bang.

"Will you read me a story, Drake?" asked Ty, cutting the beginnings of a very naughty fantasy short.

My eyes flitted to the small bookcase in the corner of the room. Hand-painted with whimsical flowers, it was lined with children's books.

"My mommy painted that bookshelf."

"She's a really good painter," I said, admiring the paintings that dotted the walls. All portraits of big-eyed children, they were clearly Dee's creations.

Another bright smile lit up Ty's face. "Do you wanna hear a secret?"

"Sure," I said though I was a little uncertain.

"My mommy wants to be a famous artist. She has ever since she was my age."

"Maybe that'll happen some day." I wondered how much Tyson knew about Dee's sordid childhood, but this wasn't the time to pry as she continued.

"After the summer, my mommy's going to be an art teacher at my new school."

"I know."

"Drake, are you going to miss my mommy after she stops being your helper?"

Her question caught me off guard; my breath caught in my throat. "I am."

"A whole bunch?"

"Yeah, a whole bunch."

"She's going to miss you a whole bunch too."

I processed her words. Had Dee shared her personal feelings about me with her precocious daughter? I fought the urge to probe and instead asked what book she wanted me to read.

"A fairy tale."

"Which one?"

"Cinderella. That's my favorite."

I searched the bookshelf and found it readily. Thank God, it wasn't the Disney version. Disney was my father's biggest competitor though ironically he'd started his lifelong career in animation there.

Holding the book, I scanned the small room for a place to sit. The pickings were slim—either Dee's bed or a wicker rocking chair, which was occupied by Froggie. Ty made the decision for me.

"Sit on my bed, Drake. That's what my mommy does."

"Um . . . okay." Apprehension was rising in my chest. I'd never read a goodnight story to a kid before.

Doing as she bid, I sat down on the edge of the bed and opened the book, making sure to position it so Ty could see the pictures as I read it. She leaned forward to make sure she could, brushing against me.

"Once upon a time . . . " I began. To my astonishment, by the third page, I was really into it and acting out all the characters. Ty giggled at my sugary sweet impersonation of Cinderella and broke into laughter at my falsetto voice for the two stepsisters and drag queen impersonation of the evil stepmother. It felt so good and natural to entertain her; I almost didn't want the story to end, and when I got to those two words, my heart sunk a little.

"Drake, read me another story!" Ty begged. "Please, pretty please?"

I inhaled a deep breath. "I wish I could, but I promised

your mommy only one book."

I expected the feisty little girl to put up a fight, but instead she asked me a question.

"Do you like my mommy?"

I faltered for an answer. "Sure. She's really nice."

Ty folded her arms across her chest and cocked her head. "No, I mean do you *really* like her? The way Prince Charming liked Cinderella and wanted to marry her."

My throat and chest both tightened. I was at a loss for words. A wry smile curled on Ty's ruby lips.

"I saw you and Mommy kissing on the roller coaster today."

I gulped. "You did?"

Her saucy smile widening, she nodded. "Yup."

I held my hands up in surrender. "Guilty as charged."

"What does that mean?"

"It means I *really* like her."

"Are you going to be her boyfriend like Brock is with Aunt Lulu?"

Boyfriend? "Do you think your mommy *really* likes me?"

"Totally!"

Again at a loss for words, I changed the subject. "Listen, your mommy *isn't* going to like me anymore if you don't go to sleep."

"Okay. Tuck me in."

"Do you want to take your cape off?"

"No. I'm gonna wear it all the time. Tonight, I'm gonna be a princess like Cinderella. Thank you for giving it to me."

"You're welcome." I smiled as she slid down on the pillow and then adjusted her comforter so that it covered most of her petite body. Slowly, I rose from the bed.

"Drake, wait! You're forgetting something."

Hmm. Maybe she liked to sleep with a stuffed animal or

something. I eyed a teddy bear on her nightstand and placed it next to her.

She rolled her eyes at me. "No, silly. You're forgetting my goodnight kiss. My mommy always gives me one before I go to sleep."

"Oh." Without saying another word, I bent over and placed a chaste kiss on her forehead. A whiff of her essence drifted up my nostrils. Sugar and spice and everything nice . . .

She smiled as I straightened. "And my mommy always says 'I love you from here to the moon and back.'"

I laughed. "That's what my mom always said to me." Effortlessly, I repeated the words back to her.

"Me too."

I warmed at her words. I wasn't big on kids, but this little girl was stealing my heart. She smiled again at me.

"Drake—"

"Yeah?" *Now what?*

"Thanks again for my cape and the *bestest* day ever!"

"I had the *bestest* day too." And I really meant it. I gave her another quick kiss.

"Good night, Mighty Girl. Sleep tight." I turned out the light and headed toward the door. My mind wandered to Dee and my cock stirred. The *bestest* day ever wasn't over yet. It was only going to get better.

CHAPTER 23

Dee

Clean up was a breeze, thanks to the paper plates and plastic utensils I used. I simply wiped them off and tossed them into our recycle bin. All I had to wash were a few serving plates and pieces of silverware. Scrubbing the stubborn frosting off the cake knife with a sponge, I thought about the great day Ty and I had. All thanks to Drake. My blood pulsed through my veins at the thought of him. Memories of the day whirled around in my head, and as I relived his kiss—oh, that incredible kiss!—a wistful smile spread across my lips and a tingly feeling flooded me. As I let out a sigh, a pair of large hands cupped my shoulders and a warm breath skimmed the back of my neck.

"Can I help?"

Drake. Both the sound and touch of him sent a rush of goosebumps to my flesh. "Thanks, but I'm almost done."

"There's got to be something I can do."

Take me in your arms. Smother me with another kiss. My eyes darted to the counter where the leftover ice cream cake was beginning to melt. "You can put the cake in the freezer." *And your tongue in my mouth before my heart melts.*

"Sure." He sidestepped to the cake, but before grabbing the platter, he dipped his long middle finger into the chocolate frosting and then sucked it off. My insides fluttered as I watched him lick his luscious lips.

"Mmm. That cake was so frickin' good. My mother always got me a birthday cake from Baskin Robbins."

And my mother never got me a single one. Pushing the painful memory aside, I told him how thoughtful it was of his mother to get Ty a skating outfit. I was as blown away as Ty was.

"It came from her heart. And she's serious about the skating lessons. I think she's fallen in love with your little girl."

"That's not hard to do."

"I know."

Finishing the dishes, I processed his words and spun around.

"Did you have any problem getting her to sleep?"

He grinned. "Piece of cake. No pun intended."

I hoisted myself onto the kitchen counter, keeping my eyes on him as he put the cake in the freezer. He noticed the fortunes we'd gotten earlier glued to the fridge with the silly sperm magnet and grinned. I thought he'd make a smug comment, but he didn't so I continued.

"Really? It usually takes me an hour. That's amazing. Thanks."

"Any time." He shut the freezer door and headed back my way. He stood directly in front of me, his hands anchored on the counter.

"Ty is really something."

Smiling, I took what he said to be a compliment. "Yeah, she's really special."

"You know, she's really mature for her age."

"What makes you say that?" Of course, I already knew the answer to that question as Ty had been around adults most of her life and had endured many of my hardships. But

I still wanted to hear his thoughts.

"We had a really grown-up conversation."

I raised a brow. "About what?"

"About you."

My heartbeat sped up and my muscles tensed.

"She said you really like me."

I gulped down a breath of air. I'd never told her anything of the sort, but my precocious daughter was wise and perceptive way beyond her years. My heart thudded, the obstructive lump in my throat hindering my speech as my new boss tilted my chin up.

"Do you?"

"I'm not sure what you mean," I replied, finally finding my voice.

"Yes, you do."

I gulped again as Drake held me fiercely in his gaze.

"She saw us kiss on the roller coaster."

"Oh, Geez!" I bit down on my lip. "That must have really upset her."

Drake grinned again. "Actually, she found it very impressive."

A mixture of mortification and desire swept through me as I felt myself heating. His eyes burned into mine and I knew I was succumbing to my need for him.

"Dee, I need to tell you something." His voice was soft and lower. "I really like you too."

"You do?" I squeaked.

"I find everything about you attractive."

I felt myself flushing. My pulse quickening.

"I feel a connection to you. And to Tyson too. I don't know why . . . I just do. I'd like to spend more time with you—"

I cut him off. "You shouldn't get involved with me. I come with too much baggage."

"Like what?"

"For starters, there's Kyle." Just the mention of his name put a fowl taste in my mouth.

Drake's eyes darkened "He's garbage."

"I'm technically still married to him."

Drake's voice softened. "Not forever." Then hardened. "I'll eliminate him."

"Drake, he'll always be in my life. I have a child. More baggage."

"Ty . . . she's an asset. She's a part of you I find so attractive."

I warmed at his words. It meant a lot to me that he adored Ty and the feeling seemed mutual.

"I'm a single parent. My daughter will always come first."

"Kids always do come first."

"I suck at relationships."

He chuckled. "I suck at them too. I've never even been in one. So we're about even there. You might actually be ahead of me."

He just wasn't going to let me win; I dug deeper, combatting tears forming behind my eyes. "Drake, I'm a nobody from the wrong side of the tracks. You're rich and successful . . . you deserve better." Pulling out my last card, I felt like I was stooping as low as I could get.

Tenderly, he tilted up my chin until my eyes met his. He held me captive in his gaze. "Bullshit. You underestimate yourself, Dee. You've done a great job raising a great kid all by yourself. You're smart, you're talented, you're on a good path . . . and you're fucking sexy as sin."

Me sexy as sin to this sex god?

Why do you think I kissed you on the roller coaster today?"

"I-I don't know."

"Then let me show you why." Before I could utter another word, he cradled my face in his warm hands and captured my lips with his. Not resisting, I surrendered, taking his mouth and then his tongue. For the moments that passed, he was my universe. As he gnawed and sucked me, I heard myself moan with rapture.

"I love the taste of you," he murmured as he began to nuzzle my neck, trailing ticklish kisses from behind my ear to a spot just below my chin that drove me crazy.

"D-baby, you taste so fucking good. I could eat all of you."

Oh, God. What he was doing to me with his words and tongue! My panties were melting and my toes were curling. "Drake, please . . . I'm not good enough for you."

He blew a breath of hot air against my neck. "Maybe, it's the other way around. That I'm not good enough for you."

Squeezing my eyes closed, I flung back my head, my breathing growing audible. "No, Drake. You're perfect." *Too perfect.*

He kissed that sensitive spot one more time. "Let's find out."

"Is it hot in here?" I mumbled absently, my body temperature rising like mercury.

"No, baby. It's hot in *here*." I gasped as he reached for my hand and put it to his crotch. A hard, thick, searing mound met my palm.

"D-baby," he breathed into my ear, "I can't tell you how much I want my cock inside you. I want to sink it into your sweet pussy and make you come so fucking hard you won't be able to walk. I'd take you right here—on the counter—but the way I'd take you to the moon and back, I'd make you scream so loud you'd not only wake up your daughter but the entire universe."

I was speechless. The intense ache for him made it impossible to talk. I wanted him so badly between my legs I *could* scream. Biting down on my tongue, I impulsively began to rub his cock. The friction of my hand against his hardness and his jeans set my palm on fire.

"Fuck," he groaned. "That feels so good." He groaned again. "Dee, I want you to do something for me."

My eyes met his, my mind, my body crying out *anything*. Still rubbing his cock, I let him lift me off the counter.

"Get down on your knees."

His words spun around in my head as I silently did as he asked. He lifted my hand off his cock and—WHOOSH!—unzipped his fly. Before I could blink, out sprung his cock. Eye-level with me, it was enormous. Close to ten steely inches of virile magnificence. My breath caught in my throat. Nothing had prepared me for seeing his cock in its pure glory. Or the package that came with it. Kyle's dick was the only other dick I'd experienced, but it didn't compare with this towering monument of manhood. Shoving Kyle to the back of my mind as Drake shoved down his jeans, my startled eyes shot up to his face. His eyes smoldered with lust as a wicked smirk lifted a corner of his lush lips.

"Dee, do you know when you clamped your lips around that corn dog today, it totally turned me on? I wanted my hard cock in your mouth. So fucking badly."

My eyes dropped down again to his cock. My heart was racing with anticipation. He wanted me to blow him. Blow this beautiful monstrosity. It's what I wanted to do too.

Curling my hand around the thick base, I leaned in a bit and wrapped my mouth around the wide crown.

He hissed. "Yeah, baby. Go down on me and suck me hard."

Without overthinking it, I slid my mouth down his velvety shaft. I was surprised how much of him I could take in. Heated, he tasted delicious, a manly mixture of sweet and salty. When I got close to the base, I slid my mouth back up swiftly now that his erection was slick with my saliva. I swirled my tongue around the crown and heard him hiss again as I went back down as far as I could. The tip of his cock hit the base of my throat.

"Christ. I love fucking your mouth. Don't stop. You're doing it just right."

Carried away with lust, I began to rhythmically bop up and down his extraordinary length, picking up my pace with each successive glide. Fixed on the extreme pleasure I was giving him. All I could think about was how much I wanted to make him come as his erection filled my mouth, and a jumble of moans, groans, and "oh yeas" filled my ears. I lost sense of time and place. His cock was my everything, his pleasure my world. As I went down on him one more time, his cock pulsed against my palate.

"D-baby, I'm going to come in your mouth," he rasped out. "Fill it with my cum."

On my next rapid heartbeat, a grunt catapulted from his lungs and he combusted. His hot release coated my throat like lava, and as he withdrew from my mouth slowly, I swallowed and gazed up at him. His head arched back, he blew out a long, harsh breath.

"Are you okay?" I asked, my voice small.

He lowered his head and met my gaze. His eyes smoldered. "Am I okay? No, Dee, I'm not okay."

My heart skipped a beat; terror ripped through me.

"You just fucking blew me to pieces. That was the best blowjob I've ever gotten. Stand up."

Shaking and speechless, I rose to my feet. My knees weak, he hauled me closed to him until we were just a breath apart. His heart beat against mine and just as fast.

"Drake, it's been a really long time since I've had any kind of sex with a man." *Let alone ever kissed someone like you*, I added silently.

He smiled and placed a chaste kiss on my forehead. "You could have fooled me."

Cleaning himself up with a dampened paper towel, he tucked his still swollen cock into his jeans and zipped up his fly as insecurity and second thoughts flew back at me.

"Drake, we shouldn't have done this."

"I have no regrets." He said it like he meant it.

"Well, I do. Besides all the baggage I come with, Hanson Entertainment frowns upon fraternization. I can't afford to lose my job."

Affectionately, he flicked my nose. "Don't worry about it. I'm going to talk to my father tomorrow morning at our breakfast meeting."

"What are you going to tell him?"

"The truth."

A heated stretch of silence filled the air between us. I don't think either of us wanted to face the truth or define it. I was scared; given my situation, a relationship with this gorgeous man-god didn't seem feasible, and if it was only a fling, I feared hurting everyone involved and above all my precious daughter. Nothing good could come out of any kind of relationship with Drake Hanson.

Drake gently traced my silent lips with a finger and then cupped my shoulders.

"You need to go," I blurted out.

His eyes locking with mine, Drake let go of me. "D-baby, it's better that way. I don't trust myself to sleep on the couch without ravaging you. And I have things at home I need to prepare at home for my meeting with my father."

My heart heavy, I nodded, wishing he'd contested me. Ravaged me and stayed.

"Will you be okay?" Concern laced his voice.

I nodded again. Silently.

"You'll make sure all your windows and doors are securely locked and your alarm is on?"

I nodded one more time. "Yes. I'll walk you to the door."

We reached the front door in no time.

"Dee," he said softly as if my simple name was a prayer. Before I could unlock it, he plastered me against the wood, pinning my arms above my head and slamming his lips once more on mine. It was an impulsive, passionate, fiery kiss. A kiss that didn't want to say goodbye. Before I stopped breathing, he pulled away.

His eyes seared into mine. "That was just a small thank you for giving me the *bestest* day of my life."

Bestest. Ty's favorite word. As the syllables vibrated in my ears, he let go of me and I moved away, my body weak, my bones liquid. With a trembling hand, I unlocked the door and then swung it open. Without saying another word, he stepped outside and walked toward his car. Standing in the doorway, I let the cool evening air revive me.

"Drake," I called out. But it was too late. He peeled off the curb and was gone.

With a weighty heart, I closed the door, making sure to double lock it before I sagged down against it. Crouched, I folded my arms around my knees and silently cursed Drake for giving me the *bestest* day too. Damn him. And damn me for letting him.

CHAPTER 24

Drake

On my way to the Polo Lounge, my father called to tell me he was going to be twenty minutes late. An unexpected conference call with Gunther Saxton and his investment team had come up.

It was fine by me. When I got to the famed Beverly Hills Hotel dining room, I was shown to the corner booth where we met for breakfast every Monday. Our regular waiter immediately brought me a pot of coffee and some cream, and I told him I'd order my usual eggs Benedict once my father showed up.

Ignoring the familiar movers and shakers around me, I poured myself a cup of the strong brew and my mind immediately drifted to Dee. I glanced down at my cell phone. It was almost eight o'clock. She'd likely be taking Tyson to school and then heading into the office. I thought about texting or calling her but refrained.

I couldn't get Dee out of my head. This girl was under my skin and in my bloodstream, making a beeline for my heart. I was breaking all my rules—from never mixing business with pleasure to never going beyond a one-night stand though technically I hadn't slept with her. And worst of all, she was married. Despite all these major NOs, I'd never felt this way about any woman before, and on my way home last night, I'd seriously asked myself the question: Could my temp possibly be my forever?

Taking a sip of the steaming coffee, I contemplated what I should tell my father about her. As the caffeine activated my senses, I decided less was best. He didn't need to know about her past or the fact that she was still married. That she had a child wouldn't likely disturb him. He loved kids. I was, however, on the fence about whether I should tell him that she worked for me. While she was only temporary, Hanson Entertainment frowned upon fraternization. Finishing my coffee, I cast my eyes down again at my cell phone. I still had time to kill so I decided to call Brock's office to see if I could meet with him sometime this week. His devoted secretary Stella would likely already be in, and sure enough, she picked up on the first ring. Glad as always to hear my voice, Brock's flirty assistant told me he could fit me in this morning at eleven. I checked my schedule. Perfect. I could head over to his office, which wasn't far, straight after breakfast. And then I could do a meeting with an art director over lunch in Century City before heading to The Valley for our weekly *Danger Rangers* recording session. Then, it hit me. I was going to be out of the office all day. I wouldn't see Dee. Maybe that was a blessing in disguise because I wouldn't have to sit behind my desk and fantasize about bending her over it and fucking her from behind. And I wouldn't have to worry about hiding my insta-boner at the sight of her luscious curves in one of her tight little skirts. Or talk about last night.

After I ordered another pot of coffee, my phone pinged. It was an email from Dee and in the subject line was one word: *Today.* I clicked it open and read it.

Drake~
Is there anything you need me to do for you today?

~*Dee*

Spread your legs was on the top of my long list, but there was no way I could risk writing that with Gunther carefully scrutinizing Hanson Entertainment and possibly having access to emails on the server. Out of the blue, a brilliant idea flashed in my mind. Tyson had mentioned wanting to meet the Danger Rangers while she was in the hospital, and today was as good a day as any. I sent back my reply:

Please pick up Tyson after school and bring her to the Danger Rangers recording session in North Hollywood.

Dee returned the email instantly.

Seriously? She is going to be so thrilled!

Wearing a smile, I responded with a happy face emoticon as I caught my father ambling my way out of the corner of my eye. Wearing his customary navy blazer, a pair of khakis, and sneakers, my handsome tanned dad, who didn't look a day over fifty, took a seat across from me and apologized for being late.

"How did it go with Gunther?" I asked after our waiter took our orders.

My old man took a sip of his coffee. "He's watching our every move like a hawk. He's concerned about our upcoming development slate."

"Don't worry. We've got a lot of shows in the works."

My father nodded with approval. "Where do we stand with Peanuts?"

Peanuts, the number one kids' network, was our bread and butter. We'd yet to get a new series green lit by Jennifer Burns, who ran it. She was looking for something fresh and different that would appeal to girls, and not one of the series concepts we pitched to her fit the bill. I couldn't lie to my father; it would only bite me in the ass.

"We're still going back and forth... close but no cigar."

My old man pinched his lips. Nope. He wasn't happy. "Son, it's critical that we sell at least one show to Peanuts. Gunther is about to put a very big offer on the table, contingent on that."

"Like how much?"

"The number 1.6 billion has been floating around."

"Jeez." That was a shitload of money. The pressure was on. Our breakfast orders arrived and my father continued.

"Son, I've made it loud and clear to him that I want you to run the company. That's what I've spent my life grooming you for. Hanson Entertainment will always be run by a Hanson. And that's a deal breaker."

It's true. I'd grown up watching cartoons with my old man and giving him input. And after I graduated UCLA, he'd put me to work right away... making me experience every department. Almost ten years at the company and now the Head of Development, I wasn't sure I'd ever have his business acumen.

"I want this deal to happen. Saxton Enterprises is a good fit for our company and it'll take care of generations of Hansons to come."

My father's fantasy—the Hanson dynasty. Both my parents were only children as was I, well for almost my entire life. There weren't a lot of us if you didn't count the many little Hansons resulting from my sperm donor days. Something my dad knew nothing about. Inwardly, I shuddered as he lifted his forefinger.

"... Which brings me to my final point. As I've mentioned to you, family values are very important to Gunther. He's been married forty years to the same woman and has three children plus six grandkids. He condemns drugs, cheating, and frivolous sexual behavior." My father took a bite of his scrambled egg whites and then looked me in the eye. "He still has a bit of a problem with you."

Here we go again. The you-better-settle-down-or-else lecture.

"He's perceives you as a player. Someone who's got his dick in every It Girl in Hollywood. This image doesn't sit well with his notion of a family-oriented entertainment company. He believes that image is everything. How can moms trust our products and be loyal to them when the head of the company is screwing every babe on the planet?"

Rage pulsed through me. While Dad seemed to like Gunther a lot, his puritan values irked the shit of me. People like that were self-righteous because they were hiding something. I wasn't even sure I wanted to stay at the company once he took it over, but I wasn't about to give my father a major coronary. He wanted this deal more than anything.

"Dad, I've been making a major effort to lie low until the deal is done." I paused. "And I'm seriously involved with someone."

His brows lifted to his forehead. "Oh, so when were you going to tell me?"

"Well, I guess this is as good a time as ever."

"Is it Krizia?"

"No." *Never.* "Someone new I met through work."

"Oh, she's in the kids' biz?"

"Indirectly." *Moms are in the kids' biz.* "She's an artist."

He quirked a small smile. My father liked artists and performers. He'd married my mother, a star figure skater.

"Mom's already met her." I paused. "And her daughter."

Dad's eyes widened. "*Her* daughter?"

"Yes, she has a six-year-old. I'm surprised Mom didn't tell you."

Dad furrowed his bushy dark brows. "Yeah, she did mention you coming by on Saturday with your new temp and her daughter now that I think about it. She couldn't stop talking about that sweet little girl. But I don't think she had any idea the two of you were involved."

"We weren't. Things have moved forward quickly."

"She's still working for you?" My father's voice took on a challenging tone.

I took another sip of my coffee, draining the cup. "Yes, until Mona gets back."

"When will that be?"

"In a few weeks."

My father narrowed his steel blue eyes. "Just keep things out of the office. I can't afford for you to screw things up, pun intended. Understand?"

Relieved, I nodded. My fantasies would need to remain exactly that. Fantasies. I couldn't risk blowing my father's deal.

He asked for the check as our waiter passed by. "I'd like to meet her, but I'll be leaving for Germany this morning with Krizia's father to meet with Gunther's people and will be there until the end of the week. Why don't you bring her to the gala at our house on Saturday night?"

"Her name is Dee. And I will."

Dad clasped his hands together with approval. "Excellent. Gunther and his wife will be sitting at our table."

My chest tightened. Now, I just had to ask Dee to the event and hope she'd agree to come.

CHAPTER 25
Drake

Brock's corner office was located on the twenty-fifth floor of a towering steel and glass building in the heart of Century City. It was furnished in a manner that was as sleek as he was with high-end Italian furnishings and a built-in bookshelf filled with volumes of leather-bound law tomes. On the walls, numerous awards and degrees were interspersed with abstract paintings. Windows enveloping the office offered sublime views of verdant Beverly Hills, downtown LA, and the Pacific Ocean.

Keeping things casual, Brock sat in one of the Barcelona chairs, dressed in an impeccable, custom-tailored three-piece suit, crisp white dress shirt, and a spiffy blue tie that brought out the color of his eyes. Sitting angled to him on the rather uncomfortable leather couch, I was wearing my customary jeans, T-shirt, and Nikes. His efficient secretary Stella had brought us both bottled waters.

After a few sips of water and some light conversation about our next hockey game, I cut to the chase. Brock billed his clients at $500 per hour, and I didn't want to take up a lot of his time since he was doing me a favor.

"I need some legal advice."

Brock's brows jumped up. "Dude, you're in some kind of trouble?"

I cleared my throat. "No, it's more about Dee."

"Don't tell me, bro, you knocked her up."

I let out a nervous laugh. "That wouldn't be possible. I haven't even banged her."

"Man, what are you waiting for?"

"It's complicated. Not counting the fact that she works for me."

"She's your temp, right?"

"Yeah . . . but I'm feeling something long-term with her."

"Oh, so you're wondering how you should deal with your regular secretary who's on leave so she won't hit you up with a wrongful termination lawsuit."

"Not at all. It's nothing like that." I took another swig of my water. "It has to do with Dee. She's married."

Brock looked surprised. I surmised that her sister hadn't shared this with him for whatever reason.

"And it gets worse. The asshole was incarcerated."

"What did he do?"

"He assaulted her when she was pregnant. Almost caused her to lose her kid."

"Jesus."

"Why didn't she divorce him while he was in prison?"

"She tried, but he hired a clever lawyer who found a loophole."

"Do you know his name?"

I closed my eyes, searching my memory. Damn my inability to remember names. "I think it was Luis Romero."

"Ramirez?"

I nodded. "Yeah, that's it".

Brock's face hardened. "I know him. He's a fucking scumbag. Plays dirty and uses Mob connections to payoff law enforcement agencies, judges, and other court officials up in Fresno."

"Well, I guess he had enough connections to get Dee's husband, Kyle McDermott, paroled. And now he's in LA. He broke into Dee's apartment last week, demanding to see their daughter."

Brock listened intently as I continued.

"I think the motherfucker was high on something. He assaulted Dee again."

"Shit."

"If I hadn't shown up at her apartment, he might have raped her or done something worse."

"Jeez. Did he hurt her or the kid?"

"No. But he left me with this memento." I pointed to the small scab on my forehead, which was now fading. The memory of Dee lovingly taking care of me popped into my head but only for a fleeting moment.

Brock eyed my face. "Crap. He could have beat the shit out of you."

"Actually, it's the other way around. I could have beat the shit out of him if he hadn't fled." I exhaled a breath. "Seriously, I would have killed the fucker for touching Dee if I could have."

"I'm glad you didn't. You would have needed a criminal defense attorney, not me."

Brock knew the extent of damage I was capable of on the ice. I'd knocked out a few players' teeth over the course of my hockey career and sent several to the emergency room for stitches. I'd lost count of how much time I'd spent in the penalty box.

"Did you or Dee file a police report?"

I shrugged. "No, I wasn't thinking straight." In retrospect, maybe it was for the best. The last thing I needed right now was a media shit storm—getting my name smeared all over the news in the midst of my father's big takeover. And that was the last way I wanted my father to find out about

Dee's checkered past.

"Brock, I'm worried about Dee and Tyson. I don't think they're safe. Or Lulu for that matter. They have security bars on their windows and an alarm system, but I'm still worried."

Brock's expression softened. "You really care about this girl, don't you?"

I took in a deep breath and looked him in the eyes. There was no hiding my feelings about Dee. I wore them on my sleeve.

"Yeah, I do. I have some kind of weird connection to her. And to her little girl too. When I'm around her, an explosion of fireworks goes off inside me. Dee does things to me no woman has. It started from the minute she stepped into my office."

"Get out. Love at first sight for LA's biggest player?"

My cheeks flushed. "I think that title belongs to you, but yeah."

"So, why haven't you fucked her?"

Hunching, I rested my elbows on my thighs and slid my head between my fists. "I'm taking it slow. I don't want to hurt her or her daughter, and I guess I don't want to get hurt either. I don't know how to do serious relationships and this one has disaster written all over it. To use her own words, she comes with a lot of baggage I don't know how to handle."

"Is there an issue with fraternization?"

"Yes and no. I told my father about her, but left out the sordid details. For now, he's okay with her being my temp and having a kid. The bigger issue is what if her past leaks out in the middle of the Saxton Enterprises deal."

Soaking in my words, Brock ran his hand through his perfectly groomed light brown hair. I could tell from the intense expression his face that his sharp legal eagle mind was at work. After a few minutes, he broke his silence.

"Listen, Drakester. You're right. This is complicated. There are a lot of issues at stake here, but you've got to prioritize."

I cocked my head, my ears perked.

"Number one on the list is Dee's safety and that of her daughter." He took a sip of his water. "And Lulu's too."

I detected unease in his voice. I wasn't sure if Dee had told Lulu what had happened the other night with Kyle. What was obvious was that Dee's sister was more to Brock than a passing fling. Still pensive, he stroked his chin with his thumb.

"Do you or Dee know where this asshole lives?"

I shook my head.

"Do either of you have his driver's license or license plate number?"

"I don't," I replied, regretting that I didn't chase after him. "Dee might."

"Find out. And I'm sure she must have his Social Security number. If she doesn't, I can get it from the Fresno County sheriff's office."

"Where are you going with this?"

"We need to find out where this douchebag lives. Once we have that info, we can get a restraining order that won't allow him within one hundred feet of Dee and her daughter. And if I have to, I'll put a few of my peeps on him to make sure he stays away."

While this all sounded good, it didn't stop the motherfucker from stalking them or endangering their lives in the meantime. They needed 24/7 protection, not something understaffed LAPD could provide. Brock cut into my mental ramblings.

"Once we locate him, we can also serve him divorce papers. California is a no-fault state. While his scumbag lawyer can contest it and draw things out, ultimately no one can force a man or woman to stay in a marriage. Where it may get dicey is with the kid, but with his criminal record, Dee may have a good shot of getting full custody of Tyson. I'll be glad to represent her."

At his words, a heavy weight lifted off my chest. "Thanks, man. You make it sound so easy. I'll take care of all of Dee's attorney fees."

Brock broke into a smile. "Bro, you don't owe me shit except for the money I have to outsource to my informants, which shouldn't be much."

My brows lifted. "No way. I can't let you take on this case for gratis. C'mon, man, I owe you something."

Brock twisted his lips in thought and then flashed a wry smile. "How 'bout this . . . make me Best Man at your wedding and be sure your lovely bride throws her bouquet to her sister."

My heart palpitated at this possible reality. "Deal."

"Good," he said, glancing down at his fancy watch. "Listen, man, let's talk more tomorrow. I need to head downtown to a mediation; it's a high-profile case involving a big reality TV star. Another sperm donor dispute. Seems like a few recipients found out his identity and are suing him for major child support. I'm trying to prove that the sperm bank screwed up."

At this news, the good feeling I had dissipated and a knot formed in my stomach. Brock knew nothing about my college sperm donor days. After all these years, I shouldn't be worrying, but something deep in the pit of my gut told me my past was going to catch up to me. Sooner than later. I had another pressing issue to discuss with Brock, but this wasn't the time.

"Good luck, man," I said, rising to my feet as Brock strode over to his desk to retrieve his briefcase.

"Thanks." We walked to the door together. "And get me that info as soon as you can."

As we exited his office, he gave me a man pat on the back. "Hey, and maybe later this week we can go out on a double date."

My mind jumped to Dee. Date was four-letter word I'd never done and I was already contemplating something much longer.

CHAPTER 26
Drake

One of my many job responsibilities, and among my favorites, was overseeing *Danger Ranger*s recording sessions. Our in-house studio was being refurbished—updated with the latest state-of-the-art equipment to impress my father's courter, Gunther Saxton—so we were now temporarily holding them at a studio in North Hollywood, not too far away from our headquarters.

Why did I like them so much? They were fun. I got to kick up my legs in the control room with the voice director and audio engineer and watch the actors do their job in the soundproof recording booth. Jennifer Burns, the head of Peanuts TV, was also usually there, and it was an opportunity to schmooze her, something I excelled at doing. I'd inherited this social skill from my father, who was indeed the King of Schmooze. His ability to charm powerful network executives, whether they be personable ones like Jen or tough cookies like some of her competitors, had a lot to do with his success as well as the pending deal with Gunther Saxton, who was notorious for his ruthlessness.

"I love this episode," said Jen before we moved on to the next line. She was seated between the director and me, taking notes.

"Me too." I honestly did. Now in its twenty-second

season and still going strong, the Danger Rangers were being threatened by the latest villain to land in Bay City. The Exterminator, a half-racecar cyborg, who wanted to eliminate the Rangers.

While the pace was fast, the atmosphere was laid back. The fun part for the actors was that they could come to work in their pajamas if they wanted and they didn't have to memorize their lines. Furthermore, being a voice actor often let them play a role that they were not normally associated with . . . like Brandon Taylor, America's number one action hero, who was guest-starring as the evil Exterminator. Charlie Atlas, our flamboyantly gay voice director, was a hoot, throwing the actors hilarious jibes, while getting them to deliver their lines perfectly in just a few takes.

"Taylor, give me a grunt," he shouted out.

"Ugh!" huffed Brandon.

"Jesus, Brandon. Don't give me a grunt that sounds like you're ramming your wife."

All of us burst out in hysterical laughter, including Brandon and the other actors.

"Charlie, what exactly do you want?" asked Brandon, still laughing.

"Pretend you're the Incredible Hulk and you're mad as hell."

"Okay."

"Line 228. Take two," called out the engineer.

Taking a couple fortifying breaths, Brandon got back into character and scowled. On Charlie's count of three, he let out a thunderous grunt that almost knocked the other actors off their stools.

"Keep that," an elated Charlie told the engineer and then met Brandon's gaze through the glass window. "That was so gorgeous I came in my pants!"

More laughter all around. Like I said, Charlie was uninhibited and outrageous. Thank God, parents and kids didn't know what went on behind the scenes of our G-rated cartoons. For laughs, storyboard artists liked to occasionally draw the Danger Rangers with big dicks bursting through their latex superhero outfits, and writers liked to sneak in lines like "Fuck off, asswipe" to keep the network executives and broadcast standards peeps on their toes. My mind flashed to Dee and her precocious daughter. As much as Tyson wanted to meet the actors who played the Danger Rangers, maybe it wasn't a good idea to have asked them to come to the racy recording session.

"Yo, Charlie. My temp and her six-year-old daughter will be here soon. Do you think you could tone it down a bit?" *A bit?* By a landslide.

"Honey, just call me Glenda, the Good Witch of the North," he retorted in an overly effeminate falsetto voice. I fucking loved Charlie. A total pro, he was simply the best.

Fifteen minutes later, Dee and Ty arrived. We were on a roll, more than halfway through the script.

"Hi, Drake!" shouted Ty, running over to give me a hug.

"Shh!" I put a shushing finger to my mouth.

"Okay," she rasped back softly as she peered through the window. "Are those the Danger Rangers?"

"Yes. You'll get to meet them soon."

"YAY!" She gave me another hug.

"Oh my goodness, what an adorable little girl!" exclaimed Jennifer. Wearing shorts, a *Danger Rangers* T-shirt, and her red cape, my favorite little girl indeed was the epitome of cuteness. I could just eat her up.

"Hi, Drake," said another soft, raspy voice that made my cock stir. Dee. I turned and met her gaze. As our eyes locked, a spark of electricity lit up the air between us. Dressed in jeans and a jersey that revealed the contours of her perky boobs, I had to will myself not to take her into my arms and consume her. I also had to will my cock to behave.

"Make yourself comfortable," I told her in a business-like voice, pointing to the vacant chair next to mine.

"Drake, can I sit on your lap?" asked Ty, her big smile melting me. The small gap between her front teeth only added to her cuteness. I had a gap like that, too, when I was a kid.

"Sure," I said as Dee sat down and Ty hopped up on me. As the strawberry scent of her hair wafted in my nose, a big part of me (no pun intended) wished it was Dee sitting on my lap and I was inhaling her.

Charlie cut into my fantasy. "Everybody, let's take five. When you guys get back, we'll wrap this baby up."

"There's a baby here?" asked Ty, full of innocence, her eyes circling the small room.

I chuckled as did Jennifer. This little girl was so damn adorable. "What Charlie means is that when the cast gets back we'll finish up the recording session."

"I get it!" beamed Ty as the cast removed their headsets and dissipated to take a short break. Right about this time, the accommodating studio always had a tray of delicious, freshly baked chocolate chip cookies waiting in the kitchen for the staff and actors. Usually, a PA brought in a plateful for Charlie, Jen, the engineer, and myself, and today was no different. They arrived just after I introduced everyone.

"Yum!" squealed Ty, taking one giant bite after another.

"What is your red cape for?" asked Jen, the mother of two young children.

"Drake gave it to me for my birthday," replied Ty proudly. "It's magic."

I shrugged nonchalantly as Ty jumped off my lap.

"I'm Mighty Girl!" She flexed her slender arms like a weight lifter. "I can be anything I want. And today, I'm a superhero like the Danger Rangers!"

As she fearlessly leaped across the room, my eyes jumped from Dee's mortified expression to Jen's excited one.

"Drake, after the recording session, let's talk. You've just given me a great idea."

I shot her a puzzled look. She shot me back a wink that had me guessing and could drive me crazy. Network executives had so much power. Much more than Ty's imaginary superhero. Another voice diverted my attention.

Brandon Taylor. Wearing low-slung sweats and a V-neck T-shirt, he entered the booth.

"How am I doing, guys?"

I watched as Dee's jaw dropped to the floor. "Oh my God! You're Brandon Taylor! I love your show."

The dashing actor was the star of the highest rated show on TV—*Kurt Kussler*. A cocky mega-watt smile curled on the action hero's lips, and his famous violet eyes twinkled. "Thanks. Will someone introduce me to this beautiful woman?"

My eyes fixed on Dee's face, her expression wavering between awestruck and love-struck. Her eyes were batting a hundred miles a minute and her mouth was still wide open. White-hot jealousy heated my bones as I reluctantly made the introduction to Hollywood's number one heartthrob—*People Magazine's* "Sexiest Man Alive." What woman didn't love him? My nerve endings crackling, I had to remind myself he was happily married and a family guy. But my jealousy reared its ugly head again when I made the introduction and he bent to kiss Dee's hand.

"Why are you kissing my mommy?" challenged Ty, hopping back on my lap. "Only Drake's allowed to kiss her!"

I felt my face reddening. Dee's was turning crimson too. All eyes fell on me.

"Kids," I mumbled with a dismissive shrug, thankful that the cast was filing back into the recording booth.

"I guess that's my cue," said Brandon as he pivoted toward the door. "See you guys later."

"By the way, Brandon, you're rocking it," commended Charlie just before he disappeared.

My pulse rate calmed down as the actors returned to their places and put their headsets back on. Mikes stood before them along with stands holding the recording script.

"Okay, boys and girls, let's wrap this episode up. Don't forget there's a six-year-old sitting next to me so you need to behave."

"Yes, Mommy!" the cast shouted out in unison in child-like voices.

Ty giggled. "They're funny!"

With Charlie pulling all the punches, the rest of the session went smoothly—and tastefully. Now almost six o'clock, we had one last scene to record—the climatic scene where the Rangers save the citizens of Bay City from the evil Exterminator and then destroy the monster.

"Okay, cast," Charlie thundered, "I need some loud screaming. You're the citizens of Bay City and the Exterminator is coming after you."

The cast did as he asked, but I had to agree with Charlie. They sounded lame.

Charlie turned to us. "Okay, troops, we need reinforcements. Get in there and give it all you've got."

"Oh boy! Does that mean we get to act with the Danger Rangers?" asked Ty, her eyes bright with excitement.

I gave her an affectionate noogie. "Yup. C'mon, Mighty Girl. Let's kick some butt!"

"Yay!" she squealed as I stood up and carried her.

Dee flung me a nervous look. "Drake, I'm not sure about this."

"C'mon, Dee. We need you. You're a great screamer."
Oh was she! My cock twitched at the thought.

"Honestly, Dee it'll be fun," Jennifer added, giving me a suspicious look.

In no time, we were all in the booth, sharing mikes with the actors. I was still holding Tyson, but had repositioned her so she was facing the mike. Dee was standing beside me and I was grateful she was sharing the Purple Ranger's mike and not Brandon's. The Danger Rangers all fawned over Tyson. She was in seventh heaven.

Charlie gave us the cue to scream. "Okay, boys and girls. On my count of three, scream like you mean it. One . . . two . . . three . . ."

A deafening roar broke out in the room. A decibel louder than everyone, Dee was in rare form. Orgasmic.

"Cut! You guys fucking nailed it!" shouted a jubilant Charlie. I cringed at his language, but I think it went over Ty's head. "Let's do the Rangers' final bit and we're out of here."

"Charlie, wait," intercepted Jen. "I'd like to give Tyson a line to say before we move on."

"Sure. What do you have in mind?"

"Go, go, Danger Rangers!"

Charlie spoke directly to Tyson. "Sweetheart, do you think you can do that?"

"Piece. Of. Cake."

Everyone laughed at her words, and then on Charlie's cue, she shouted the words into the mike.

One take. "Sweetheart, that was *fuh* . . . freakin' perfect."

"Totally!" Jen agreed as I high fived her. *My little star.*

We stayed in the booth while the cast finished up with the epilogue—the Danger Rangers going back to their civilian identities and celebrating their victory.

It was a wrap, but the sweetest wrap ever with all of the cast giving hugs to Tyson and telling her to come back anytime.

I set Ty down and we filed out of the booth.

"Drake, I'm going to take Ty to the restroom and then head home." Dee paused and met my gaze. "This was so much fun, especially for Tyson."

No one looking, I smiled and then flicked her nose. There was a lot more I wanted to flick, and not with just with my fingers. "Wait for me in the reception area before you leave. Okay?"

She nodded and then took Ty's hand, heading in the direction of the restrooms. I returned to the control room where Jennifer was gathering up her notes and belongings. She cut to the chase.

"Drake, I'm crazy about that little girl."

"Me too." *And her mother.*

"I've been looking desperately for a girl empowerment series to add to our lineup and I think I found it today."

My eyebrows shot up. "What are you talking about?"

"*Mighty Girl.* The next *Kim Possible*. A series about a little girl who believes she can be anything . . . do anything . . . with her magic red cape."

My breath caught in my throat. "Jen, are you kidding?"

"No, Drake. I totally see the series. And that little Tyson is pure magic. I'm thinking CGI, but I really want Tyson to voice the character. She's got true talent and her raspy voice is infectious. I think this can be our next breakout hit."

"Seriously?" My heart was racing.

"Seriously. I think you can talk her mom into it."

"What makes you say that?"

"Because she's totally into you and you're totally into her."

"It's that obvious?"

Jen rolled her eyes. "Duh."

Feeling my cock strain against my fly, I heaved a sigh. "I've never had a relationship."

"You should talk to Blake. He could give you some pointers."

Her husband, Blake Burns, the head of Conquest Broadcasting, Peanuts' parent company, had been a notorious Hollywood player until he met Jen. They were now one of Tinseltown's most respected power couples. I forced a small smile.

"Things are more complicated than they appear."

"Because she has a child?"

"That's the fun part." I took another steeling breath. "Because she's married."

"Oof. I wasn't expecting that."

"I wasn't either." When I stopped to think about it, everything about Dee had caught me off guard. Even her very first appearance in my office. And something told me there were more surprises ahead. Maybe I should get off this bumpy ride while I still had a chance. Before I hurt both her and her little Mighty Girl. Before they hurt me.

"And, it gets more complicated."

Jen's brows lifted and then she glanced down at her watch. "It's going to have to wait. I've got a fundraiser to attend at my son's pre-school and am meeting Blake there in a half hour. Call me, Drake, and we'll do lunch. In the meantime, I want to put *Mighty Girl* on the fast track and try to get a toy deal at the licensing show. The merchandising upside, in my opinion, could be phenomenal."

The word "merchandising" was like the sound of a slot machine landing on the three cherries. Sirens and . . . *Cha-ching! Cha-ching! Cha-ching!* The kids' biz wasn't really about cartoons. It was about all the ancillary merchandise—the toys, the apparel, the electronics, and much more. The animated series, *Danger Rangers,* hadn't made my father rich. It was all the action figures, vehicles, and video games that retailers couldn't keep on the shelves that had netted him a fortune. Mega-hits like *Danger Rangers* were few and far between. Maybe *Mighty Girl* was the next one? Was my red cape really magic?

I hugged Jen goodbye before she headed to the parking lot where her car was parked. With my laptop bag slung over my shoulder, I hurried to the reception area where Dee and Tyson were waiting for me.

"Do you have dinner plans?" I asked Dee.

"I was just going to drive through an In-N-Out Burger and then head home."

"The one near Highland?"

"Yes, that one."

"Meet me there and I'll buy dinner. I have something really exciting to tell you."

"Yay!" shouted Ty. "Can I have a vanilla milkshake?"

I smiled at her. "Mighty Girl, you can have anything you want."

One quick stop for gas, and I got caught in the LA rush hour traffic. It was fucking insane, making me wish there really was an Exterminator who could wipe out every douchebag on the road. To make matters worse, the parking lot of the mega-popular hamburger joint was totally full so I had to circle around the congested area three times until I finally found a spot a few blocks away. Rattled, I sprinted across the pavement, hoping Dee and Ty were still there. I'd tried to call Dee on my cell several times, but kept getting some stupid message: "We are unable to complete your call at this time. Please try your call later." This happened a lot in LA.

There were just too many people in this goddamn city.

I flew into the In-N-Out, and to my relief, I spotted Dee and Ty seated at a booth. They had eaten, the remains of their orders still on the table. Just seeing them—*my* two girls—made me feel better, and I could feel the tension oozing out of my system. I darted up to them, taking the empty seat next to Ty who was facing Dee.

"I'm sorry I'm so late. The traffic was horrendous."

"Does that mean it sucked?" asked Ty.

"Ty!" gasped a blushing Dee.

Giving Ty a noogie, I smiled the big, heartfelt smile that only she could put on my face. "Yeah, Mighty, it sucked." *Fucking sucked.* I loved that this child spoke my language.

"Drake, get something to eat," insisted Dee, recovering from Ty's precocious but unnerving comment.

"I'm good. I'm not that hungry."

"You can have the rest of my burger," Ty offered.

Okay, a small lie. I was a little hungry. "What kind?"

"A cheeseburger with everything on it except onions. I hate onions! Ewww!" She adorably scrunched up her face with disgust.

My favorite kind of burger and I, too, hated onions. "Are you sure you don't want it?"

"Drake, I want you to have it," she replied, handing me the half-eaten burger off her red plastic tray.

"Thanks." As I prepared to take a bite, she grabbed a fry and dipped it into her milkshake. Left-handed like me, I couldn't believe my eyes.

"Mighty, you always dip your fries into your milkshake?"

I watched as she stuffed the shake-coated fry into her mouth.

Dee answered for her. "Yes. She always has."

"That's so weird," I mumbled, reaching across the table

for a fry. "I do that too. For as long as I can remember." I dunked the fry into her milkshake and followed suit.

"Mmm," I moaned, savoring the flavor of sweet and salty in my mouth.

"That's so cool, Drake. We're twins!"

Dee rolled her eyes. "You guys are so weird."

"Drake, can you wiggle your ears?" asked Ty, her voice animated.

I watched as she demonstrated and then I wiggled mine. It was a talent I'd inherited from my old man. *Like father like son*.

"What about you, Dee?" I asked while Ty giggled and continued to wiggle hers.

"I can't."

So like father like daughter? Ty caught my attention before my mind dwelled on Kyle.

"What about this?" she asked, sticking out her tongue and then curling it to touch the tip of her button nose.

"Uh-huh." My voice was garbled as I mimicked her. "Dee, can you do this?"

My eyes stayed glued on her as she stuck out her tongue and struggled to make it reach her nose. Impossible. Both Ty and I burst into laughter.

"Give it up, Mommy."

I loved watching Dee's tongue in action. "Dee, don't worry. Your tongue has many other special talents."

Giving up, she flushed at my words. God, she was cute. My cock stirred in my jeans at the memory of last night's blowjob.

"You should at least try one of these." I dipped another fry, the longest and thickest one, into the milkshake and offered it to Dee.

"I'm not sure about this."

"C'mon, Mommy. It's super duper yummy."

"Okay. I'll try it," Dee said hesitantly as I extended my arm in her direction, holding the fry erect between my fingers. My gazed fixed on her lips as they went down on the tip of the fry and she slowly sucked off a layer of the creamy milkshake. It was so fucking erotic. My cock flexed beneath the table as the image of it coated with my creamy cum flashed into my mind. I could actually feel Dee's fuckable mouth on my erection, licking and flicking. In the presence of her sassy six-year-old daughter, I was thankful that my dirty thoughts couldn't be heard or seen though, by the heated look on Dee's face, I wondered if she could read my mind.

Slowly, she slid the fry into her mouth, nibbling on it as if to make it last.

"Mmm," she hummed, her lips brushing against my fingers when she got to the end. "That was amazing."

My blood was heating, my erection straining. "So, you like the combination of sweet and salty? It's a special delicacy."

"What's a *delicassy*?" asked Tyson.

"Um, uh, something's that's yummy to suck on like um, uh . . . "

"A chocolate covered banana," chimed in Dee, her cheeks reddening.

"Or a perfect cherry," I deadpanned, stretching my leg beneath the table until the toe of my Nike hit her pussy and rubbed it lightly.

She squirmed in her chair, my little circles growing faster and deeper. There was no doubt in my mind I could bring her to an orgasm, and man, did I want to, but there was no way I could do that with Tyson here. Okay, I was bad, but not *that* bad.

A cocky grin on my face, I waited for her to give me a signal to stop or say something, but instead she circled her body, pressing into my shoe with each rotation. I sheepishly narrowed my eyes at her, knowing full well I was stimulating her clit. She bit down on her lower lip, her arousal making me crazy with lust.

"Mommy, what are you doing?" asked Tyson, cocking her head.

"Dancing."

"Your mommy's a very good dancer," I chimed in, enjoying every minute of my ministrations and recalling how good she felt in my arms the night we danced together.

"But Mommy, there's no music playing."

"Sometimes, cupcake, you can hear music in your head." Impassioned, her gaze zeroed in on me. "So, Drake, what's the exciting news you want to share with us?"

With her state of arousal and mine, I'd almost forgotten the big news. Still rubbing her clit, I blurted it out.

"Jennifer Burns, the head of Peanuts TV, wants to develop an animated series based on Tyson."

"Oh my God!" Dee yelled with a jolt, every diner turning to look at her. Holy fucking shit! I'd just given her an orgasm.

"Mommy, I'm going to be a cartoon?"

With a flushed Dee in a state of shock from both the news and her orgasm, I answered for her.

"Yup. She wants to call it *Mighty Girl*."

"What's it about?"

"It's about a little girl with a magical red cape who can be anything she wants—from a superhero to a fireman to a writer."

"Like me and my red cape."

I nodded. "Exactly."

"Wow! That's so cool! Wait till I tell all my friends at school!"

A sudden alarm button inside me went off. Anything

Hanson Entertainment put into development had to be kept top secret so competitors wouldn't beat us to it. "Can you do something for me, Mighty?"

With a big smile, she nodded.

"You've got to promise to keep it a secret." I put a shushing finger to my lips. "Can you do that?"

She nodded again.

"Pinky shake?"

A big grin whipped across her face. "Pinky shake!" she shouted out, offering me her little finger. The deal was sealed and somehow with our pinkies locked together I felt even closer to this special little girl and her mother. The connection between us was magical. Electrical. Real.

"Drake, what does this all mean?" asked Dee, recovered from her covert orgasm.

"It means that your lives are going to change in a big way."

I walked Dee to her truck, and while she threw her bag into the trunk, I lifted Tyson into her car seat.

"Drake, do you wanna sleep over again?" she asked as Dee returned to buckle her up.

"No, cupcake, that's not a good idea," Dee retorted, spitting out the words.

"But, Mommy—"

"No 'but, Mommy.' Play with your new iPad. Drake and I need to talk for a few minutes and then we're going straight home."

"Are you gonna kiss him, Mommy?"

Dee slammed the door shut and then faced me squarely.

"Listen, Drake, I need to be honest with you."

"You want to kiss me?"

"That's not funny."

"It wasn't supposed to be."

"You've got to stop."

"Stop what?"

"Everything you're doing. We shouldn't get involved."

"I'm confused. What's going on?"

"I'm having second thoughts. You're bad for me. And I'm bad for you. I don't want this to escalate any further."

"I don't fucking believe you."

"Believe it."

"And believe that you didn't want to suck me off last night or let me toe fuck you under the table a few minutes ago? Or kiss you on the roller coaster?"

"That was different. I was scared. I wasn't in control."

"You could have gotten up from the table just now. You weren't roped down although you tied to a chair is quite an entertaining image."

Though the sky was darkening, the blush on Dee's cheeks shone in the evening air.

"This is hard for me, Drake."

"Yeah, it's hard for me too."

Not giving up, I pinned her against the car door and pressed my erection against her to let her know how *really* hard it was.

She blew out a breath. "Listen, Drake, we really need to end this."

I swept a strand of hair off her face. "Why?"

"The timing. It's all wrong."

I let out a frustrated breath of my own. I didn't want to lose her. I *couldn't* lose her. The timing was all wrong for me too. There was the pending *Mighty Girl* deal—another conversation—and there was the pending Saxton deal. My father, happy that I was serious about someone, was looking forward to meeting and introducing her to Gunther at the upcoming gala. And he would be over-the-top happy to finally have a new series on Peanuts. My mind worked feverishly for a solution. A few moments passed... and Bingo!

"Listen, Dee, I have an idea. Let's just pretend we're involved until my father's deal goes through. We're talking a couple of weeks, and after that, you're free to do what you want. By that time, you won't even be my temp and we can re-evaluate things."

"What will it involve?"

"Being discreet. I told my father about you and he's adamant that we keep our relationship out of the office. But he is eager to meet you."

"He can stop by my desk and see there's *nothing* between us except a wall."

Damn this girl. What kind of game was she playing?

"That won't be possible. He's out of the country. He wants you to come to the gala he and my mother are hosting for Gunther Saxton on Saturday night."

"As your—"

"Date." I did it... I said the word. It wasn't that hard.

"What if I say no?"

"You can't say no."

"What do you mean?"

"It's part of your job responsibilities. Paragraph five, line three: 'The assistant must attend all business-related events as requested by her superior and will be paid overtime in accordance with company policy.'" I was totally making this shit up, but Dee fell for it.

She narrowed her eyes at me. "Fine."

I let her go and she rounded the truck, getting into the driver's seat. Seeing this fiery woman behind the wheel of a pickup was fucking sexy as sin. Following her, I held the door open as she buckled herself in.

"Please let go of the door."

I smirked. "Good night, Dee. See you in the morning. We need to discuss the *Mighty Girl* deal first thing."

"Let me sleep on it."

Let me sleep on it with you.

With this thought on my mind, I watched her slam her door shut and pull out of the parking lot with a vengeance.

Sweet vengeance.

CHAPTER 27
Drake

After Dee took off, I walked back to my car at a brisk pace. Despite the whirling dervish of emotions spinning in my head—Dee was totally mind fucking me—every nerve in my body was on high alert. Now past eight o'clock, the sun had set, and the late May sky was now a sun-kissed navy, a few pink streaks holding out until night fell. I walked faster. Even with the mayor's attempt to clean it up, this still wasn't the greatest of neighborhoods. The dimly lit streets were littered with garbage, but worse, the nocturnal animals—thugs, drug dealers, and prostitutes—were already trolling the pavement.

I managed to get to my car in one piece, and as soon as I turned on the ignition, I put my convertible top up. In my stressed-out state from the rush hour traffic, I'd foolishly forgotten to do that. I was lucky my one hundred thousand dollar Gran Turismo was still in once piece, too, as car thefts and vandalism went with the territory.

Eager to get home, I pulled out of my spot and headed down Yucca. As I turned onto Selma, my eyes almost popped out of their sockets. Holy fucking shit! Could it be? Pulling over into a red zone, I brought my car to a screeching halt and jumped out. Dodging an oncoming car, I darted across the street. A drug deal was going down in more ways than one.

"What the hell are you doing with him?"

At the sound of my voice, Krizia, wearing a ski cap and dark glasses to mask her identity, leapt to her feet from a squatting position, leaving her partner in crime's exposed cock dangling. It was fucking Kyle! His beady eyes met mine.

"Fuck," he grumbled, tucking his limp dick back into his jeans as fast as he could. Zipping up his fly, he took off like the wind.

"You motherfucker!" Shoving Krizia out of my way, I chased after him.

With me right behind him, he jumped into his car, an old Dodge Camaro, and started it up.

"Open up, you motherfucker!" I shouted, trying to yank the door open, but the asshole had locked it.

"Fuck off, asswipe." With me still clinging to the door handle, he peeled off the curb, leaving me in a cloud of dust.

Fuck. Fuck. Fuck. Fuck. He was out of sight before I could memorize his license plate number. Memorizing anything had never been my forte and was one of the reasons I could never be an actor. With rage bubbling in my blood, I spun around and caught Krizia running toward her Mercedes parked at the end of the street. Adrenaline mixed with my rage. *She* was *not* going to get away. No fucking way. Not without explaining what she was doing with Dee's piece of shit future ex. And telling me what she knew about him.

Jet-propelling myself, I caught up with her as she was opening her car door and rammed into her, slamming the door shut with the force of my body. Flipping her around, I pinned her against the car with both my hands and hipbones.

"Let go of me, Drake! You're hurting me," she yelled, futilely trying to writhe herself free. She was no match for my strength. Or my fury.

"What the hell were you doing with that motherfucker?"

"What did it look like?"

I held her fiercely in my gaze. Rage pulsed through me. I knew the answer. Just as I'd always suspected, Krizia was a drug addict.

"That's right. I was blowing him. Why blow my money when I could blow him for some extra coke."

"What do you know about him?" I made a conscientious decision not to tell her about his relationship to Dee or about his criminal past.

"Nothing except for his first name."

"Bullshit. You must have his phone number."

"He calls me from an undisclosed number. We make an arrangement. We meet. I get my shit. And that's it."

"I don't fucking believe you."

"Jesus, Drake. Do you seriously think I get involved with my dealers? They're good for one thing. Getting me what I need. Now, let go of me."

My anger succumbing to frustration, I pushed off from her and forced myself to take a deep breath to stop myself from kicking her car door or bashing the roof with my fist. Or tossing her aside.

Free of me, she slipped off her glasses and knitted cap, then shook loose her mane of red hair. She was undeniably stunning but as toxic as they come.

Her poisonous green eyes met mine. "So, are you going to tell your daddy about my little habit?"

I narrowed my gaze at her. With my father's pending billionaire dollar takeover, this wasn't the time to shake things up. Moreover, knowing Krizia's twisted mind and the way she could spin a story, there was a good chance she'd incriminate me and make my dad think I was doing drugs. Just what "Mr. Family Guy" Gunther Saxton, who was also her client, would need to hear to call the whole deal off.

Right now, I needed Krizia on my side and for reasons beyond the deal. Maybe she could lead me to Kyle.

"Listen, Krizia. I'll make a deal with you. I'll keep my mouth shut, but if you learn anything more about that asshat, let me know."

"Fine, but fat chance I'll be seeing him again. Thank you for 'blowing' my deal." With a huff, she got into her car and sped off.

As her car faded into the distance, my mind switched channels. A very real fear set in. Maybe the motherfucker was on his way to Dee's house. She didn't live far.

Fuck. He had a big head start on me. I sprinted across the street to my car. Buckling myself in, I floored it and then speed-dialed her. It went straight to her voicemail. Fuck. Why wasn't she picking up? More games? Weaving in and out of the traffic on Sunset, I tried again. Fuck. Again, no answer. This time I left her a message to make sure the house was locked and to call me right away. I waited five minutes to hear back from her. But nada. Crazed, I called her again and again, but call after call, no answer. Panic set in. My heart beating like a jackhammer, I prayed nothing had happened to Dee. Or her Mighty Girl.

CHAPTER 28

Dee

Tyson sound asleep, I took a quick shower and made myself some tea. Shrouded in a terrycloth robe, I settled onto the couch and nursed my hot beverage. I couldn't get Drake's proposition out of my head. He wanted me to be his pretend girlfriend. The more I thought about it, the more it enraged me. He was using me though I wasn't sure for what purpose. Whatever the reason I didn't like it one bit. In fact, maybe I wouldn't even go through with it. Taking another sip of my tea, I wished my sister were home. I needed a sounding board because when it came to Drake it felt like someone stabbed me in the brain. I couldn't think straight. I'd be lying if I said he didn't affect me. He did on every level, playing with my heart, my body, and my mind. And the epicenter of carnal lust, my soul.

As I set my mug down on the coffee table, a loud pounding at the door startled me. My heartbeat accelerated and every nerve in my body stood on edge. Oh, God! Kyle?

"Dee, are you there? Fucking open up!"

I heaved a sigh of relief. It was Drake. But as soon as I exhaled, my relief morphed into anger. What was he doing here? I thought I made it loud and clear to stay away. Tightening the belt of my robe, I headed to the front door and unlocked it.

"Dee, are you okay?" The words spilled out of his mouth.

I studied him. He looked totally disheveled, worry etched deep on his face.

"I'm fine. Why are you here?"

The expression on his face softened a little. "You scared the shit out of me."

"What are you talking about?"

"Why didn't you answer your phone? I called you a dozen times."

"I heard it ringing, but it was in the trunk."

"What about five minutes ago?"

"I was in the shower."

His eyes roamed down my body. I was suddenly very conscious of the fact that I was stark naked beneath my robe.

"Tell me what's going on."

"It's fucking Kyle. I ran into him right after In-N-Out."

My heart dropped to my stomach. "Oh my God. Are you okay? Did he hurt you?"

"I'm fine. I was worried he was going to come here and harm you and Mighty."

"Oh, Drake!"

"Thank fucking God, the two of you are okay."

Before I could take my next breath, he hauled me into his strong arms and all the anger I harbored melted away. His beating heart sang in my ears. One arm still roped around me, he stroked my damp hair before tenderly kissing my scalp.

"Jesus, Dee, I couldn't live if something happened to you or Ty."

"We're good; we're good," I repeated softly, realizing how much we meant to him. "Come on in. Would you like some tea?"

Cradling my face in his large hands, he chuckled. That

sexy sparkle in his eyes returned. "A whiskey would be more like it, but for you, I'll settle."

Five minutes later, we were stretched out on the couch both drinking tea, me spooned against his body. In between sips, he nuzzled my neck.

"What are you wearing beneath your robe?" he breathed against me.

A coy smile, which he couldn't see since my back was to him, curled on my lips. "Use your imagination."

"Mmmm." I could hear the smile in his voice. "You're such a tease."

"I'm just pretending."

Without warning, his hand slipped under my robe and crawled between my legs. I jolted, almost spilling my tea.

"Jesus, Dee. You're so fucking wet for me. This is pretending?"

He continued to caress my sensitive slick folds, my wet heat dripping down my inner thighs. The bundle of nerves between my legs buzzed with electricity as he rubbed his thumb over it. Closing my eyes, I arched my head back as I moaned with ecstasy. Oh God, what was he doing to me?

Then, suddenly, the sound of the front door opening clicked in my ears. My eyes popped open and I straightened up. Drake heard it too.

"Fuck." He jumped to his feet and grabbed the lamp on the end table, yanking the electrical cord out of the wall socket.

"What are you doing?"

"Stay right here," he whispered as my heart pounded with fear.

Stealthily, with the base of the lamp in his hand, he tiptoed to the front door. I thought my heart would leap out of my chest as the door swung open. And then my eyes grew as wide as saucers.

"Jesus," mumbled Drake.

"Drake, what the heck are you doing with that lamp in your hand?"

Lulu! As Drake lowered his arm, I let out a sigh of relief. "We thought you were Kyle."

Lulu's brows jumped to her forehead. "Dee-Dee, what are you talking about? Kyle's in jail."

Drake shot me a puzzled look. "She doesn't know?"

I looked my confused sister straight in the eye. "Lou, he's out. He's here in LA."

Her jaw dropped to the floor. "What?"

"C'mon, Lou. We need to talk."

Several cups of tea later, my sister knew everything that happened last week.

"Jesus, Dee-Dee. Why didn't you tell me?"

"I didn't want to worry you."

Lulu rolled her eyes at me. "The fucking scumbag could have killed you. And Drake too."

Drake's face darkened. "It's the other way around. I could have killed him."

Still in her workout clothes, Lulu sat back in her chair and met his angry gaze. "I wish you had."

Calming down, Drake filled Lulu in on his recent encounter with Kyle. Though he didn't go into much detail, I learned that Kyle was dealing drugs again. Which meant he was probably shooting up heroin or doing crystal meth.

"I'm worried about your safety. And Ty's too. He knows where you live."

"We're moving out at the end of the month."

Drake's lips pressed into a thin line. "That's not soon enough."

"What do you propose?" asked my sister, her tone challenging.

"That I stay here until you move."

Before either my sister or I could reply, Drake's cell phone rang. He pulled it out of his jeans pocket and gazed at the caller ID screen.

"Shit. It's my father. He's calling from Germany. I have to take this."

My eyes stayed on him as he spoke to his father. The tense expression on his face worried me.

"Seriously?" He paused for a beat. "Fine. I'll be there." Then he ended the call.

"What's the matter?" I asked.

"I have to go to fucking Germany. Gunther Saxton wants me to give a presentation of our development slate to his investors."

"I'll help you get it together in the morning," I offered, my mind jumping to the *Mighty Girl* cartoon, something we hadn't really discussed.

Drake looked at me glumly. "That's not going to be possible. I have a plane to catch in three hours."

"Gah! Is there anything I can do to help?" I asked while my sister took our depleted mugs into the kitchen.

Drake thought for a moment. "Yes. Forward all the recent photos and videos you took of Tyson in her red cape, and anything else you may have, to our art department so I'll have something to show them by the time I land."

He stood up and then helped me to my feet. Facing me, he cupped his hands on my shoulders. Our eyes locked.

"I hate leaving you, Dee." He took a fortifying breath. "I'm going to ask Brock to look after all of you when I'm gone. Maybe he can arrange for some surveillance."

I nodded like one of those bobble head dolls Ty collected. His warm breath heated my cheeks and his touch was making my bones melt.

"When will you be back?"

"Saturday. In time for the gala."

I forced a small smile. "Do you still want me to be your pretend girlfriend?"

"No, D-baby."

My heart sunk as he flicked my nose.

"I don't want you to pretend. I want you to be my *real* girlfriend."

And with that, his mouth consumed mine in a passionate kiss that I wanted to never end.

CHAPTER 29
Dee

The week with Drake away in Germany went by quickly. Though there was a nine-hour time difference, we managed to talk several times a day. A lot of our conversations were about *Mighty Girl*. In his absence, I had taken the lead on the development, my artistic background making it easy for me to communicate with the character and storyboard artists as well as the animators, who were whipping up a short CGI sizzle reel to convey the look and feel of the series. I had to say I was totally awed by how they captured Ty's likeness and sassiness just from the photos and videos I'd provided. I was also awed by the speed at which the Hanson Entertainment creative team worked. Drake brought in Jaime Zander's agency ZAP! to work with the Hanson team to create the promo script with input from Peanuts executive, Jennifer Burns, and by Wednesday, I was back at the recording studio with Tyson to record her lines. My little Mighty Girl nailed it, and I couldn't be prouder or more excited, especially after I heard that the reel was received with a standing ovation by both his father and Gunther. When Drake got back from Germany, he was going to negotiate our deal. He mentioned royalties, an executive producer fee, and back end participation, but I had no idea what all those things meant.

And then there were the other phone calls, the ones from his hotel room . . . his bed. The caring ones making sure that Ty, Lulu and I were all safe and sound. And the toe-curling ones that shot hot tingles to my core and wet heat between my legs. Drake had only one rule: we couldn't text or send personal emails. He was too afraid that Gunther's Gestapo-like aids would intercept them. Any evidence of our sexual intimacy or talk about Kyle could jeopardize his father's deal.

Saturday came before I knew it. At seven a.m., a phone call woke me up. Drake. He was at the Munich airport, about to board his father's private plane, and would be at my house by six. After he said goodbye, I was too wound up to stay in bed. Attending tonight's black tie gala at his parents' house had my stomach in knots. I was super nervous about meeting both his father and Gunther. How was I supposed to behave? What should I talk about? And most worrisome of all, what was I supposed to wear? I wasn't exactly the kind of girl who had a closet full of evening gowns. In fact, I didn't own one and I hadn't had time to go shopping during the week. Maybe Lulu had something I could borrow, but chances of one of her dresses fitting me were slim. We had totally different body types. Lulu was tall and lanky with legs that went on for miles while I was average in height and what one would call curvy. Maybe later today, when my little sleepyhead woke up, we'd go shopping—find a thrift store or resale shop and get lucky with a slinky gown and some strappy heels. It would be great if Lulu could come along as she had a great eye and great taste, but Saturday was her busiest day with clients. As I padded around the kitchen making a pot of much needed coffee and contemplating the day ahead, the doorbell rang. Who could be here so early in the morning? My heartbeat quickened at the thought it might be Kyle, but I took comfort in remembering that the drugged out former musician was never up at this early hour.

Heading to the door, I peeked through the peephole and smiled with relief. It was my sister Lulu, her hands full—a cardboard tray with two coffees in one hand and a small bag in the other. Unlocking the door, I swung it open.

"Hi," I said softly, not wanting to wake up Ty. "What are you doing here? I thought you had a client this morning."

She stepped inside. "I did, but while I was driving to her house, she called me to cancel because she had menstrual cramps. So I headed over to Donut King and picked up some coffee and donuts. I don't have another client till ten."

"Thanks," I said, grabbing one of the coffees and following Lulu to the couch where we sat down, sitting cross-legged facing each other. The way we used to as kids when we played cards.

"Have a donut." Lulu handed me the bag. Inside were three donuts—two of them glazed and the other a pink frosted one with rainbow sprinkles. "The pink sprinkled one is for Ty," she said as I curled my fingers around one of the glazed ones.

"That is so sweet of you. She'll love it. That's her favorite."

Smiling, Lulu bit into her donut. "Holy cow. These are good. The next best thing to sex."

I gulped down my yummy biteful. "I wouldn't know."

Lulu rolled her eyes at me. "C'mon, sis. Don't tell me you and Drake haven't slept together."

I shook my head. "We haven't even gone out on a real date."

Lulu tore off a piece of her donut. "What the heck are you waiting for? Your vagina is going to dry up and crumble."

Lulu had a way with words. She could always make me laugh. Rather than telling her that he made me as wet as

Niagara Falls whenever he was with me, I iterated all my excuses . . . that it was difficult with Ty around . . . that I was still technically married . . . that I'd been hurt once, both physically and emotionally. I didn't want to get hurt again.

"Dee-Dee, you've got to move past Kyle. Drake's a great guy and he's crazy about you."

"How do you know?"

"He told Brock."

My brows shot up. "He talked to Brock about me?"

Lulu rolled her eyes again. "Duh. Brock's his best friend. Guys talk about more than just sports and the number of times they've gotten laid." She stuffed the glazed chunk into her mouth. "And he's crazy about Tyson too."

I couldn't deny that. Everything he did made Tyson's world brighter. Around him, my precious baby was a like a mega-watt light bulb.

I took a sip of my steaming coffee and then set the cup down on the coffee table. Planting my elbows on my thighs, I sunk my head between my hands and sulked.

"But, Lou. There's still the availability issue. Maybe that's why he likes our relationship. He's a player; he doesn't want commitment. He can justifiably walk away anytime because I'm still married."

"Bullshit. He's not walking away. He asked Brock to look into facilitating your divorce. Brock will represent you."

"Huh!?" My head shot up. "Drake never told me that."

"Maybe he wanted to surprise you."

"With Brock's exorbitant bill?" Anger crept into my voice. "There's no way on earth I could afford Brock."

Lulu held me steadfast in her gaze. "Drake offered to pay for Brock's services, but Brock didn't want his money. He's going to handle your case free of charge."

"What?" *Why?* My initial shock was overpowered by

other emotions. Ones that I couldn't put into words but were strong enough to put tears in my eyes.

With a warm smile, my sister tenderly brushed away a few that escaped. "It's simple, sis. Drake really cares about you. You're not a one-night fling for him."

Blinking back my tears, I soaked in her words. They weren't enough for me. "But there's still Kyle; he's going to be in my life forever."

"Screw Kyle. Stop thinking about the asshole. Trust me, Brock's a genius at what he does. He'll get him out of your life for good . . . sooner than later." She gave me hug. "Now, let's focus on Drake. When are you seeing him again?"

"Tonight. He's on his way back from Germany and I'm supposed to go with him to a gala at his parents' house . . . as his girlfriend."

"That's awesome."

"Except I have a big problem. It's black tie and I have nothing to wear. You don't by any chance have an hour or two this afternoon to run around with me and Ty looking for a gown?"

"Sorry, I'm all booked up. But you're in luck. I have something better. Don't move. I'll be right back."

My eyes stayed on her as she polished off her donut and scurried off in the direction of her bedroom. Before I could finish my coffee, she was back, holding up a long black garment bag.

"What's that?"

Her face lit up with excitement. "You're not going to believe this . . . "

"Believe what?"

"One of my new clients is Zoey Taylor."

My eyes went wide. "*The* Zoey Taylor who's married to Brandon Taylor?" I quickly told my sister that I'd recently met Brandon at a voice recording session I'd attended with

Tyson. Zoey, his former assistant, was the star of the popular sitcom, *Perfect 10.*

"Uh-huh. That one. And look what she gave me yesterday."

My gaze stayed on her as she unzipped the garment bag and removed the contents. I gasped.

"Oh my God, it's gorgeous!" Dangling from Lulu's hand was the most stunning gown I'd ever set eyes on. A halter-neck red sheath edged with beadwork—almost identical in color to the magic cape that Drake had given Ty.

"It's an Armani and has your name written all over it."

"What do you mean?"

"It's yours. Zoey wore it once to the Emmy's, but it doesn't fit her anymore. And even if it did, she can't be seen in the same thing twice. So she gave it to me . . . except it's not designed for my straight as an arrow body. But it'll look divine on you with your curves."

I moved closer to inspect the gown. On closer look, I saw it had a thigh-high slit and was meticulously made. The rich, silky fabric felt so good to the touch.

"Try it on," insisted my sister.

"Right here?"

"Yes, unless you want to wake up Ty."

"Okay," I conceded as Lulu slid the gown off the padded hanger.

I quickly undressed, and with Lulu's help, the gown was on me. The dress fit me like a glove, clinging to every curve and accentuating my cleavage with its deep, plunging neckline that nearly met my navel.

"Oh my God, Dee-Dee, you look amazeballs!

"I do?"

"Trust me, I'm your mirror and I say you do. When Drake sees you in this, he's going to want to fuck you senseless."

"Wow, Mommy! You look so beautiful!"

At the sound of Ty's bright voice, I spun around, almost losing my balance. Shit. I hope she didn't hear what Lulu just said.

"Where are you going in that pretty dress?"

"I'm going to a party tonight with Drake."

"Cool! He's going to love that dress!"

I loved my baby girl. She didn't just make statements; almost everything that came out of her mouth could be punctuated with an exclamation point. Her unbridled enthusiasm was contagious. No wonder everyone fell in love with her. Including Drake.

My cell phone rang. Charging, it was in the kitchen.

"I'll be right back." I might as well get used to walking in this slinky dress.

When I returned to the living room, Ty was devouring the pink frosted donut Lulu had bought for her. All the excitement I'd felt about tonight left the room.

"What's the matter, Mommy?" asked my sweet, perceptive daughter.

I inhaled a sharp breath through my nose and shrugged. "I can't go to the gala tonight."

"Why?" asked my sister.

"Ty's sleepover has fallen through. Chandra is sick with a stomach bug."

My sister wiped off a few sprinkles from Ty's frowning lips. "That's not going to stop you. I'll watch Ty."

"But don't you have a date with Brock?"

"Actually, that didn't work out either. Believe it or not, he's got to fly to Miami tonight for some crazy, unexpected deposition that's taking place early Monday morning. It was the only flight he could get. So Aunt Lulu is free to spend the night with her favorite niece."

"YAY!" shouted Ty, wrapping her arms around my

sister.

We exchanged a smile. God, did I love my sister. Maybe one day, Ty would have a sibling she could count on and love as much.

~

Ty and I had a fun mother-daughter day out. A stop at Payless shoes netted me a cheap but attractive pair of metallic silver heels and a dressy red satin clutch, and Ty made out with a new pair of sneakers that lit up when she walked in them. Afterward, we ventured for the first time into a Vietnamese restaurant where we devoured Pho, a delicious noodle soup with mixed vegetables and chicken. Down the street was a cheap nail place. We both indulged in mani-pedis. I chose a fire engine red polish to match my dress, but Ty went all out with a different Crayola color on each finger and toe. On the way home, we stopped off at Kentucky Fried and picked up a bucket of crispy chicken and a quart of mashed potatoes. My on-the-go sister didn't like to cook nor was she very good at it, but she could at least heat up the chicken and potatoes.

We got home at three-thirty. Drake had texted me to confirm that he would be here at six to pick me up, so I wanted to give myself plenty of time to get ready. To feel relaxed, not rushed, though all afternoon I felt flutters in my chest every time I thought about my evening ahead with him. I was as nervous as I was excited.

Parking Ty in the living room with the TV turned to *Danger Rangers*, I took a long hot shower. As the hot water beat down on me, I did something I rarely did—I made myself come, imagining Drake's deft hands between my legs. I needed the release if I was going to make it through the night ahead. Butterflies were still flitting around in my tummy and my heart was hammering.

Getting ready was a group project. My baby girl was so excited I was going out on a special date with Drake.

"How do you know what a date is?" I asked as she sat on the bathroom counter blow-drying my hair while my sister rolled my long, thick, wet tresses around a brush.

"Gosh, Mommy! Everyone knows what a date is. It's when a boy takes a girl out and then he kisses her. Like on *The Bachelor.*"

A shockwave wound through me. "Since when do you watch *The Bachelor,* young lady?"

"Aunt Lulu lets me watch it all the time with her."

I shot my sister a scathing look. She flashed a guilty as charged smile at me. "Chock it up to female bonding. We're both rooting for Greg and Lynette to end up together."

I rolled my eyes. I needed to have a come to Jesus meeting with her. But on second thought, it was probably meaningless. In this world of social media, kids these days knew everything. They grew up so fast.

"Are you going to kiss Drake again?" asked Tyson.

My breath hitched. Not so much because of my six-year-old's audacity, but more because of the very real possibility.

"Of course she is," responded my sister before I could get my mouth to move.

"Lucinda!" I always called her by her real name when I got mad at her.

"Deandra, he's not going to be able to keep his mouth off you."

Tyson giggled. "You should let him do kissy lips with you, Mommy. Drake's a super duper kisser."

I saw myself blush in the mirror. My sassy girl was right. Right as always. Drake was an amazing kisser and the thought of his lips consuming mine sent shivers down my spine while the rest of me heated.

Forty-five minutes later, my makeover was complete. With Ty's help, Dee had arranged my hair into a sexy, messy bun and applied just the right of amount of makeup on my face, insisting I wear her red lipstick to match my dress. And she'd given me her cubic Zirconia earrings, the perfect finishing touch. A little before six, I glanced in the floor length mirror that Ty and I shared. I barely recognized myself. I looked ... well, uh ... as Ty put it, like a princess. A modern, sexy one. The doorbell rang. My pulse went into overdrive and my stomach fluttered. Drake.

I was shocked by my own image, but nothing prepared me for seeing Drake in a tux. My heart flipped. He looked dazzling ... totally swoon-worthy ... his hair slicked back, his sapphire eyes glimmering, and a megawatt smile beaming on his breathtaking face. My body temperature soared as the butterflies came back in a swarm. I suddenly wished I had a fan that matched my dress. In fact, any fan.

"Hi," I squeaked. *Be still my heart!*

"Hi," he said back, his gaze transfixed on me.

Ty, already in her jammies, raced over to him. "Doesn't my mommy look pretty?"

I flushed while Drake's eyes raked over me and then met mine again.

"She looks beautiful."

My skin prickled at his words and I felt myself turn almost as red as my dress. "Thanks," I murmured.

"You guys have a great time," chimed in Lulu, sparing me from having to say more.

"Be good," I told Tyson, bending down to give her a light kiss on her forehead, not wanting to ruin my lipstick. "And don't wait up for me."

She looked up at Drake with a mixture of adoration and conspiratorial mischief in her eyes. "Have fun with my mommy."

He effortlessly lifted her into his arms, not the least bit concerned she'd mess up his sexy-as-sin tux. Something about this big, strong, stunning man in his formal wear hugging my sweet little girl made my heart melt. I watched as she straightened his slightly off kilter bow tie. Able to hold her up with one hand, he ruffled her hair. "Thanks, Mighty." He shot me an unnerving wink. "I plan to."

CHAPTER 30

Dee

Drake's parents' house looked even bigger and more beautiful than the first time I saw it. Though it was only dusk, it was all lit up and resembled a palace right out of a storybook. A parade of fancy cars and limos were lined up in the circular driveway, waiting to be valeted. We were next in line.

"Drake, I'm nervous. I've never been to something like this."

"Relax, D-baby. You're with me. You have nothing to worry about."

The uniformed parking attendant opened my door and took our car as soon as Drake rounded it. Taking my hand, he led me to the vast backyard.

My heart thrumming, I took in the scene. It *was* a scene . . . at least three hundred glamorous people dressed to the nines, the bejeweled women mostly in black. I suddenly felt conspicuous in my red dress regardless of how gorgeous it was.

Drake's parents spotted us instantly.

"Darling, how good to see you again," breathed Drake's stunning mother, giving me a kiss on each cheek. "You look beautiful. What a fabulous dress!"

Twitching a small smile, I thanked her for the compliment.

Drake introduced me to his father. Orson. Though probably in his early sixties, he looked a lot younger, with his athletic physique, thick wad of salt and pepper hair, and bronzed, taut skin. Though taller and bigger in frame, Drake was definitely a cross between his beautiful platinum-haired mother and his handsome father.

I held out my hand and he shook it warmly. "Drake didn't tell me how pretty you are."

"And dear, wait until you meet her daughter," added Drake's mother. "She's absolutely darling."

"You'll have to bring her over again. My wife is eager to teach her how to figure skate."

"I will," I said nervously, catching sight of a dapper silver-haired gentleman with eagle-like features coming our way. Dressed in an impeccable tux with his hair slicked back, he exuded wealth and power.

"Well, *hallo, hallo, hallo.*" His voice was deep and bore an accent.

"Gunther, welcome to our home," beamed Drake's father, giving him a manly pat on his back. "Is your wife here?"

"Unfortunately, Ingrid wasn't feeling well after the long flight. She's resting at the hotel."

"Sorry to hear that. Give her our best."

Gunther's attention shifted to Drake. "So, young man, looks like you made it back in one piece."

"Good to see you again, Gunther." Shaking his hand, Drake eyed him coldly.

Gunther's steely eyes drifted to me. He just didn't stare at me; he leered at me, eyeing me from head to toe and staying on my exposed chest way too long. The way he looked at me made me want to jump out of my skin.

"So, who is this beautiful *fräulein*?"

Drake's father introduced us. He called me Drake's girlfriend. I twitched a nervous half-smile at Gunther, who I learned was on the verge of buying Hanson Entertainment. Drake had never told me this. Now I understood the magnitude of the "deal." What was at stake.

The mogul's lips thinned into a salacious grin as he took my hand and lifted it. I stood as still as a statue as he kissed my knuckles.

"*Enchanté*, my dear. We must spend some time together."

From the corner of my eye, I caught Drake's jaw tightening. Possessively, he wrapped an arm around me, making some kind of statement. Looking across the lit-up yard, Drake's father's attention was diverted.

"Gunther . . . Saul Bernstein, the Chairman of Conquest Broadcasting, and his wife Helen are here. Alexis and I will introduce you."

"Drake . . . Dee," chimed Drake's gracious mother, "we'll catch up with you later." She gave us each a double-cheek kiss before breezing off with her husband and Gunther.

Releasing his arm from my shoulder, Drake stood by me stiffly. "I need a drink." His voice was tense. "Do you want something?"

"Just a glass of white wine with a little ice."

"Stay here. I'll be right back."

My eyes followed him as he hurried off in the direction of one of the outdoor bars. Maybe some alcohol would help me relax. While Drake's parents couldn't be nicer, I felt out of my element. I didn't belong among all this Hollywood glitterati. It seemed like everyone knew each other, and except for the Hansons, I knew no one. My encounter with Gunther had only made me more uneasy. He creeped me out. Not looking forward to spending more time with him, I inwardly shuddered.

"Hey, Dee, is that you?" came a vaguely familiar voice.

I turned to the right, and coming at me was Brandon Taylor with his wife, Zoey. The star of my favorite sitcom, *Perfect 10*, I recognized her instantly. He introduced us. To him, I was merely Drake's assistant. Zoey couldn't be sweeter, but my pulse pounded in my ears as she complimented my dress. Oh shit!

"An Armani, right?"

"Yes." I quirked a nervous smile.

She smiled back at me. "You wouldn't believe it, but I owned the same dress . . . "

Oh yes I would!

" . . . but I literally gave it away yesterday. I must say it looks so much better on you than it ever did on me."

"Thanks." *If she only knew*.

Brandon took his wife's hand. "Dee, we've got to go mingle, but if you and your daughter ever want to come to the set of *Kurt Kussler*, just let Drake know."

"Or to *Perfect 10*," added Zoey.

Feeling more relaxed, my smile grew genuine and widened. I thanked them both for their kind offers before they skirted off.

I blew out a breath. Well, I got through that unexpected encounter, but I was alone again and antsy. Where was Drake? What was taking so long?

"Well, if it isn't the temp. Derinda, right?"

Another familiar voice from behind me broke into my thoughts. I spun around and recognized her immediately. Krizia. The Hansons' public relations exec. I took in the statuesque beauty's appearance. She was impeccably dressed in a strapless black gown that showed off her lithe, toned body and her glorious shoulder-length red hair. In her slender hand was a goblet filled with red wine.

"Hi, Krizia," I mumbled. "By the way, it's Deandra."

"Whatever." She gave me the once over. "Are you here by yourself?"

"No, I'm here with Drake."

"Oh, are you taking notes for him?" Her snarky voice dripped with sarcasm.

Screw her. I flashed a smug smile, pleased that my inner bitch was making her debut. "I'm here as his date. He wanted me to meet his father and Gunther Saxton."

She rolled her bile-green eyes at me. "Do you honestly believe you're marriage material for a man like Drake?"

Her comment caught me off guard. Marriage was not on my brain. Given my situation with Kyle, it couldn't be. And truthfully, I hardly knew Drake. Taking a sip of her wine, my unwanted companion pursed her lips.

"Drake's father wants him to settle down; it can make or break the Saxton deal. Drake and I have a history together. Our parents are dear friends, and my father is Orson's financial advisor. Both Orson and Alexis adore me as does Gunther."

I didn't know much about Krizia's background, but it didn't surprise me that she came from privilege with her haughty entitled behavior. Willing myself to be brave, I fired a question at her.

"Are you saying you're right for him?"

She scoffed. "What I'm saying is you're not. You're just hired help who gets paid to serve him coffee in the morning and suck his dick at night."

Rage hurtled through me. I wished Drake would get back. My eyes darted around the never-ending yard, but he was nowhere in sight. My blood curdled as she continued.

"You're just a 'temporary' diversion. As soon as you're gone from Hanson Entertainment, you'll be a skeleton in his closet like the rest of his hook-ups. It won't take him long to realize that I've always been the one for him."

I'd never been a competitive or confrontational person, but I had enough of this venomous bitch. I drew in a long, steeling breath.

"It was nice seeing you again, Krizia. I'll tell Drake you said 'hi.'"

She narrowed her eyes at me as I pivoted on my heel and stalked off. "Wait a second, Deidre," she snapped before I took two steps. "I just need to ask you one thing."

Against my better judgment, I spun around and faced the bitch. A smug smile tugged at her full lips. "Weren't you waiting for a drink?"

"Yes, I was." Before I could blink an eye, Krizia hurled the contents of her wine glass at me. I gasped with shock as the red wine splattered all over me . . . both on my exposed chest and my beautiful red dress. Tears stung my eyes as I stared down at the dark crimson liquid dripping down my cleavage and saturating the silk fabric of the gown. My mouth agape and quivering, I gazed up at Krizia.

She smirked. "Enjoy the rest of your night, Deanna, or whatever your name is. The wine's on me."

No, the wine was on me. Literally. My eyes watering, I brushed away the deep burgundy rivulets still dripping down my chest as she triumphantly slithered away. My gown was soaked. Stained. And ruined. As a rebel tear crawled down my face, a welcomed voice drifted to my ears.

"Sorry it took so long. The line at every drink station was crazy."

Drake. Holding two drink in his hands, a white wine for me and some cocktail for him, he strode up to me.

"Drake, I need to go home."

His eyes fell on me and grew wide. "Jesus. What the fuck happened?"

"Krizia," I spluttered, holding back more tears.

Drake's face darkened like the sky. "Fucking crazy bitch." He plunked the two drinks onto the hors d'oeuvres tray of a passing waiter and gripped my hand. "Come with me."

Five minutes later, we were inside Drake's parents' house in one of the luxurious guest bathrooms. Bigger than the bedroom Ty and I shared, it was all rich marble and bronze, the walls covered with an elegant floral wallpaper. An intoxicating scented candle lit it up in a soft amber glow.

"Step one," Drake said, dabbing a damp hand towel on the main area of the stain, the halter covering my left boob. "The key is to blot, not rub."

"Do you know what you're doing?" *Totally turning me on!* As he applied pressure, my nipple responded to the friction, growing hard beneath the thin silk fabric. I'm sure he could feel it peeking as well as my heart pounding.

"Thanks to my mother, I'm an expert on red wine stains. I've watched her remove them from tablecloths a gazillion times at dinner parties."

I watched as he continued to dab, my eyes darting back and forth from his hand to our reflection in the large gold-leafed mirror above the sink. He was standing so close I could feel his warm breath on my cheek. The light, manly scent of his cologne mingled with the vanilla scent of the candle, creating a heady combination. Taking a break, he looked down at his handiwork and smiled coyly.

"It looks good." He eyed my breast, a mixture of pride and lust flickering in his eyes. "Onward."

"You're ruining your mother's beautiful towels."

"She won't care. Remember, I told she doesn't believe in loving things that can't love you back."

"I shouldn't love this dress so much," I sulked, still convinced it was ruined.

He set the wine-stained towel on the marble counter and

then cupped my shoulders. "You should because I love you in it. You look sexy as sin."

At both his sweet words and gentle touch, goosebumps erupted along my arms. "Thanks," I gulped. "What's next?"

He flashed a confident, oh so sexy grin. "Step two."

Retrieving the hand towel, he dipped it into a bowl of warm sudsy water.

"It just takes patience and a little dishwashing liquid mixed with water." He applied the towel to my breast, again blotting the stain, but now squeezing the nipple with his fingers as he did. White-hot sparks of arousal shot to my core. It was if a power cord was attached to my pussy.

"This is challenging," he breathed against my neck, still working my breast.

Oh God, was it. I wanted his luscious mouth all over me in the worst way. My breathing grew harsher. "I bet it's not as hard as it was removing chunky barf bits," I randomly spewed, harkening back to our very first encounter in his office.

"D-baby, it's harder." On my next rapid heartbeat, he pressed my hand to his crotch. Holy shit. His cock *was* hard as a rock! Make that a volcano.

A wicked smile played on his lips. "I'd say I'm going to great lengths to get rid of this wine stain."

Oh was he! His enormous rigid length filled my palm as his eyes burned into mine. Grabbing another hand towel, he performed the third step—soaking the towel under the faucet to wash off the suds from the fabric. He should have just used my panties—they were soaking wet too.

"Are we done? We should get back to the party."

"No, D-baby, not yet. There's a secret fourth step."

My eyes stayed on him as he snatched a hair dryer that was hung on the wall. He flicked it on and aimed it my boob. Hot air blasted out of the nozzle.

"What are you doing?" I asked, the heat and the hum making me flush with lust.

He circled the dryer all around my breast. "Blow-drying the stain. My mother's trick. It'll prevent a permanent watermark from setting in. How does it feel?"

"Is the temperature in the room rising?" As the hot air blew on my flesh, his eyes began to smolder.

"No, D-baby, it's you. You're fucking hot as hell."

He aimed the dryer at my neck and then waved it all over my upper body, sending chills down my spine. His free hand made its way to the slit of my dress and slid up my leg, blazing a trail of fire over my skin.

"Mmmm. You've got fabulous legs. This dress was made for them."

When he reached the apex of my inner thigh, he slipped his hand under my thong. I moaned as his fingers caressed my slick, fiery folds.

"Christ. You're so fucking hot and wet for me."

He wasn't kidding. The lacy fabric of my thong (a birthday present from my sister) was so soaked it needed to be rung out. Maybe Drake should be blow-drying my crotch, not my dress.

He continued to caress my now throbbing pussy, rubbing my clit with his thumb, while my hand vigorously rubbed his monstrous concrete erection. The dryer buzzed in my ear. A lot more buzzing was going on. Every nerve. Every cell. Every molecule of my being. My skin was prickling, the hair on the back of my neck bristling, every follicle, every inch of me sizzling with electricity.

"D-baby, I'd like to suck you dry. And then bury my cock inside your sweet pussy and blow your brains out."

"Are you saying you want to fuck me?

"Yeah. I've wanted to fuck you since the day I met you."

Krizia's earlier words flashed into my head. My hand

jumped off his cock. "Drake, I don't want to be one of your hook-ups."

"Come on, Dee. How could you say that?" Putting the blow dryer down, he drew me closer to him, his eyes intense. "Do you honestly think I'd introduce one of my hook-ups to my father? Or spend the amount of time I do with you . . . and Tyson? Or for that matter, struggle to get this damn wine stain out of your dress? Seriously, baby, if you were one of my hook-ups, you'd be bitching at me, demanding a brand-new dress, and I'd say fine . . . just send me the bill. See ya. You're not like that. And that's one of the many things I like about you. I actually more than like you. I care about you. And I've never cared about a woman before." He blew out breath. "Speech over. The. End"

I hung my head in shame. A roller coaster of emotions whipped through me, desire sitting in the front seat right next to regret. I returned my hand to his still hard cock, letting it warm my palm.

Pressing his thumb under my chin, Drake tilted my head. "Look at me, Dee."

By force, I met his eyes as all my insecurities poured back into me. "Drake, Maybe Krizia is right. I'm not good enough for you."

His eyes darkened with anger. "Fuck, Krizia. She's a sick bitch. I don't give a shit about what she thinks or says. She means nothing to me. You *are* right for me. And I'm going to prove it once and for all right now."

On my next heated breath, he flipped me around so I was facing the mirror with him standing directly behind me. Clutching the edge of the counter, I met his reflection in the glass. His eyes glinted with lust. And so did mine. Wanting him as much as he wanted me, I watched as he hiked up my dress and then yanked down my thong. His large hands gripped my butt, squeezing and massaging it.

"Dee, you have a gorgeous ass. One day I'm going to fuck it, but right now all I want is your tight little pussy." One hand slid between my legs, stroking my very wet folds.

I moaned and my back arched at the exquisite sensation. How long had it been since a man had given me so much pleasure? And affection. Had one ever?

I moaned again, this time louder, as his thumb moved back to my clit, rubbing the hypersensitive bundle of nerves. Wetness poured down my inner thighs as he sped up the rotations.

"Sometimes, you have to rub, not dab," he breathed against my neck.

Rubadubdub. I was coming apart.

CHAPTER 31
Drake

My cock was a greedy bastard. A needy son of a bitch. I was a guy who liked to fuck. Fuck hard and fuck a lot. Come when I wanted. And as I pleased. Making my partner orgasm first was not high on my list of priorities. My cock was a taker of pleasure, not a giver. I liked to fuck and forget, then move on. The countless women I'd screwed and never saw again was nothing to be proud of.

But with Dee, things were different. She wasn't just another random lay with nice tits and a fine ass, though she scored through the roof in those departments with her perfect knockers and firm round cheeks. As much as my heavy cock ached to be inside her and I was bursting with pent up sexual energy, I was determined to pleasure her every way I could. I didn't just want to fuck Dee Walker. I wanted to do as many possible things as I could to her. Taste her. Lick her. Kiss her. Pummel her. I wanted to see her come again and again and above all hear her scream my name on her lips over and over until she was hoarse and couldn't walk. As I caressed her slick folds and rubbed her sweet, responsive clit, everything about her turned me on. The way she arched her back. The way she fucked my thumb. The way she flushed from her cheeks to her chest. The way her eyes smoldered with lust in the mirror. The way she moaned and groaned.

"Oh my God, Drake," she breathed out as I plunged a finger into her entrance. "What are you doing to me?"

"D-baby, doing what I want. What you want." Nuzzling the back of her neck, I began to pump my long rigid finger in and out of her hot, wet, tight as fuck pussy. God, she felt so fucking good. I was just warming her up for what was to come, no pun intended. My erection strained against my trousers and I let her know by pressing it against her buttocks. I could easily get off just by dry humping her, but that's not what I wanted. I wanted to be inside her in the worst way, but right now her pleasure trumped mine. Putting a woman's needs before my own was something new to me, but I more than liked it. My cock pulsed with anticipation as I watched her come undone in the mirror. Tortured ecstasy washed over her face as whimpers replaced the harsh pants that escaped from her lungs. She looked beautiful.

"Oh, Drake," she screamed out as she finally shattered all around my finger. Her body slackened as she rode out her orgasm. Curling my arm around her waist to hold her up, I pulled out my digit and told her to keep her eyes on me in the mirror as I sucked it. Fuck. She tasted delicious. I couldn't wait to fuck her. Taste more of her. Lick every inch of her body.

"Drake," she murmured, all flustered, "we should get back to your parents' party."

"D-baby, the party can wait. But I can't."

My cock was aching for her. Ready to explode. Taking her hand, I led her out of the bathroom where a surprise awaited us.

Fucking Krizia. Venom poured out of her eyes.

"Well, well, well, if it isn't the knight in shining armor and his damsel in distress."

"Get out of my way, Krizia," I gritted, my words as

sharp as a sword.

"Fuck you, Drake. You're going to be sorry you ever met this little whore."

My blood curdling, I could feel Dee's hand trembling in mine. "Ignore her, D-baby."

Without wasting a second, I brushed past the pyscho bitch and swept Dee to the grand staircase that led to the second floor of my parents' house. So eager to get her into bed, I would have taken two steps at a time, but she was in no condition to keep up with that pace. In fact, if she stumbled one more time, I was going to have to carry her. She managed to a make it to the top of the winding stairs where another surprise awaited us. My mother. I faltered for words.

"Hi, Mom. What are you doing up here?"

"I just came up to get a shawl. It's gotten a little chilly outside." Her eyes flicked to Dee.

"Dear, are you cold? I have dozens of shawls and can lend you one."

"Um, uh, I'm actually hot."

She wasn't kidding. She was on fire. "Actually, Mom, Dee is feeling a little faint and feverish."

My mother studied her face. "Yes, she does look rather flushed."

The flush of her orgasm was still burning brightly on her cheeks. I couldn't wait to bury my cock in her pussy and keep her blazing.

My mother adjusted her pashmina wrap around her shoulders. "Drake, darling, why don't you have her lie down for a bit."

"That's what I was thinking." So I can spread her legs and ravage her.

"Dee, darling, I hope you feel better and we'll see you

downstairs shortly at the party. You made a wonderful impression on Gunther. He's eager to spend more time getting to know you."

The mention of Gunther's name made every muscle in my body tense. The image of him leering at Dee flashed in my head. Though my father had thoroughly researched him and decided he was the right person to buy Hanson Entertainment, something about him rubbed me the wrong way. His slickness? Eyes that roamed in all the wrong places? His distrust of me? My father was usually a great judge of character so maybe it was just me—my growing possessiveness of Dee and need to protect her.

"Thanks, Mrs. Hanson," she said, her voice as unsteady as her legs.

"Alexis," my mother corrected with a warm smile. "I do hope you children will be able to join us later."

"We'll try, Mom." I gave her a quick peck on the cheek before she sauntered downstairs and we headed down the long antique-filled hallway.

"Where are we going?" asked Dee.

A few minutes later, we were in my former bedroom. Nothing had changed since I'd moved out except it was a lot neater. My eyes took it in . . . the massive platform bed impeccably made up with a gray spread and fluffy Egyptian cotton pillows . . . my hockey sticks stacked perfectly by size in the corner across from my guitar . . . my trophies lined up immaculately on the built-in shelves . . . and my favorite possession—a large signed poster of my idol, Wayne Gretsky, hanging above my desk on the padded charcoal wall. Dimming the recessed lighting, I spun Dee around and kissed her madly. As her soft moans filled my mouth and my ears, I spied with one eye the words my sports hero had handwritten on my poster:

You miss 100% of the shots you never take.

I was going to take a shot at Dee Walker. And I wasn't going to miss.

CHAPTER 32

Dee

What was I doing?

It was plain, raw, and simple. I was letting my sexy as sin boss kiss me everywhere he could and undress me as I feverishly grappled with the buttons of his shirt.

"Is this the bedroom where you grew up?" I panted out as he unzipped my gown.

"No, this is the bedroom where I'm *going* to grow up. Fuck a woman like a man. Give her a fucking she'll never forget."

His eyes gleaning with lust, he slipped the slinky dress down my arms and then over my hips before it fell to my feet. Managing to step out of it, I stood before him in just my lacy red thong and metallic heels, his mouth trailing kisses down my neck. Goosebumps popped along my arms while white-hot tingles danced down my spine to the mound between my thighs. My clit still quivering, I was dripping with desire for him. On fire.

His shirt wide open, exposing those ripped-from-a-magazine abs, he took a step backward and eyed my dimly lit body. My bare breasts rose and fell with my heavy breathing as he studied me.

"Jesus Christ, Dee. You're so fucking beautiful."

No man had ever called me beautiful. The word vibrated

in my ears like a tuning fork.

"Spectacular," he added as he cupped my full breasts with his big hands. He massaged them hungrily, his thumbs running over my already hard nipples. Another stream of wet heat shot to my molten center. I moaned as he groaned.

"I can't get enough of you." His hands too occupied, he ordered me to undo his pants. As his mouth went down on my right breast, sucking in as much of it as he could, I fumbled with the fastener, my hand more than once grazing over his enormous erection. The heat beneath the fine wool fabric was palpable. So was his bulge. I swear he was about to burst right through his fly.

Once I unhooked the fastener, his hand met mine and he helped me slide down the zipper. *Whoosh!* I glanced down. Holy cow! He was commando! A museum-worthy specimen of mankind that possibly had no rival.

"Feel me, baby," he whispered, releasing my breast from his mouth. "This is what *you* do to me."

My fingers curled around his mammoth cock. He hissed as the thick hot velvet singed my palm. Wrapping his hand around mine, he rubbed the wide crown against my abdomen while his other arm, drew me closer.

"D-baby, I want to bury my cock inside you. Make you come like there's no tomorrow."

My heart thudded as my emotions wrestled. Actually it was more like a tug of war, with fear on one side of the rope losing a futile battle to desire. A heated battle between body and mind, any form of rationality going by the wayside. I faltered for an excuse.

"Drake, are you sure? You're my boss and you know my situ—"

"Hush. Put this on me." Cutting me off, he reached inside the breast pocket of his tux jacket and pulled out a small foil packet. A condom. My eyes stayed on him as he tore it open and handed me the sheath. My pulse in overdrive, I did as he commanded, rolling the latex over his rigid length. God, I loved the way his weighty cock felt in my hands, but how would this mighty pillar feel inside me? Would he fit? Would I know what to do?

"Drake, it's been a long time . . . " *Almost seven years.*

"Don't worry." His eyes smoldering, he yanked off his bowtie before stripping off his jacket and shirt. Then off went his shoes and trousers. Before I could soak in his amazing body or say another word, he hauled me so close we were flesh to flesh, his hard chest pressing against my soft breasts, his hard cock pressing against my wet center, and heat to heat, he sealed my mouth with a fierce, passionate, all-consuming kiss. And then he tore off my panties. On my next rapid heartbeat, I was in his powerful arms, and in one more, I was flat on his bed, my body caged in by his. Anchored on his elbows, he spread my legs wide with the force of his knees and then one-handedly lined up his cock with my entrance. Oh my God! The reality of the moment hit me hard. Drake Hanson was going to fuck me! And I was going to let him do it! As he inserted his cock, inch by glorious inch, nothing but the sensation of his wondrous fullness filled me. There was no room for second-guessing, no room for regret. I winced as I felt myself stretch to accommodate his size.

"Am I hurting you?" he asked as he pushed inside me.

His words whirled around in my head as he took me to the hilt. Kyle, the only man I'd ever been with, had never asked me that. All he ever did was hurt me inside and out. Drake was so different. So caring. So loving. And oh so big! Shoving Kyle and all I hated about him to the back of my mind, I shook my head.

"Are you sure?"

I nodded. "Oh, Drake, you feel amazing!"

Smiling, he kissed me and then grunted as he gave another hard thrust. "You feel fucking amazing too, D-baby. So hot... so wet... so tight. I'm going to apologize now because I'm going to fuck you hard. So hard I'm going to have to carry you home."

"No apology needed," I managed, my legs wrapping around his hips as he began to pummel me. "It... it... feels so good. Oh, God. I've wanted this... you... so badly. Please don't stop."

He didn't stop. Instead, he sped up his thrusts, slamming into me with more force again and again. Each time rubbing against my clit and hitting a spot deep inside me I never knew existed. A hypersensitive spot that was doing crazy things to my body, things I'd never felt before. An orgasm of epic proportions was about to crash through my body.

"Drake," I cried out. "I'm going to come."

"Yes, baby, come for me. Come for me hard. Come for me loud. I want to hear you scream out my name."

Every feeling, every emotion, every particle of energy surged through my body seeking an escape. I whimpered. I sobbed. I shrieked. On his next powerful thrust, everything broke loose, and I roared out his name so loudly I barely heard my next words.

"I love you."

CHAPTER 33
Drake

Thank the Gods of Rock, my parents had the smarts to soundproof my room when I was a teenager so they didn't have to hear me blast my music. If they hadn't, the cry of my name on Dee's lips would have surely had someone at their party calling 9-1-1.

Her whole body shook as she fell apart around my cock, the multiple spasms coming in rapid succession. My own epic orgasm followed quickly with one more hard thrust into her juddering pussy, and a loud feral grunt that obliterated whatever she was muttering as she rode her orgasm out with mine. Breathing heavily, I collapsed onto her heated body and felt the rise and fall of her chest beneath mine. She wrapped one arm around me and ran the fingers of her other hand through my hair. It was without a doubt the best fuck I'd ever had and all I'd intended was to give her one she'd never forget. Her ecstasy had become mine.

We stayed in this position for several minutes until our breathing calmed down though I could still feel our hearts pounding in unison. Rolling off her, I slipped off my condom and tossed it, then repositioned her so that our slick bodies were flush and her head rested on my chest. I liked having her brain on my heart almost as much as I loved having my cock in her pussy. They were both heady feelings, no pun intended.

Tracing circles around her exquisite puckered nipples, I blissfully hummed until her phone rang. *Shit.*

"Ignore it."

"I can't. Maybe something is wrong."

"Don't go there," I said, my pulse quickening at the thought of Kyle. "It's probably just your daughter."

She bolted to a sitting position. "I hope so."

"Hurry back," I said as she slipped out of the bed. My eyes stayed on her fuckable ass as she stumbled to her bag, which was on the floor next to her dress. Burying my worry, I silently chuckled, amused by the fact she wasn't walking too well. I could hear her curse under her breath with every step. When she bent down to pick up the bag, her gorgeous ass rose in the air and her perfect tits dangled like ripe fruit. She was a sight to behold. I couldn't resist her in that position and hopped out of the bed to join her. Finding her phone, she flinched as I wrapped my arms around her waist and trailed kisses down her spine.

"Drake, stop! It's Tyson."

Phew! As she stood up, one of my hands crawled down to her still soaked pussy. I stroked it while planting kisses on the nape of her neck. A sweet little voice invaded my ears.

"Hi, Mommy! Can you see me? Aunt Lulu showed me how to use FaceTime on my new iPad."

"What?" stammered Dee.

"Mommy, I can see your boobies!" An explosion of laughter spilled from the cutie pie's lips.

"Oh my God!" Frantic, Dee reached for her dress and quickly covered up her luscious tits. I fought hard to hold back my own laughter.

"Mommy, is that Drake with you?"

Smiling, I waved. "Hi, Mighty!"

"Hi, Drake. Are you having fun with my mommy?"

"Oh yeah." I could feel Dee tense up, but I was enjoying every second of this virtual encounter.

"Guess what, Mommy?"

"What?"

Tyson grinned broadly and for the first time I noticed the big gap. Dee gasped.

"I bit into a piece of chicken and my front tooth came out."

"Oh baby." Dee's voice was suddenly watery. "Did it hurt?"

Tyson shook her head. "Nope, not even a teensy-weensy bit. Wanna see it?"

Dee hesitated and then said sure. Ty proudly held up a baggie containing the tiny baby tooth. I chimed in.

"That's so cool, Mighty. Do you know who's going to stop by your house tonight when you're sleeping?"

"The Tooth Fairy!" she shouted gleefully.

"And she's going to leave you money."

"How much is she gonna leave?

"A lot."

"Yay!" Ty jumped up and down as Dee snapped her head and shot me a what-the-fuck look.

"I'm gonna go to sleep right now in case she comes early."

Dee turned her attention back to the phone screen. "Sweet dreams, cupcake. I love you from here to the moon and back. MWAH!"

"Me too! Night, Mommy! Night, Drake!"

The screen went dark and *my* girl began to snivel. A pang of guilt trickled through me.

"Dee, I'm sorry. I didn't mean to embarrass you."

She turned to face me, tears streaming down her face. "It's not you, Drake."

I brushed her tears away, but they kept falling. "I don't

understand. Everything's good." *So good.* "What's the matter?"

She sniffled. "It's my baby girl. She's growing up so fast. And I wasn't there when she lost her first tooth."

Suddenly, I understood. A life-changing once-in-a-lifetime event. A milestone. Taking her dress from her and tossing it onto a chair, I lifted her into my arms. She folded her arms and legs around my neck and hips, putting her head to my heart. I loved the way it felt. Holding her this way was both empowering and sexy. She looked so beautiful, tears and all, as she gazed up at me. Her forehead touched mine.

"I'm a mess," she blubbered.

A hot, wet, sexy mess. The fact that she wasn't the center of her universe totally turned me on. The fact that I had to work hard to be a part of it turned me on even more. I kissed the top of her head and then kissed away her tears.

"Hey, I can take you home if you want," I said earnestly.

She cradled my face and her glistening eyes locked with mine. "It's okay, Drake. Just hold me."

I could hold her forever. Words unspoken, I carried her back to the bed and set her down. Spread out, her body shimmered like porcelain against the dark comforter. The urge to kiss every part of her again consumed me. My cock stiffening, I crawled onto the bed and began to trail kisses up her inner thighs. She moaned. Her sweet pussy was one kiss away. I could already taste it on my lips. Gently, I parted her legs and buried my head between them. My mouth touched down on her wet heat and I began to lap it up like honey. I'd never been so intimate with a woman nor so determined to pleasure one. I couldn't get enough of her. She was like a drug. I sucked, licked, and kissed her still swollen nub as her hips rocked into me, writhing and wiggling. Moans turned into whimpers. Whimpers into screams.

"Oh my God, oh my God," she cried out again and

again.

I felt like I was a god. *Her* god, exerting my power over her body. My goddess.

"Oh my God, I'm going to . . ."

Come. Yes, baby. Come all over my face.

CHAPTER 34
Dee

We missed the rest of the party, fucking until Drake ran out of condoms and sucked every orgasm out of me. He wanted to take me to his place, but I needed to go home. To put some Tooth Fairy money under Tyson's pillow and be there for her when she woke up. Had Tyson not lost her tooth, I'd likely be doing the walk of shame in the morning. And my sassy little girl would have called me on it.

We drove there in silence, letting Frank Sinatra fill the air between us. My mind was in a fog and I was still throbbing from all the incredible sex. I tried to make sense of this crazy night, but couldn't. I'd let my sinfully sexy boss fuck my brains out. Now what?

Despite the Sunset traffic, we got to my place in less than forty-five minutes. With both my car and my sister's in the driveway, Drake parked his Maserati on the street. The lights in the house were off which meant everyone was asleep.

"Let me walk you to the door," insisted Drake as I undid my seatbelt. His first words since we left his parents' house.

"Okay." As soon as I uttered the word, I wished I hadn't.

Rounding the car, he escorted me to the entrance of my house, his hand planted on the small of my back. Why did this little gesture make me feel so special? So adored. So cherished.

"So, I guess it's time to say goodnight to the Tooth Fairy," he said softly as I retrieved my keys from my bag and unlocked the front door.

"Shit." I fished again through my bag.

"What's the matter?"

I pulled out a crumpled dollar bill. "This is all the cash I have."

Drake rolled his eyes. "A buck that looks like it's been through the ringer for your kid's first tooth?"

Shame crept through me. My voice grew small. "Maybe you can take me to an ATM?"

He chuckled. "I. Don't. Think. So." Then he reached into his breast pocket and pulled out a bill. "Here. This is better."

My eyes grew wide as he handed it to me. Holy shit! It was crisp, brand-new hundred-dollar bill. "Drake, I can't take this."

He laughed again. "No backsies."

He sounded resolute.

"I'll pay you back when I get my pay check."

A smile stayed on his face. "You can pay me back another way . . . "

A sudden pang of anger ripped through me. A trigger. If he thought I was going to fuck him, he was dead wrong. No way was I going to accept the money and be at his beck and call. That was my mother. That wasn't me.

My turn to say: "I. Don't Think So."

To rub salt into an open wound, he laughed again. "Oh, my sexy Tooth Fairy. You've got such a dirty mind. As much as I'd like to fuck you till the cows come home, that's not what I had in mind."

Blushing, I shot him a puzzled look.

His face softened. "I'd like to be with you when you put

the *dinero* under Mighty's pillow." He paused. "Can I come in?"

The genuine sweetness in his voice melted my heart and dispelled the rage. With a smile, I told him he could and then pushed the door open. As he followed me in, I told him we should take off our shoes so we wouldn't wake up Tyson. Or my sister.

"Do you have a piece of paper and some crayons or colored pencils?" he asked as he slipped off his left shoe.

"Of course."

"Good. We need to leave a note from the Tooth Fairy."

"Um . . . right." Why didn't I think of that? When I was giving art lessons, kids would always show me the notes they got from the Tooth Fairy. Maybe because I never got one?

Five minutes later, we were sitting side by side at the kitchen table with leftover Kentucky Fried, two glasses of milk, and a box of Oreos. Neither of us had eaten all night and we were suddenly ravenous. Along with the food, colored pencils were scattered on the table. While I drew a picture of the Tooth Fairy on a sheet of paper, Drake munched on an Oreo, eating it just the way Ty did . . . splitting it open and licking off the frosting first. Except when he licked the frosting, it was so damn sexy.

"You're such a good artist," commented Drake after devouring the cookie.

"Thanks." I had to admit my whimsical Tooth Fairy with her purple tutu, gold crown, and magic wand was almost marketable.

Drake snagged the paper with the drawing. "Okay, now let me write the note so Ty won't recognize the handwriting and will think it's really from the Tooth Fairy."

In no time, our teamwork paid off. The note, thanking Ty for her beautiful shiny tooth and commending her good brushing and flossing, was written though I made Drake add a P.S. after "Love, The Tooth Fairy" saying that since this was Ty's very first tooth she was getting a little extra. Drake added quotes around the word "little" and then drew a funny picture of a tooth that looked like a cartoon character. As if we were two proud parents, we admired our handiwork. To say I was not touched by the care Drake put into the note would be a lie. The all-night sex we had might have been electrifying, but our joint arts and crafts project aroused me in another equally powerful way. For lack of better words, a comfy, cozy crackling fireplace kind of way. Sparks were flying between us, the heat rising. Our thighs touching, I felt closer to this gorgeous man-god than I ever had.

"How did you lose your first tooth?" I asked as he folded the note into an envelope along with the hundred-dollar bill.

"Skating. I slammed into the wall of the rink and almost knocked out the same front tooth that Ty lost. It was hanging by a thread and was a bloody mess. My father pulled it out when he got home. My mother almost fainted."

"Eww." Thank goodness, that hadn't happened to Ty. I would have totally freaked.

"It looked much worse than it was. And I scored big with the Tooth Fairy," he added with a chuckle. "What about you?"

A lump formed in my throat as the painful memory surfaced. I could still feel the sharp whack to my face as if it were only yesterday. My head involuntarily jerked at the sensation. There was no magic fairy for me. Just ugly reality.

"Dee, are you okay?" asked Drake.

I nodded, wanting to open up to him. "My mother, in one of her drunken fits, whacked me when I was five and knocked out my two front teeth."

Drawing in a breath, I closed my eyes and saw crimson red behind them. Blood everywhere. I could even hear five-year-old me crying, my mother shrieking madly.

Drake cupped my face and I opened my eyes. His face somber, his gaze penetrated mine. "Oh, baby. I'm sorry. I wish I could make everything right for you. Trust me, Ty is never going to have to go through what you have. I'll kill anyone who ever lays hands on her. And I mean that."

My mind quieted and then his lips touched down on mine. This kiss. Oh, this kiss. Laced with chocolate, it was like none other. Slow and tender. Sweet and tender. Warm and tender. Giving and tender.

I could have let him kiss me all night, but I finally pulled away. "C'mon, let's take care of this."

"Good idea." My eyes fixed on him as he licked the envelope with the note and hundred-dollar bill. Oh, what that tongue could do!

A few moments later, we were in the bedroom I shared with Ty. The nightlight was on, and my heart swelled with joy at the sight of my little girl fast asleep with a small smile curled on her rosebud lips. Bending down, I reached under her pillow for her tooth and then replaced the plastic baggie with the envelope Drake was holding. Before rising, I planted a small kiss on her forehead.

"Does she always wear her red cape to bed?" whispered Drake as I stood up.

"Yes. She rarely takes it off. It makes her feel safe."

As we watched my precious little girl breathe softly, her chest rhythmically rising and falling beneath the comforter, Drake squeezed my hand.

"You're so lucky to have her."

"I know."

"My mother always wished she could have had another little girl like Ty."

My eyes widened. "But don't you have a sister?"

"I did. Her name was Mia."

Did?

"She died when she was five. A freak accident. A tree branch fell on her."

"Oh my God. I'm so sorry."

"I was only three-months-old at the time. Though my parents never talk about it, I think it was really hard on them."

I could only imagine. My stomach painfully twisted at the thought of losing Ty. Nothing could possibly be worse than losing a child you loved. *Absolutely nothing.*

"Do you want to have more children?" asked Drake, breaking into my chilling thoughts.

The question from the beautiful man who had lost his sister caught me by surprise. Unsure of why he was asking me this, I spoke the truth.

"Only if the right man comes along. Ty would love a little brother or sister, but it's hard enough being a single mom and raising one child. Every child deserves a father . . . a loving father."

"They do." Drake's voice was soft but reflective. In an effort to change the subject, I led him out of the room and walked him to the front door. Before I could open it, he spun me around and pinned me against it. His warm breath heated my cheeks as he traced my lips with a finger. Desire swirled through me. I had the burning, desperate urge to have his lips on mine again . . . his lips on me everywhere.

"You know, we're not going to see each other for a week."

His words free-fell in my head. It took me a few moments to process them and then I remembered. He was leaving early tomorrow morning for another weeklong business trip—this time to New York. The Licensing Expo. I had spent a good part of the week finalizing meetings, making dinner reservations, and pulling together materials he needed, including the *Mighty Girl* presentation. I nodded silently in acknowledgement.

"I'm going to miss you," he said softly, stepping into his shoes.

"Don't worry, I'll keep everything together at the office." I made myself sound as professional as possible, which was kind of ridiculous with him standing a kiss away from me.

He quirked a small sexy smile that rendered me breathless. "I mean *really* miss you." Tilting up my chin, he looked at me intensely. "I had an amazing time tonight."

"Me too," I managed, not letting him know that I'd had the best night of my life.

"I don't want you to see anyone else while I'm gone."

"What do you mean?"

"I mean . . . I'm falling for you, Dee Walker. I want you to be exclusive to me. I want you to be mine. Mine alone."

My heart pounding, my stomach knotting, I played with the edges of his undone bowtie. "Oh, Drake, this is so complicated."

"It's even more complicated for me, D-baby. You have no clue. There's a lot to figure out."

Was he referring to his non-committal womanizing ways or was he referring to Kyle? Or both? Or something else? I decided not to question him and ruin the evening. His unwavering gaze held me captive.

"I want you to be careful when I'm gone. Keep the doors and windows securely locked. The alarm on at all times. And if you see that bastard anywhere near here, you call Brock. He's got your back."

"Okay."

"And one more thing . . ."

Without warning, he hauled me into him and captured my mouth with his. The kiss, so hot and passionate, blazed through me, turning my insides liquid. With stars in my eyes, I melted into him as our mouths and tongues melded. He finally pulled away but kept my head in his hands.

"Send me a photo of Mighty when she wakes up in the morning."

And with that he was gone.

CHAPTER 35
Drake

Why did the sex with her have to be so sublime? Why did the whole night have to be so sublime?

My M-O was to fuck and forget. Roll on, roll off. My cardinal rule was to never get emotionally involved with a woman and never let anyone spend the night in my bed. Maybe she didn't physically sleep over, but the memory of her kept me up in more ways than one. My cock erect and restless, I relieved myself, reliving our night together. Her coming over and over. All over my face. My hand. My cock. She was the perfect fit. The perfect fuck. The perfect woman. I felt totally connected to her.

And it was so much more than just the incredible sex and the fact that she was insatiable. I felt connected to her in another powerful way that had nothing to do with my cock. It had everything to do with my heart. All the emotions she made me feel. Who would have thought that I could get off on writing a note from the Tooth Fairy over milk and cookies? Every minute with her made me drunk with lust . . . and love. And there was her magical little girl who somehow connected our hearts, made us inseparable. Together, they brought out a fierce need for me to possess and protect them. A need to take care of them every way I could.

I was already up when my alarm sounded. My morning

wood throbbed.

Fuck this shit.

Change of plans.

I wasn't going to New York.

At least alone.

Grabbing my cell phone from my nightstand, I made three calls.

The first to my mother.

The second to Brock.

The third to Dee.

Cha-ching! Cha-ching! Cha-ching!

CHAPTER 36
Dee

I couldn't believe it! I was on a plane about to land in New York.

Drake had convinced me to go with him. Ordered me was more like it as he needed my help at the licensing show. He had arranged for Ty to stay at his parents' house; his mother was thrilled to have her, delighted to take her back and forth to school as well as excited to start her ice skating lessons. My precious cupcake was equally excited, especially when the big limo came to pick us up . . . to drop Ty at the Hansons' house and then take Drake and me to LAX. There was only one stipulation—I needed to be home by Friday for Ty's kindergarten graduation. It was something I couldn't miss. Drake agreed; he promised Ty he'd be there too.

Right after we touched down at JFK airport in the early evening, Drake took me shopping. Somehow, thanks to his fashionable mother's influence, he'd managed to convince Barney's on Fifth Avenue to stay open late just for us. While casual attire suited Los Angeles just fine, I needed a sophisticated New York wardrobe for the Licensing Expo. So our Town Car made a stop at the chic department store, where with the help of a personal shopper, Drake bought me a dozen designer dresses and matching red-soled stilettos, enjoying every minute of my fashion show as I paraded in and out of the dressing room. I should also mention that on the way out, he couldn't resist buying me an insane amount of sexy lingerie that matched every outfit. Armed with garment bags and shopping bags, we headed to the Walden Hotel where we ordered room service and made endless love. If Drake had his way, we would have never left the room.

The Licensing Expo began on Monday and we quickly got into a routine. A quick, early morning fuck in bed or in the shower followed by breakfast and then a Town Car picked us up to take us to the Javits Center where the show was being held.

Wow! I'd never seen anything like it. It was a circus! Pure bedlam. The dizzyingly expansive space that seemed to go on for miles was filled with aisles and aisles of vendors from around the world marketing their wares to countless buyers who likewise expanded the globe. There were costumed characters galore and I even saw a dog that could perform a hundred tricks, his owner promising he'd be bigger than Lassie. Everyone was out to make a buck.

The huge Hanson Entertainment booth was located in a prime location . . . just as you walked into the exhibition hall. Dozens of buyers were milling around it, many clamoring to take photos with the costumed *Danger Rangers*. Orchestrating these photo ops was my main responsibility along with maintaining Drake's hectic schedule while he and his head of licensing met non-stop with new and existing licensees. Drake's main focus was to get a major toy deal for *Mighty Girl*. If Tyson didn't need to practice all week for her kindergarten graduation ceremony, Drake would have brought her along. He was convinced my loveable, spunky little girl with her red cape could have charmed the pants off anyone and cinched a deal. He was right.

I saw Drake in an entirely new light. He was more devastating than ever, as if that was possible, dressed in custom-tailored suits that showcased his tall athletic physique, and coordinating silk ties that complemented his sparking blue eyes. He was alive and animated, the consummate showman who could woo buyers and make them want to partner with Hanson. With endless meeting after meeting, we hardly had a minute to spend with each other. But at least a few times a day, Drake managed to get me into one of the small meeting rooms for a delicious kiss that melted me as much as energized me.

Evenings were consumed by cocktails with prospective licensees, business dinners at posh restaurants, and then more drinks back at the hotel. Worn out by the end of the long day, we couldn't wait to retreat to our luxurious suite and just be with one another. To fuck our brains out until we fell asleep. I'd never slept as well as I did in Drake Hanson's loving arms.

The week went by quickly. With our crazy schedule that began at the crack of dawn and usually ended around midnight, sometimes later, I really never got to see the sites of New York. But truthfully, the only site I longed to see was my gorgeous man. And he was all mine.

There were only two downers. So far, Drake hadn't been able to secure a toy deal for *Mighty Girl*. Most of the big toy companies like Mattel and Hasbro already had a popular girls' toyline. Drake tried to convince them that *Mighty Girl* was different . . . that it was inspirational and educational, not just aspirational, and stood apart from all the Bratz, Disney Princesses, Wonder Women, and Strawberry Shortcakes out there. Sadly, no one got the concept.

And sadly, for me, I missed *my* little Mighty Girl terribly. I managed to FaceTime with her at least twice a day. She was having the time of her life. She gave me a grand tour of the Hansons' mansion that rivaled Jackie Kennedy's tour of the White House and included a detailed account of her pink fairy-tale-like room with its princess canopy bed. She also kept me abreast of her skating progress. To my amazement, thanks to Drake's mother, she had become quite the little skater, able to glide on her blades expertly both forward and backward and even do a small arsenal of tricks. She couldn't stop talking about how nice Drake's parents were, including his father, who taught her how to play checkers and make cookies in her new Easy Bake oven. Drake's super rich parents were spoiling her, and I was worried if she could adjust back to our simple lifestyle. How could I compete with my meager earnings? The only thing that gave me hope was that she couldn't wait for me to come home.

I'd be home soon. I sighed as I gazed out the window of our hotel suite. In a few hours, Drake and I would be on a plane heading back to LA. Thirty stories above the street, I drank in the early evening beauty of this magnificent, towering city, hoping one day to return, this time with Ty and take in all the sites. As I fantasized riding in a horse-drawn carriage through Central Park with Ty snuggled next to me and the man I loved on the other side holding us both close to him, a warm breath grazed the back of my neck, and in the glass, I could see Drake's reflection. My skin heated. He was bared to me, every ripple of his incredible body glistening against the glimmering New York skyline.

"Let's leave this city with something to remember," he whispered in my ear as one hand curled around a breast, massaging it, and the other slid under the waistband of my sweat pants until I was melting with need.

His nimble fingers caressed my slick folds. "Jesus, D-baby, you're always so fucking wet and ready."

I moaned at both his touch and words. His voice was low

and gravelly. So full of raw lust. Removing his hand from my breast after tweaking my nipple, he yanked down my sweats.

"Spread for me," he ordered before sucking my neck and arousing me further. Not wearing panties, I was so wet there was a river between my legs.

Breathlessly, I did as he asked. Then, my eyes flitted to the throngs of people scuttling along Park Avenue and at the endless stream of cars and cabs cruising along the wide two-way street. Despite how miniscule they appeared from my vantage point, a shudder shimmied through me.

"Drake, don't you think people will see us?"

He chortled. "It's New York, baby; nobody gives a shit."

And as he started to rub my throbbing clit, the truth was the whole world could be watching and I wouldn't give a shit. Groaning with ecstasy, I arched my head back and gripped his powerful thighs as he rubbed his already sheathed concrete-hard shaft against my backside.

"I'm going to fuck you against the window, and when I'm done, I'm going to wipe my cock on the pane and leave Manhattan with a souvenir. Spell out with my cum: Drake & Dee were here." He swallowed a smug laugh. "Make that . . . Drake & Dee *came* here."

So turned on and needy for him, I was in no condition to make a witty comeback. "Oh, Drake, I want you so badly inside me. Fuck me now. Please."

"Christ. I love it when you beg."

On my next heated breath, he began to push his huge cock inside me, and as he filled me, I leaned forward, squeezing my eyes shut and pressing my warm hands against the cool glass. I groaned again once his magnificence was deep within me, and after he pulled out halfway, he began to bang me without mercy. My hands pressed so hard against the window I thought I might knock it out and we'd go tumbling thirty stories to the ground.

"Baby, don't worry," Drake grunted out, punctuating each thrust, as if reading my mind. "If you go, I go. But you'll be coming so hard you won't know what hit you."

"Oh, God," I cried out as he pummeled me harder and faster, his hands gripping my hips as they rocked into him.

"Don't hold back. When you come, I want you to scream so loudly the hotel staff hears you." He thrust again, even deeper. "No, make that all of New York. They'll be singing my name on Broadway."

Between pants, whimpers, and a loud chorus of "Oh, Gods," I felt myself building rapidly toward an out of this world climax, the sensation of a massive orgasm rising inside me like a wildfire. And then almost on the verge, I heard my cell phone ring.

"Fuck." We panted out the word in unison.

While Drake didn't stop pummeling me, my eyes blinked open, startled by how much my hot breath had fogged up the window. Lifting my palms off the glass, I straightened up as the phone kept ringing.

"Drake, I've got to take this. It's probably Ty. Or it could be the airline or driver."

Drake blew out a hot, frustrated gust of air and then slowly pulled out of me. "We're not done here," he breathed against my neck as I slid up my sweats. I sure didn't want Ty to catch me with them down, and to my relief, Drake put on a robe as he followed me to my phone. Retrieving it from my bag, I sat down on the scrumptious king bed, Drake huddling close to me.

Sure enough, it was my daughter on FaceTime. Even though she'd called at the untimeliest moment, my heart lit up at the sight and sound of her. Just out of school, she was eager to tell me how well her final kindergarten graduation rehearsal went. The big event was taking place tomorrow at noon LA-time.

"Drake, are you still coming to my graduation?"

"Mighty, I can't," he answered.

What!?

A frown tugged on my little girl's face. While my eyes widened, hers watered. "But, Drake, you promised!"

"I'm sorry, Mighty. A couple of important meetings I had today got canceled, and now I have to do them tomorrow."

I shot him an angry look. Why hadn't he told me? I was going to have to fly home by myself tonight to a broken-hearted little girl.

"Listen, Mighty, I'll see you on Saturday, and I'll bring you a special graduation present."

The tears were now falling. "I don't want a present. I just want you to be there to hear me sing."

Her disappointment escalated into soft sobs. "Come home soon, Mommy!"

"I will, my baby. I will."

My heart was now breaking; a toxic mix of disappointment, distrust, and disdain coursed through my veins. I needed to end this. Get away from him. I didn't need a man in my life who could hurt my precious daughter.

"Mommy, I have to go," she sniffled. "Drake's mommy is giving me a skating lesson."

"I'll call you from the airport to say goodnight."

"Okay, Mommy. I love you from here to the moon and back."

"The same, baby, the same."

The screen went dark. I threw my phone into my purse, and on my next breath, I felt Drake nuzzling my neck.

"How about we finish what we started before you

leave?"

"Stop it," I barked, leaping to my feet. I began to toss garments into my suitcase.

"Jesus. What's the matter?"

Everything. Rage rose in my chest. "How could you disappoint my daughter like that? How could you not tell me you weren't coming back with me tonight?"

"It happened last minute. I was going to tell you just before Tyson called you."

Just after you fucked me? Fuming, I gave him the silent treatment. I didn't want to waste words on him. I continued to haphazardly pack my bag.

"Aren't you going to take your new dresses back with you?"

"I have no room for them in my suitcase, and to be honest, I don't have any need for them in LA." *And I don't have any need for you.* On Monday, I was going to look for a new temp job that would hold me over until I started my teaching position in September.

I zipped up my bag and threw on a hoodie. I was comfortably dressed for the long flight home. *Alone.*

"I'll call someone to take down your bag. The car will meet you in front of the hotel at six. And there'll be someone to meet you at baggage claim when you land at LAX."

"I don't need anyone to take down my bag. I'm perfectly capable of doing it myself." I wheeled the bag to the door, Drake trailing behind me.

Before I could crank the handle, he spun me around and pinned me against the wall. "Listen, Dee, I'm sorry. I can't go back to LA without a toy deal. The Saxton deal is dependent on it."

"Good luck," I said, my tone as cold as dry ice. "Now, let go of me. I don't want to miss my plane."

He stepped away. Jerking the door open, I stormed out. As it closed behind me, I heard Drake bang it and curse under his breath.

Fuck him.

CHAPTER 37
Drake

A cocktail of guilt, remorse, and anxiety whipped through me as I sat in the back seat of the Town Car that was inching up Park Avenue in the stop-and-go rush hour traffic. I felt like a total shit for not flying back to LA with Dee for Tyson's graduation. And Dee's reaction only made feel like a bigger dick. Balls. I never thought her little girl would cry like that. I could lose them both; the possibility was very real. Maybe, just maybe, things would work out.

I had one more shot to score a major toy deal for *Mighty Girl*. My pitch to Sarah Greene-Golden. I inhaled a steeling breath as the car finally pulled up to her majestic apartment building on the corner of Park and Eighty-Fifth Street.

After I slid out, the doorman pointed the way to the elevator, which took me directly up to Sarah's penthouse apartment. It was the epitome of Park Avenue elegance with spacious hi-ceiling rooms, Art-Deco furnishings, and sweeping views of the city.

"Thank you for letting me meet with you tonight instead of tomorrow," I said as she ushered me into the antique-filled living room. The attractive, twenty-something rising star in the toy industry had just had a baby with her billionaire husband, Ari, who headed up a Fortune 500 pharmaceutical company. She was on maternity leave from Ike's Tikes, where she was Vice President of Development. Tall and lanky with a mane of long dark hair, it was hard to believe she'd recently given birth.

She laughed. "No, thank you. You're saving me a trip downtown. I'm sorry I had to cancel our meeting today. I totally forgot that our nanny wasn't available to watch the baby."

I began to relax, taking a seat on a velvet armchair next to her. My laptop bag was on my lap. "Your place is amazing."

"Thanks. We're actually going to redecorate shortly to make it more kid-friendly. Antiques and toddlers don't mix well."

I chuckled, reminded of all the damage little-demon-me caused in my parents' grandly furnished house. I shared this silly tidbit with her and then we chitchatted a little about the licensing show and the kids' biz. It was time to get down to business, but as I unlatched my laptop bag, Sarah's husband strode into the room. Tall, muscular, and casually dressed in khakis and a polo shirt, the movie-star handsome golden-haired man closely resembled Chris Hemsworth. I stood to shake his hand as Sarah introduced us.

"I'm about to pour myself a Scotch. Can I get you anything?"

I declined, content with the bottled water and hors d'oeuvres that Sarah had laid out on the coffee table. As I took a sip of my Evian, a child's voice drifted into my ears.

"Daddy! Guess what!"

I looked up and racing toward us was a cute little boy wearing a karate gi. About the same age as Tyson, he was the spitting image of Ari with sandy hair and bright blue eyes. Beside him was a buxom Hispanic woman with sparkling dark eyes, who I assumed was the nanny.

"What, buddy?" asked Ari, lifting the boy into his arms. This must be Sarah and Ari's son.

"I got my yellow belt!"

"Way to go!" Ari's eyes flickered with pride and joy as they high-fived. *Fatherhood.* A twinge of envy zipped through me as Ari introduced me to his son, Ben. The youngster's eyes lit up.

"Cool beans! You make the *Danger Rangers* cartoon? I watch that show all the time. It's on in a few minutes."

Still smiling, Ari affectionately ruffled his son's unruly hair. "C'mon, let's get you washed up, into your PJs, and we'll watch it together so Mommy and Drake can do their work."

"I'll get dinner prepared," said the nanny in Spanish. "Señora Golden, will Señor Hanson be joining us?"

I politely declined and then pulled out my computer, setting it on the coffee table so Sarah could see the screen.

"What's your new show about?" she asked as the others disappeared.

"The demo piece speaks for itself."

Bending forward, I loaded up the CGI snippet our animation team had put together and hit play. My stomach knotted as Sarah watched it.

An animated little girl with a red cape and long pigtails flew onto the screen, morphing into different characters, one after another.

"I'm Mighty Girl and I can be anything I want when I wear my magic red cape. A fireman! A policeman! An astronaut! A superhero!"

She leapt into the air, her cape flying behind her. *Whoosh!* Our company logo appeared, and before the screen faded to black, I shut my laptop.

Sarah met my anxious gaze, folding her hands on her lap. "Drake, I'm going to cut to the chase." My heart thudded. "I love this. It's exactly what Ike and I have been looking for."

YES! She was referring to her boss, Ike Abrams, the head of Ike's Tikes. Adrenaline was pumping through my veins as she continued.

"An aspirational girls' series skewing to girls 4-6. It's so empowering. And the possibilities are endless. I totally see this. It's the next *Dora the Explorer*. I want to be a partner. What inspired this?"

"A special little girl I know." As the image of Tyson wearing her red cape flashed through my mind, Ari's smooth voice sounded in my ears. He was ambling back into the living room, holding a small pink bundle in his arms.

"My princess, look who's up!" he beamed, coming toward us.

Sarah stood up, her eyes twinkling. "Drake, meet our little angel, Rosie."

Hesitantly, I rose, my eyes transfixed on the tiny, cocooned baby in Ari's strapping arms. His expression oozed with paternal joy as he wooed her with funny little sounds and baby talk.

"She's beautiful," I said. Truly she was, with her ivory skin, chocolate brown eyes, and tuft of dark, silky hair. She already looked a lot like Sarah.

"Thanks," said Ari, rocking her gently. "Do you have kids?"

A lump formed in my throat as my pulse quickened. How should I answer that question? Should I tell him this baby daddy had dozens? Hundreds?? Thousands? That maybe . . .

Sarah cut my thoughts short. "Drake, do you want to hold her?"

My stomach tightened. I hedged and hawed, but Sarah didn't give me a chance. Taking the baby from Ari, she gently set her in my arms. "Here. Just be sure to hold her head up."

"Hi," I said softly, casting my gaze at her. She felt delicious. So amazing. Her sweet, intoxicating baby scent infected every one of my senses. To my astonishment, she stared up at me and curled her rosebud lips into a smile. I swear she had super powers—able to turn every bone in my body into liquid. As I held her with awe, Sarah planted a tender kiss on her silky scalp.

"This is *my* Mighty Girl. She can be anything she wants . . . even President of the United States."

Back in the Town Car, I pumped a fist. Yes! We had a toy deal.

I made three quick calls.

One to my father to tell him the great news.

One to my licensing guy, asking him to handle my remaining meetings.

One to our travel department to book me a flight.

Three hours later I was on a Red Eye, heading back to LA.

CHAPTER 38
Dee

It was the cutest thing I'd ever seen. Thirty-five little boys and girls, wearing royal blue caps and gowns, were seated on stage in two long rows. Tyson was seated in the middle of the front row, waiting to be called by her teacher, Mrs. Dunne, to come to the podium and receive her diploma. With her last name starting with "W," she'd be the last one to be called up.

I was seated in the front row of the auditorium. My sister to the right of me, I kept my eyes focused on Ty, taking photos to avoid looking at the empty chair next to me. The one that had been reserved for Drake. I didn't want to think about him. I wanted this to be a happy day for my daughter and me. *Fuck him.*

Mrs. Dunne was on the kids whose last names began with "T." It would be Ty's turn any minute. Suddenly, a loud pounding sounded on the doors to the auditorium. The pounding continued. In fact, it got louder. More relentless.

"Someone, open up!" I heard a muffled voice shout out.

A parent in the back row rose to open the doors. All eyes, including mine, turned to the drop-dead gorgeous man standing in the back. His eyes darted around the auditorium before landing on me, and then he dashed down an aisle. My heart leapt into my throat. Oh my God!

"Drake," squealed my daughter as her name was called. "YAY! You're here!"

"Hi, Mighty!" he shouted back as he took the empty seat next to me, breathless.

With a smile that lit up the room, my little girl bounced up from her seat and ran up to the podium where her teacher shook her hand and handed her the diploma.

"Now, let's have a big shout-out for all our kindergarten graduates," Mrs. Dunne thundered. "One, two, three."

On her count, all the smiling children flipped the gold tassels on their caps to the left and then tossed the caps into the air. As they went flying, applause and cheers erupted. Drake let out a deafening wolf whistle. Our focus on Tyson and her classmates, we still hadn't made eye contact. My heart, however, was doing somersaults. I couldn't believe he was here.

Mrs. Dunne signaled for the audience to calm down. "And now, the conclusion of our ceremony. Please join us as Tyson Walker leads us in "If You're Happy and You Know It."

Tyson skipped up to the mike that was placed in the middle of the stage. At the top of her lungs, she began to sing the song, her classmates and the audience joining in.

I couldn't clap loud enough . . . I couldn't shout "Hooray" loud enough. Nor could Drake. As the song came to an end, the cheering audience gave the children a standing ovation. As they all took a bow, Drake spun me around so I was facing him and then dipped me before smacking my lips with his. If all eyes were on us, I wouldn't know.

He'd come back for me. Come back for *us*. I'd never been so happy in my entire life.

CHAPTER 39

Drake

It was the perfect night for a celebration. Tyson was celebrating her kindergarten graduation with a pizza party at her friend Chandra's house. Gunther Saxton, who was still in LA, had called for one to toast my toy deal and the imminent acquisition of Hanson Entertainment—now a handshake away.

Musso & Frank Grill on Hollywood Boulevard was the oldest restaurant in Tinseltown. Opened in 1919, the iconic eatery still retained its original character with its high ceilings, wood paneling, and red leather booths. The classic steakhouse menu was also basically the same . . . except for the prices. As you walked into the restaurant from the parking lot through the back entrance, the restaurant's original menu was framed on a wall. You couldn't miss it. In 1929, the price of a filet mignon was a dollar. Today the same steak cost fifty. Times had indeed changed.

The maître-d' led Dee and me to a table in the larger of the two dining rooms. We walked hand in hand, Dee's soft and warm. My father and mother were already seated along with Gunther and his wife. She was what I expected—blond and buxom with a toothy smile and a Botox-filled face as taut as a tightrope. Unlike my mother who whispered wealth with her understated beauty and style, this woman screamed money with her blinding bling everywhere.

"Hi everyone," I said enthusiastically, as Dee and I took our places, facing each other at the end of the table. My father was seated at one end, Gunther at the other, close to Dee and me. There was one empty chair. I wondered if it was reserved for Karl Vanderberg, my father's financial advisor.

My parents welcomed us, and after shaking my hand, Gunther introduced us to his wife. Ingrid. I, in turn, introduced her to Dee. Gunther's lecherous eyes stayed on my girl, lingering on her hint of cleavage. I wanted to rip his eyeballs out of their sockets. My gut still told me Mr. Family Man was not to be trusted.

"So lovely to finally meet you," gushed Ingrid. Her voice was breathy, accented, and affected.

"The same," replied Dee, demurely.

"Gunther told me you're a single mother."

"Y-yes. My husband passed away several years ago."

"You're so young to have endured that tragedy."

Dee took in a shaky breath and agreed.

My mother chimed in. "She has the most delightful little girl."

A nervous Dee twitched a small smile and thanked my mother for the compliment before she continued.

"Ingrid, you have to meet her."

"I would love to."

My turn. I inhaled a deep breath to fortify myself. "Everyone, we have some exciting news to share with you tonight."

Dee shot me a puzzled look as a red-jacketed waiter brought a bottle of champagne to our table. He poured us each a glass.

I curled my fingers around the stem of the saucer-shaped glass and raised it. "Here's something to toast to. Something

I believe will seal the deal between my father and Saxton Enterprises." All eyes were on me. "Dee and I are getting married."

Shouts of congratulations and applause drowned out Dee's gasp. I gave her a kick under the table for her to go with the flow. Yes, I'd acted impulsively and recklessly, but behind the façade was sincerity and passion. I hadn't yet figured out how to make Dee my wife, but right now this was what was needed to make my father's billion-dollar dream come true. And to let Gunther Saxton know that Dee was mine.

"Wonderful news! And can we expect some more little Hansons in the near future?" asked Gunther, reaching for his champagne glass.

Dee still couldn't get her mouth to close. I answered for the both of us. "Yes. We plan to have a big family. Lots of little Hansons." *In addition to all the unknown ones running around out there,* I added silently, still never able to forget my sperm donor past.

A massive smile exploded on Gunther's face as he lifted his glass. "Then, let's toast. First, to the impending nuptials of Drake and his lovely fiancée, Dee . . . and second, to my future CEO—"

"Am I missing something?" came a familiar shrill voice that cut Gunther short. "Sorry I'm late. The sudden downpour brought traffic to a standstill."

Dressed to the nines in a blood-red mini dress, Krizia strutted over to our table in her six-inch high designer heels, holding a matching monster bag along with an umbrella. My father rose.

"Actually, Krizia, you're just in time to hear the exciting news."

My blood froze before Krizia could sit down in the vacant chair. Why didn't my father tell me he'd invited her to this celebratory dinner? My heart squeezed as he continued.

"I'll want a press release issued immediately."

"Of course," replied Krizia, flashing a smug grin.

"It's official. Saxton Enterprises is acquiring Hanson Entertainment for an undisclosed sum rumored to be close to two billion dollars, and I will be retiring at the end of the year . . . leaving the day-to-day operations in the hands of my capable son." With a proud smile, he looked my way.

I quirked a nervous smile and then glanced at Dee. She looked much like she did that day at The Pier when she stepped off the roller coaster . . . like she was going to be sick.

Krizia's grin widened. "That's wonderful, Orson. I'll get on it right away."

"Orson, darling," chirped my mother. "Why don't you share the other splendid news with Krizia since she'll be helping me plan the big event."

Suddenly, I felt as sick as Dee looked. My chest tightened as my stomach knotted with deep-seated apprehension.

"Ah, yes, my dear." My father again looked my way and I struggled to meet his gaze. Then his eyes shifted back to Krizia. "Krizia, we just found out that Drake is engaged to Dee and will be marrying her in the very near future."

Krizia's mouth dropped open and her eyes bugged out. "What? He's marrying that slut?"

My father's eyes narrowed into razor-sharp blades. "Krizia, you are totally out of line. Both my wife and I are very fond of her . . . and her adorable daughter."

A fiery bolt of lightening shot through me; I felt my cheeks flaring. It might be pouring outside, but a major shit storm was in the making here in the restaurant.

Krizia's shock and rage gave way to a wicked smirk. "Well, Orson, perhaps you don't *really* know who Drake is marrying."

My father stared at her harshly. "What are you talking about?"

Krizia snickered. "Should I start off and say that your future daughter-in-law is pure trailer trash? Her mother was a drunken whore, and she doesn't even know who her father is."

My father's bushy brows arched up. "What!?"

Having my father's ear, and I suppose everyone's, Krizia continued with an insidious mixture of confidence and contempt. "That's just for starters. Did Drake mention that 'our lovely widow' is still married?"

Swallowing past the giant lump in my throat, I gave Dee another quick look. Every drop of color had left her face.

"And that her 'late' husband is still alive? And . . ."

My heart hammered against my chest so hard I thought it would jump out onto the table. The inevitable was coming.

" . . . That he's a drug-dealing ex-felon, who served time in prison for domestic violence."

She paused and a silence so thick a knife couldn't cut through it fell over the table. Finally, turning to me, my father broke it.

"Son, is this true?"

Before I could open my mouth, Krizia jumped in. "Orson, I can prove it. I have documentation right here in my bag."

Sickened and speechless, I watched as Dee slowly rose from her chair. Pale as a ghost, tears forming in her eyes, she looked squarely at my father.

"There's no need, Mr. Hanson. Everything Krizia said is true. I'm sorry that I've shamed you all tonight." Without saying another word, she grabbed her bag and fled.

"Jesus," I muttered, leaping to my feet.

"Drake, where are you going?" I heard my father shout

out. "Get back here."

It was too late. I caught up to Dee at the front entrance of the restaurant. I grabbed her by the elbow, holding her back. In my peripheral vision, I could see diners staring at us; we were creating a scene.

"Dee, wait!"

"Please let go of me," she choked out, desperately trying to free herself.

"No, Dee. We need to talk."

"There's nothing to talk about," she replied tearfully. "I've totally humiliated your family."

"It's not your fault."

Her lips quivered. "How could you do this to me? Put me in this position?"

Stupid fucking me. My impulsive charade to seal my father's dream deal had come back to bite me in the ass.

"I should have never lied. I just wanted my father's deal to go through."

"So you could be CEO?"

"It had nothing to do with that."

"Let go of me, Drake. Now!"

"I can't. I don't want to."

Then, with a sharp, sudden jerk, she freed herself and flew out the door.

"Dee!" I cried out, following her outside.

The rain was coming down in buckets. In a matter of seconds, the two of us were drenched. As she tried to hail a taxi, I gripped her by her shoulders.

"D-baby, please. I'm sorry."

"There's nothing to be sorry about. I'm the one who's sorry. Sorry for ever stepping foot in your office. Sorry for getting involved with you when I had no right to. And sorry for probably screwing up your father's big deal."

"Stop it."

Impulsively, I flipped her around, cradling her wet cheeks in my hands. My lips claimed hers, with a mix of passion and rage as the rain pounded down upon us. She gripped the lapels of my soaked jacket, balling the material with a palpable push and pull. Desperate moans, caught between desire and disgust, gathered in her throat as our warm breaths fought off the chill of the downpour and our tongues did battle, clashing madly with each other.

Finally, I broke the kiss, but my hands stayed splayed on her mascara-streaked face. "Maybe I lied, but my feelings about you are real. I'm crazy in—"

Before I could say the one word I'd never said to a woman, Dee's hand swept across my face. The swat echoed in my ears as the sting set in. Catching me off guard while I rubbed my cheek with one hand, she managed to break free of me.

"Screw you." Her voice rose with anger. "You should have thought about your actions. And I should have thought about mine." Turning away from me, she lifted her arm and yelled again for a taxi. Within seconds, one pulled up to the curb.

As she charged toward it, I seized her cold, wet hand, squeezing her fingers with mine.

"Let go of me, Drake!" Her voice was hoarse and desperate. Pained.

"At least, let me take you home," I begged as the impatient cabbie lowered the front passenger window and hollered for her to get in. Horns were honking all around us.

"No, Drake. Get away from me. I never want to see you again."

My grip loosened. She broke free of me and dashed into the cab. As she slammed the back-passenger door shut, the taxi peeled away from the curb, sending a cold splash of water all over me. I was as soaked as a drowned rat. With the rain falling on me like a spray of bullets, I buried my face in my hands and felt my heart sink to the glistening, wet pavement. Utterly defeated, I turned around and trudged back into Musso's.

No one had left the table. The only difference was Krizia was now sitting in Dee's seat. She was already moving in on me like a predatory beast. The extreme rage I felt toward her pulsed through my bloodstream. I clenched my fists by my sides so I wouldn't throw her onto her bony ass.

"Drake, please sit down," ordered my father, motioning to the chair I'd been sitting in. His words were as sharp as broken glass.

"That poor girl," murmured my mother, sitting to my left, and then asked if I was all right.

No, I wasn't all right. My heart was splintering and I was chilled to the bone. And my emotions were in a total turmoil. Anger, confusion, sadness, and regret ripped through me like shrapnel, shredding me to pieces.

"I'm sorry," I mumbled, lacking for words.

"There's nothing to be sorry about." Gunther's voice was glacial. "Krizia spared us a lot of potential headaches and embarrassment."

A triumphant smile slithered across Krizia's pursed lips as Gunther continued.

"I have a no tolerance policy for liars. Transparency is everything to me."

"Dee didn't lie," I interjected. "It's not her fault."

"Be quiet, son," chided my father. "Let Gunther talk."

Clearing his throat, Gunther looked at me pointedly. "Moreover, there's no way I could have a CEO married to a woman of that sort. We are a family-oriented business, and if her background got out, as I'm sure it would, it would tarnish our image and credibility. Image is everything."

I swallowed back the painful lump in my throat. His

words were like arrows to my chest, not because he was criticizing me, but because he was attacking Dee. My love. A good human being and mom. The woman who had stolen my heart, together with her beautiful little girl.

Gunther cleared his throat again, and then his steely eyes locked with my father's. "Orson, the deal is off."

I glanced at my father's fallen face. I'd blown it for him. And I'd blown whatever chance I'd had with Dee. I loathed Krizia, but I loathed myself more. As unbearable failure and sorrow devoured me, Gunther stalked off with his wife.

CHAPTER 40
Dee

I pressed my face against the window as the cab made its way back to my house. With the pouring rain, traffic was at a crawl and it felt like an eternity. The diverse neighborhoods we passed by along Hollywood Boulevard were a blur and couldn't distract me from my thoughts. My heartache. Tears dripped down the window, kissing the raindrops that streaked the outer glass.

With the inclement weather and Friday night traffic, it took close to an hour to get to my Silverlake residence. Having cashed my paycheck, my last one, I paid the driver and gave him a generous tip.

The lights were on, the rain still pouring. Shivering wet with a heavy heart, I ran to the front door and rang the bell. I just didn't have the wherewithal to fish for my keys or fiddle with the complicated lock. Lulu, thank God, came to the door in no time. Her eyes popped at the sight of me.

"Jesus, sis, what are you doing back so early? And look at you . . . you're soaking wet."

The pounding rain sounded in my ears and showered me with more pain than I could bear. When I opened my mouth, sobs spilled out. Loud, heaving ones. Not wasting a second, my sister wrapped an arm around me and ushered me into the house.

"Is Ty home?"

"Yes. I picked her up. She's sound asleep."

I could always count on my sister.

"Let's get you into some dry clothes."

"D-don't wake up, Ty," I managed through my chattering teeth. "I'll change into my robe. It's in the bathroom."

"I'm coming with you." Worry laced my sister's voice.

"N-no, it's okay. I'll be fine." *Fine* . . . I reflected for a moment on that four-letter word. Truthfully, I didn't think I'd ever be fine again.

"Okay. I'll make some hot tea in the meantime."

"That would be nice," I forced myself to say as I slogged to the bathroom.

Five minutes later, I was back in the living room, wrapped up in my terrycloth robe. While my chills and sobs were subsiding, I didn't look or feel any better. My unkempt hair was like a wet bird's nest, and I hadn't gotten off all the mascara from my blotchy, tear-soaked face. My head throbbed as I rubbed my burning, bloodshot eyes.

"Drink some tea," my sister urged.

Weakly, I nodded, only to break out into another heavy round of tears when I noticed the mug was a souvenir from the Santa Monica Pier . . . something I'd won playing Skee-Ball. All the memories of that glorious day whipped through my head like a roller coaster. An emotional roller coaster I couldn't get off.

"Dee-Dee, what the hell is going on?" demanded Lulu, after forcing me to take a few sips of the tea. "Why aren't you with Drake?"

The soothing, piping hot beverage coursed slowly down my throat, providing me with just enough relief to open up to Lou. In between small sips, I told her everything that had happened tonight. She listened intently with very few interruptions.

"Oh my God! How awful!" exclaimed Lulu when I came to the end of my woeful tale. "I'd like to kill that jealous bitch."

"She did it out of jealousy?"

"Of course. Why else?"

I hadn't given much thought to Krizia's motivation. I was too consumed by my mortification and hurt. Lulu's insight didn't make things any better.

"What are you going to do?"

A new emotion—confusion—mingled with my pain. I bit out my answer.

"I'm going to quit my temp job."

"Are you sure you want to do that?"

"I have to. I can't face him. And besides, his father will fire me anyway for screwing up his deal."

"It wasn't your fault." The same words as Drake's.

"I should have come out and said that I wasn't really engaged to Drake." I took another sip of the hot tea. "I don't know why I didn't."

"Bullshit. Of course you know why. It was wishful thinking. You're madly in love with him."

Lulu's words struck a deep chord inside me. We'd never talked about my feelings, but my sister was right. I was head over heels in love with Drake Hanson. And it wasn't because of all the great sex we had. It was because of all the great moments we'd shared. All the fun. All the laughter. And above all, because of the way he'd taken to Tyson and she'd taken to him. Their magical bond. Oh, God. What was I going to tell her? She was going to be heartbroken not seeing him again. The only pain worse than my own was seeing my baby girl suffer. I loved her more than life itself.

Almost on cue, her sweet, raspy voice broke into my despair.

"Mommy, what are you doing home?" she shouted out,

running up to me.

I took her in my arms and gave her a hug. She stared at me with her earnest eyes. Concern filled the rims.

"Mommy, have you been crying?"

"Um, uh . . . no." I'd never shed a tear in front of her, well at least when she could see me crying. Being brave for my daughter was part of my job.

"Yes, you have!" challenged by astute little girl. "What's the matter?"

My sister came to the rescue. "Tyson, honey, it's late. You shouldn't be up. Let's get you back in bed."

"Lou, it's okay." I ran my fingers through my daughter's silky hair. She might as well hear the truth. Or some child-friendly version of it. "Cupcake, I had a fight with Drake."

Ty scrunched up her face. "What kinda fight?"

"A grown-up fight. He said a lie about me." *A lie that I wish could be true but would never be.*

Though I'd lied to Ty about her father her entire life, I'd instilled her with the value of telling the truth at all costs.

"I'm not going to work for him anymore."

Ty frowned. "Does that mean you're never gonna see him again?"

"I'm not sure."

"But, Mommy, you have to. At my graduation, he promised he was gonna take us to New York at Christmas to skate at *Rockerfellow* Plaza. And he promised he wouldn't break his promise."

Her words gutted me. "Well, maybe not this year." *No, not ever.*

My little girl defiantly crossed her arms. "I think you and Drake should kiss and makeup."

Uncontrollably, at her words, my eyes grew watery. The mere thought of Drake's lips on mine sent my emotions into a tailspin, and I couldn't stop a few tears from falling.

"Oh, Mommy, are you crying again?"

I sniffled as she threw her arms around my neck and hugged me. God. Here she was taking care of me when I should be taking care of her. Gnawing guilt succumbed to gratitude. How blessed I was to have this incredible little girl. She was my temple. Sacred and special.

"It's gonna be okay, Mommy. Just wait and see."

The warmth of her body and her loving words brought me much needed solace. I kissed the top of her head.

"Dee, is there anything I can do?"

My sister. I glanced up at her.

"Lou, I'm going to put Ty back to bed and call it a night. Thanks for everything."

We hugged. A short ten minutes later, I was ready for bed too. I tucked Ty in.

"Mommy, do you believe in happily ever after?"

I was taken back by her unexpected question, especially in my frame of mind. I hesitated before answering.

"Yes, I do." Another lie. Or maybe half-truth. Once upon a time I did. Once when I met Kyle. And then again with Drake. But with my epic-fail pattern, this fantasy would never be a reality. When it came to finding true love, I was doomed. I didn't, however, want to blow this dream for my sweet little girl. She deserved to have it. So, I answered, "Yes, I do."

An ear-to-ear smile spread across her face. "Me too."

Fighting back tears, I returned the smile. Enough drama for tonight.

"Mommy, do you wanna sleep with me tonight?"

"Yes, my cupcake. I'd like that."

A few heartbeats later, I was in her bed snuggled next to her lithe body.

"Good night, my baby girl. I love you from here to the moon and back."

"Me too, Mommy."

I kissed the back of her head and soon she was out like a light, unaware that my tears were soaking her red cape. Drake's magical cape. If only it had the power to magically make this night go away.

CHAPTER 41

Drake

I spent the rest of the weekend in bed. Actually, make that the entire week. Right after the Dee fiasco, I did a foolish thing. While my parents left the restaurant in a huff (well, at least my father did), I stayed behind at the bar and downed a couple of Scotches. Truthfully, I lost count after two. Several women tried to hit on me and I told them I was gay. Then, too afraid to get into my car because I was positive I was going to drive straight to Dee's house and get into a major accident on the way, I took a long walk in the pouring rain along Hollywood Boulevard to sober up. By the time I got home, I was so drenched you could ring me out and I was coughing. By Monday, I was sick as a dog with some kind of God-awful flu. The kind you cough up brown shit and your throat, head, and chest hurt so fucking bad you can barely talk, think, or breathe.

What was worse, on Monday morning, in my debilitated, feverish state, I overslept and missed my weekly breakfast meeting. At ten thirty a phone call woke me up. It was my father's forever secretary, Barbara. Obviously, he wasn't talking to me. And I couldn't blame him.

"Drake, your father wants to know why you weren't at the Polo Lounge?"

"Tell him I'm sick," I croaked.

"You don't sound well at all."

I didn't tell her that I felt like I was dying. It was more than just my throat and my lungs or the raging fever. It was that pounding muscle inside my chest that was killing me. I was growing more certain by the second that I had the plague.

"I'll let him know. By the way, your temp quit."

Dee quit? At her words, I coughed up more shit, and as I did, I put my hand to my aching heart as if I was having a heart attack. Which maybe I was. The coughing spell continued.

"Drake, are you okay?" asked Barbara.

"Yeah," I rasped. *Fuck no.*

Tuesday began even worse. I woke up hacking and in a cold sweat from an awful dream. I dreamt I was stranded on the Santa Monica Pier in a horrible storm, and from my vantage point, I could see a ship being carried out to sea. On the deck were dozens of little boys who looked just like six-year-old me and among them was one little girl who looked just like Tyson. They were all reaching out to me and crying, "Daddy, save us!" A bolt of lightening flashed in the sky as thunder roared. But as I stood there helplessly and hopelessly, the boat sailed further and further away from me into the turbulent sea until, to my horror, it got caught in a mile-high wave and capsized. And that's when my eyes snapped open and I bolted to a sitting position.

Brushing sweat off my damp forehead, I tried to make sense of the dream. All day long between fitful naps and hazy consciousness, it haunted me. I was in some kind of netherworld between delirium and denial. I couldn't get the image of all those little boys out of my mind and especially Tyson. Her soulful eyes connecting with mine, her little arms reaching out for me as the ocean pulled her further and further away from me. Like a jigsaw puzzle, piece by piece, the dream revealed itself and I was frightened. The horrific dream replayed in my head over and over to the point I was afraid to go to sleep.

Wednesday began with a scare. I heard the door to my condo click open and slam shut. It couldn't be my housekeeper because she came on Fridays. Was I being burglarized? Had fucking Kyle tracked me down? Coughing, I forced myself out of bed and grabbed the hockey stick next to it to use as a weapon. As sick as I was, I was ready to pounce.

"Darling, what are you doing with that stick in your hand?"

Holy Shit! Standing at the door to my bedroom was my mother!

"Mom?" I choked out before remembering she had a set of keys to my apartment.

Wearing one of her stylish velour tracksuits, she sauntered my way. "Darling, put that ridiculous stick down and get right back into bed. You look and sound terrible."

Slowly, I did as she said. She was right about my current condition. Whatever it was had taken a toll on me. I hadn't shaved, showered, or combed my hair since last Friday and when I glimpsed myself in the bathroom mirror this morning, I met the reflection of a scary-looking Neanderthal with sunken eyes and pasty lips.

My mother tucked me in, making me feel like I was a five-year-old again. She placed her palm on my forehead as I coughed.

"You're running a fever. I've asked Dr. Brown to stop by to check you over."

Dr. Brown was our concierge family doctor. He'd been with us forever. Through strep, broken bones, stitches, bee stings, and much more. Ten minutes later I was sitting up in bed with an old-fashioned glass thermometer under my tongue and a stethoscope to my back. Removing the thermometer from my mouth, he took a peek at it and then asked me to breathe deeply in and out. It was an effort to do as he asked, the inhale and exhale both excruciatingly painful.

"What is it, doc?" I wheezed while my mother was in the kitchen heating up soup she'd picked up at Whole Foods.

"You have acute bronchitis. I'm going to call in a prescription for ciprofloxacin along with a cough suppressant and have your pharmacy send them over. Take two doses of the cipro with water immediately and then another tonight. Tomorrow, one in the morning, one in the evening. You'll likely start feeling better by tomorrow afternoon, but I want you to rest, drink plenty of fluids, and finish out the prescription."

I nodded. "Are you sure I don't have a heart condition?"

Packing up his medical bag, the good doctor smiled. "No, Drake, your heart sounds perfectly fine. And heart disease doesn't run in your family."

My mother returned with a tray holding a large bowl of soup and Dr. Brown filled her in about my condition before leaving. She set the tray down on my desk and brought me the bowl. Sitting on the edge of my bed, she forced me to have some. Despite my lack of appetite, it actually felt good to have something in me and she'd heated it just right to avoid burning my raw throat. After a few spoonfuls of the flavorful chicken noodle broth, my coughing subsided and my voice grew a little stronger.

"Mom, how'd you know to come over?"

"Your father told me you were sick and hadn't been in the office for three days."

At the mention of my father, my chest tightened painfully.

"He hasn't disowned me yet?"

"Darling, why on earth would you say that? Your father loves you. He was worried."

Her heartfelt words genuinely surprised me. I scooped up another spoonful of soup. "How's Dad?"

"Truthfully, he's suffering more than you."

"Because the Saxton deal collapsed?"

"Hardly."

My brows shot up.

"He feels terrible about that evening. Terrible for that lovely girl who had to endure so much humiliation."

I was stunned into silence.

"Drake, darling, perhaps you don't know this, but your father was hoping you might settle down with Dee. While you were away with her in New York, he grew extremely attached to her adorable little girl."

"He did?"

"I wish you could have seen the two of them together. He doted on her. It was so incredibly sweet. They cuddled together and watched cartoons. He read her bedtime stories every night and acted out all the parts. They played hide-and-seek. He took her to the park after school and taught her how to play checkers. They even baked thumbprint cookies together . . . something your father used to do with your sister but hasn't done since she left us. Your sister was the apple of your father's eye . . . he adored her and took her loss way harder than I did. I think in many ways Tyson reminded him of Mia and filled the void in his heart that's burdened him all these years. I haven't seen him so happy in ages."

As my mother shared this narrative, I could picture my father doing all these things. Suddenly, I saw him in a new light. A softer, kinder one that only the magic of a little girl like Tyson could turn on. I knew because she'd done the same to me. Dr. Brown was wrong. Broken hearts *did* run in our family.

I imbibed a few more tablespoons of the soup, each one more fortifying than the one before. Impulsively, I shared my nightmare with my intuitive mother, tweaking it slightly so that it was only Tyson on the boat. With all the drama that had gone down in the past week and my weakened state, this was not the time to tell her about my sperm-donor past.

"What do you think it means, Mom?"

"You can't let the boat sail away and sink. That little girl was crying out for you. It's not too late. Go after her. She is meant to be yours."

Yours. Mine. A new reality was sinking in.

～

By Friday, I was feeling a lot stronger. At least, physically. While I still had a nagging cough, it was nothing like it had been. My throat and head no longer hurt and my appetite was back. A sharp pain, however, lingered in my chest. Heartache. I'd tried to both call and text Dee, but to my dismay, she'd blocked my number. After taking a shower and shaving for the first time in a week, I decided I would drive over to her house with the hope of seeing her. Scratch that. With the hope of winning her back.

Though Westwood, where I lived on the prestigious Wilshire Corridor, was quite a distance from funky Silverlake, basically the other side of town, I made it to her place in no time because I'd beat rush hour traffic. It was only 7 a.m. I was sure she'd be home with Tyson.

After parking my car in front of her house, I headed to the front door. I was a little surprised her truck wasn't parked in the driveway. Only her sister's Mini occupied the space. Maybe it was in the shop for repairs or she had to take Tyson to a doctor's appointment or something. A mix of nerves and hopefulness coursed through my veins.

I rang the doorbell. I waited. No response. I rang it again, this time twice in succession. No response. One more time and then I banged loudly.

"Dee . . . are you there? It's me, Drake." *BANG, BANG, BANG*. Desperation set in. "Please, Dee, open up!"

The door finally swung open. But it wasn't Dee who stood before me. It was her sister, Lulu.

"Drake, what the hell are you doing here?"

With a heavy breath, I met her gaze. Daggers were shooting out of her eyes. Dressed in skimpy boxer shorts and a Mighty Dicks T-shirt, her hair a wild mess, she had that just-fucked look going on. But that enviable look didn't mask her rage.

"Is Dee home? I need to talk to her."

She narrowed her eyes at me. Her look became more intimidating. Daggers became poison darts.

"She's away with Tyson." She paused for a second. "She *needed* to get away. Away from you."

"Where is she?"

She scoffed at me. "Jesus, Drake, what part of she never wants to see you again don't you get?"

Her words sliced through me. Before I could respond, a familiar voice sounded in my ears.

"Hey, babe, what's going on?"

Brock. Freshly showered. Wearing just a towel around his waist.

"Hey, man." Awkwardness colored his voice as he adjusted the towel.

"Hey."

"You missed the hockey game last night. Where were you?"

"Sorry. I was sick." I coughed. "Bronchitis."

"We lost without you." He wrapped an arm around Lulu, igniting an emotion I'd never felt before. Envy. "Call me later. I may have big news."

"Sure," I mumbled as Lulu slammed the door shut in my face.

CHAPTER 42

Drake

"Who are you?" I asked the skinny, tattooed girl, sitting at the desk outside my office.

"Onyx. Your new temp."

Jesus. With her purple spiked hair and piercings, she looked more like an alien . . . one of our *Danger Rangers* villains.

"Dude, I've put all your mail on your desk. If it's okay by you, I'm going out for a smoke."

"Sure," I muttered, trudging into my office. No need to tell her I hated cigarettes and smokers.

My first day back in almost two weeks—after the week in New York and then another home sick. After my encounter with Lulu this morning, I had a setback. My heart felt like it'd been weighted down by a two-ton elephant, and my chest felt hollow. I thought about going home and crawling back into bed, but the thought of hanging at my condo with my housekeeper there wasn't appealing. Besides, I needed to have my sheets changed and truthfully, the only thing I had to look forward to all day was going home to clean fresh sheets and a made-up bed.

My desk looked like it had been hit by a scud missile. The mail strewn everywhere, so unlike the way Dee laid it out with periodicals neatly stacked and envelopes arranged by size. It was overwhelming, and I decided I'd go through the mess later in the day. As soon as I sat down, my cell phone pinged. It was a text from Brock.

Call me. You're not going to believe what I have to tell you.

Though he was my best bud, the last person I wanted to hear from at this minute was Brock the Rock. I was still reeling from seeing him with Lulu this morning, and while I knew I should be happy for him, I wasn't quite sure how his relationship with Dee's sister was going to affect our friendship. For all I knew, he was texting me to tell me they were moving in together or getting engaged. Brock was a lucky man.

As soon as I set my cell phone down, my desk phone rang. With my new temp on a break, I debated whether to let it go to my voicemail or pick it up. On the third persistent ring, I opted for the latter.

"Drake?"

I recognized the voice immediately. My father's. Every muscle in my body tensed.

"I saw your car in the parking lot. You're here?"

After a small coughing fit, I told him I was.

"Please come down to my office. I want to talk to you."

My pulse quickened. Hanging up the phone, I braced myself for an uncomfortable encounter. I hadn't spoken to my father since the Gunther Saxton fiasco last Friday night, and though my mother said he wasn't furious with me, I didn't totally believe her. My father was not one to get over things easily. Following the tragic death of my sister, he was in a deep depression for over a year that required him to seek counseling.

My father was seated at his desk when I got to his massive corner office. Another small coughing fit captured his attention, and he lifted his head from the periodical he was reading. He took off his reading glasses and his eyes met mine.

"Are you all right?"

"Yeah, I'm fine," I said after coughing again into my forearm. The doctor told me that the cough could linger for a couple weeks, but after several days of my medication, I was no longer contagious.

"Good." No smile. "Take a seat." No please. He motioned to one of the armchairs facing him. Anxiously, I sat down. His next words rattled me.

"I want you to draft a press release explaining why the deal between Hanson Entertainment and Saxton Enterprises didn't go through."

A bolt of anger ripped through me. So, this is how he was going to punish me. For screwing up the deal of a lifetime. By pouring salt in an open wound.

"Why can't Krizia do it?" It pained me to say her name.

"Because I fired her."

Despite my wide-eyed surprise, the tone in his voice didn't leave room for questioning. I was adept at writing press releases, having written them before while I worked in PR briefly after I graduated college. Grooming me to head up the company, my father had made me work in every department.

"This will help you." He slid the *Hollywood Reporter* he'd been reading across his desk. "Read this."

Hesitantly, I picked up the glossy trade magazine. My eyes scanned down the front page until it came to this headline:

Baby Daddy Drama: Escort Claims Media Mogul Gunther Saxton is the Father of Her Child

Holy shit! My eyes as wide as saucers, I perused the exclusive article, which talked about how the two of them had met and had sex in a hotel room while Gunther was in

Los Angeles last year pursuing the acquisition of our company among others. Then this: *According to Ms. Amaretto, she was introduced to Saxton by his public relations consultant, Krizia Vanderberg, at a Hollywood party.* Holy shit again! I quickly flipped to page 20 where the story continued.

High-profile divorce and family law attorney, Brock Andrews, will be representing Ms. Amaretto. In a brief press conference, he issued this statement: "Both Carmen and I are confident that the DNA testing will prove that Mr. Saxton is the putative father. Once paternity is confirmed, we will be seeking extensive damages and child support from the defendant." Mr. Saxton was unavailable for comment.

Holy fucking shit. This is what Brock wanted to tell me. I'd always suspected there was more than met the eye with Mr. Family Man, but I was still stunned and speechless.

"Drake, thank you," said my dad, catapulting me out of my shock.

"For what?"

"For saving me from potentially making a deal that would have destroyed our company. Everything I . . . " he took a beat . . . "*we* have worked for. If this scandal had erupted after we'd been acquired by Saxton Enterprises, I'm sure every one of our shows would have been yanked off the air."

"Is this why you fired Krizia?"

"No. Actually, I fired her three days ago."

Before the scandal. "For what reason?"

"For humiliating that lovely young woman. And for humiliating you."

I was speechless as a mixture of respect and love for my father surged inside me. My mother was right. Despite all my fuck ups, he cared about me . . . had my back. And he saw in Dee what I saw in her. A short but awkward stretch of silence followed. My father broke it before another coughing fit set in.

"Drake . . ."

"Yeah, Dad?"

"I had lunch with Blake Burns yesterday. He couldn't stop talking about his wife's enthusiasm for our new series—the one inspired by Dee's daughter. She has high hopes for it. How's the development going? Is there a deal in place?"

I latched onto my father's words, anxiousness filling my chest. I needed to be honest with him.

"Dad, Dee quit. She's no longer my temp. There is no deal."

"What??" His brows knitted. "Where is she?"

"I don't know."

"What do you mean?"

"I've tried calling her . . . texting her . . . emailing her . . . but no response. And now she's blocked my number."

"Then go to her house. You know where she lives."

"I did that this morning. Neither she nor Tyson was there. Her sister told me they went out of town—"

My father interrupted. "Well, they've gotta come back some time."

My chest tightened. "Her sister said that Dee never wants to see me again."

"Baloney. I saw the way she looked at you. She's totally in love with you."

"Dad, I hurt her. I acted recklessly."

"Love is reckless, son."

My eyebrows shot up. He continued.

"Do you think I pursued the rights to the Ice Capades solely to develop an animated series? No, I followed the show around the world so I could woo your mother. She was quite the ice queen in more ways than one."

I let out a soft chuckle. I never knew that.

"It took me almost two years, but I finally melted her. Do you know how?"

I shook my head.

"I never gave up. You have to live your personal life the way you live your professional life: With passion, patience, and persistence. The right one comes along only once. You gotta make things work."

Digesting his words, my eyes wandered. Behind him on his credenza, assorted photos were lined up—a photo of my stunning mother at the peak of her skating career . . . a photo of my parents dancing at their wedding . . . an early photo of our family at the beach, my sister Mia age five and me still a baby in my mother's arms . . . one of six-year-old me posing like a superhero, clad in my red cape . . . Mia's kindergarten portrait taken shortly before she died . . . and next to it, one I'd never seen before . . . a recent photo of my father with Tyson, wearing matching aprons and hands deep in cookie dough. The expression on my father's face was one of pure joy as was Tyson's, their blue eyes twinkling and their grins ear-to-ear wide. I'd not seen my father look that happy in ages. He caught me staring at the photo.

"Mom told me about the thumbprint cookies . . ."

Then my eyes traveled across two more photos . . . Mia posing on the ice in a purple skating outfit and next to it, a recent one of Tyson in her purple skating costume (and red cape), striking the same pose. In a New York minute, it all clicked. My heart began to race. I had to confront Dee. Tell her what she meant to me . . . and what Tyson meant to me. My heart beat faster. Was it possible?

My mind kicking into overdrive, I watched as my father swiveled in his chair and picked up the photo of me in my red cape. He turned around and faced me, his eyes on the photo.

"I remember when I gave that cape to you, Drake."

"Me too."

"I said you could be *anything* you want." He paused, setting the photo down. "*Be* a man, Drake. Use your balls and go after her."

My father stood up and I did something I hadn't done in a very long time. I rounded his desk and hugged him.

"Dad, thanks for everything."

"Go, Drake. I want that little *Mighty Girl* on the air . . . and I more than want her in my life."

CHAPTER 43

Dee

The impulsive trip to Las Vegas was supposed to be a fun, healing escape. Lulu had suggested it—I needed to get my mind off Drake and reboot before our big move. Bask in the desert sun, swim, drink Mai Tais, take Ty to the Vegas attractions, and maybe see a show or two. But none of that happened. Fun? It was anything but.

The road trip, which should have taken five hours, took close to ten. Torrential rain, which fell the whole way, brought traffic to a crawl, and halfway into the trip, my truck broke down. Both of us starving and needing to pee desperately, we had to wait forty-five minutes for a tow truck to come by. And then we spent two long hours at a mechanic's garage while the battery was replaced. That cost me a couple hundred bucks I couldn't afford to spare.

It got worse. The hotel in Vegas, which looked so nice in photos online, was a dive. Off the beaten path, our room was grungy and smelled of cigarettes. It was supposed to be a non-smoking room, but I quickly came to the conclusion those were non-existent in this joint. The guests inhabiting the hotel looked as seedy as the hotel itself. Not a child in sight. I tried to book another hotel on The Strip, but they were either way out of my price range or all booked up on account of some hair stylist convention happening in town.

It rained for five straight days. We never got to sit at the pool, and running around Vegas in the pouring rain with a lot of the city under construction was both nerve wracking and frustrating. To make matters worse, most of the attractions were shut down for one reason or another. Poor Ty. Disappointment after disappointment. Whatever could go wrong, did go wrong.

The huge Ferris wheel across from the MGM Grand didn't operate in the rain.

The roller coaster at Circus Circus wasn't working. And Ty wasn't tall enough to ride the bigger one at New York New York.

The animated movie at the M&M factory stopped in the middle, and the technicians couldn't fix it.

The Treasure Island pirate show couldn't go on because the winds were too high.

Taylor Swift, Tyson's favorite recording artist, was in town, but the concert was sold out with last minute scalper tickets going for five hundred dollars apiece.

The one show we were going to see got canceled because the magician fell ill.

And the striped snow tigers at the Bellagio, where the legendary fountains were shut down because of the weather, made my baby girl burst into tears.

"Cupcake, what's the matter?" I asked, lifting her into my arms.

"I'm so sad for the pretty tigers. They should be in the jungle with their mommies and daddies and brothers and sisters."

Her words totally crushed me. My sensitive, creature-loving little girl.

"They like it here." Please . . . who was I kidding?

She shook her head vehemently. "No, they don't! They want to go home!"

And then she began to bawl. Big fat tears rolled down her cheeks as her shoulders began to heave. My inner alarm siren sounded. "Honey, what's wrong?"

"I don't like it here," she spluttered. "I want to go home. I miss Drake."

She was gutting me. Her sobs like knives to my heart, I floundered for words.

"Cupcake, we can go home right this very minute if you want." I paused. "But we can't see Drake anymore."

"Why, Mommy, why?" she sobbed out, her endless tears drowning my soul.

"Drake and I aren't friends anymore." The words pained me. Killed me.

"But we had the *bestest* time with Drake."

I thought about her words. We *did* have the *bestest* time with Drake. Every time with Drake was the *bestest* time. All the fun memories spun in my head like a slow, enchanted carousel.

"I'm sorry, baby," I murmured, my voice thin and watery, before kissing the top of her head.

"Mommy, I don't understand. Drake told me he really, really liked you. The way Prince Charming liked Cinderella."

My breath hitched in my throat. "He did?"

Sniffling, she nodded, the tears still falling. "The night he put me to bed. Please, Mommy, why can't he be your boyfriend?"

Tears burned the back of my eyes. It took all I had not to cry. I couldn't let my little girl know that this was as painful for me as it was for her. I smoothed her silky hair and then brushed away her tears.

"Cupcake, it's complicated. Sometimes two people can fall in love, but it's not meant to be."

"But it was meant to be, Mommy! *It is!* The fortune

teller said so!"

Unable to console her or explain, I just let her cry in my arms.

A half-hour later, we were checked out of our raunchy hotel and driving back to LA. Already in her pajamas, Tyson quickly fell asleep in the backseat, snuggled against Froggie, who'd come along for the ride. Taylor Swift's "Sad Beautiful Tragic" played on the radio, and while the rain finally stopped, I needed windshield wipers to wipe away the tears pouring from my eyes.

Encountering both rush hour traffic and a jam up from an accident plus stopping a couple of times at drive-thrus for much needed coffee, it took over eight long, exhausting hours to make it back to Los Angeles. It was close to midnight when I pulled up to my house. To my surprise, another car was in my driveway behind Lulu's. I recognized it. A black Porsche that belonged to Brock. The living room lights were on.

Parking on the street, I quietly got out of the truck, unfastened a sound asleep Tyson from her car seat, and gathered her into my arms. She stirred a little, but didn't awaken. At the front door, I fumbled with the keys, the double lock harder than usual on account of holding Tyson. The door opened wide before I could unbolt the second lock. Handsome Brock, wearing a pair of low-slung sweats and a body-hugging Mighty Dicks T-shirt, stood tall before me.

"Hi," he said softly. "Can I help you?"

I twitched a small smile. "It would be great if you could take our suitcases out of the truck. I'm going to put Tyson to bed."

"Sure," he said as I headed to our bedroom.

Wiped out from the long ride, I tucked my sleeping beauty into her bed and kissed her gently on the forehead. "I love you from here to the moon and back," I whispered before tiptoeing out of the room. Silently, I prayed that she'd have sweet dreams and that Drake wouldn't be in them. Or in mine. When I returned to the living room, Brock had already brought in the two bags along with Froggie. The bags were parked on the hardwood floor among the many scattered sealed boxes. While I was away, Lulu had obviously packed up most of the house in preparation for our move. God bless her. A pang of guilt shot through me. Though she'd insisted on our getaway, I felt bad that I hadn't helped much.

"We didn't think you'd be back until tomorrow morning," said Brock, setting Froggie on a chair. "If you want, I'll leave."

"It's okay, Brock. Stay." Weariness laced my voice.

"Thanks. I helped Lulu pack up earlier and asked if I could stay since I have an early morning client meeting downtown. It's a hell of a lot easier getting down there from here than from Westwood."

"No problem," I replied, not asking him where he was going to sleep.

"I'll sleep on the couch," he said as if reading my mind.

"You don't have to. It's uncomfortable."

He quirked a smile. "Thanks. Where'd you go?"

Obviously, my sister had kept her word and not told him. "Vegas."

"Ah, Sin City."

"More like Suck City."

He laughed lightly. "It depends upon who you go with . . . or without."

Drake. I read more into his words into his words than I should. My heart pinched.

"You look tired, Dee."

"I am. It was long trip back." I briefly told him about the traffic, but didn't share the real reason behind my bloodshot eyes.

"Can I get you a glass of wine? Lulu opened a bottle of white and it's sitting in the fridge."

"Yeah, that would be great."

"Relax, I'll be right back."

As he strode to the kitchen, I plopped down on the couch and blew out a deep breath. The tension that had built up inside me on the way home seeped out of my body. Not until I sunk into the cushions did I realize how really tired I was. I felt like one of Tyson's ragdolls. As I tugged off my sneakers from my cramped feet, Brock returned with a glass of wine in one hand for me, a bottle of Coors in the other for him. After handing me the wine, he settled in a chair and angled it so he was facing me. He twisted off the top of the beer bottle and took a long swig of the frothy beverage. A satisfied "aah" escaped his throat after he swallowed. I followed suit and took a sip of the wine. The chilled liquid coursed down my throat and I savored how good it was. Certainly not the cheap Two Buck Chuck Lulu and I usually bought. Likely something big bucks Brock had brought over. I immediately took another sip and felt myself unwind.

Brock took another chug of his beer and then looked me in the eye. "Drake came by."

My heart stuttered; my voice stammered. "H-he did?"

"Yeah. This morning."

My chest tightened with emotion. "What did he want?"

"What do you think? He wasn't paying me a visit. He wanted to see you."

Silence.

"Your sister told him you never want to see him again."

Tears pricked the back of my eyes. "That's a fact," I

snapped, hoping my bravado would serve as dam and hold them back. "I hope you didn't tell him where we're moving to."

"Lulu swore me to secrecy. I'm a lawyer. I respect secrets."

"Thank you," I said, my voice softening to almost a whisper. I took another sip of the wine to moisten my dry mouth and to soothe my pain.

"Drake looked like shit."

My brows lifted and my heart skipped a beat. "What do you mean? Is he okay?" *Fuck me for caring.*

"Not really. He's been sick as a dog. Bronchitis."

A pathetic "oh" fell from my lips. It actually pained me to say the one little word when what I wanted was to call him. Find out how he was. See what he needed. Ask what I could do to make him feel better. Desperation coiled in the pit of my stomach. The need to be with him pounded through my veins.

"I'm sorry to hear that," I muttered.

"I'll let him know." Brock's voice dripped with sarcasm.

I chewed my lip and then drank more of my wine.

Setting his beer down on the coffee table, Brock kept his gaze on me. His eyes grew intense, his jaw tightened. I'd never seen him like this. His lawyer face?

He heaved a breath and folded his arms across his tight abs.

"Listen, Dee. I'm going to level with you. Drake is like a brother to me. I've known him my whole life. I know him inside and out. And let me tell you, I've never seen him like this. He's a fucking basket case."

"Bronchitis can wipe you out," I said defensively and unconvincingly.

"Screw the bronchitis. He'll get over his fucking cough. But he's not going to get over you so quickly. Or Tyson."

My heart hammered in my chest. I was at a loss for words. His eyes not wavering from me, Brock went on.

"Trust me, Drake's had a lot of women, but I've never seen him act this way over anybody. He's crazy about you and Tyson. And I swear, the guy's never wanted to settle down and have a family."

"He's a player," I bit out, my defenses in high gear.

"Maybe he was once, but he's changed. You and your little girl changed him. I'm going to tell you a secret. He's asked me to help you find a way to get a divorce from your prick of a husband."

"Why didn't he tell me himself?" I blurted, not telling Mr. Secret Keeper that I already knew this from my sister. Anger joined my whirling dervish of emotions. "In case he changed his mind?"

"Jesus, Dee. You so fucking underestimate him. You may think he's an asshole, but you know what, he's a really good guy. Make that a great guy. The real deal. I swear he'd kill for you and your little girl."

The intensity of his words got to me. The dam holding back my tears broke loose. They rushed out of my eyes like a raging river.

"But I'm so wrong for him. I'm an embarrassment to his family. I saw the way his father looked at me when Krizia told him about my past." I brushed away the tears, but they kept spilling down my cheeks.

Brock's expression softened. "Drake's a big boy. His own person. He's been rebellious his whole life. And sometimes he acts before he thinks . . . goes by his gut. He didn't blurt out you two were engaged to please his father. He did for himself . . . because he really wants you in his life." He took another chug of his beer. "Listen, Dee. You've got to stop playing the Kyle card. I'm pretty damn good at what I do, and with time, I'll get him out of your life, once and for all. You know, as a lawyer, sometimes I have to be a psychologist. I have to figure out what makes people tick. What they're afraid to admit. What walls they hide behind." He paused. "Do you know what the wall you hide behind is called?"

With a sniffle, I shook my head. My eyes met his.

One word. "Fear."

Bull's-eye. An arrow straight to my chest.

My lips trembling, I simply nodded. Brock was right; I didn't need a lecture. I'd lived my whole life in fear. Afraid to pursue my dreams. Afraid to stand up to Kyle. Afraid to leave him. Afraid to tell him my deepest, darkest secret. And now I was afraid to face the possibility of another man hurting me—and my baby girl—the way Kyle did. The long and short of it, I was afraid of falling in love. Afraid to admit it. But it was way too late. I was helplessly, hopelessly in love with Drake Hanson. My hand flew to my aching, breaking heart. I was bleeding tears.

"Dee?" The familiar but groggy voice of my sister spared me from saying anything. Wiping away my tears, I craned my neck and caught sight of her. She was wearing boxers and a tank top that showed off her lanky, toned body.

"I thought you weren't coming back until early tomorrow morning."

"We left early. I'm sorry; I should have called you."

"Ty's asleep?"

"Yeah, sound asleep." It was too late to go into our disastrous trip to Vegas. And emotionally, I was too worn out to talk about it.

Lulu's heavy-lidded eyes shot to Brock. "Baby, maybe you should go."

"It's okay, Lou. I already told him to stay. I'm going to hang out here and finish my wine," I added, giving Brock no choice but to sleep with my sister. "See you in the morning."

Brock smiled. "Thanks again. I promise to be out of here before you and Ty wake up."

My eyes followed him as he ambled over to my sister and sweetly kissed her. Bidding me goodnight, he wrapped an arm around her shoulders and ushered her back to her bedroom. A wave of sadness and self-pity swept over me.

I didn't just finish the wine. I guzzled it. Drunk with emotion and overwhelmed with heartache, I once again did something I refrained from doing, living under the same roof as my daughter. Shoving down my jeans, I spread my legs and slid my hand under the waistband of my undies until two fingertips found my throbbing clit. Circling it vigorously like a finger-painting child, I fantasized about Drake and came in no time. Maybe I'd temporarily put out the fire between my legs, but the flames blazing in my heart persisted. Before I burned up with remorse and sorrow, I closed my eyes and let sleep consume me.

CHAPTER 44

Dee

Saturday. It was moving day. Everything was packed. Boxes filled with wrapped dishes and glasses as well as others filled with Ty's picture books and my art supplies lined the living room floor. All my paintings were off the walls, each bubble-wrapped and packed in a carton. Ty's ginormous plush frog, Froggie, sat upright against one of them. He was coming in the truck with us. Froggie looked sad, at least I thought he did. Tears welled in my eyes at the memory of Drake winning the oversized amphibian at the Santa Monica Pier. And the incredible evening that followed. Though I'd only been in this house for a short time, it held so many memories for me. It was impossible for me to mentally pack them away. Everywhere I looked I thought about Drake.

Soon the house would be demolished, making room for a condo complex that would stretch across the empty lot next door. I only wished my memories of my time with Drake would be demolished along with it. Not a minute went by without thinking about him. Despite my conversation with Brock last night, I knew the chances of having Drake back in my life were slim. Yes, yesterday he'd come by to see me. But opportunity didn't knock twice. It was time to let him go.

The moving van would be here shortly. Lulu and I had hired some cheap students with a van to help us with the big stuff and to collect some of my furnishings, which were in storage. Hopefully, Lulu, who had run out to pick up some donuts and coffee, would be back before they showed up.

With a heavy heart and a little time on my hands, I did a final check. One painting remained. One I'd secretly started and almost forgotten. I'd hidden it under my bed. A portrait of Drake carrying Ty on his shoulders the day we all went to The Pier. I had committed that image to memory. Staring at it, my eyes watered. I had captured the moment perfectly, the sparkle in Drake's beautiful blue eyes and the glee written all over my baby girl's face. Heaving a deep breath, I debated whether I should leave it behind. Let it be demolished with the rest of the house. Before tears erupted, I impulsively carted it into the living room and decided it would come with me in the back of the pickup. I wasn't sure if I'd hang it in my new place, but one day, I would have the courage to finish it. I wanted Ty to have this painting. To know there once was a good man in her life, who loved her with his heart and soul. As if she was his very own. Maybe one day they would connect again.

Setting the painting against a wall, my eyes darted from corner to corner. All looked good. Despite my gloom, I reminded myself that Ty and I were going to a better place to live, not too far away. With the substantial fee our landlord had given us for evacuating the premises before Lulu's lease was up, I was able to afford a nice although small two-bedroom apartment in a secure apartment building where visitors had to use an intercom system to have tenant access. Lulu was moving into a one-bedroom in the same building though I had a hunch she would be moving in with Brock sometime soon.

"Mommy, when will the movers be here?" asked Ty,

running in from the backyard where she'd been playing. Amazingly in good spirits and excited about our move, my sweet, precious girl was wearing overalls and the empowering red cape Drake had given her. I didn't think she'd ever take that cape off. And truthfully, I hoped she wouldn't for a long, long time. Besides my souvenir mug from the Santa Monica Pier and some photos, which I couldn't bring myself to delete, it was my one other connection to Drake. And a very special one.

"Very soon," I answered.

And then, the doorbell rang. The movers? I wasn't sure since I didn't hear a truck pull up to the house. Perhaps, they had to park it down the street. And then a loud knock followed. My heartbeat sped up. Was opportunity knocking again? Could it possibly be Drake?

With Ty following me, I hurried to the front door and peered through the peephole. I blinked hard. It wasn't who I expected. What was *she* doing here? Bile rose up in my throat. She was the last person I wanted to see.

Krizia. My eyes met hers. "What do you want?"

"Please open up. I just want to talk to you for a few minutes and apologize for my behavior."

A sickening feeling fell over me as I weighed her words, wondering how she knew where I lived. Had Drake told her?

"Please. I'll only be five minutes. It would really mean a lot to me."

"Mommy, who's there?" Ty's words drifted into my ears as I pondered what to do. The last thing I wanted was a confrontation with Krizia. Moreover, what good would her apology do me? It would be like rubbing salt in a wound and only burn a bigger hole in my heart.

"Please, Deandra. I'm not leaving until you open the door. I need to unload."

She sounded desperate and sincere. And she actually got

my name right. I hesitated. Then, with a shaky hand, I undid the double lock and swung the door open.

I immediately regretted my decision. Towering over me in her stilettos and sexy ensemble, she treated me to a slow, poisonous smile. I felt sick to my stomach.

"Come on in." The sooner she left the better.

"Get out of my way, bitch!"

Oh my God! That voice! My heart leapt into my throat. I blinked my eyes one time too many. Before I could blink again, Kyle shoved Krizia aside, sending her crashing to the pavement, and then burst into the house.

"What are you doing here?" I asked in a panic. Madness flickered in his eyes. He was definitely high on something.

"Mommy, who is this man?" asked Ty, fear rising in her voice as she clung to me.

My heart racing, I urged her to run to our bedroom and lock the door.

But it was too late. Before Ty could take a step, he snatched her from me.

"Mommy!" she screamed.

"Oh my God! Let go of her!" I clawed at Kyle like a wild animal as he tore out the door, throwing a screaming Tyson over his shoulder.

"What the fuck, Kyle? What are you doing?" I heard Krizia mumble, stumbling to her feet. Ignoring her, I almost knocked her down again as I bolted out of the house, adrenaline pumping through my veins.

"Ty, baby!" I cried out at the top of my lungs, running after her down the narrow, serpentine street. My worst nightmare was happening. And with each step, they were getting further and further away from me.

"Mommy!" wailed my baby girl, reaching out for me.

"Ty!" I shrieked, my sobs clogging my ears. My heart was cracking over every nook and cranny of the uneven sidewalk. My lungs and limbs were burning. Every breath, every step hurt. Oh my God. Oh my God. Oh my God. How could this be happening?

"Somebody help me!" I yelled out to a neighborhood of deaf ears. "PLEASE!" Why didn't anyone hear me?

I was at least fifty feet behind them when Kyle reached his Dodge. Tears blinded my eyes as he skidded up to the driver's side and yanked open the door. My feisty little girl was pounding and kicking him.

"Stop it, you little brat," I heard him growl.

"Let her go!" I pleaded. *Oh, please let her go!* Panting, I kept running, my eyes on Kyle as he flung Ty into the vehicle and then hopped into the driver's seat. He attempted to start up the rundown car, but the ignition wouldn't catch. Luck! It gave me more time to catch up to them. But as I jet-propelled myself forward with all the muscle power I had left, the unfathomable happened. My foot caught in a sidewalk crack and I felt myself lurching forward. Oh God, no! I was about to take a tumble. Trying to stop the momentum, I took two awkward steps forward, but nothing could stop me from falling to the pavement. As I hit the ground, burning pain seared my palms and knees. I'm sure I'd scraped them and torn my jeans, but without looking at the extent of the damage, I scrambled to my feet as Kyle tried to start his car again. This time the motor rumbled.

Then, as I stood up, a familiar voice startled me.

"Dee, what's going on? Are you okay?"

Drake! He was in his convertible heading up the street. Oh my God! What was he doing here?

"Drake! Kyle's got Tyson!" Frantically, I pointed at him, taking off in his car.

"Fuck!"

My heart beating out of control, I clasped my hand to my

mouth as Drake cranked his wheel and made a lightening-sharp U-turn that screeched in my ears and left tire tracks on the street. My heart in my throat, I trailed behind him as he zoomed down the narrow, twisty street that could barely fit two cars in hot pursuit of Kyle. *Oh dear God!*

Driving recklessly at some ridiculous speed, Kyle was almost down the hill where the road made a hairpin turn. As he rounded it, a large moving van came into view and climbed up the street. I stopped dead in my tracks. Everything happened all at once. As a horn blasted from the van, Kyle's car slammed head on into it, the explosive crash clamoring in my ears. "Noooooo!" I screamed as Drake's car came to a screeching halt. My heart literally stopped as I watched him jump out and sprint down the street to the scene of the accident. With a mixture of adrenaline and dread pumping through my veins, I ran toward it too, my heart now pounding so fast and furiously I thought it would ricochet out of my chest. Through my glazed eyes, I saw Drake run up to the passenger door and yank it open. On my next excruciating breath, Ty was lying limp and unconscious in his powerful arms. Oh, my baby! My poor baby! She was hurt! Hysterical sobs wracked my body as I began to think the worst. *No, oh no! Oh, please God, NO! You can't take her from me!!*

Holding her in his arms, Drake dashed onto the tree-lined street. "Dee, call 9-1-1!" I heard him shout out. Fuck. I didn't have my phone. Had it fallen out of my pocket when I fell? Or was it back at the house? Oh my God! Oh my God! Oh my God!

A horn wailed in my ears like a siren. And then—BOOM!—Kyle's Dodge burst into flames. All I could see ahead of me was a thick cloud of black smoke and a massive fireball. The air was heavy with the smell of the smoke, burning rubber, and charred flesh. *They were gone. NOOOOOOO!* The earth opened up beneath me and everything faded to black.

CHAPTER 45
Drake

The ambulance siren blared in my ears.

They were taking Ty to Children's Hospital, which happened to be the closest hospital to Dee's house. A few minutes away . . . with no traffic.

The poor little thing was strapped onto a gurney, which made her tiny form, look so frail and vulnerable. An oxygen mask covered her face and she was wrapped in a thick blanket. At this point, the paramedics didn't know the extent of her injuries, but what I surmised was that she was in critical condition. She was hanging on to life by a mere thread.

The moving van driver had miraculously escaped the harrowing crash without as much as a scratch and felt terrible about the fatal incident. Both the cops and I assured him it wasn't his fault.

Kyle didn't make it. After his car burst into flames, the motherfucker was burnt beyond recognition. Under different circumstances, I may have rejoiced—ding-dong, the fucker's gone—but all that mattered to me right then and there was the condition of Dee's precious little girl. Krizia had joined me at the scene of the accident, tearfully begging for forgiveness. The crazy bitch had no clue that when Kyle had asked her to help him get access to Dee in exchange for some blow that he was going to kidnap her daughter. I had no interest in her tears or rant and, in my rage, told her to fuck off. There was someone far more important who needed my attention. My support. And my love.

Sobbing softly, Dee sat huddled next to me, my bomber jacket over her halter-top to keep her warm. My arm was wrapped around her. She had fainted at the sight of Kyle's car blowing up, but fortunately hadn't sustained any major injuries except for a few minor cuts and scrapes from her earlier fall, which the paramedics patched up.

She shivered against me. "Oh, Drake, I'm so scared."

"D-Baby, she's going to be okay," I assured her, lying through my teeth as I brushed away her tears. The truth was I wasn't sure, but I couldn't share this with my vulnerable, beautiful companion. I squeezed her shoulders, feeling closer to her than I ever had. Tragedy, I realized, had a weird way of bringing people together, and for a brief moment, I thought about the untimely death of my sister, who I'd never gotten to know. It could have separated my parents, but instead it made them stronger. Cemented them forever.

Uncertainty coursed through me as we raced up Sunset Boulevard, weaving in and out of the minimal Saturday morning traffic. I called my parents to let them know what had happened so that arrangements could be made to give Tyson the best medical care possible. Being major benefactors of this renowned hospital came with benefits as they should. Both my parents, who had in a short time grown very close to this special little girl, insisted on joining us at the hospital. I told them not to come until I called them. Fingers crossed that phone call would come with good news.

Then, I gave my phone to Dee so she could call her sister Lulu. With all the fire trucks and police cars at the scene of the accident, she was trapped on the street. Driving behind the van, she'd witnessed the whole thing, not knowing who was involved. She promised to get to the hospital as soon as she could. All she could do for now was send prayers and positive thoughts. God knows, we needed them.

After a long fifteen minutes, the ambulance pulled into the emergency entrance of the hospital. The paramedics pushed the back doors open, and I hopped out and then helped Dee, who I feared would collapse again if I didn't hold on to her. With my arm wrapped around her waist, our eyes stayed on the stretcher as the paramedics worked quickly to slide it out with our little Tyson fighting for her life. A team of doctors and nurses met us at the entrance.

"Drake, are you sure she's going to be okay?" asked my teary-eyed companion.

I was about to say yes. But as Ty was transferred to another gurney, she began to convulse. Her little body shook violently.

"Move it! Move it!" shouted one of the medics.

"Oh my God! What's happening?" Dee cried out.

"She's going into cardiac arrest!"

Jesus.

"Where are you taking her?" I blurted.

"Straight to surgery."

"Oh my God," Dee gasped again as the emergency team charged through the automatic doors. We kept pace with them as they raced to an elevator, everything a blur. Holding Dee's ice-cold hand, I knew in my heart we were racing against time.

CHAPTER 46

Dee

Drake gripped my hand as we waited with baited breath for some news about Tyson. After being admitted to the hospital, she'd been rushed to the Hanson Trauma Center and was now undergoing surgery. My heart ticked with each minute of the clock, my stomach twisted into a painful knot. I hadn't stopped praying. Only prayers could keep my mind off two frightening words: what if.

Finally, after three excruciating hours, a doctor headed our way. She was wearing scrubs and had her surgical mask strung on top of her head. Probably in her forties, she adjusted her half-moon glasses as she approached us. My heart beat faster with each step she took. Still holding hands, Drake and I jumped up from the leather couch in unison.

"Mr. and Mrs. Hanson? I'm Dr. Wang, your daughter's surgeon."

I didn't even bother to correct her. "Is she okay?" I blurted out, my heart beating a gazillion miles a minute.

The doctor lifted off her glasses and pinched the bridge of her nose. She looked weary and stressed. I thought my heart would combust or beat out of my chest as she blew out a breath.

"Your daughter sustained major trauma to her body and is bleeding internally."

"What does that mean?" Panic peppered my voice.

"We can't find the source of the bleeding. She's lost a lot of blood and needs a transfusion."

"Then give her one," I barked.

"There's a problem."

A giant lump formed in my throat. *A problem?* Drake squeezed my hand as I asked what it was.

"Your daughter has a very rare blood type. And the hospital doesn't have any available. We're looking for donors and calling local blood banks."

Silently, I processed her words. I knew this when she was born, but truthfully had never thought much about it. Or ever thought it would be a matter of life or death.

"Is it AB negative?" Drake asked matter-of-factly.

Oh my God. How did he know this?

Returning her glasses to her nose, the doctor nodded. "Yes."

Drake heaved a deep breath, his chest rising and falling. "That's my type. Tell me where to go."

Anxiously, I waited for Drake to return. The thought of losing my little girl consumed me—every breath, every heartbeat, every cell of my body. How could I live without her? She was my everything. I loved her more than life itself. A little voice in my head said don't go there, but another kept screaming the worst possible scenario so loudly my head pounded. Closing my eyes, I rubbed my temples, trying to assuage the madness.

I so wanted Drake to come back. He was my only solace in the sea of despair that was drowning me, pulling me under. Thank God, he had the same rare blood type as Tyson. What were the chances of that? Maybe it was a sign from God that things would turn out okay. "Oh, please God, please," I prayed softly. "Don't take my sweet little girl from me. Please." Tears seeped out of my eyes. "Oh God, do you hear me?"

The sound of footsteps broke into my prayers. Blinking my eyes open, I looked up. It was Drake.

He stopped midway; our eyes met, mine watering, his filled with worry. And then totally distraught, I sprung out of my seat and ran into his arms. The waterworks broke loose and I cried my heart out as he held me tightly. Stroking my hair as I soaked his shirt, he just let me cry for as long as I needed. Losing track of time, I cried until I could cry no more and then looked up at him with my stinging eyes.

His face pinched, he looked tense. Slowly, he tilted up my chin with his thumb. My voice thin and watery, I thanked him for donating his blood. A miracle of miracles.

He held me intensely in his gaze and then took a deep breath.

"Dee, does Donor 5262 mean anything to you?"

My heart practically stopped as my jaw dropped to the floor. The floor felt like it was going to open beneath me. My breath hitched in my throat, his words stunning me into silence. Oh my God!

Drake rubbed the bandage on his upper arm that was covering the site where they must have drawn his blood . . . Tyson's blood.

"I need to eat something and we need to talk."

CHAPTER 47
Drake

The hospital cafeteria was busy. It was filled with weary-looking hospital personnel, but mostly worn out, worried parents. It saddened me that so many people had sick or injured children, and I was among them. My only solace was that they were getting the best care possible at this world-class hospital.

Dee and I both ordered burgers and large coffees and found a table for two in the corner. We hadn't spoken a word since I asked her that one question. I had many more to ask, but I had to get something off my chest first.

I took a sip of the steamy coffee to fortify myself and then it just spilled out. "Dee, I am donor 5262."

My eyes stayed on her as she lowered her lidded cup to the table. A look of shock washed over her face. She blinked hard several times, processing my words. Her mouth parted, but words didn't come out.

"I'm Tyson's *real* father, right?"

She nodded silently, still too shocked to speak. A short, intense silence stretched between us and then she broke it.

"I-I can't believe it."

There was no denying it. I had all the proof I needed.

Dee nervously picked at her burger. "I've never told a soul about what I did. Not even my sister. Kyle was on a downward spiral, going into bouts of deep depression and reckless behavior; our marriage was on the rocks. I thought that having a child would turn him around and save our marriage, but it wasn't possible with him. He was infertile from all the booze and drugs though he didn't know that. Determined, I read about sperm donation and learned about a sperm bank in Los Angeles."

The one in Westwood. I knew it well. Dee continued.

"So, when I went to visit my sister, one fateful weekend seven years ago, I made secret arrangements to visit the sperm bank to pick out a donor."

"Why did you pick me? There were dozens to choose from."

"I picked you because you sounded amazing and had many of Kyle's attributes—or should I say former ones. Your profile said you were tall, athletic, smart, funny, and healthy. Blue-eyed with dark hair." She paused. "Oh, and you played the guitar and sang like a rock star."

While I could have lived without the mention of Kyle, my lips twisted into a smile. "I *am* all that, but I lied on my application about a few things."

Dee cocked a brow. "You did?"

"I had lousy grades, not a 5.0. I majored in fucking, not physics. I wore braces. And I was allergic to bees. Sorry about that."

Dee quirked a little smile, the first since the accident. "How many times a week did you go there to um . . . uh . . . "

I cut her off. "You mean to jerk off in a jar? Three times a week all through college. I got calluses, but it paid me well."

"You needed money?"

"Yeah. My father had me on a strict allowance and I needed extra bucks to support my lifestyle. Plus, he wanted me to get a job while I was in college to learn some real-world responsibility. So that was my job. I found it on a bulletin board at the campus coffee shop. Jerking off for dollars. Wank. Bank. And go. At the time, it was the best job in the world."

"You regret it now?"

If she'd asked me that question a few weeks ago, the answer would have been a loud and clear yes. The stupidest thing I ever did. But now, I felt differently.

"No." I paused thoughtfully. "I made Tyson . . . with you . . . and I don't regret that at all."

"Really?" Her voice was small and unsure.

"Yeah, really. I love that kid like she's my own." I paused for another moment. "What am I saying . . . she is my own. *Ours.*"

"Ours," Dee repeated, her voice as soft as a prayer.

"I fell in love with her the minute I met her. And as time went on, my feelings grew and I began to suspect she could be mine. There were too many weird similarities . . . the color of her eyes . . . that gap between her teeth . . . the way she took to the ice . . . her left-handedness . . . those silly things we could both do like wiggle our ears and touch our tongues to our nose."

"She even eats Oreos just the way you do," Dee interjected with another small smile.

"A girl after my own heart." I chuckled.

"When did you first suspect she was yours?"

"Maybe when my mother said Ty reminded her of my sister. It took a while. The clues kept adding up, but I was in denial. Then when I was sick this past week, I had a weird dream about her. The dream clicked when I saw side-by-side photos of my sister and Tyson in my father's office; they could almost be twins. And then tonight, when I found out about her blood type, I was 99.9% positive she was mine."

"Why not 100% sure?"

"I needed to hear it from you."

Needing to take a break, I took another sip of my coffee.

"Dee, did you ever think I was Tyson's father?"

"N-no, never; I still can't believe it." A new wave of tears streamed down her cheeks. Taking my unused paper napkin, I reached out and dabbed them away. I took in her face. Even with the bloodshot eyes, blotchy skin, and swollen lips, she was beautiful. In fact, more beautiful than ever at this moment, knowing that she was the mother of my child.

She sniffled. "Oh God, Drake. This is all too much for me. What if we lose her?"

I narrowed my eyes at her. "Stop it. Don't go there. We're *not* going to lose her. She's my kid. She's got my blood and genes. And she was wearing my cape. She's got superpowers. She's Mighty Girl and she's going to live. You got that?"

Tears still trickling, Dee bopped her head up and down. I think I convinced her, but the real truth was I hadn't convinced myself. I was worried sick, but I didn't want to show it. I had to be strong for the both of us. For the woman I loved with all my heart, body, and soul. The woman who was the mother of my child. If Tyson died, I would die, too, because she was a part of me.

I took a bite of my burger while Dee took in a shaky breath. Another question was on my mind, but she beat me to one.

"What should we do?"

"About me being Tyson's father?"

Biting down on her lip, she nodded.

With a small smile, I took Dee's hands in mine. They were still icy cold, but I was going to warm them up.

"It's simple."

"Simple?"

"We're going to become a family."

"Huh?"

"Don't 'huh' me, Deandra Walker. You love me as much as I love you."

"You love me?"

"Yeah, I love you like crazy. I think I loved you from the moment I met you."

"Really?"

"D-baby, do I have to prove it to you by standing up on this table and shouting out how much I fucking love you? So loudly everyone in this hospital will hear me, including our daughter?"

I pushed my chair back and started to rise.

"Wait! Don't do that."

"I won't if you answer one question."

"Anything."

"Will you marry me?"

Dee's kissable mouth fell open. But before she could utter the one word I yearned to hear, my cell phone buzzed. She quickly reached for it and saw the text message.

"Tyson's out of surgery!"

"C'mon, let's go." Leaving behind the rest of my burger, I leaped up and rounded the table. Grabbing Dee's hand, our fingers entwined, we jogged out of the cafeteria.

My question wasn't going to get answered. And now there was an even more important one weighing on my heart.

Was our precious little girl going to be okay?

CHAPTER 48

Dee

As soon as we darted out of the elevator, Dr. Wang met us in the reception area.

"Is she okay?" I blurted out, Drake folding his brawny arm around my shoulders and holding me firmly. I was wound up as tight as a spool of thread, my heart beating in a wild frenzy.

A small smile appeared on the doctor's weary face. "I have good news for both of you."

My heartbeat sped up when it should have slowed down. "Yes?"

Her smile widened. "Your daughter is a fighter. We were able to identify the source of the bleeding and cauterize it. Thanks to the transfusion, she pulled through the surgery without a hitch. I'm happy to tell you that except for a few small scars, she's going to be just fine."

A mixture of elation and relief bubbled through my bloodstream like champagne. "Oh, thank God." I broke away from Drake and hugged the doctor.

"Doctor, can we see our little girl?" asked Drake, his excited voice mirroring my own emotions.

Our little girl. His words melted me.

"Yes. She's in recovery. Follow me."

Five minutes later, Drake and I, hand in hand, were

standing by Tyson's bedside. Her eyes were glued shut and she was hooked up to all kinds of IVs and monitors, and there was a breathing tube in her nose. Having been here only a few weeks ago for her bee sting, a sense of déjà vu gnawed at me.

Drake squeezed my hand. "She's beautiful, our little girl. You know, she really does look a lot like me."

Through my happy tears, I laughed. "You are so damn conceited. Everyone's always said she looks a lot like me."

"Well, everyone's wrong," he retaliated. "We'll see . . ."

His voice trailed off as Tyson stirred. Her eyelids fluttered and then slowly she blinked them open.

Still holding Drake's warm hand, I ran the fingers of my free hand through my baby's silky hair, her long pigtails fanned out on the pillow like angel's wings.

"Hi, sweetie," I said softly.

"Hi, Mommy." Her voice was a mere rasp, but it was enough for me. "Where am I?"

"You're in the hospital again."

"I got stung by another silly bee?"

My pulse sped up and my chest tightened. Sucking in a breath, I proceeded cautiously.

"Do you remember what happened?" Dr. Wang had explained to us on our way here that there was a possibility Tyson wouldn't remember the kidnapping or accident. And might never. Post traumatic stress disorder. Fingers crossed she wouldn't.

She blinked her eyes several times as I held my breath. "Mommy, I remember you getting ready for our move to our new apartment. Then, someone came by and rang the door bell."

My heart hammered, my muscles clenched. Did she remember more? I bit down on my lip as her eyes shifted to Drake.

"Hi, Drake. Did you come by to kiss and make up with my mommy?"

As I let out a loud sigh of relief, Drake cracked that dazzling smile. "Yeah, Mighty Girl. I took her out for lunch."

"Did you have fun?"

"We had a blast." The double entendre of his words was not lost on me. I quickly shoved the memory of Kyle's car crashing and exploding to the back of my mind, focusing on the what is, *not* the what if.

"Cool," replied Tyson as Drake affectionately flicked her button nose.

"What would you say if I asked her to marry me?"

Tyson's eyes grew as round as Cheerios. "Wowee!!! What did she say?"

Bursting with joy, I turned to face Drake. His smoldering eyes held mine with a mixture of tenderness, anticipation, and love. I suddenly realized I was free to say the one word that was on the tip of my tongue.

"Cupcake, I said . . . yes." *A million times yes!* "YES! YES! YES! YES!" I repeated as Drake swept me off my feet and spun me around. Setting me down, he planted a hot kiss on my lips.

"Yay! Does that mean Drake is going to be my daddy?"

"Yup. I'm going to be your daddy. Starting right now. You better get used to me spoiling you every minute of the day." He winked at me. "And your mommy too."

CHAPTER 49

Tyson

Three months later

Do you wanna know what I wished for when I blew out the candles on my birthday cake?

I was supposed to keep my wish a secret, but I guess since it's coming true I can tell you.

I wished for my mommy to marry Drake. He was the nicest man I ever met and I could tell my mommy really liked him and he really liked her. And he liked me a whole bunch too.

I wished for him to marry Mommy so he could become my daddy. I always wanted a daddy. And then I found out he really was my daddy. It's kinda "complicated"—Mommy used that big word– when she tried to explain to me how it all happened. I kinda understand. She really wanted a baby, but she couldn't have one by herself. So she went to this place and got some sperm put into her. I knew what sperm were—Chandra's daddy, the *gynosaurus*, gave me a sperm magnet that he got at some big doctors' meeting. They're white and squiggly (and I think they have eyes and can see), and are very good swimmers. When they meet a mommy's eggs—I bet they look like that pretty glass egg in Drake's parents' house—and fall in love, a baby is made. That's how I was made. With Mommy's egg and Drake's sperm. I can't wait to tell my all my friends in school that I know how babies are made. They think some bird with a big beak delivers them in a diaper or they grow in mommies' tummies, but they're wrong.

Today, my mommy and daddy are getting married. I've never been to a wedding before. It's so much fun. And as the flower girl, I get to wear this really pretty dress. It's long and white and super frilly. Kinda like a dress Fancy Nancy would wear, but it's even prettier. Drake's mommy, my new grandma, bought it for me.

The wedding's taking place in the backyard of Grandma's big house. There's like a gazillion people watching Mommy and Daddy get married. Including all the Danger Rangers! It's my turn to walk down the aisle. I practiced last night at the rehearsal so I know just what to do. I just have to smile at all the people and throw petals from the basket of flowers I'm holding. Drake is waiting for me at the altar and gives me a thumbs up with a big smile. He looks so handsome! Standing next to him are Aunt Lulu, the maid of honor, in her red dress that matches the color of my cape, his friend Brock, the best man, and my grandma.

When I get to the altar, Drake gives me a big hug and a lot of people in the crowd say awww! And then that famous "Here Comes the Bride" song starts to play. I turn around and watch Mommy walk down the aisle. Drake's daddy, my new grandpa, is holding her arm. She looks so pretty in her Cinderella dress—like a princess—and she's smiling, but I think she's a little scared.

"I love you, Mommy!" I shout out and everyone laughs. So do Drake, Aunt Lulu, and Brock, who makes the crowd laugh louder when he whistles at her. Uncle Brock is funny! Mommy thinks he's going to marry Aunt Lulu and he'll become my *real* uncle.

Mommy and Grandpa make it to the altar, and Daddy

takes Mommy into his arms. They look so happy together. Letting go of Mommy, Daddy takes her hand and mine too. The reverend who's marrying them starts to speak; he looks like Santa Claus and has a very deep voice.

Blah, blah, blah, blah, blah. Why do wedding ceremonies take so long? On cartoons and in my picture books, they just say "I do" and live happily ever after. The reverend stops talking (Phew! Finally!), and Mommy and Daddy exchange their vows. I listen carefully to what Drake is saying . . . he says he's marrying the two of us, both Mommy and me . . . that he'll cherish and take care of us forever. Mommy has tears in her eyes; I don't understand why she's crying. Weddings are supposed to be happy, right?

When Drake finishes, Mommy recites her vows. She talks about how much she loves Drake and how lucky she is to have found him.

"Thank you for being part of my life. And *our* precious daughter's too. We will love you for eternity." Her voice sounds small and lots of tears are pouring down her cheeks. I squeeze her hand. "Don't cry, Mommy," I tell her. She squeezes my hand back.

Mommy and Daddy exchange rings. The reverend pronounces them husband and wife. They kiss and everyone shouts YAY! Me too! Yay for my mommy and daddy!

I turn to face the crowd and sing out as loud as I can.

"If you're happy and you know it, clap your hands!"

Clap! Clap!

Everyone joins in as I sing the rest of the song . . . "If you're happy and you know it and you really want to show it, shout hooray!"

"Hooray!"

Hooray for my mommy and daddy. After the wedding, they're going on a honeymoon, and I'm staying with Grandma and Grandpa at their big house. I can't wait. Me and Grandpa are gonna bake cupcakes. And Grandma's gonna give me more ice skating lessons and teach me new tricks.

Mommy says I'm the luckiest little girl in the world.

I am!

Me . . . Tyson "Mighty" Hanson.

CHAPTER 50

Dee

"Drake, where are you taking me?" I asked, blindfolded and nestled against him in the backseat of a limo. By the swift, even speed of the vehicle, I was pretty sure we cruising down one of LA's many intertwining freeways.

"It's a surprise, my beautiful wife," he replied with mischief in his voice.

Wife. He called me his wife. It was my new favorite four-letter word (and his too), and it had taken me little time to get used to.

"By the way, you look sexy as sin in that lacey black mask," he whispered against my neck before nuzzling it. "And it looks hot as hell with your wedding gown still on. I'm almost tempted to fuck you right now in the limo, but we're almost at our destination."

"Drake, you're making me crazy," I moaned back as he kissed that sensitive spot under my chin that got to me every time.

"That's my job. Tell me, Mrs. Hanson. Are you wet with need?" he breathed, his hand starting at my ankle and making its way under the layers of tulle that adorned my gown.

I arched my head back as his hand climbed up my thigh

and slipped under my garter and panties. He stroked my sensitive folds, his thumb rubbing my pulsing clit.

"Jesus, D-baby, you're sopping wet for me. God, you make it so fucking hard . . . to resist you."

In my mind's eye, I could picture his rock-hard cock straining against his trousers. That ginormous tent. It was amazing how clearly one could see blindfolded. He brought my hand to his crotch and confirmed what I imagined. Beneath my palm was that hard, hot mound of flesh that was setting me on fire. He was as ready for me as I was for him.

"Are you sure we don't have time for a quickie?" I murmured, fighting the urge to pull down his fly.

He laughed. "You horny little girl. That's not the way I want to fuck you. No quick in-and-outers tonight. I'm going to fuck you like there's no tomorrow." The car slowed down and then came to a stop. "Besides, we're here at our destination."

"Can I take my mask off now?" I asked, at once a little disappointed and a lot excited.

"Not yet."

I heard the passenger door open and a familiar roar sounded in my ears. I let out a gasp. Was it what I thought it was? I wondered as Drake helped me out of the car and then lifted me into his strong arms.

"Drake, are we at—"

"Yup." I could picture the proud smirk on his lips. I wanted to bite it off. "We're at the Santa Monica Pier. I thought we'd start our first night as husband and wife off with some fun and excitement."

"Didn't we have enough fun and excitement at the wedding?" I asked, the memories of the unforgettable evening swirling in my head as he hauled me across the boisterous pier. I bet all eyes were on us—this gorgeous as a movie star man in a tux carrying his masked bride in her wedding dress toward the amusement park. Still tipsy from all the champagne I drank at the wedding, I felt myself heating and my heart racing as deafening screams filled the warm night air. *Gah!*

"Are you taking me on the roller—"

"Yup. I've pre-arranged everything so we don't have to wait in line."

I gulped. From the growing sound of the screams, we were very close to the ride.

"That's the only ride we're doing. You'll be riding me the rest of the night. And I have a very tasty corn dog waiting for you later."

The rest of the night sounded mouth-watering, but the thought of riding the roller coaster made my stomach knot. You'd think having done it before would make it easier and less intimidating, but knowing how scary it was made it only scarier.

"Am I going to have to wear this mask?" I stammered.

"No, D-baby, I'm going to take it off once we get seated. I want you to see the view at night. Plus, I already miss seeing your eyes."

A few minutes later, we were in the back seat of the last coaster car. The safety bar down, the car was ready to take off. My mask now sitting atop my head, I had to say that The Pier looked beautiful at night all lit up. Like a box of glittering jewels. Then, to my surprise, in the clear navy sky, a Goodyear blimp floated by.

"Look at the blimp," I shouted out to Drake, pointing at it and happy for the distraction.

He looked up and then I couldn't believe my eyes. The LED panel lit up and words that lit up my heart scrolled by.

D-baby, I love you from here to the moon and back.

"Oh, Drake!" I cried out, flinging my arms around him as the coaster took off. As the car slowly started its ascent, he cupped my head in his hands and kissed me passionately. I was lost in him. At the apex, he broke the kiss, and the screaming that would last all night long began as we plummeted down the track.

"Baby, you can scream louder than that," he said with a laugh as he bunched up the voluminous skirt of my wedding gown. Once again, his hand crawled up my leg, making its way between my thighs.

"Drake, what are you doing?" I asked in a panic as the coaster whipped around the track.

"Practicing what I preach. I'm going to take you to the moon and back."

I gasped again as his fingers returned to my clit. He began to rub it vigorously.

"I only have three minutes to make you come, baby."

Oh, God! I didn't think I'd last that long as I squeezed my eyes shut and gripped the safety bar. The feeling of going over the edge in more ways than one consumed me. The soaring pleasure this man was giving me competed with the roar of terror that spilled from my lips. I was more than going to fall off this thrill ride; I was going to fall off the earth as he took me to the edge. I gripped the safety bar more forcefully, worried it wouldn't hold me in when I came. In my heart, I knew Drake was loving every second of this extreme torture. Loving every tortured moan and groan that fled from my O-shaped mouth.

I screamed. I cried. I whimpered.
I prayed. I swore. I begged.
"Drake, please make me come!"
"Hold on, baby!"

Then as the car swerved around another sharp curve, he plunged a finger into my pussy. He pumped it up and down while his other fingers continued to work my needy clit. Oh dear Lord! My life was going to be over. I clenched my muscles around his long, thick digit, hoping by clinging to it I wouldn't fall off the coaster.

As my body climbed to its apex, waves of ecstasy began to roll through me, and as the coaster came to a halt, I fell apart. In record time.

I opened my eyes, noticing people in line were giving me funny looks. Why was this crazy woman in a wedding gown still shrieking and panting when the ride was over? Because I was still riding my roller coaster of an orgasm out.

Lifting the safety bar, Drake stepped out of the car and then helped me out. I wobbled. My legs were like Jell-O from my outrageous orgasm. He held me up and steadied me.

"D-baby, that was amazing. I fucking love this roller coaster."

"Oh my God, that was amazing," I breathed out, smoothing my gown. Beneath the layers, I was still pulsing between my thighs.

"C'mon." Drake looped an arm around me as we made our way back to the limo. "There's one last thing we need to do before we head over to the hotel."

We were staying at the oceanfront Casa Del Mar, steps from The Pier, before we flew off to Cabo in the morning.

"Like what?" I asked, hoping it wasn't another ride.

"We need to visit someone special."

He has a friend here? Gah! I was in no condition to make friendly conversation.

Without questioning him, I let him lead the way along the crowded pier, and five minutes later we were standing once more before none other than the mechanical fortune teller.

"Say hello again to Zoltar."

"Drake!" I laughed, now recovered from my orgasm. "He can't hear me."

"Be nice to him. He holds a lot of power. I want to know what our future has to bring."

I couldn't believe we were doing this again, but I gave in to his whim. Making me go first, I inserted a dollar bill, courtesy of Drake, and waited patiently for my fortune to spew out. When it did, I read it immediately and burst into laughter.

"What does it say?" asked my new husband.

I rolled my eyes. "It's the same fortune as last time. *You will meet a tall dark handsome stranger.*"

He chortled. "Well, it did come true." He flicked my nose. "You just better not meet another one, Mrs. Hanson."

"Ha-ha. Very funny. Now, your turn." I watched as he repeated my actions. His brows knitted as he read his fortune.

"C'mon, tell me. What does it say?"

"It says: *A surprise awaits you.*"

He showed it to me. "That is so generic. Do it again."

"Fine." I watched as he inserted another dollar into the machine before retrieving his new fortune. "What does this one say?"

This time a wicked smile lifted his lips. "*You will be fucking someone's brains out soon.*"

"I don't believe you. Show me."

"I'll show you." Slipping the fortune into his breast pocket, he hauled me into him and gave me a fierce, passionate kiss. As he held me, he pressed my hand against his crotch. His hard, hot, pulsing length seared my palm.

"Trust me, D-baby," he breathed in my ear. "Zoltar is *never* wrong . . ."

EPILOGUE
Drake

One Year Later

Shortly before Dee and I got married, I came clean about my sperm donor past with both my parents and my buddy Brock. Brock assured me that I had nothing to worry about; the sperm bank was legit and would adhere to keeping my identity secret. In the unlikelihood some mom or kid ever did come after me, he said he'd have my back and cited some California law. Well, that was reassuring. Yeah, right. I found out there were exactly a dozen little Drakesters and Drakettes running around out there. Let me re-phrase and add a word . . . *only* a dozen. While you'd think I would be relieved, my ego was somewhat deflated. I thought with my profile and genes, hundreds of women would have picked me to be their baby daddy. Guess not . . . there were dudes out there who were more appealing than me. Or better liars. Only one thing mattered: the woman, who I fell heels in love with and whose child is the apple of my eye, chose me.

My parents had a more positive reaction than I anticipated. My mother thought I was heroic—giving a family to so many women and couples who yearned for one. I thought my father would fall off his rocker, but he simply rolled his eyes. I'd done a lot of dumbass things in my life, but this wasn't one of them. Marrying Dee Walker was the smartest thing I ever did and they had a granddaughter they simply adored. And more.

Today's our first anniversary. It's hard to believe a year's gone by. So much has happened. We have a lot to celebrate.

"Happy anniversary, D-baby." Spooning her warm, bare body in my arms, I nuzzle the back of her neck.

"Mmmm." Her sexy, groggy moan knocks at my morning wood. My erection presses against her as she acknowledges our special day. "Are you going to bring me breakfast in bed?"

I wish she could see the fiendish smile on my face as I respond. "Baby, I'm going to *give* you breakfast in bed." On my next breath, I wrap my hand around my length and guide it into her. As she moans again, my other arm wraps around her soft belly and I begin to grind into her. Her moans turn into groans as she rocks her hips back to meet my thrusts. Gripping her harder, I grind deeper and faster. Her groans grow louder, more desperate. Oh, what a beautiful morning. Oh, what a beautiful day.

"Drake, we're going to wake everyone up," she pants out.

"I don't give a fuck if we wake the whole neighborhood up," I grunt, bringing us both closer to the edge and to the reality we actually may wake the neighbors of the tawny Santa Monica neighborhood we now live in. I can feel my balls tightening, that tingling between my legs. I want us to come together so fucking bad.

"Oh my God, oh my God, oh my God," she shrieks as my breathing grows harsher.

"Hold on, baby." A few more deep thrusts and bam! We both detonate. With a scream, she shudders against me as my own body jerks forcefully. My nuclear release spills into her atomic pussy. Insane pleasure blasts through me as her body unleashes one crashing wave after another around my explosive cock.

"Holy fuck," I mutter before kissing her everywhere I can.

"Drake, I'm going to feel this all day."

A few minutes later, she's rolled over, her naked body against mine and her head on my beating heart. Our go-to after sex position. Sunlight streams through a crack in the drawn curtains. I steal a glance at my sexy wife and harden at the sight of her. She's got that gorgeous just-fucked look going on. That slight flush. Her hair a sexy tousled mess. Her lips stretched wide with a dreamy smile. My cock is crying out for more: I'm insatiably yours.

My thumb circles her puckered nipples that complement her spectacular, still swollen tits and then I trace her luscious lips. "How 'bout you suck my cock and then we'll take a quick shower together?"

She twists her lips as if in deep thought and fiddles with her wedding ring. A trinity ring . . . the three diamond stones symbolizing the past, the present, and the future. Dee, Ty, and me. Our eternal union.

"C'mon, Dee. I'm hard again. I'm making it so easy for you." I put her hand to my rock-hard cock to make sure she knows. "All you have to do is wrap your sweet lips around it."

My eyes stay on her as her lips curl into a seductive smile. I mentally punch the air. Score one for me. She sits up, crawls down the bed, and just when I think she's going to go down on me, she scoots off. What the fuck!?

I shoot up to a sitting position. "Where are you going?"

Heading across the room with a sexy bounce in her gait, she looks over her shoulder. "I'm giving you a time out."

"Seriously? Have I been a bad boy?"

'You've been a *very* bad boy. And I loved every minute.

I have something for you."

Okay, she's got me intrigued, but I swear tonight I'm going to tie her up. Fuck her until she's begging me to stop. But I won't. I'll show her how naughty I *really* can be. My eyes stay on her fuckable ass as she squats down and slides a large, flat gift-wrapped box out from under our dresser. She carries it to the bed and hands it to me.

"What's this?" I ask as she hops back onto the bed and sits cross-legged, facing me.

"Your anniversary present. Open it."

Eagerly, I tear off the paper and the big bow and then slide out the contents from the box.

"Careful," says Dee. "It's fragile."

Encased in bubble wrap, it must be a framed painting or photograph. With Dee's help, I remove the wrapping, and my eyes grow wide. Holy shit! It's an oil painting of Tyson and me at the Santa Monica Pier, my sweet Mighty Girl riding piggyback on my shoulders. Her sixth birthday. The magical day our roller coaster of a life took off.

"Do you like it?" asks Dee.

"Fuck. I love it." I smack a kiss on Dee's lips. "Is this what you were secretly working on in your studio?"

Dee has a studio in our spacious backyard where she paints. We converted the guesthouse. Last month, she had her first major exhibition at Jaime Zander's art gallery and it was a huge success. Instead of teaching, she now paints full-time, but on weekends, gives painting lessons to a few lucky kids. It allows her to be a stay-at-home mom and have a fulfilling career at the same time.

After a nod, a wistful smile crosses her face. She casts her eyes down at the painting and then back at me. "That day will always be special to me."

I tenderly brush the side of her face with my fingertips. "How, baby?"

"It was the day I fell in love with you. I saw the way you connected with Ty and her with you. That connection was so powerful. So beautiful. And I knew then how much my . . . *our* . . . baby girl needed a loving father in her life . . . how much I needed you."

Her voice grows watery and trails off. I carefully set the painting on the bed and then tap my thigh. "Come here, baby."

I watch as she repositions herself on my lap, her bent legs straddling me and her arms wrapped around my neck. Her soulful brown eyes lock with mine and I think about how our little girl brought us together. I move in for another passionate kiss when the bedroom door handle jiggles and is followed by a loud knocking.

"Mommy, Daddy, open up!"

Ty. "Coming." I wish, but I'm not going to let an opportunity pass. My mouth consumes Dee's with a hot, tongue-driven kiss. I force myself to pull away and before heading to the door, grab the pajamas strewn on the floor after last night's love making. We scramble to put them on.

"Happy Anniversary, Mommy and Daddy!" shouts out my Mighty as I swing the door open.

I give her a big hug and lift her into my arms. "What's that?" I ask after noticing the folded piece of paper she's holding.

"It's your card! I made it myself!"

"Cool! I want to read it with Mommy."

A few seconds later, we're all on the bed. Dee and I take turns reading the adorable card with the whimsically drawn family aloud. The little girl with pigtails is wearing a red cape just like the one Mighty is wearing over her PJs.

Me: "Happy Anniversary to the Bestest Mommy and Daddy in the World!"

Dee: "Love, Your Cupcake ("Mighty") and Milo."

A big red heart and lots of X's and O's follow.

"Oh, cupcake!" gushes Dee with a kiss. "I love this! Such a perfect picture of us."

"Me too," I add, smacking a kiss on her other cheek. "Thank you, sweetheart!"

A smile as wide as the sky lights up my precious girl's face. She's missing several teeth now, and the front one has come in crooked just like mine did when I was her age.

"I signed Milo's name for him. I couldn't get him to hold the crayon."

Dee and I laugh while Ty's attention shifts to the painting on the bed. "Mommy, did you paint this?"

Dee grins. "Yes, cupcake. I made it for Daddy for our anniversary. I want him to hang it in his new office."

I now occupy my father's large corner office. After the Gunther Saxton debacle, my father decided not to sell our company but to retire anyway. Following the overnight success of *Mighty Girl*, he handed me the reigns and I'm now President of Hanson Entertainment.

"I know exactly where it's going to go . . . on the wall right across from my desk so I can see you all day long," I tell my daughter.

"YAY! What did you get Mommy?"

My pulse rate quickens with excitement. I have the most fucking awesome present for the love of my life—a pair of dangling diamond earrings, each heart-shape diamond symbolizing the two other loves of my life. My little gems. Just as I'm about to retrieve the little box hidden under my pillow, a loud wail sounds.

"Mommy, Milo is up!"

Our three-month-old son. Conceived on our wedding night. Though I wasn't wearing protection, Dee was still on birth control. The chances of getting her pregnant were slim. What can I tell you? My sperm are still Olympians. And

Zoltar was right as usual . . . a surprise awaited us.

The wail grows louder as we hop out of the bed. What a set of lungs this kid has! A screamer just like his mother. My present will have to wait. Tonight, over a romantic dinner at the Casa Del Mar hotel, I'll give the woman I love with all my heart, body, and soul the earrings. I would give her the world if I could.

A few moments later we're gathered in the nursery adjacent to our room. I lift my baby boy up from his crib and he calms. His eyes, the color of mine, gaze up at me. He coos and this little miracle, the spitting image of me, totally melts my heart. My eyes follow his around the room Dee hand-painted. A colorful mural with barnyard animals and a cow jumping over the moon. Yup, I'd made many babies. But this one was as special as the little girl who changed my life forever. His wide eyes land on the three colorful words painted above his crib and he coos again. I smile. Yeah, my little man, you were . . .

MADE WITH LOVE

Tyson

Twenty Years Later

When I was little, Dad told me I could be anything I wanted to be when I wore my red cape.

I no longer wear that cape, but its powers have stayed with me.

An Olympic figure skating champion at the age of eighteen, I'm a writer now, a bestseller in love with a Pulitzer prize winning ginger, who's convinced he once barfed all

over my father.
>This is *my* story . . .
>All I will tell you is . . . .
>*They lived happily ever after.*

THE END

Thank you so much for reading *Baby Daddy*. I hope you enjoyed reading it as much as I enjoyed writing it and that you fell in love with Drake, Dee, and Tyson. As a special bonus, here's a link to *Trainwreck*, Ari and Sarah's story. Ari Golden is a sexy as sin billionaire who lets aspiring toy designer Sarah Greene into his life despite the dark secrets they both harbor. Told in dual POV, it's filled with steamy passion, suspense, and many twists and turns. And it's **FREE!**

ACKNOWLEDGMENTS

As always, it takes a village to write and publish a book. A big shout out to all of the following:

- ♥ My Bestest Betas: (In alphabetical order) Auden Dar, Kashunna Fly, Dawn Myers, Kristen Myers, Kim Pinard Newsome, Jenn Moshe, Karen Silverstein, Jeanette Sinfield, Mary Jo Toth, Shannon Meadows Heyward, and Joanna Halliday-Warren
- ♥ My Eagle-Eyed Proofreaders: Mary Jo Toth and Gloria Herrera
- ♥ My Amazing Cover Artist: Arijana Karcic, Cover It! Designs
- ♥ My Fabulous Ebook and Paperback Formatter: Paul Salvette, BBebooks
- ♥ My Dear Friend and ARC Formatter: Sean Hennessey/Zirconia Publishing
- ♥ My One and Only Assistant: Gloria Herrera
- ♥ My Wonderful Family: My hubby and college-bound daughters
- ♥ My Hard-Working Release Blitz Organizers: Kylie McDermott, Jeananna Goodall, Jo Webb/Give Me Books and ALL the amazing bloggers, who spread the word about this book
- ♥ My Friend, Dr. Eliran Mor, who gave my girls the sperm magnet that inspired this story
- ♥ The Lovely Rebecca Friedman for making me re-think

- the original title and reader Eve Recinella for making me re-think the original blurb
- ♥ My Faithful ARC Readers: You know who you are! Thank you for all your unbelievably kind words! You've made me cry happy tears!
- ♥ The one and only Raine Miller, for her kindness and beautiful words
- ♥ The Incomparable Lauren Blakely, who managed to read and review *Baby Daddy* in the middle of all the amazing books she's writing. I adore this superwoman!

And last but not least, thank you to all who believe in me and purchased a copy of *Baby Daddy*. If you loved it (and I hope you did!), please leave a review—even a short one. Reviews help others find my books and mean the world to me. Always remember, my beautiful Belles, you are the reason I write. *Endless Love,* the long-awaited sequel to my critically acclaimed tearjerker, will be coming in Fall 2017. I can't wait to bring it to you! Be sure to add it to your Goodreads TBR list and look to pre-order it on my website.

Goodreads: ENDLESS LOVE
Website: nellelamour.com/endless-love

MWAH!~ Nelle ♥

ABOUT THE AUTHOR

Nelle L'Amour is a *New York Times* and *USA Today* bestselling author who lives in Los Angeles with her Prince Charming-ish husband, twin teenage princesses, and a bevy of royal pain-in-the-butt pets. A former executive in the entertainment industry with a prestigious Humanitas Prize for promoting human dignity and freedom to her credit, she gave up playing with Barbies a long time ago, but still enjoys playing with toys with her husband. While she writes in her PJs, she loves to get dressed up and pretend she's Hollywood royalty. Her steamy stories feature characters that will make you laugh, cry, and swoon and stay in your heart forever.

To learn about her new releases, sales, and giveaways, please sign up for her newsletter and follow her on social media. Nelle loves to hear from her readers.

Check out her cool website:
www.nellelamour.com

Sign up for her fun newsletter:
nellelamour.com/newsletter

Join her on Facebook:
facebook.com/NelleLamourAuthor

Follow her on Twitter:
twitter.com/nellelamour

Email her at:
nellelamour@gmail.com

Follow Her on Amazon:
amazon.com/Nelle-LAmour/e/B00ATHR0LQ

Follow her on BookBub:
bookbub.com/authors/nelle-l-amour

BOOKS BY NELLE L'AMOUR

Unforgettable
Unforgettable Book 1
Unforgettable Book 2
Unforgettable Book 3

Alpha Billionaire Duet
TRAINWRECK 1
TRAINWRECK 2

An OTT Insta-love Standalone
The Big O

THAT MAN Series
THAT MAN 1
THAT MAN 2
THAT MAN 3
THAT MAN 4
THAT MAN 5

Gloria
Gloria's Secret
Gloria's Revenge
Gloria's Forever

An Erotic Love Story
Undying Love

Seduced by the Park Avenue Billionaire
Strangers on a Train
Derailed
Final Destination

Writing as E.L. Sarnoff
DEWITCHED: The Untold Story of the Evil Queen
UNHITCHED: The Untold Story of the Evil Queen 2

Boxed Sets
THAT MAN TRILOGY
THAT MAN: THE WEDDING STORY
Unforgettable: The Complete Series
Gloria's Secret: The Trilogy
Seduced by the Park Avenue Billionaire